THE
INVISIBLE

Also by Andrew Britton:

The Assassin

The American

THE
INVISIBLE

ANDREW BRITTON

KENSINGTON BOOKS
http://www.kensington books.com

7

Britton

KENSINGTON BOOKS are published by

Kensington Publishing Corp.
850 Third Avenue
New York, NY 10022

All Kensington titles, imprints and distributed lines are available at special quantity discounts for bulk purchases for sales promotion, premiums, fund-raising, educational, or institutional use.

Special book excerpts or customized printings can also be created to fit specific needs. For details, write or phone the office of the Kensington Special Sales Manager: Kensington Publishing Corp., 850 Third Avenue, New York, NY, 10022. Attn. Special Sales Department. Phone: 1-800-221-2647.

Kensington and the K logo Reg. U.S. Pat. & TM Off.

Library of Congress Card Catalogue Number: 2007939103
ISBN-13: 978-0-7582-1335-8
ISBN-10: 0-7582-1335-2

First Hardcover Printing: March 2008

10 9 8 7 6 5 4 3 2 1

Printed in the United States of America

For my grandmother, Eunice Britton

ACKNOWLEDGMENTS

To Linda Cashdan of *The Word Process*, for her editorial guidance early in "the process." Thanks again for your input. To Erika Lease, M.D., for her invaluable contribution on the medical side of things. To Carol Fitzgerald and everyone at bookreporter.com, for designing and maintaining my Web site. To Connie Asero and everyone who participated in the Crystal Coast Book Festival. It was an extraordinary event. Thanks for letting me be part of it.

Thanks to everyone at Kensington, especially Steven Zacharius, Robin E. Cook, Laurie Parkin, Maureen Cuddy, Michaela Hamilton, and Doug Mendini, a true fixture on the trade show circuit. To Meryl Earl, who has somehow managed to get my books published in a multitude of languages, none of which I understand. To Rosemary Silva, for her outstanding work with the copyediting. Also thanks to Alex Clarke and the entire team at Penguin Books for their continued support in Australia and the U.K.

To my editor, Audrey LaFehr, for her enthusiasm, encouragement, and exceptional patience. Thanks for everything.

To my agent, Nancy Coffey, for many, many things. If I had to name them all, the acknowledgments would be longer than the book itself. So thanks for all that you do. Let's hope this is just the third of many.

And to Dezzy Murphy and the other Irish climbers who conquered Concordia, thanks for inspiring the prologue.

An "invisible" is CIA-speak for the ultimate intelligence nightmare: a terrorist who is an ethnic native of the target country and who can cross its borders unchecked, move around the country unquestioned, and go completely unnoticed while setting up the foundation for monstrous harm.

THE KARAKORAM HIGHWAY (KKH), PAKISTAN

In Rebeka Česnik's opinion, the view, even when seen through the cracked window of the ancient bus winding its way down from Kashgar to Islamabad, was simply magnificent. Perfect. Stunning in every conceivable way. These were the words she had used to describe every trip she'd ever taken, and her effusive comments always made her friends and relatives smile, though it had taken her quite a while—the better part of her life, in fact—to understand just why that was.

Her mother had been the one to finally let her in on the joke. That had been a few years earlier, shortly after Rebeka joined Frommer's as a travel photographer. At the time, the observation had struck her as not only true, but slightly humorous. Even now the memory made her smile, but she couldn't dispute her mother's words.

It's a good thing you took up photography instead of writing, she had said, *because no matter where you go, your descriptions are always the same. Every place you visit is just as perfect as the last.*

It was a true enough statement, Rebeka supposed, though she'd never really dwelled on her lack of verbal creativity. All she cared about was her traveling and her art, and to her great satisfaction, she'd been able to make a successful living with both. She'd always had the ability to pick out a unique, compelling scene, but that wasn't enough for her. Nor was it enough to satisfy her extremely demanding employers. Instead, her goal was to pull the readers into the photograph, to draw them away from the article itself. It was a lot to aspire to, as the magazines she worked for employed some of the best writers in the business. Moreover, it was nearly impossible to capture the grandeur of the things she saw on a regular basis. Still, judging by the awards and accolades she had racked up over her short career—including the prestigious Hasselblad Award in 2006—she had managed to make her mark in an industry brimming with talent, and that was no small feat.

Rebeka had embarked on her current career after winning a regional photography contest at seventeen years of age. She'd started shooting on an amateur basis in 2002 with a secondhand Minolta Dynax 8000i. The camera had been a gift from a spoiled cousin who'd since moved on to more expensive hobbies, and she'd fallen in love with it instantly. Her love of travel, however, dated back to her childhood, and she sometimes wondered why it had taken her so long to work her two favorite hobbies into what had become a spectacular career. She had grown up on the Soča River in the Julian Alps, not far from the famed Predjama Castle, and she credited the gorgeous scenery of her childhood with sparking not only her interest in nature, but her desire to see as much of it as possible.

Since leaving Frommer's the previous year, she had embarked on freelance assignments for *Time, Newsweek, Le Monde, National Geographic,* and *Naša žena* in her native Slovenia, just to name a few. Those assignments had given her the opportunity to visit fourteen countries over the course of two short years, in addition to the twelve she'd already seen, and she had thoroughly documented her journeys—not only with her camera, but also in her journal, by far her most treasured possession. Every assignment carried with it the promise of a new adventure, but as she stared out the window, ignoring the unpleasant sway of the bus on the steep mountain road, she couldn't help but think that the snowcapped peaks surrounding the Hunza Valley had surpassed her wildest expectations. A brief shower earlier in the day had given way to a spectacularly clear blue sky, and the afternoon sun made the snow-topped spires in the distance glisten in ways she could never hope to capture on film. It didn't happen often, but there were times when she knew she could never do justice to the scenery, and while those moments were among the most thrilling of her personal life, they were hard to accept professionally. Still, she wouldn't have traded the sight for anything.

After a while the bus rocked slightly to the right as it swept around the mountain, and the splendid sight of Tirich Mir—the highest peak in the Hindu Kush range—faded from view as the bus began the long descent into Khunjerab National Park. Disappointed with the change in scenery, Rebeka turned in her seat and let her gaze drift over her fellow passengers. The vehicle was filled to capacity, which wasn't surprising, given the time of year. Many were climbers destined for the world's most challenging peaks, and they were assured of permits only during the summer months. She had traveled with these people for weeks on end, and she'd come to know most of them fairly well.

Sitting directly across from her was Beni Abruzzi, the rakish, handsome, long-limbed climber from Brescia. He was talking—with animated gestures, as always—to Umberto Verga, his stocky Sicilian cousin. Umberto rarely spoke, and when he did, it sounded more like a series of grunts than actual speech, but Beni was only too happy to pick up his cousin's slack. He'd served as a *caporal maggiore,* an infantry corporal, in the Italian army. He'd also spent some time in Iraq, a fact he'd mentioned more times than Rebeka cared to remember. Abruzzi had spent hours bragging about his military exploits, and while Rebeka believed most of his stories, she wasn't impressed in the least. Unsurprisingly, the Italian's gaze was presently fixed on the trio of pretty Norwegian nurses who had joined them in Tashkurgan. That had been two hours earlier, and forty minutes before the bus crossed from China into Pakistan via the Khunjerab Pass, the highest point on the Karakoram Highway.

There was also the downtrodden group of Danish climbers who'd arrived at K2 four days earlier with the goal of summiting, only to turn back at base camp in Concordia, and a small knot of aging Canadian trekkers. There was even a renowned American geologist by the name of Timothy Welch. The professor emeritus from the University of Colorado seemed to spend a great deal of time staring at his hands and muttering under his breath, which Česnik found both amusing and a little unnerving.

Beni managed to catch her eye, but she turned away before he could fix her with his usual lascivious stare. To cover her reaction, she hastily pulled her journal out of her Berghaus pack, undid the clasp, and started to scribble a few notes, catching up on the events of the past few days. It was hard to concentrate under the lean climber's intense gaze. She'd done her best to make her disinterest clear, but her efforts had clearly been wasted. Although she was just twenty-three—the same age as Abruzzi—Rebeka had accomplished a great deal in her young life. For this reason, she tended to look down on many people her own age. She knew it was snobbish, but she couldn't help it; she was a driven woman, and that meant things like men, sex, and partying didn't figure high on her list of priorities.

At the same time, she knew her looks had given her a considerable boost in her current career—that they would have helped her in *any* career. She took this in stride, though, and it didn't change the way she viewed her success. After all, she'd seen the recent U.S. edition of *Outside* magazine, and her picture on the page of contributing journalists had not been any larger than that of the editor in chief, a decidedly unattractive Swede in his midsixties. This discovery had only confirmed what she already knew: that it was her talent—not her looks—that had made her one of the world's most sought-after young photographers.

She looked up, startled out of her reverie as the bus shuddered, the driver downshifting suddenly. Craning her neck, Rebeka saw a number of vehicles parked alongside the road up ahead, men milling about on the paved surface. As the bus rolled forward, the scene came into focus, and she saw something that chilled her blood.

Rifles. Every man in sight was heavily armed, and there were plenty of men. Judging by the low rumble of voices in the surrounding seats, everyone else was just as confused and concerned as she was. Passports and visas were frequently checked on the KKH, but this wasn't one of the scheduled stops. As far as Rebeka knew, they still had miles to go before they reached the next Pakistani checkpoint. Tensions between General Musharraf's government and that of Indian prime minister Manmohan Singh had been rising steadily over the past few months, but this was the first time she'd seen any tangible evidence of the escalating situation.

She only hoped she was right, that it wasn't something else entirely. Bandits had always been a problem on the Karakoram Highway, though guarding against them was usually just a matter of taking the proper precautions, such as not traveling alone or after dark. As it stood, it was midafternoon, still light, and they were nowhere near the Line of Control—the heavily guarded border that separates the disputed territory between Pakistan and India. In short, these were about the best conditions a traveler on the KKH could ask for.

The bus ground to a gentle halt, and the doors at the front banged open. The air in the vehicle seemed unusually thick, and no one was making a sound. Rebeka realized they were waiting to see what would happen, just as she was. But then a man appeared at the front, and the collective tension seemed to drain away. The man standing next to the driver and surveying the passengers was wearing the uniform of a Pakistani army captain. Rebeka felt her breath come a little bit easier, and she wasn't concerned in the least when the captain asked them all to disembark and present their passports. Realizing that the soldiers might poke through their belongings, she slipped her journal under her coat. She wouldn't be surprised to get back on and find some items missing from her pack, and while most of it was replaceable, the journal was the one thing she couldn't bear to lose.

She was sitting near the back of the vehicle, so she had to wait for the passengers up front to disembark. As they began to line up on the side of the road, documentation in hand, Rebeka saw a rare opportunity and decided to take it. The soldiers seemed to be unusually wrapped up in their task, so she dug out her camera—a Canon EOS-1V with an 85mm lens already affixed—and carefully lifted it above the ledge of the window. She took a few quick shots with the flash disabled, hoping to capture her fellow passengers' frustrated expressions. It wasn't part of her assignment, but she happened to know a freelance writer who was doing a story on corruption in the Pakistani army, and she thought she might be able to get some mileage out of the photographs.

Once she'd fired off a half-dozen shots, Rebeka quickly lowered the camera and checked to see if anyone had noticed. It didn't look like it, but either way, she had run out of time; the front of the bus was nearly empty, and a young soldier was striding toward the open doors.

Rebeka quickly ejected the film, dropped it into a spare tube, and slipped it into her pack. She had just gotten to her feet when the soldier reached the back of the bus and gestured toward the camera. Shouting something she didn't understand, he grabbed her free arm with his left hand, then reached for her camera with the other. She pulled it away instinctively, but he leaned in and managed to knock it out of her hand. Then, as she watched in disbelief, he kicked it toward the back of the vehicle.

"What do you think you're doing?" she shouted in English, tugging free of the soldier's grasp. "Do you have any idea how expensive that was? As soon as we get back to Islamabad, I'm going to—"

She never got the words out. The soldier slammed a fist into her stomach, then slapped her hard across the face. Rebeka's knees banged against the edge of the seat as her body followed the blow. She hit the plastic cushion hard, tears springing to her eyes as she struggled for air. Momentarily stunned, she didn't fight as the soldier reached down and wrapped a hand in her hair, yanking her to her feet. Hunched forward and crying out with pain, she reached behind her head and frantically tried to pull his fist apart as he marched her to the front of the vehicle. Once they had reached the driver's seat, he released her and shoved her hard down the stairs.

Rebeka tumbled through the open doors. As she hit the ground awkwardly, something gave way in her shoulder with an audible pop. Although her head was swimming with confusion and fear, she instantly tried to prop herself up using her right elbow. It was completely instinctive, but it was also a huge mistake; her shoulder instantly screamed with agony, and she screamed in turn, collapsing onto her side. Ten seconds later, the young Pakistani stepped off the bus and walked past her, carrying the broken remains of her camera.

Her fellow passengers were starting to resist, having realized that something was wrong. Shifting her weight to her left elbow, Rebeka managed to sit up and take in the scene, though her vision was still slightly blurred. She watched as Umberto Verga stepped forward and spat a few words in halting Punjabi to one of the guards, who immediately tried to push the hefty climber back into line. Verga barely moved, but his face turned red with indignation. Taking another step forward, he slapped aside the barrel of the Pakistani's rifle. Rebeka watched in a daze as Verga repeated his question in English, and although he was standing about 30 feet away, he was shouting so loud, she could hear every word.

"What the fuck did you hit her for?" the Sicilian bellowed, spit flying out of his mouth. His heavily bearded face was just a few inches from that of the soldier. "Who do you think you are, you little shit? Do you have any idea what you're starting here?"

She was vaguely surprised to see Umberto jumping to her defense, especially since he had never muttered more than a few words in her direction. But her surprise quickly turned to horrified disbelief when the Pakistani took two steps back, whipped the AK-47 up to his shoulder, and squeezed the trigger. A number of rounds punched into Verga's barrel chest. The Sicilian took two uncertain steps back, then spiraled to the ground, shock carved into his weathered face.

For a moment, there was nothing but stunned silence. Then the passengers started to scream, everyone running in different directions. Unfortunately, there was nowhere to go. Nothing but flat plains in every direction, all of which led up to mountainous peaks, and the soldiers had clearly planned for this possibility. They had arranged themselves in a semicircle around the bus, and they didn't seem to panic as the passengers scattered. Instead, they fanned out to a greater degree. Strangely enough, nobody fired a shot. Above the panicked screams, a sonorous voice pleaded for calm in cultured English.

Rebeka, still propped up on her left elbow, watched it all unfold in a dreamlike state. Part of her was hoping she was right, that it *was* just a dream, but she couldn't deny what had happened to Umberto Verga, and she couldn't deny what was happening now.

A sudden noise caught her attention, and she realized the bus was pulling away, the rear tires kicking up a spray of crushed gravel. She felt pebbles stinging the right side of her face, then heard a high-pitched whine as the vehicle shifted into second gear. A hoarse voice carried over the cacophony, giving a command in Punjabi. It was the same voice that had called out in English earlier, but it had taken on a different, harder tone. The next thing she heard was the sound of gunfire, immediately followed by splintering glass. There was a loud thump, the sound of a vehicle crashing into a shallow ditch. Then there was nothing, save for a few distant sobs and the steady hum of an idling engine.

Looking around, Rebeka saw that the soldiers had taken on a less threatening posture, their weapons pointed toward the ground, faces fixed in neutral expressions. The leader seemed to be holding court, his rifle slung over his chest, hands raised in a calming gesture. He was speaking in English, but Rebeka couldn't make out the specific words, her ears still ringing from the earlier blow. Whatever he was saying seemed to be working; her fellow passengers had mostly lapsed into silence and were moving back toward the soldiers cautiously. As Rebeka watched from a distance, Beni Abruzzi stumbled forward and dropped to his knees beside his cousin's body, his mouth working silently. The other passengers seemed equally glued to the disturbing sight, but nevertheless, they kept moving forward. It was as if they recognized the futility of running, that for the moment, their best option was to comply, to adhere to their captors' demands.

Captors. The word seemed to lodge in her head for some reason, even though these men were dressed as soldiers. To the north, a rapidly approaching truck was kicking up plumes of dust on the KKH, its windshield sparkling in the pale yellow sun. The armed Pakistanis didn't seem to notice the vehicle, which gave Rebeka a very bad feeling. After what they had just done, they wouldn't be looking for extra attention. As her head cleared, the truth started to dawn, piece by piece, like a jigsaw puzzle coming together before her eyes. Only this puzzle was forming a picture she didn't want to see: the soldiers were expecting the truck.

They didn't need the bus, because they had the truck. They were going to leave the bus all along, because it served as a message. The bus was proof of what had happened here, and the truck was taking them somewhere else.

They were being kidnapped.

When the truth hit her, Rebeka was overcome by a wave of foreboding. She had read accounts of journalists who'd been caught up in similar situations, but she also knew of the larger number who had not survived to tell their tale. Still, despite the fear that clenched her gut, she didn't visibly react. Instead, she just stared around, wondering if any of her fellow travelers had figured it out. Part of her wanted to fight this injustice, so she staggered to her feet and hunched over at the waist for a second, trying to stop her head from spinning.

Once she'd pushed down the worst of the nausea, she straightened and turned to look for the leader, the man who'd calmed the other travelers with his gentle command of the English language. Rebeka couldn't pick him out, but she did see the cargo truck, which had come to a halt 20 meters away. Her fellow travelers were now facedown on the ground, their hands being tied behind their backs.

Most were lying passively, but a few were struggling, and two or three weren't moving at all. Looking closer, she realized that the still fig-ures were bleeding profusely from head wounds. She didn't think they'd been shot—she hadn't heard any additional gunfire—but even from a distance, she could recognize how serious their injuries were.

A soldier was moving toward her, boots crunching over the coarse gravel, his rifle slung over his chest. He smiled, produced a strange-looking length of cord, and gestured for her to turn around. She did so slowly, struggling to suppress her fear. Her hands were pulled gently behind her, then bound securely with the plastic restraints. Feeling a tap on her uninjured shoulder, she turned once more. This time, however, the soldier was no longer smiling. Holding his weapon in both hands, he pulled his arms in tight at shoulder height, then whipped the butt of the rifle forward, directly into her face.

Rebeka saw a flash of bright light, then felt a sudden, blinding pain, her head snapping back with the force of the blow.

Her legs gave way, and everything went blessedly, mercifully black.

CHAPTER 1

ORAEFI, ICELAND

The whitewashed hotel at the foot of the Svínafellsjökull Glacier was simple, comfortable, and nearly empty, even though the roads were clear and spring had just given way to the short Arctic summer. In short, it was everything the lone traveler had been looking for when he'd walked into town two days earlier, legs aching from a day's worth of arduous trekking. It had been nearly three weeks since he'd departed the sprawling capital of Reykjavík, based 200 miles to the west, and he'd spent most of that time crossing the bleak Icelandic wilderness on foot. The Skaftafell Hotel seemed almost luxurious after his previous accommodations, a cramped, foul-smelling hut on the Morsárdalur mountain track. Still, he would have been satisfied with much less.

Southeastern Iceland was only the latest stop on what had become a prolonged expedition to some of the world's most challenging environments. Ryan Kealey wasn't exactly starting from scratch, as he'd spent his teens and early twenties hiking and climbing in places ranging from Washington's Mount Rainier to Ben Nevis in Scotland, but he'd never pushed himself as hard as he had in recent months. He knew where this sudden desire to test himself had come from, but while he had tried to address the source, he'd been unable to come up with any real answers. In large part, this was because he couldn't find the woman who'd caused him so much pain and frustration, despite his best efforts and high-level connections.

She'd walked out in January, four months after a terrorist attack in New York City that had nearly claimed her life. Kealey had waited for two months, putting out feelers, calling in favors, but it had gotten him nowhere. By the time March rolled around, he'd finally admitted defeat, accepting that she didn't want to be found. He'd pushed it aside for another few weeks, but then, tired of sitting around with nothing to do but think about her, he'd decided to strike out on his own. His only goal at the time was to clear his head, lose himself in the raw, primitive beauty of the world's most isolated regions.

That had been three months earlier. Since then he'd climbed Denali in Alaska, Kilimanjaro in northeastern Tanzania, and Mount Cook in the Southern Alps of New Zealand. He'd crossed Chile's Atacama Desert at its widest point, scaled Morocco's High Atlas Mountains, and completed the 60-mile, six-day Paine Circuit in Patagonia. He had beaten his body to the point of sheer exhaustion and then had pushed harder, but nothing had helped. It had taken him half a year to figure it out, but the truth had been staring him right in the face the whole time. No matter what he did or where he went, he couldn't stop thinking about Naomi Kharmai.

Kealey had been sorting it through in his mind since the day she'd disappeared, trying to figure out what he could have said or done to stop her from leaving. It was hard to pick out the worst part about the whole situation. It was all bad, but some aspects were worse than others. When he thought about it honestly, it wasn't the fact that she had left that troubled him most. What really bothered him was her inability to face the past. The terrorist attack that nearly claimed her life the previous September had left her scarred in more ways than one, and while Kealey had done his best to help her through it, she had never fully recovered. At least not on the inside. In fact, the last time he'd seen her, she was still very much in denial.

It weighed heavily on him, and it was hard not to feel a sense of personal failure. If she had left because she needed more than what he had to offer, that would have been one thing. It would have been hard, but he could have dealt with it. What concerned him was that she might have gotten worse since walking out—that she might have spiraled further into her inner sanctum of guilt, grief, and depression. He didn't want to push her, but he would have given anything to hear her voice, if only to know that she was still alive.

Shifting the weight of the pack on his shoulders, Kealey crossed the dark gravel expanse of the parking lot, heading toward the hotel's main entrance. Stopping well short of the building's lights, he looked up and appraised the clear night sky. The stars had come out an hour earlier, and they were shockingly bright, given the dimly lit surrounding countryside. Svínafellsjökull towered behind the low-slung building, the glacier itself a dark silhouette against the deep navy backdrop. Ribbons of green light seemed to ripple and dance in the crisp, clean mountain air. The aurora borealis—better known as the northern lights—was something that he'd never seen before landing in Keflavík, and the sight was at once ethereal and incredibly eerie.

After admiring the view for a few minutes more, Kealey pulled open the door and nodded hello to the plump, smiling receptionist. She returned the gesture and went back to her crossword puzzle as he climbed the stairs, making his way up to the bar on the second floor. The worn oak doors were propped open, dim light flickering into the hall. Stepping into the room, he pulled off his wool knit watch cap, ran a hand through his lank black hair, and started toward the bar. The walls were paneled in pale oak, uninspired prints hanging around the room and above the fireplace, where a small fire was burning. The dark green couches, shiny with wear, complemented the worn carpet perfectly, and burgundy velvet drapes hung behind the bar itself, where a morose young man stood guard behind the small selection of taps. Kealey had just finished ordering a beer when he sensed movement over by one of the large windows. He turned and stared for a few seconds, appraising the solitary figure. Then he lifted a hand in cautious greeting. Turning back to the bar, he revised his order, his mind racing. Less than a minute later he was walking across the room, a pint glass in each hand, wondering what might have brought this particular visitor halfway around the world.

Jonathan Harper was seated with his back to the wall, his right foot hooked casually over his left knee. He was dressed in dark jeans, Merrell hiking boots, and a gray V-neck sweater, but despite his youthful attire, the deputy DCI—the second-highest-ranking official in the Central Intelligence Agency—looked far older than his forty-three years. His neat brown hair was just starting to gray at the temples, but his face was gaunt, and his skin was shockingly pale. His mannerisms were even more noticeable. He seemed shaky and slightly guarded, but also resigned, like an old man who senses the end is near. All of this was to be expected, though, and Kealey knew it could have been worse. In truth, the man was extremely lucky to still be alive.

Kealey placed the beers on the water-stained table, shrugged off his jacket, and slid into the opposite seat. They appraised each other for a long moment. Finally, Harper offered a slight smile and extended a hand, which the younger man took.

"Good to see you, Ryan. It's been a long time."

"I suppose so," Kealey said. He leaned back in his chair and crossed his arms in a casual way. "About seven months, I guess. When did you get here?"

"I flew into Keflavík this morning, but the bus only arrived a few hours ago."

"Sorry to keep you waiting. How have you been?"

"Not bad, all things considered." Harper took a short pull on his lager, coughed sharply, and wiped his mouth with the back of his hand. "The doctors are happy enough, so I guess that's something."

"And Julie?"

"She's fine. I think she secretly enjoys having a patient again, though she'd never admit it."

"Knowing her, it wouldn't surprise me at all," Kealey replied. He knew that Harper's wife had worked for years as a head nurse at the Mayo Clinic in Rochester, Minnesota, one of the best hospitals in the country. The smile faded from his face as he debated going forward with his next question. Finally, he went ahead and asked it.

"What about Jane Doe? Any luck on that front?"

"Not a thing. I'm starting to think we'll never find her. Even if we did, it's not like we could hand her over to the FBI. There just isn't enough evidence to charge her with anything. They never found the gun, you know."

Kealey nodded slowly. Eight months earlier, the newly appointed deputy director had narrowly survived an assassination attempt in Washington, D.C. The attack had taken place on the front step of his brownstone on General's Row, just as he was stretching after his morning run. Harper had been facing away from his armed assailant when the first shot was fired. The .22-caliber round penetrated his lower back, then ricocheted off the third rib and up through the right lung. The second and third rounds had torn into his upper arm as he turned toward the shooter, and the fourth had punched a hole in his chest, missing his heart by less than an inch.

The woman had been moving forward as she fired, and by the time the fourth round left the muzzle of her gun, she was less than 10 feet from her target. As she approached to fire the fatal shot, a D.C. Metro police cruiser had squealed to a halt on Q Street, lights flashing. The police officer's arrival on the scene had been pure chance, nothing but luck, but it had saved the deputy director's life. The woman fired at the officer as he stepped out of the vehicle, killing him instantly, but the distraction gave Julie Harper—who had been making coffee when the first shots were fired—the chance to open the door and pull her husband inside to safety.

Unfortunately, the would-be assassin managed to escape in the ensuing chaos, even though the Metro Police Department was able to seal off the surrounding streets with astonishing speed. What followed was one of the largest manhunts in U.S. history, but despite the enormous resources it had thrown into the search, the government had yet to track her down.

The CIA had looked harder and longer than anyone else, of course, and in time, they'd managed to dig up a few tenuous leads. "Jane Doe" had been involved with a former Special Forces soldier named William Vanderveen. In 1997, while on deployment in Syria, Vanderveen had made the decision to sell his skills to some of the world's most dangerous terrorist organizations. From that point forward, he'd earned—through countless acts of cold-blooded murder—his status as one of the most wanted men in the world. The connection between Vanderveen and the would-be assassin was based on photographs taken in London by Britain's Security Service, MI5. The men who took the shots were assigned to "A" branch, Section 4, the "Five" unit tasked with domestic surveillance. The shots showed Vanderveen and the unknown woman walking side by side in the heart of the city, but despite the excellent image resolution, the photographs had proved useless. The Agency's facial recognition software had failed to find a reliable match in the database. MI5, the French DGSE, and the Israeli Mossad had also come up empty, as had a number of other friendly intelligence services.

In other words, the woman was a black hole, a nonentity. Kealey knew how much it bothered Harper that she'd never been caught, but as he'd just said, there had been no progress on that front. This realization brought Kealey to his next point.

"John, it's good to see you again, but what exactly are you doing here?"

The deputy director didn't respond right away. Instead, he picked up his beer and swirled the contents thoughtfully.

"I'm surprised to hear you ask me that first," he finally said. "I thought you might be wondering how I found you." He looked up and studied the younger man. "You know, I have a few questions of my own. For instance, I'd like to know why you haven't set foot on U.S. soil in two and a half months. I mean, I spend half that time looking for you, and when I finally catch up, I find you . . ." He trailed off and lifted his arms, as if to include the whole country.

There was an unspoken question there, but Kealey wasn't sure how to answer it. When he'd set out three months earlier, it was without a plan. Without a real idea of what he was looking for. But whatever it was, he'd found it on the alpine tundra and the vast, seemingly endless ice fields of Iceland. He'd found it in Alaska, Tanzania, Patagonia, and all the other places he'd seen in recent months. For lack of a better word, it was solitude, the kind of terrain where one could walk for days without hearing a sound other than the wind. It was what he had wanted at the time—what he still wanted, to a certain degree—and he couldn't explain why. Naomi's disappearance had played a role, but that was only part of it. Something else had instilled in him the desire to get away from it all, though he had yet to identify the secondary cause for his restless behavior.

"I'd also like to know where you picked up a French passport in the name of Joseph Briand," Harper continued. He paused expectantly. "I don't suppose you'd be willing to volunteer the information."

Kealey gave a wan smile, and that was answer enough.

"I didn't think so. It's funny, seeing how you don't even speak French. A Saudi passport would have been far more—"

"Comment savez-vous que je ne parle pas français?"

"Okay, so you speak a *little* French." The older man couldn't conceal a small, fleeting smile of his own. "It's good to see you're expanding your horizons."

"Just trying to keep my mind active."

"Sounds like you're ready to return to the ranks."

"Not in this lifetime." Kealey shook his head and looked away. "And if that's why you're here, John, you're wasting your time. I'm not interested. I've done my part."

"We've already played this game, Ryan, on more occasions than I care to recall. You say the same thing every time, but when it comes down to the wire, you always—"

"I meant it when I said it before," the younger man shot back. "And I mean it now." His face tightened suddenly, his dark eyes retreating to some hidden point in the past. "I just didn't walk away when I should have. That was my biggest mistake. There was always something else that had to be done. Before it was Vanderveen, and at the time, it seemed like the right thing to do. But you know what it cost me to track him down, and then last year, with Naomi . . ."

Harper nodded slowly, his face assuming a somber expression. "I know what it cost you, Ryan, and I know what it cost Naomi." He hesitated, then said, "You may not believe this, but I personally advised the president against bringing you into this matter. I told him everything you just said to me. I told him that you've done your part. That you wouldn't be interested. He didn't want to hear a word. After what you did in New York last year, he won't have it any other way. As far as David Brenneman is concerned, you're the first and only choice, at least when it comes to the current situation."

"And you couldn't say no to the president," Kealey said sarcastically. "Is that it?" He didn't bother asking what "the current situation" was; simply put, he didn't care to know.

"That's part of it," Harper conceded. "But there's another reason you need to be involved, and once you hear me out, I think you'll feel the same way."

Kealey studied the older man for a long moment without speaking. Jonathan Harper was one of the smartest people he knew, but he could also be extremely manipulative. They had known each other for nearly a decade, ever since Harper had first "sheep-dipped" him for an off-the-books assignment in Syria. "Sheep-dipping" was a term that referred to the temporary recruitment of active-duty soldiers for "black," or deniable, operations. Usually, the CIA had a hand in the process, and Kealey's first task was no exception. At the time he had been a captain in the U.S. Army's 3rd Special Forces Group, and that assignment—the assassination of a senior Islamic militant—

had changed him forever, as well as putting him on the path to a new career.

Since then, he and Harper had become good friends, but the job always came first, and Kealey knew the other man wouldn't hesitate to impose on their relationship. He had done it before, and Kealey had always been up to the task. He wanted to refuse this time and knew he would have been justified in doing so. But while the older man's face was as implacable as ever, there was something in his tone that gave Kealey pause. He could tell there was more to the current situation than Harper was letting on, and that made the decision for him.

"Okay," he said. "I'll hear what you have to say, but I'm not committing to anything. Let's get that straight from the start." Kealey lifted his glass and drained the contents. "What's this about, anyway?"

Harper pushed a plain manila folder across the table, then rose and collected their empty glasses. "Read through that, and then we'll talk."

CHAPTER 2

ORAEFI

"This guy doesn't have much of a track record," Kealey said ten minutes later. He closed the folder and tossed it onto the table. "And there's nothing in that pile of paper to suggest he's a threat. At least not to us."

"Have you ever even heard of him?" Harper asked. He had returned with two fresh beers a few minutes earlier, but had sat quietly as he waited for Kealey to finish reading.

"The name seems familiar, but no, I don't really know who he is."

"Well, allow me to enlighten you, as the file is a little thin when it comes to his background. Amari Saifi is forty years old, Algerian born, and a former paratrooper in that country's army, hence his nom de guerre, Abderrazak al-Para. He's also a senior figure in the GSPC, otherwise known as the Salafist Group for Call and Combat. Since it came to prominence in the late nineties, the GSPC has been responsible for countless acts of terrorism in Algeria, most notably the kidnapping of thirty-two European tourists in 2003. That incident was masterminded by Saifi, and it was also what brought him to the attention of our government. To be fair, we weren't really interested in the act itself. We were more concerned with how it all turned out in the end."

"What do you mean by that?" Kealey had looked through the file with a slight degree of interest, but he didn't know anything about Saifi or the GSPC, so it didn't make much sense to him. One thing in particular had left him confused. According to the attached documents, the GSPC was committed to establishing an Islamic government in Algeria, which made it a rebel group with a limited objective and, presumably, a limited network. In other words, funding and active members were probably hard to come by. He didn't understand why this ragtag group should concern the CIA *or* the president, especially since it had all but disbanded in recent years.

"After several months of secret negotiations," Harper continued, "the German government capitulated and offered Saifi a ransom of six million dollars in exchange for the hostages, which he accepted. All were returned safely in two stages, except for one woman, who apparently succumbed to heat exhaustion in the Sahara Desert. That was where the hostages were being held. Is any of this ringing a bell?"

"Not really." Kealey wasn't impressed. The size of the file—a few articles and some grainy photographs—said one of two things, at least in his opinion. Either Saifi wasn't that big a deal, or there just wasn't a lot of background on him. The deputy director's next words, however, made the distinction clear.

"Ryan, I don't get the feeling you're taking this seriously, so let me say it in plain language. Simply put, Amari Saifi is probably the most dangerous person you've never heard of. Besides the kidnapping, he was directly involved in the murder of forty-three Algerian soldiers over a period of fourteen months. He was also linked to a number of bombings in neighboring Mauritania, though his involvement was never confirmed. Again, that was in 2003, but he's been active with the Salafists since 1992.

"In March of 2004, Saifi was traveling on foot through the Tibesti Mountains when he was apprehended by another rebel group, the Movement for Democracy and Justice in Chad. That's the MDJC, for the sake of brevity. Sixteen of his men were also captured in that incident, but Saifi was the only one who really mattered. The rebels instantly knew what they had, as by that time, Saifi had essentially established himself as the bin Laden of the Sahara."

"So they decided to auction him off to the highest bidder," Kealey guessed.

"Exactly. Unfortunately for the rebels, however, there were no takers, at least not at first. Strangely enough, even the Algerian government didn't seem to be in that big a rush to get their hands on him.

We never figured out why, but it was probably because they didn't want to risk their diplomatic relationship with the Chadian government."

"Why didn't we step in?"

"The same reason," Harper replied. "We were tempted to make an offer, as Saifi was already on the State Department's list of wanted terrorists, but it never happened. After much debate, the president decided he couldn't deal with the rebels directly, because it would undermine the Pan Sahel Initiative, which was in its infancy at the time. Especially since the initiative was specifically aimed toward curtailing terrorist activity in North Africa, and the Chadian government pretty much viewed the MDJC as a terrorist organization. Anyway, al-Para was eventually remanded to Libyan custody, and from there, the Algerians finally stepped in. A trial was scheduled for June 2005, but Saifi never stepped foot in the courtroom. He was sentenced *in absentia* to life in prison, and according to the Algerian interior ministry, that's where he currently is."

Kealey looked up quickly, confusion spreading over his face. Then he flipped open the folder and pulled out a number of pictures. He turned them around so the other man could see, and said, "According to the time and date stamp, these pictures were taken two weeks ago. If this is Amari Saifi, how did he get out of prison, and why are the Algerians covering it up?"

Harper nodded slowly. "Good questions. Unfortunately, we don't have any answers at this time."

"Are we sure this is him?" Kealey asked, tapping the face in the photograph.

"Beyond a doubt. We used an older photo for comparison and ran them through the facial recognition software at Langley. We got a hit on eighteen nodal points, and as you know, fourteen nodes are enough to make a positive match."

Kealey leaned back in his seat and lifted his glass, thinking it through as he nursed his beer. After a couple of minutes had passed in silence, he said, "There's one thing I still don't understand, John. Why does this concern us?"

Harper turned his head to the right. While they'd been talking, a young woman had entered the room and taken a seat at the bar, facing away from them. After studying her dispassionately for a moment, he turned back to Kealey.

"Have you been keeping up with the news?"

"No."

"You must know about the situation in Kashmir, though."

Kealey nodded slowly. Several months earlier, the Israeli government had announced its commitment to a large armament sale to India. The deal—reputed to be worth nearly eight hundred million dollars—included a dozen Hermes 180 unmanned aerial vehicles, fifty Raytheon battlefield surveillance radars, and twenty-five SPYDER mobile firing units. Perhaps the most controversial part of the deal, each SPYDER unit carried four missiles capable of engaging aerial targets from a distance exceeding 15 kilometers. When news of the impending sale became public, the Pakistani president, Pervez Musharraf, had immediately launched a very vocal, public campaign condemning it. He'd implored the United States to step in and call a halt to the sale, but his pleas had fallen on deaf ears. To make matters worse, the Indians were seeking additional hardware from Israel, including submarine-launched cruise missiles, and Israel looked ready to deal.

In response, the Pakistani army had begun increasing its presence on the disputed border in Jammu and Kashmir. Over the course of two short months, more than 10,000 troops had amassed on the Line of Control, and India had responded in kind. The White House had remained relatively quiet on the matter, and while many other world leaders had made remarks pleading for restraint on both sides, President Brenneman had yet to directly intervene in the Israel-India deal. Many saw this as a tacit approval of the transaction, including General Musharraf, who had recently boycotted a White House function while attending a peace symposium, of all things, in Washington, D.C.

"Secretary Fitzgerald arrived in Islamabad several hours ago," Harper said. Brynn Fitzgerald was the acting secretary of state. Two months earlier, her predecessor had suffered a fatal heart attack while attending a summit in Geneva, and Fitzgerald had been elevated to the top job, making her just the third woman to hold that position in U.S. history. The president, impressed with her work in the past, had immediately submitted her name to the Senate Committee on Foreign Relations, but the Senate as a whole had yet to confirm the nomination.

"She's expected to meet with Musharraf both tonight and tomorrow," Harper continued. "With any luck, she'll be able to convince him that we have limited influence over whom the Israelis do business with. Needless to say, it won't be an easy sell. Everyone knows that Brenneman could squash that deal with a single call."

"I agree," Kealey said. "But what does this have to do with Amari Saifi?"

Harper pointed toward the photographs spread over the table. "These images were captured by a professional photographer named Rebeka Česnik. She, along with fourteen of her fellow passengers, disappeared on the Karakoram Highway in Pakistan two weeks ago. Three other people were killed as the kidnapping took place, along with the driver of the bus. Their bodies were left behind, along with the bus itself and all the passengers' luggage."

"If everyone is missing or dead, how did we get these shots?"

"Apparently, the kidnappers didn't realize that Česnik had removed the film from her camera. She hid it in her pack, and they settled for taking her camera. At least, that's the assumption, as it was never recovered."

"Okay, but how does this figure into Fitzgerald's visit? And why is Amari Saifi, the leader of a North African terrorist group, operating in Pakistan all of a sudden?"

"Fitzgerald is going to make a few gentle inquiries in Islamabad," Harper said in response to the first question. "She'll inquire about their efforts to track down the kidnappers, but Saifi is off-limits until we have more information on what he's doing there. When the secretary of state meets with Musharraf tomorrow morning, she won't mention al-Para once. You may not be aware of this, Ryan, but twelve American tourists have gone missing in Pakistan over the past several months. Some disappeared individually, others in groups of two or three. A ransom demand has yet to be made, and nobody's claimed responsibility. We're looking at Saifi for all of it. It's almost an exact replication of what he did in Africa, only this time he's taken our people, which makes it our business."

"So to summarize, the president wants the hostages released unharmed as soon as possible, and he's asked you to get it done."

"Exactly."

"Why should I care?" Kealey said, looking directly into the other man's eyes. A brief, awkward silence ensued. "I don't work for the Agency anymore, John. I don't want to leave you hanging, but I want to be involved even less. Besides, it sounds like you need someone who speaks the languages. Someone who knows the area. More importantly, you need a place to start. A lead of some kind."

"We have a lead," Harper assured him. "All we need is someone to follow it up. That is, someone with a proven track record. Someone such as yourself. Remember, Ryan, the president asked for you by name on this. What happened in New York is not exactly a distant memory. He remembers what you did there. He remembers how many lives you saved that day, and he's grateful for it. He wants someone who knows how to get results."

"Then we're back to why I should care."

The deputy DCI leaned back in his seat and shook his head wearily. He looked for all the world like a guidance counselor who'd failed to get through to a wayward student. Instead of answering the younger man's question directly, he pointed toward the other side of the room. "See that woman over there?"

Kealey turned in his seat to study the small, slender figure at the bar for the first time. He couldn't see her face, but nevertheless, it clicked in a matter of seconds. His mind went blank, and it was like the air had been sucked right out of the room. For once, he'd been caught completely off guard.

"That's why," Harper said. His voice carried a hint of regret, as if he'd been pushed into something he found distasteful. "That's why."

CHAPTER 3

ISLAMABAD, PAKISTAN

The three-story apartment building, located in the G7/1 sector of Islamabad, was just one of many similar dwellings on Khayaban-e-Suharwardy, a major street that marked the southern edge of the Pakistani capital. On the third-floor balcony of the end unit, close to the point where the thoroughfare met the Sahar Road, a solitary figure lifted a cigarette to his lips with a shaking hand. As he breathed in the calming smoke, he gazed out across the lush green grass and narrow, sinuous canals of Sector H7. In the distance were the lights of the Rose and Jasmine Garden, and beyond, the dark silhouette of the sports complex. The night air was warm and still, and traffic was almost nonexistent at three in the morning. It was quiet and peaceful, a marked contrast to the constant, clamorous din of the daylight hours. Behind him, through the open patio door, his wife stirred, moaned softly in her sleep, then fell silent once more.

A lifelong insomniac, Naveed Jilani frequently ventured onto the balcony to gather his thoughts and while away the early-morning hours. On this occasion, though, he wasn't just trying to pass the time. Instead, he was completely focused on the day that lay ahead. The fear and stress had been building up for the past two weeks, and he knew he hadn't hidden it well. He didn't know when his wife had first caught on, but he felt sure she had sensed it right from the start. Parveen was a fine woman, a good wife, an attentive mother to their three-year-old son. She was accustomed to his dark moods, his prolonged bouts of strained silence, and she knew when to give him his space. Being the devoted wife she was, she'd sought to relieve his stress in other ways, but even her gentle touch in bed had not been enough to quell his fears. It was something he could not have explained to her. She wouldn't have understood, and he had no desire to trouble her with the true cause of his anxiety. She wouldn't have been able to fix it anyway, but he couldn't fault her for that. Even in the early hours of the morning, when the regret and bitterness left their deepest impressions, Naveed couldn't bring himself to blame her. Sometimes it seemed as if his whole life had been leading up to this point, and there was nothing that he—or anyone else—could do to change it.

Jilani had been born in 1975 in the city of Quetta, less than 100 miles from the Afghan border. His mother had died of cancer when he was ten years old, and owing to his father's lack of funds and interest, he was sent to live with his uncle in the slums of Karachi. Syed Jilani had tried and failed at many things by the time his nephew came to know him, but from 1979 to 1984, he found a degree of success in Afghanistan, where he fought with distinction alongside the mujahideen. In the years that followed, his hatred for America became increasingly virulent, despite the fact that the West had funded and armed the Afghan fundamentalists in their extended war against the Soviet forces. Still, his feelings for the West didn't preclude him from taking full advantage of the U.S. weapons and ammunition left over from the conflict in Afghanistan. It was a dangerous, highly illicit enterprise that required more than one set of hands, and when he first began smuggling arms from Afghanistan into neighboring Iran and Pakistan in 1997, Syed Jilani knew exactly where to turn for help.

During his time in Afghanistan, the elder Jilani had formed lasting partnerships with men who knew how to use their positions for monetary gain. One of these contacts was an army lieutenant and a member of Inter-Services Intelligence. The only son of a construction magnate, Benazir Mengal was connected at the highest levels to Afghan warlords, Pakistani generals, and prominent figures in the emerging Taliban, and that made him the perfect man to facilitate Syed Jilani's cross-border activities.

Naveed was fifteen years old when he met Mengal for the first time, and he had been instantly drawn to the charismatic Pakistani soldier. The reason for his adulation was simple: Mengal was an easy man to admire. Unlike Naveed's father and uncle, he had succeeded brilliantly in everything he'd ever tried. He was handsome, intelligent, and possessed of a natural spark that allowed him to draw people in with incredible ease. From the very start, Naveed could see how Mengal affected the people around him, including his uncle. Syed Jilani, normally brash and quick to temper, was quiet and respectful in Mengal's presence, as were his like-minded acquaintances. In short, Ben Mengal was everything Naveed Jilani wanted to be, and he'd modeled his whole life on that principle. At least he'd tried. Whether or not he'd succeeded was another matter entirely.

He'd tried to join the Pakistani army shortly after his eighteenth birthday, but a thorough physical had revealed a heart defect that precluded his entrance. Naveed had desperately searched for a loophole, but when it became clear that all avenues were blocked, he'd turned to his mentor for help. By that time, Mengal was a lieutenant colonel and a department head with Inter-Services Intelligence. His influence alone would have been enough to cut through the bureaucratic restrictions, but on a calm summer day in 1993, he'd met with Naveed to explain the situation. He had described the limited opportunities the army would offer, due to the younger man's nonexistent education, and he'd proposed an alternative: a career in government service.

Naveed could remember that conversation in its entirety. He had been hesitant at first, but Mengal had soon won him over. He made quiet, sincere promises based on his position, and in the years that followed, he'd come through in spectacular fashion. For a man of thirty-four with no university training and a limited knowledge of English, Naveed Jilani had achieved a position of remarkable influence in the Pakistani government. But Mengal's work behind the scenes was not born of generosity, and two weeks earlier, he had asked his young friend to repay the favor.

Naveed did not often hear from the general in person, but while the call had merely caught him off guard, the favor had left him stunned to his core. He had agreed, of course—he had long known he was incapable of refusing Ben Mengal—but the conversation, which took place in the back room of a madrassa in Peshawar, had caused him to rethink his entire association with the former army officer. The truth was, Naveed knew next to nothing about the man who had single-handedly made his career. Since that troubling meeting, he'd done his best to learn more about his benefactor, but unfortunately, that was easier said than done.

Rumors about Mengal abounded, but few could be confirmed. It was said that his ailing father had recently disowned him, thereby depriving him of the vast fortune he was set to inherit. Naveed wasn't sure if that was true, but he knew that Mengal had been asked to step down in the wake of 9/11. That event hadn't come as a surprise to anyone. Since the fall of the Taliban, Mengal and his ilk had become a liability, an uneasy reminder of Musharraf's former alliances. To make matters worse, it was widely assumed that Mengal had a direct connection to senior members of al-Qaeda, including the director himself. Those associations, whether real or imagined, had brought him to the attention of the Western intelligence services. But that had been years earlier, and since severing his links to the army and the intelligence community, he had largely gone unnoticed. From 2001 until the present day, Mengal was practically a black hole, and it was largely assumed that he had retired to a life of quiet solitude.

Naveed Jilani did not buy into the rumor. He wasn't an educated man, but he'd worked closely with career diplomats for the last sixteen years. He knew how to read people, and he knew better than to dismiss a man like Ben Mengal. In twenty-five years of government service, the general had built himself a reputation that stood apart from his position with the Pakistani army. He had also sewn the seeds for a number of future enterprises, none of which required the thin veneer of authority. Still, nothing could have prepared Naveed for what the older man had asked of him two weeks earlier. He still couldn't believe he'd agreed to Mengal's request, but in the end he had, and that was all that mattered. He had no choice now but to follow through with it. In less than twelve hours, he was going to help the general strike a blow against the West that would be felt for years to come, and there was nothing he could do to stop it—nothing he could do to extricate himself from an act that would soon place him square in the path of a vengeful nation, the most powerful on earth.

Behind him, his wife called out softly, imploring him to come inside. Naveed took one final drag on his cigarette, then flicked the butt over the iron rail and exhaled a narrow stream of smoke. He gazed up at the clear night sky and whispered a silent prayer. He did not ask for the strength to do the right thing; he had already made his decision. Instead, he asked Allah to look over his wife and child.

He asked that someday, whether it was five years from now or twenty, they might come to understand. He knew he had no right to ask such things; it had been many years since he'd set foot in a mosque, and his faith—even under the guidance of his devout uncle—had been tepid at best. Given the magnitude of the task he was facing, though, he felt sure that God would understand. Taking one last look at the empty sky, he turned and went inside, then closed the door behind him.

CHAPTER 4

ORAEFI

As he stared across the room in disbelief, Ryan Kealey fought to push down a surge of rising emotions. He was doing his best to keep them in check, but it just wasn't working. Shock, anger, relief, and confusion were all hitting him hard, but the anger was steadily winning out. It was immediately obvious that he had been kept in the dark for a reason other than the one he had settled upon a few months earlier. After much internal debate, he'd decided that the woman he was currently staring at had left him simply because she needed some time and space to herself. It was the only thing that made sense, because their relationship could not have been better. With her sudden reappearance in this particular place, though, it was all too clear how wrong he had been.

"You knew?" he finally asked. It was a struggle to keep his voice under control. He had about a million questions to ask, but for the most part, he was still trying to figure out exactly what was happening here. "You knew where she was the whole time?"

"It was her decision to keep it from you," Harper explained quietly, "and she came to me in the first place. I want to emphasize that."

"When?" Kealey managed to ask. His gaze was locked on Naomi Kharmai. Her shoulders seemed tense, as though she could feel his attention, but he knew it was all in his mind. There was no way she could know the conversation had turned to her. She wouldn't be able to hear them; the small fire didn't do much to heat the large room, and the heating system was obviously in disrepair, as it was unusually noisy. "When did she contact you?"

"It was the first week of February. She was a wreck at the time, falling apart at the seams. If you could have seen her the day after she called, the first time I saw her, you'd know what I'm talking about. In other words, I didn't have a choice. That's what I'm trying to tell you, Ryan. There was no way I could have turned her down, not after what she's done for us. Not after the sacrifices she's made."

Harper paused to gauge the younger man's reaction. When Kealey remained silent, he shifted uneasily, then went on with the story.

"She didn't want to come to Langley. Not at first, and not as a visitor, so we met at a coffee shop in Georgetown. It was a pretty short conversation, and she did most of the talking. Basically, she wanted to come back into the fold, but she didn't want to go back to London, and she didn't want to return to the CTC. She wanted something else, and I made it happen."

"What did she want?"

"To be completely honest, I didn't even hesitate," said Harper, pushing on. It was as if he hadn't heard the question. "She was already more than qualified, and you know what I'm talking about, because you've seen it yourself. For one thing, she has a gift when it comes to languages. It's amazing, really. She just soaks them up like—"

"John, what are you trying to say?" Kealey asked, making an effort to control his rising temper. He couldn't believe that he hadn't been told about this earlier. "What did she want from you?"

"Training," the other man answered simply. "She wanted training."

Kealey wasn't sure how to respond to that. As he tried to interpret the cryptic remark, Harper stood and collected his coat.

"I'll let her explain the rest. As for what we discussed earlier, you're already booked on a flight tomorrow evening. It's not binding, of course, but I always travel hopefully. Take some time to think it over, but I need your decision by noon. That's when the last bus leaves for Keflavík. And Ryan?"

"Yeah?"

"Don't go too hard on her. She could use your support."

Harper had paused on the way out the door to murmur a few words in her ear, but five minutes had passed since then, and Naomi still hadn't moved. She hadn't even glanced over her shoulder. From where he was sitting, Kealey couldn't see her face, so he had no way of knowing what she was thinking. He could read her body language, though, and her tense, constant movements were saying a lot. She seemed to be pushing a glass back and forth in a deliberate way, as though turning something over in her mind, or deciding how best to approach their unexpected reunion.

Unexpected on his end, Kealey corrected himself. She must have known this was coming for quite some time. He desperately wanted to jump up and walk over, but he knew it was better to let her make the first move. They hadn't seen each other in half a year, after all, and there was no point in pushing things now.

It was a lot to take in. Her sudden reappearance had hit him hard, and he was still trying to figure out how to react. Unfortunately, he had run out of time to think it through. Without warning, she had climbed off her stool and started across the worn carpet. A few seconds later she slipped into the seat that Harper had just vacated, folded her arms across her chest, and fixed him with a steady stare. Her mouth was set in a straight, tight line. There was nothing apologetic about the way she was looking at him; in fact, it was just the opposite. It was almost as if *she* were upset with *him,* which didn't make sense at all.

"Naomi," he said slowly, shaking his head. He wasn't sure what to say. "I can't believe it. I mean, I haven't seen you in months, and now you just . . ."

"I know. I didn't mean to catch you off guard. It just kind of happened that way."

"How have you been?"

She opened her mouth to respond, then clamped it shut and looked away. It was a trite, obvious question, but it was the way he had asked it that made all the difference. The concern in his voice could not have been more genuine, and judging by the small frown that had crossed her face, he'd taken her by surprise. She probably expected him to be angry, Kealey realized, and on some level, he was. For the moment, though, he was just relieved to see her again.

She was still distracted, so he took a second to look her over. The white cashmere sweater she was wearing was one of her favorites, as familiar as her snug, worn jeans and clunky heels. Her shimmering black tresses drifted around her face and over her shoulders, her bangs sweeping from left to right across her forehead. It was a slight variation on her usual style, and it served to conceal most of the pale, crooked scar that bisected her right cheek. It was the only mark on her otherwise flawless caramel-colored skin, which only made it that much more noticeable.

Most of all, he was struck by her posture, which was hard to read. She looked aggressive and defensive all at once. Her arms remained folded across her chest, and her jaw was clenched tightly shut. It was almost as if she were daring him to question the choices she'd made since their last conversation—the choices she'd intentionally kept from him for months on end.

Kealey couldn't tell how much was show and how much reflected an actual change in her personality, but he didn't think that her recent training at "The Farm"—the Agency's main training facility near Williamsburg, Virginia—could have changed her this much. It was more likely that the trials she had gone through the previous year were really to blame. It was strange to see her this way, stripped of her innocence and naiveté. Mostly, though, it was just good to see her again, to know that she hadn't succumbed to her inner turmoil.

"I've been doing okay," she finally responded. The words caught Kealey off guard; he'd forgotten he'd asked the question. "Better since I went through the course at Camp Peary, anyway. What did Harper tell you?"

"Nothing, really."

"He must have told you something," she pressed. "What did he say?"

"He said you wanted to train." Kealey hesitated. "Is that what you were doing at Peary? Training to go into the field?"

She nodded slowly. "You may not believe this, Ryan, but it was the right decision. The best thing I could have done, really. I needed a change, but it wasn't just that. I needed to . . ."

"To what?" he asked, once it became clear she wasn't going to finish.

She shrugged and looked away. She was trying to project a degree of determination, but she couldn't seem to pull it off. It was just as he'd thought; she might have changed on some level, but despite her best efforts, she hadn't been able to fix what was truly wrong. It didn't surprise him at all. From personal experience, he knew that the wounds inside—the ones that didn't bleed and couldn't be seen—were usually the worst, if only because there was no clear way to repair them.

"I can't really explain it," Naomi said, "but trust me, it was all for the best. It wasn't about you, by the way. That's not why I left, but . . . look, that's beside the point. I'm here because I wanted to talk to you. To tell you in person. I think I owe you that."

"Tell me what, exactly?"

"That I'm ready to go back to work." She paused for a second to gauge his reaction. "Harper offered me this assignment himself. He said I was perfectly suited for it, given the Pakistani angle. There aren't too many people who speak Punjabi in the Clandestine Service."

"Surely more than one, though," Kealey said, unable to keep the skepticism out of his voice. Although he cared about what she was saying, she had yet to bring up what mattered most, at least to him. He was trying to push down his bitterness, but he couldn't hold it back entirely. "Interesting how you were the first person he thought of."

She looked at him sharply. "What's that supposed to mean?"

"Nothing. I don't—" He stopped himself abruptly, not wanting to continue down this road. The last thing he wanted to do was start an argument. He desperately wanted to know what was going on in her mind, but he couldn't force it out of her. If he pushed her away, she might disappear for another six months, and he didn't think he could bear to lose her again. "I know you're capable, Naomi. That isn't the issue here. I just . . ."

"What?"

"I don't think you're ready." She started to interrupt, but he held up a hand to stop her. "Just hear me out. You've done more in the past couple of years than most field operatives do in ten, and you deserve the chance to do more, if that's what you want. But you have to give it time."

"I *have* given it time." She looked away, as though gathering her strength, then turned back to him, a hint of frustration rising to the surface. "I've given it nearly a year. What do you think I should do? Just quit? Harper picked me for this himself. *He* thinks I'm ready. Doesn't that mean anything to you?"

"He doesn't think you're ready, Naomi. That was a lie. Don't you see what's going on here?" He shook his head angrily, wishing he could make her understand. It was all coming up, all the frustration and pain of the past six months, and despite his best efforts, he could no longer hold it back. "It's all bullshit. He's just using you to get to me. I'm sure you—"

"That's so arrogant," she said, bolting up in her seat. Her dark green eyes were wide with anger as she punched a finger across the table. "I should have known you'd say something like that. You may not believe it, Ryan, but I *have* changed, and I'm more than capable of doing what needs to be done. Ask the instructors at the Farm if you don't believe me. Ask them about my scores on the range. I'm not an analyst anymore, and I'm not going to step aside. If you don't want any part of this, there are plenty of qualified people at Langley who'd love to fill your shoes."

"Look, I'm not trying to say you don't have what it takes," he said, backpedaling quickly. Then he caught himself and stopped. He couldn't keep playing it safe; he had to tell her what he really thought. He desperately wanted to keep things civil, but she was the one who had walked out without saying a word. She was the one who'd left him hanging for months on end, and now she was dropping another bombshell: the fact that she'd just taken on another, much more dangerous role at the Agency, barely ten months after a lesser role had nearly taken her life. It was just too much to take in at once, and her aggressive attitude was only making things harder. "I just don't want you to jump into something you can't handle." He lowered his voice and leaned forward, imploring her with his eyes. "Have you really moved past it, Naomi? Do you really believe what you're saying right now? I was with you when you went through the worst of it, remember?"

Her face darkened as she stared across at him; clearly, she wasn't prepared to back down, much less admit he was right. "Ryan, you haven't seen me in six months. I don't care what you believe. I'm not the same person I was back in January, and you know what? I'm not entirely sure I want to work with you on this. Especially if you're going to fight me the whole way."

Kealey looked at her in disbelief, at a complete loss for words. It was clear she'd been expecting an argument from the very start, and she wasn't about to deprive herself. In short, she was telling the truth. She *was* acting like a completely different person, so unlike the woman he'd known six months earlier. So unlike the woman he loved.

"What about us?" he asked quietly. He deeply resented being forced to ask the question; it felt too much like he was pleading with her. But he had to know, and she was clearly unwilling to broach the subject. "I thought we had something good. Is that over now? Is that what you're trying to tell me?"

She didn't respond for a long time, but a familiar look crossed her face, and for a split second, she was the same person she'd been the last time he saw her: hurt, scared, and vulnerable. When she finally spoke, it was in a low voice, her eyes aimed down at the table. "I don't know, Ryan. Please don't make me think about that right now."

He hesitated, unsure of how to proceed. "Naomi, I—"

"Look, I can't think about it," she repeated, snapping her defenses back up in a heartbeat. She looked annoyed, as if he'd tricked her into giving something away. "Besides, that isn't the issue here. I just want to know one thing, okay? Are you in or out? If you don't want to go after Saifi, if you don't want to help find those missing tourists, just say so. I can do it myself."

"Is that what you want?" he asked. He kept his voice low and calm, ignoring her show of bravado. "Do you want me to turn Harper down? Would that make it easier for you?"

She searched his eyes for a few seconds; clearly, she was trying to assess his sincerity. "It's up to you, Ryan. I can't make the decision for you. But if you don't think I'm ready, we're obviously not going to be able to work together. Maybe you should . . ." She looked away uneasily. "I don't know. Maybe you should tell him you don't want any part of it. Maybe that would be best for both of us."

He shook his head and looked down at the table. Her words had stung him deeper than she could have possibly known. When he finally lifted his head, he realized she was no longer glancing away. She was staring at him intently, waiting for his answer. Her stubborn, uncompromising gaze knocked something loose inside, and when he spoke, his words were just as hard and combative as hers.

"Unfortunately for you, Naomi, you can't stop me from getting involved. I really don't want any part of this, but I can already tell you're not going to give me a choice. So if I can't talk you out of it, then I guess you've found yourself a partner. Bear in mind, though, that I'm only doing it for one reason."

"Yeah?" She squared her shoulders, her eyes flashing in response to his tone. "And what's that?"

Kealey stood up and snatched his jacket off the back of his chair.

"To make sure you don't get yourself killed." He turned again and walked to the door, regretting the conversation more and more with each weary step he took. He didn't know what could have happened to change her this much, but he knew he wouldn't rest until he had figured it out. In the meantime, all he had to do was keep her out of harm's way. *Easier said than done,* said a little voice inside, but he pushed it down. He had done it before, and he'd do it again. He'd do whatever it took to keep her safe, regardless of how she felt about it.

CHAPTER 5

ISLAMABAD

In his twenty-two-plus years with the Bureau of Diplomatic Security, Special Agent Mike Petrina had been charged with a wide range of duties. He'd couriered documents, investigated passport fraud, and protected senior U.S. officials in thirty-four countries on six continents. In that time, he'd witnessed some truly historic events, but he'd also experienced those rare, worrisome moments where the prevalent mood was downright hostile. Nosing a Suburban through a crowd of angry protestors could be dangerous enough, but that was a regular occurrence, and he'd endured far worse. In the fall of 2000, he had been standing a few feet away when Madeleine Albright first set foot on North Korean soil. He could remember the trepidation he'd felt when the first female secretary of state shook hands with Kim Jong Il, and he could recall—with crystal clarity—the plastic smile of the reclusive communist leader, as well as the icy stares of the North Korean soldiers standing guard. While the current situation wasn't quite as bad as that, the mood in the room was undeniably tense, and it was getting worse by the minute.

The wood-paneled press room of the presidential palace was filled to capacity with journalists and cameramen. Small, ornate chandeliers hung overhead, illuminating the crowd and the smiling portrait of Muhammad Ali Jinnah, the founder of Pakistan. As far as Petrina could tell, Jinnah's was the only smiling face in the room. Two polished lecterns were standing before the portrait, positioned less than 3 feet apart. Behind the lectern, to the right, was the Pakistani foreign minister, Malik Bokhari. The lean, angular Pakistani was dressed in a dark suit and red tie. To his left was acting Secretary of State Brynn Fitzgerald. From where he was standing, Petrina had an excellent view of both officials, as well as the crowd, and the collective tension was hard to miss.

"Madam Secretary," came a voice from the crowd. Petrina instantly looked for the speaker and picked out Susan Watkins, the senior correspondent for CNN. The foreign minister had already finished his prepared remarks, as had Fitzgerald, and they had moved into the question-and-answer phase of the briefing. "I'd like to refer, if I might, to Israel's recent decision to complete a major arms sale to the Indian government. I assume President Brenneman has had time to reflect on that announcement, and given the sensitive nature of such a transaction, I was wondering if he might have reconsidered his decision to—"

"Ms. Watkins, I've already addressed this," Fitzgerald interjected. "The president has no intention of interfering with Israel's foreign affairs, and he's made it clear to everyone that this is a situation that can only be resolved by dialogue between the affected nations."

"By which you mean India and Pakistan."

"Yes."

"But surely he recognizes the international call for American engagement on this issue, especially since the United States is the largest exporter of arms to Israel in the first place, and now they're selling off the very weapons we provided them with."

Fitzgerald looked down and met the other woman's insistent gaze, but to her credit, her diplomatic façade didn't slip an inch. "I hardly think that's a reasonable statement, Susan, and it's also a fairly simplistic way of viewing this situation. Israel has a major domestic arms industry, and according to the documents I've seen, more than one hundred fifty million dollars of the proposed sale will be used to purchase the Hermes 180 UAV. The Hermes 180, of course, is an unmanned aerial vehicle manufactured by Elbit Systems Ltd., a company based in Haifa. So the Israeli government is well within its right to make that technology salable on the international market. And on a more general note, the proposed sale to India in no way violates Israel's commitments to the United States on foreign arms sales. If you'll recall, the standards I'm referring to were drawn up after Israel considered a lesser sale to China in 2004. In that case, there were issues involving the unauthorized sale of sensitive American technology, which doesn't apply in this situation. And Israel signed a memorandum of understanding to that effect in 2005. To date, they've adhered to the letter of that agreement. So, to reiterate, we see no basis for disrupting this sale."

"But isn't it true, Dr. Fitzgerald," Watkins persisted, "that the Pakistani defense minister sent a letter to the Pentagon asking the United States to reconsider its stance, citing the damage the sale would cause to regional security in South Asia? Mr. Bokhari, if you would care to comment on that also."

Fitzgerald didn't respond for a long moment. Her counterpart turned toward her, awaiting her reaction, and the cameras started clicking away. Petrina winced involuntarily from the sidelines. Although she had an excellent rapport with the diplomats and world leaders she'd met so far, Fitzgerald's previous position hadn't prepared her for this kind of exposure. When the cameras were rolling, the slightest hesitation could have disastrous effects, as it automatically fostered the impression that the speaker in question was concocting a lie. Petrina just hoped she had the presence of mind to realize that before she answered the question.

"I haven't had the chance to examine that letter," Fitzgerald finally said. "Nor am I aware of its exact contents, so I can't—"

"But you are aware of its existence, correct?" asked another reporter.

"Yes," Fitzgerald replied, her voice taking on a sharper edge. "And so is the president. But as I said before, he—"

"Dr. Fitzgerald, if I may," her counterpart interrupted. Fitzgerald nodded once, reassuming her neutral expression.

"Of course, Mr. Bokhari."

Malik Bokhari turned back to the reporter who'd posed the question. "It's true that we have appealed to many American leaders on this matter, not just the president. In fact, President General Musharraf has personally reached out to several influential members of Congress. Obviously, we're vastly concerned over Israel's proposed arms sale to India, and the escalating number of soldiers on both sides of the Line of Control is a testament to the dire nature of the situation. Pakistan has no intention of provoking a conflict in the areas of Azad Kashmir, but any further attempts by the Indian government to increase its military readiness will be met in kind, and any incursion on territory controlled by Pakistan will be met with swift and harsh resistance."

The silence in the room was deafening as the foreign minister paused to let these words sink in. "I'd like to emphasize the fact that Pakistan has not sought additional arms or munitions since this impending sale was made public. We have no desire to be seen as the aggressors in this situation, and we seek only a return to normal levels of readiness. However, we do not believe that this can happen until India demonstrates its goodwill by canceling the upcoming purchase."

Bokhari paused and turned to Fitzgerald. "Do you have anything to add?"

"No, that's all." Fitzgerald appeared slightly shaken, but she offered a tight smile and extended her hand, which the foreign minister took. "Thank you for having me, Mr. Bokhari."

"Thank you for coming, Madam Secretary."

The press pool erupted in a flurry of questions as both speakers turned away from the crowd and walked to the rear of the room, where a member of Bokhari's entourage was waiting to open the door. As Fitzgerald followed the minister through, Petrina closed the distance between them smoothly and adjusted the Motorola microphone/receiver system positioned in his right ear, which allowed him to communicate without the use of a PTT (press to talk) button. He was a little shocked by what had just transpired, as it was rare to hear such vitriolic remarks in a public forum, but he couldn't dwell on the minister's words. He still had a job to do, and he wouldn't relax until the secretary was back on the plane and cruising at 35,000 feet. Brynn Fitzgerald's first official trip as secretary of state had just come to a close.

"Edsall, this is Petrina. The briefing just finished. Where do we stand?"

There was a crackle of static over his earpiece, then the reply. "We're right on schedule. The flight plan is filed, and the plane is fueled up and ready to go. The route is in order."

"Chase cars?"

"They're in position. We're waiting on you, over."

"Good," Petrina replied. He glanced over and saw that Fitzgerald was engaging in a few last-minute pleasantries with a member of the

Pakistani Secretariat. "She's finishing up in here. It could be ten. It could be twenty. I'll let you know. For the moment, just have everyone hold their positions."

"Got it, boss."

Fifteen minutes later, Fitzgerald stepped out into the hazy afternoon air. The cameras were still rolling, the press pool having moved to the bottom of the stairs. The motorcade was waiting a few steps beyond the assembled journalists. The acting secretary of state smiled in her practiced way—she'd gotten the hang of that already—and turned toward the foreign minister, shaking hands with him one last time. Standing at Fitzgerald's side was the U.S. ambassador to Pakistan, Lee Patterson.

Patterson was a twenty-year veteran of the Foreign Service and a career diplomat. The tall, patrician Bostonian was one of the better-known members of the diplomatic community, as he'd inherited a substantial fortune several years earlier. His 1 percent stake in Texas Instruments alone was worth nearly twenty-one million dollars, making him one of the wealthiest public servants in the world. Once the last polite farewells were out of the way, they descended the stairs side by side, surrounded by members of Fitzgerald's permanent detail. As the head of that detail, Special Agent Mike Petrina walked directly behind the acting secretary of state, his watchful eyes shielded by a pair of black Ray-Bans.

As soon as they hit street level, the doors were pulled open on the waiting vehicles. Petrina waited until Fitzgerald and Patterson had climbed into the rear seat. Then he shut the door after them and climbed into the front.

"All set, ma'am?" he asked over his shoulder.

The secretary of state broke off from her animated conversation with the ambassador. "Yes, we're ready to go, Mike."

"Would you like me to . . . ?"

She knew what he was asking. "If you don't mind."

Petrina pushed a button to raise the partition behind the front seats, giving the officials some privacy. Although the secretary of state had the same controls at her disposal, she always waited for Petrina to suggest their use. Fitzgerald's unfailing courtesy was just one of the reasons he had come to not only respect, but genuinely like the acting secretary of state.

Turning to the driver, he said, "Let's keep the speed above sixty once we hit the main road."

The driver nodded once as Petrina relayed the instruction to the lead vehicles. Then he waited for the cars ahead to pull out of the compound. Soon they had left the presidential palace behind and were streaking down Constitution Avenue, toward Chaklala Air Base, where the State Department's Boeing 757 was fueled and waiting. Formerly part of the U.S. Air Force's fleet, the plane had been specially reconfigured to meet the secretary of state's needs. Essentially, it was a less elaborate version of Air Force One, but for anyone accustomed to flying coach, the soft leather seats and surplus of legroom would have seemed impossibly luxurious.

Petrina leaned back in his seat, ran a hand over his shorn scalp, and tried to relax. They had been in Pakistan for less than twenty-four hours, but his nerves had been stretched taut the whole time. Few countries could top the Islamic republic when it came to anti-American sentiment, and that attitude was largely responsible for the extreme security measures that had surrounded Fitzgerald's first official visit. For starters, the press pool had been supplied with a false time of arrival; instead of arriving at midday, the secretary of state's plane had landed the previous night under cover of darkness, with the running lights off and the interior shades drawn. A number of false convoys had been dispatched from the airport several minutes before Fitzgerald made the short trip to the diplomatic enclave in Islamabad, and police checkpoints had been set up throughout the city.

Everything that could be done to ensure the secretary of state's safety had been put into effect, but Petrina knew he'd feel more secure when they reached the air base, and he'd feel even better once they were wheels up. Judging by the elevated voices drifting through the thin partition, the person he was currently charged with protecting felt exactly the same way.

"Lee, what the hell just happened in there?" Brynn Fitzgerald demanded. She angrily brushed some lint from the sleeve of her navy pantsuit as she glared at the man sitting next to her. She knew that Petrina and the driver could probably hear every word through the thin partition, but she was beyond caring. "I thought you said they had tempered their position on this."

"Well, that's the impression I got when I met with the chief of protocol last week. He assured me that—"

"I don't care what he told you." The acting secretary of state strained to keep her voice at a reasonable level. "I was just blindsided in front of the pool, not to mention the foreign correspondents. Do you realize how bad that's going to look when it airs? The president is going to be furious."

Lee Patterson sighed and looked out his window, doing his best to avoid her incriminating gaze. "I don't know what to tell you, Brynn. They obviously reconsidered their stance. Kashmir is an incredibly sensitive issue for them, okay? For all intents and purposes, they've been fighting over that land since 1947, and the recent military buildup is just part of the problem. There's also a lot of posturing going on right now, and there was no way the Pakistanis were going to pass up the opportunity to make a powerful statement with you in the room. If you'll recall," he continued carefully, "I told you the press briefing was a bad idea when we spoke on Friday, but you—"

"Lee, we both know it wasn't an option. I had to go on record with both sides. Otherwise, we might as well have canceled the whole trip." Fitzgerald pushed out a short breath between pursed lips, then swept a strand of errant hair away from her face. "Look, I know it wasn't your fault, but now that it's done, we have to engage in some serious damage control. Any suggestions?"

Patterson turned slightly in his seat to face her as he gathered his thoughts. They had known each other for many years, but he'd never seen her as stressed as she was now. They'd first met as second-year students at Northwestern Law. In the years that followed, their friendship had been cemented through mutual respect, a shared political outlook, and the fact that they took genuine pleasure in each other's company. That was as far as it went, though. Neither of them had ever sought anything more, and while Patterson was devoted to his wife of twenty-three years, he occasionally wondered about what might have been. At forty-eight years of age, Brynn Fitzgerald was still a very attractive woman. Although time had left its mark around her eyes and mouth, her stylishly cut reddish brown hair had yet to show a trace of gray, and her sea green eyes were just as bright and intelligent as they'd been when she was twenty-two and cramming for the Massachusetts bar exam.

Still, while she'd retained her sturdy good looks, Patterson could tell that her premature rise to the top was taking its toll. It was all a matter of timing, he knew; given another few years, she probably would have been offered the job regardless. Brynn Fitzgerald was one of the most accomplished women in government service. She had served on the boards of numerous Fortune 500 companies, and she'd earned honorary doctorates from no less than seven schools, including Harvard, Yale, and the University of Notre Dame. She was also a prolific author, having written or collaborated on five books since 2001. There was a lot about the woman to admire, Patterson thought, which probably explained why he hadn't pursued her with greater effort. On some level, he found her very intimidating, and he knew he wasn't alone in that respect.

"Well," he finally responded, "it seems to me that the president's main objection lies with dictating foreign policy to Israel. He really doesn't want to do that, or even give the appearance of doing it. If we could block the deal by offering some kind of economic aid package to India, or by increasing aid to Israel directly, he'd be able to defuse the situation without losing face."

"Maybe," Fitzgerald said, without enthusiasm, "but unless we can stall delivery of the aid package until the end of the year, it still reeks of compromise. It doesn't matter where it goes—Israel or India—the reason behind it will be extremely transparent."

"Stopping this escalation is worth the political fallout," Patterson countered. "After all, the stakes are huge. India and Pakistan have a combined troop strength of more than two million, and both countries have access to enormous troop reserves in the event of a large-scale conflict. Those are facts that we can't afford to overlook."

"Not to mention the nukes," Fitzgerald muttered. She had recently been briefed on both countries' nuclear capabilities, and she knew how dire the situation actually was. According to the CIA's latest estimates, Pakistan had somewhere between twenty-eight and forty-two weapons prepped for delivery, while India had between forty and fifty. Even if those numbers were off by 10 percent or more, the devastation that would result in the event of a nuclear exchange would be unthinkable.

"Exactly," Patterson agreed. "This isn't exactly a new scenario, you know. In 1999 a similar situation cropped up, and both countries went as far as to state that all military options were on the table." The ambassador paused to let that carefully worded statement hit home. "Brynn, you really need to sell some kind of interjection to the president. The deal has been on the table for months now, and the Israelis are ready to move. Once the money changes hands, we won't be able to control what Musharraf does next. I mean, we won't have any influence at all."

"I'll talk to him. You should know he's really adamant on this, Lee, but I'll do my best."

"Good. And thank you." Patterson felt some of the tension in his shoulders start to dissipate. As the U.S. ambassador to Pakistan, he faced strong opposition—sometimes outright antagonism—on a daily basis, and the events of the past few months had only made matters worse. He'd met the president on several occasions. Patterson knew him to be a stubborn individual, but the acting secretary of state was just as strong willed. If anyone could convince David Brenneman to change his mind, it was Brynn Fitzgerald.

"What about our missing tourists?" Patterson asked. He had been present only for part of the bilateral discussions. "What did they have to say about that?"

"ISI is putting in the resources, but as you know, ten of those people disappeared in mountainous areas during periods of bad weather, so there isn't much chance they'll be coming back." The Directorate for Inter-Services Intelligence was easily the most powerful of Pakistan's three major intelligence agencies. For this reason, it was heading up the search for the missing Americans. "There's no dispute that some of them *were* actually kidnapped, but there's also a good chance that some simply got trapped in a snowstorm. Or fell into a crevasse. Take your pick. Most of them applied for climbing permits to begin with, which is something we should really have taken into account from the start."

The ambassador nodded slowly, but he couldn't disguise his unease.

"What are you thinking?" Fitzgerald asked.

Patterson took his time in framing his response. "Brynn, I've been here for nearly four years now, and I've seen just how deep the anti-American sentiment runs in the general population. I've done my best to change that, but I have to tell you, I've learned to expect the worst. So when I hear the Paks have concocted a story that covers all the bases, I can't help but take it with a grain of salt."

Fitzgerald permitted herself a brief smile, then caught herself and glanced away to lessen the blow. "I hear you, but it's like you just said. You've been facing off with these people every day for the past four years, so you might not be the most—"

"I have nothing against the Pakistani people or their govern-ment," Patterson interjected testily. "And I resent any suggestion to the contrary. I've—"

"Lee, I'm sorry." Fitzgerald lightly gripped his arm and saw his ex-pression soften immediately. "I didn't mean to suggest that you're bi-ased against them. I know you better than that. I'm just saying that you might not be the most impartial observer. I mean, let's face it. You've been on the firing line for years now. I'm sure it hasn't been easy."

"It hasn't been easy, but you don't have to placate me." He leveled her with a steady gaze. "We've known each other too long for that. Just listen to what I'm telling you, okay? You have to have eyes in the back of your head around here. If they have the evidence, that's one thing, but you can't take anything at face value." He hesitated briefly. "I don't want to overstep my bounds here, but you're new to the job, Brynn, and sometimes it shows. It's a whole different game when your name is on the letterhead."

It wasn't the best analogy, but she knew what he was getting at. There weren't many people who could speak to her so candidly, but Lee Patterson happened to be one of them. "I appreciate the advice, Lee, and believe me, I depend on you more than you know. I realize this is a challenging assignment, but I'm glad you're the one standing post. I mean that."

"Thank you." He grinned and shot a glance at his watch. "You know, it's a shame you couldn't stay for one more day. It would have been good to catch up some more, and there are plenty of people at the embassy who didn't get the chance to meet you. It would have made for a nice little photo op."

"I know, but I'm scheduled to meet with the president in the morning, and there's no way he'll let me push it back."

"It was a good trip, though?" Patterson knew that Fitzgerald had visited numerous South Asian countries on her first official trip, in-cluding Afghanistan, Bangladesh, Bhutan, and India.

"It was . . . *enlightening*. As you just said, things are very different when you are given top billing. Everything seems a little more scripted, but I guess that's just diplomacy at work. It was a productive couple of weeks, though, and that's the main thing."

Patterson grinned again. "So, in other words, you're looking for-ward to going home."

"Not as much as you might think," Fitzgerald muttered. She looked out the window absently. The green-brown Margalla Hills could be seen in the distance, but she wasn't focused on the passing scenery. Instead, she was thinking about her upcoming meeting with the president, as well as his probable reaction after the disastrous press conference she'd just departed. "In fact, I think I'd prefer to stay right here."

CHAPTER 6

RAWALPINDI, PAKISTAN

The Suburban carrying Brynn Fitzgerald and Lee Patterson was the fifth vehicle in the motorcade making its way from Aiwan-e-Sadr, the presidential palace at the top of Constitution Avenue, to the air base south of Islamabad. Four cars back, Naveed Jilani, the senior assistant to the Pakistani chief of protocol, was doing his best to disguise his rising tension. He was waiting on the phone call that would seal the commitment he'd made two weeks earlier, and while he didn't regret his decision, his sense of personal conviction wasn't doing much to relieve his physical discomfort. He knew that what he was presently feeling was only to be expected, that the cold sweat running over his skin was completely natural, along with the tight ache in his chest and the sick feeling in the pit of his stomach. When the call finally came, the shrill tone caused him to jump in his seat. Lifting the phone to his ear, he recognized the gravelly voice on the other end immediately.

"Naveed, is that you?"

"Yes, it's me."

"I assume Mirza is with you."

Jilani instinctively glanced to his left, where Ghulam Mirza, the chief of protocol, was studying his schedule for the following day. "Yes."

"Which car are you in? The last?"

"No." Jilani paused to wipe the sweat from his forehead. He could tell that Mirza was listening to his end of the conversation, which was only making him more nervous. "That is much too late. I think we should move it up a couple of hours."

"The third from the last vehicle?"

"Yes, that's right."

"Good. Now, the secretary of state. Which car is she in?"

"I think it's the fifth number in the book," Jilani said. He glanced out the window for the tenth time in as many minutes. Although he had not been informed of the motorcade's specific route, he made the trip to Chaklala Air Base dozens of times each month in the course of his duties. He knew all of the roads by heart, and he had already figured out which route they were going to take. It was simply a process of elimination. "I can be there by ten. Unfortunately, I have prior obligations. Call Bashir if you need someone to sit with her."

There was a pause as the other man interpreted. The crude code had been decided upon at the meeting in Peshawar. Jilani had just stated that the secretary of state was in the fifth vehicle. He'd also informed the general that the motorcade would cross a narrow bridge on Airport Road in approximately ten minutes. Jilani didn't know the specifics, but he knew that armed gunmen were waiting on the road in question, as well as on two other frequently used routes from Aiwan-e-Sadr to the air base.

"So she's in the fifth car," Mengal repeated. "Are you certain? Because there's no room for—"

"I'm certain." Jilani froze involuntarily, his hand like a stone around the fragile plastic. It was the first time he had ever interrupted Benazir Mengal, and for a second, he felt something close to blind panic. "Forgive me, I didn't—"

"I understand." The older man's voice had dropped to a dangerous murmur. "You've been under a lot of pressure, Naveed, but you've done well, and I'm grateful for your loyalty. Remember, when you hear the first rocket, put your head down and stay very still. You have nothing to fear. My men are well trained, and they won't miss. Is there anything else you wish to tell me?"

"No, that is all."

"Then good-bye, my friend, and good luck. *Asalaam aleikum.*"

"Yes, *wa aleikum asalaam.*"

The phone went dead in Jilani's ear, and he lowered it slowly to his lap. His mind was blank, and it was some time before he realized that the chief of protocol was asking him a question.

"Who was it, Navi?"

"A personal call, *janāb*." Jilani avoided his superior's curious gaze as his mind kicked back into gear. For the first time, he found himself wondering just how much his life was worth, given the circumstances. He could not think of a single reason why the general's people would make the effort to spare him when the attack started, and this realization—the fact that he was completely expendable—was deeply unsettling. "My wife's brother. Parveen has been ill for some time, so her doctor scheduled some tests at the hospital. We're waiting for the results now."

The other man removed his glasses, his thin lips creasing into a frown. "That explains a great deal. You've been very distracted over the past few weeks."

"Forgive me, but—"

"It doesn't matter," Mirza said, waving away the apology. "I just hope it isn't serious. Your wife's illness, I mean."

"I wouldn't be too concerned, *janāb*." Jilani averted his eyes once more and tried to stop his hands from trembling. "I'm sure everything will be fine."

CHAPTER 7

RAWALPINDI

As Brynn Fitzgerald's motorcade moved steadily toward his position, Benazir Mengal tossed his phone to one of his subordinates, then quickly relayed the news he'd just been given. As the young man dialed through to the other members of the team, Mengal pinched the tip of his nose and studied the road to the rear of his vehicle. By chance, he had been waiting on the exact route the Americans had decided upon. It was just one of three possibilities, but it comprised the shortest distance between the presidential palace and the air base, which made it the most likely choice. It was a fortunate coincidence, Mengal thought, as it allowed him to gauge the lay of the land one last time.

The iron truss bridge, which crossed a small gully filled with brush, small trees, and litter, was less than 100 yards away. The road beyond was lined on both sides by small houses and shops. It was a poor sort of place, a general air of neglect and poverty hanging over everything in sight. Airport Road was one of the major routes between Islamabad and its sister city to the south, Rawalpindi. As a result, both sides of the narrow road were occupied by pedestrians and people on bicycles, and there was a fair amount of vehicular traffic on the bridge itself.

"General?"

He turned to face his subordinate, who had the phone pressed to his ear. In his distracted state, Mengal had not heard it ring. "Yes?"

"The motorcade just passed through a checkpoint less than a mile from here. It's time for you to leave. The second vehicle is waiting."

Mengal nodded brusquely. "The men are ready?"

The former soldier gestured toward the bridge. A heavy Nissan truck had just started to cross from the north, its bed covered by supporting poles and a thick canvas tarp. "They're ready. We have a spotter in place. He'll remain on the north side until the motorcade approaches, and then he'll place the call."

"Good."

The subordinate shifted impatiently as Mengal stared at the approaching vehicle. The cars behind the slow-moving truck were honking incessantly, the drivers clearly impatient to get to the other side. Mengal felt no sympathy for the people delayed on the bridge; in fact, he was vastly reassured by the heavy traffic. It would require the motorcade to slow dramatically as it approached the crossing, making it an easier target. Once the first rockets were fired, the cars that were hit would serve as obstacles for the following vehicles, and the high number of civilian casualties would only add to the confusion. In short, it was the perfect place for an ambush. Mengal had seen it work before.

Still, the retired general couldn't shake the uneasy feeling that had seized hold of him hours earlier. It was something he rarely experienced, but he believed in precedence. He believed in tactical decisions based on past success, and given what was about to take place, he couldn't help but reflect on recent events in his country's history. Troubling events that reeked of failure. Pervez Musharraf had miraculously escaped no less than three assassination attempts over the course of his presidency. Two of those attempts had come in 2003, and on one of those occasions, Musharraf's survival could be directly attributed to a jamming device that blocked all cell phones within several hundred meters of his motorcade. Through Naveed Jilani and his close relationship with the American embassy, Mengal knew that the vehicles in the embassy pool did not employ such devices. However, this was a minor detail, and one that didn't concern him either way. Technology could be easily defeated; it didn't count as a real obstacle. The former general was far more concerned with the human element of the secretary's security.

In Mengal's mind, this was the most probable barrier to success. During his military service, he'd once attended a welcoming ceremony for President Clinton at Chaklala Air Base. He had seen the Secret Service in action. He remembered how alert they'd been, the way they moved in synchronous, rehearsed fashion. In particular, he recalled the way they had watched him with ill-concealed suspicion. It was almost as if, even then, they could see into the darkest corners of his mind. He had quickly realized they had a file on him, and since that incident, he'd come to appreciate just how thorough the Americans were. The secretary of state was protected by a different agency, Mengal knew, but her security would be just as vigilant. He couldn't be sure, but he suspected her permanent detail was composed of at least seven men. Probably closer to ten. He had superior numbers at his disposal, but the Americans held the advantage in so many ways. The agents were trained to the point where they reacted instinctively and correctly every time, and they enjoyed access to the best weapons money could buy.

Mengal's men had all served under him at some point, and most had fought in the volatile Northwest Frontier Province. They were hardened combat veterans, and he was confident in their abilities. Still, there was a noticeable divide in terms of training and weaponry, a divide that could not be ignored. Then again, he had speed and surprise on his side, two essential elements of any successful ambush. Ironically, the Diplomatic Security Service also relied heavily on these elements, especially when moving a senior official in and out of hostile territory.

And this *was* hostile territory, at least as far as the Americans were concerned. There could be no mistake about that. Rawalpindi was home to army headquarters and a number of lesser military complexes, and Mengal knew the area like the back of his hand. It was a key advantage. He knew what would happen in the aftermath of the attack. He knew precisely where the police would set up their emergency checkpoints, and he knew which roads they would overlook. More importantly, he knew exactly how to find the small clearing where, in twenty minutes' time, he was scheduled to meet a pilot assigned to ISI, a man who'd once served under him at the Mountain Warfare School in Abbottabad. A man who knew the meaning of loyalty. If all went according to plan, Mengal would be onboard when the helicopter lifted off, but he wouldn't be the only passenger.

"General."

Mengal turned to his left, where one of his men was gesturing insistently toward the waiting sedan. "Of course." The general walked to the car and slid into the passenger seat. A man was already waiting behind the wheel. "Drive."

CHAPTER 8

RAWALPINDI

Special Agent Petrina absently tugged on the credentials still clipped to his suit jacket as he glared through the windshield of the armored Suburban. It was called "forward orientation," and it was one of the first things he'd learned at the evasive-driving course he'd attended twenty years earlier. There had been additional courses since then—for obvious reasons, DSS agents underwent constant training, even to the point of relearning fundamental tasks—but the general principles remained the same. The reason behind forward orientation was as simple as it was obvious: looking as far forward as possible allowed one to identify potential threats before they became a real hazard. Unfortunately, it wasn't much help at the moment, as they were hardly moving at all.

They'd been able to maintain a high rate of speed along Islamabad's broad avenues and boulevards, but traffic had slowed dramatically over the past few minutes. The road ahead was lined with cars, and beyond, Petrina could make out iron support beams towering over the traffic. Pedestrians and people on bicycles were streaming by on either side of the motorcade, but people on foot weren't much of a danger to the heavily armored vehicles. Petrina was more worried about the beams in the near distance, which could only belong to a small bridge. With this realization, his dark mood grew darker still. Bridges were natural choke points. Typically, they were avoided at all costs; it was a maxim of any protective detail, and it should have been caught by the advance team.

He turned to the driver. "Why the hell did we pick this road? There have to be faster routes between the palace and the air base."

"It was Edsall's call," the driver protested, waving an angry hand at the traffic in front of them. "There are construction crews on the other routes. We didn't have time to clear them out, and this was the best alternative."

"That isn't saying much. He should have brought this to—"

Petrina stopped talking when a clear voice sounded over his earpiece. "Mike, we've got a truck parked off the side of the road up ahead. It's about two hundred feet from our position."

"Where's the driver?"

"The hood is up, and the driver appears to be checking something in the engine compartment. He looks pretty pissed. Over."

"Yeah, I see it," the lead agent responded, tilting his head to see around the line of cars. The transmission was coming from the third car in the motorcade, which was already halfway over the bridge. The traffic had started to move a little, and the principal vehicle—the Suburban carrying Petrina, Fitzgerald, and Patterson—was nosing up to the bridge. "The cargo area is covered . . . Can you see inside from where you are?"

"Negative, Mike. I suggest we call our escorts and ask them to check it out on foot. Over."

"Jesus Christ," Petrina muttered under his breath. The whole situation was going from bad to worse in a hurry, and it was exactly why he'd suggested the use of aerial transport in the first place. Helicopters were much harder to target than vehicles on the ground, and they also had the advantage of unlimited air space. Unfortunately, the secretary of state had personally requested a vehicular motorcade, citing the fact that one had been used in India. It would have been noticed if different security measures—especially those that were obvious—were employed in different countries, and it would have set the wrong tone for the discussions at Aiwan-e-Sadr. Petrina could understand her reasoning, but it didn't change the fact that they were taking a serious, unnecessary risk in the name of diplomacy.

Still, that decision had not been his to make, and he couldn't change it now. What happened next, on the other hand, *was* up to him. The last thing he wanted was to have the secretary of state's vehicle on the bridge in the event of an attack, as they would be completely boxed in. The first two vehicles in the motorcade were marked Pakistani police cars; Petrina could see their lights flashing up ahead. The officers were armed only with handguns, and they wouldn't be much use in the event of a well-planned attack. On the other hand, they were best prepared to deal with this particular situation. Not only did they know the language, but the driver of the truck would be more likely to cooperate with his own countrymen.

"Okay," he said at length. "Ask them to approach on foot, and have them perform a visual check on the cargo area. Over."

"Will do," the other agent said. Petrina listened as the request was relayed to the lead cars over a secure channel. The police officers agreed a moment later. Just then, he heard the small motor kick in as the partition behind the seats came down. He turned to face the officials in the backseat.

"What's going on, Mike?" Fitzgerald asked. The answer became immediately clear when she looked through the windshield. "Oh, I see. Isn't there another road we can take?"

"I'm afraid not, ma'am." Petrina's voice was low and tight; he was embarrassed that he'd allowed this to happen on his watch. "The police are going to try and clear the road. It shouldn't take too long."

The cars edged forward again. Up ahead, the police officers had stepped out of their vehicles and were moving toward the truck. As he watched through the windshield, Petrina inadvertently nudged an object on the floor, by his right foot. The weapon—a Heckler & Koch MP5 with a 3-round burst trigger group—was perfectly suited to his current task. It was easy to use, extremely versatile, and accurate out to 200 meters in the hands of a skilled operator. A 30-round magazine was already loaded, the first round chambered. The safety was on. The weapon's proximity afforded Petrina a small degree of comfort, but he knew it wouldn't make much difference if the worst were to happen.

The detail leader tried to push away his lingering doubts as the Pakistani officers finished questioning the driver. As they moved toward the back of the truck, Fitzgerald said something behind him. Petrina was turning to address her when something flashed in the corner of his eye. A split second later, the vehicle was violently rocked by a pressure wave and the deafening sound of a massive explosion. Swinging back to the front, Petrina looked on in disbelief as the shattered remains of the truck crashed to the ground, some of the burning debris landing in the trees on either side of the road.

Most of the blast had clearly been pushed out the back of the vehicle; the officers had been killed instantly, along with the driver of the truck. Both police cars had been pushed off the road, completely gutted by the force of the explosion. As Petrina took in the devastation, he focused on the third vehicle in the motorcade. The armored Suburban had been flipped onto its side by the blast, and from the state of the vehicle, it didn't look as if the agents inside had survived.

Less than two seconds had elapsed, but for Mike Petrina, it felt like an eternity. He couldn't react; all he could think about was how fast it had happened. Nothing could have prepared him for the speed of it, but as intense as it was, the shock couldn't last. Petrina was too well trained for that. He forced himself to block out the sounds of fear and disbelief in the backseat, listening instead to the frantic traffic coming over his earpiece. "Get us out of here!" he screamed to the driver as he reached for the MP5 at his feet. There was nothing he could do with the weapon, but that didn't stop his instinctive reaction to arm himself. A split second later, the driver threw the SUV into reverse and slammed down on the accelerator. The Suburban rocked to the right as the driver swung the wheel to the left, Petrina shouting orders over the secure channel the whole time.

He looked out the passenger-side window to see the doors on the incapacitated SUV being pushed up and out. He was hit with a sudden wave of relief; at least two of the agents had survived. *Go,* he found himself willing them. *Get out of there.* Both agents started to climb out of the vehicle, but they never made it. A pair of projectiles streaked in from the tree line. Both burrowed into the vehicle, one after the other. The explosion that followed tore apart what remained of the Suburban in a flash of blood, orange flame, and black smoke. More rockets followed, targeting the fourth vehicle in the motorcade.

"Let's go!" Petrina screamed at the driver. On some level he knew he was taking his anger, fear, and frustration out on the nearest target, but he couldn't restrain himself. "Move this fucking truck! *Move!*"

The driver didn't respond, intently focused on completing the J-turn. He slammed the SUV into drive and stamped on the accelerator, the vehicle shooting forward. Suddenly Petrina had new sight lines to focus on, and he commanded his mind to adapt, his eyes scanning back and forth for new threats.

He didn't have to look far. As the Suburban accelerated back in the direction they had come from, Petrina caught sight of a Nissan truck identical to the one that had just exploded. He opened his mouth to shout a warning, but before he could, the truck slammed into the back of the last car in the motorcade, which was still facing south. The impact wrenched both vehicles to the side of the road. As Petrina watched in horror, more projectiles flashed in from either side of the road. Two punched into the vehicle that had just been struck, another Pakistani police car. Three additional rockets—something in Petrina's mind screamed, *RPGs,* but he couldn't be sure— tore into the 10-passenger van carrying the press pool. The first warhead penetrated the rear windshield, traveled 3 additional feet, then detonated in another cloud of fire and smoke. The second and third warheads shredded what remained of the vehicle, then lifted it into the air.

Petrina whipped around to check on his principal. Brynn Fitzgerald was down on the floor behind the front seats. Lee Patterson was on top of her, shielding her body with his. Petrina realized that he must have told them to get down at some point, though he couldn't recall doing so.

Satisfied with what he saw, he turned again to face forward. The driver screamed a warning, and Petrina opened his mouth to react. He had just enough time to see something dark and small moving toward them with incredible speed. It slammed into the front grille, then punched through the radiator and into the engine block. He didn't hear the explosion, but he saw the flash, felt the searing heat and the sense of everything collapsing around him. Then everything went black.

For Naveed Jilani, the end didn't come nearly as fast; in fact, he almost made it through the entire event. Despite the fear that wracked his body, he'd done exactly as Mengal instructed. He'd dropped his head and wedged it between his knees when he saw the cargo truck explode on the other side of the bridge. With his head down, he didn't see the rocket that skipped off the pavement and hit the rear fender of his own vehicle, 4 inches to the left of the fuel tank. The resulting explosion sent shrapnel tearing through the backseat. Ghulam Mirza was killed instantly, but Jilani narrowly escaped the whistling shards of steel and fiberglass. Seconds after the deafening noise stopped, he felt a stinging pain all over his body. His eyes flew open, but it took his mind a few seconds to register what was happening. And then it hit him: he was on fire. Every square inch of his flesh was burning, his suit melting into his skin . . .

He found himself wrenching off the door handle, trying to get out. He couldn't concentrate on the task; the plastic was sticking to his hand, burning a hole right through his palm, and the screaming . . . The screams were just so loud; he couldn't get them out of his mind. Jilani never had the chance to realize that the screams he was hearing were his own. He took a deep breath to let out another howl of agony, inadvertently pulling superheated air into his lungs. He managed two more breaths before his respiratory system shut down entirely. Then the noise finally stopped, and the darkness pulled him into a deep, cold sleep.

CHAPTER 9

ICELAND

Ryan Kealey was seated near the back of the 14-passenger Mercedes minibus, staring absently out the window. He'd been arranging his thoughts for the last hour as the vehicle sped west on Route 1. Otherwise known as the Ring Road, the two-lane highway encircled the better part of the island, linking most of the country's major cities in the process. The afternoon sky was overcast, dark cumulus clouds towering high over the barren, rocky soil. Everything was marked in tones of black, brown, and gray, except for the dirty white snow on the peaks to the north. A light drizzle obscured the passing terrain, the cold drops clinging to the vehicle's windows, but even on a clear day, there wouldn't have been much to see. At least not in this part of the country. Iceland offered some amazing sights to the perseverant, physically fit traveler, but simply taking in the scenery from a moving vehicle wasn't enough. In order to fully appreciate the landscape, one had to be willing to venture off the main roads.

Kealey was that kind of traveler. Over the past couple of weeks he had laid eyes on a number of natural wonders, including the multitiered waterfall at Gulfoss, the Strokkur geyser, and the chaotic ensemble of hot springs, lava fields, and rhyolite hills at Landmannalaugar. They were amazing sights, but he'd happened across them purely by accident. He would never have seen them otherwise, and in truth, he'd gotten more out of the lunarlike ice fields of the interior than he had out of the common tourist attractions. As he stared out at the passing terrain, he felt a small tinge of regret; he was sorry to be leaving so soon.

Shifting his weight on the seat, he allowed his gaze to drift around the vehicle. Although it was the height of the tourist season, he and Naomi Kharmai were the only two passengers. She was on the seat directly across from his, her small body curled up on the warm plastic. Looking over, he could see only the top of her dark head and the left side of her body. A thick woolen sweater, positioned between her hands and the right side of her face, served as a makeshift pillow, and she was snoring lightly. They had left the hotel two hours earlier. Harper had beaten them to the punch, having departed for Keflavík International at eight in the morning. The deputy DCI would have waited for the last bus, as he'd indicated to Kealey the previous night, but it hadn't been necessary. Kealey had made his decision much sooner than anyone had the right to expect, including himself.

Following his awkward conversation with Naomi in the bar the night before, he'd walked straight back to his room on the ground floor. He'd lain on the narrow bed for nearly an hour, staring up at the ceiling, thinking it through. Part of him wanted to go back to the bar, to change the whole course of the conversation, but the rational part of him said it wouldn't have made a difference. So much of it didn't make sense. Naomi's combative attitude was something he'd seen before, but never to this extent. It was almost as if she'd relegated him to some embarrassing point in her past, along with their relationship.

That was bad enough, but he was just as confused by her decision to train as a field operative. Kealey wasn't sure what had brought about this unexpected decision, but that was only part of the issue. He was just as troubled—perhaps even more so—by Harper's ready, unquestioning acceptance of her sudden transformation. And she *had* changed; there was no denying it. He remembered the way she had been when he first met her: strong but innocent, smart but naïve, young but wise beyond her years in so many ways. Despite having seen some horrific things in her short career, she'd managed to retain an air of youthful exuberance for longer than anyone could have expected. Now, though, it seemed as if everything she had seen and suffered through over the past couple of years had finally caught up with her. It was inevitable, Kealey knew, but that didn't make it any easier to witness. Simply put, she had been pushed too hard for too long.

At least, that had been his initial, albeit reluctant, assessment. He had gone to Harper's room just after midnight to accept the assignment, and evidently, the deputy DCI had relayed the information to Naomi shortly thereafter. She had banged on his door just after 7:00 AM, and when he'd pulled it open, he had found a completely different woman from the one he'd seen the night before. Despite the early hour, she was showered, dressed, and ready to go. She was smiling, alert—almost hyper, in fact—and she seemed to have forgotten all about their earlier confrontation. Not about to let it go that easily, Kealey had tried to get her to open up over breakfast in the hotel's ground-floor restaurant, but she had ignored his attempts to uncover the past six months of her life. Instead, she'd abruptly shifted the conversation back to the task at hand. Kealey was frustrated by her closed-off demeanor, but, unwilling to provoke another argument, he'd followed her lead reluctantly.

Admittedly, the longer she had talked, the more the case began to seize his interest. It presented an interesting scenario, and now, as Naomi slept deeply on the other side of the narrow aisle, he thought back to the makeshift briefing she'd provided him with. It was mainly geared toward their sole lead with respect to the whereabouts of Amari Saifi. According to the Agency's latest information, the person who might possibly lead them to the Salafist leader was another Algerian, a man by the name of Kamil Ghafour.

The details Naomi had offered were sparse, but they were enough to paint a general picture. Before his arrest in 2002, the twenty-eight-year-old Ghafour had been a committed, albeit low-level, member of the Armed Islamic Group. Otherwise known as the GIA, the group was committed to replacing the current government of Algeria with an Islamic state. The mandate was identical to that of the GSPC, which had separated from the GIA in 1998. The difference was that the GIA was still very much an active organization, whereas Ghafour had largely fallen off the grid.

He'd been released from prison two months earlier under an amnesty agreement for convicted terrorists. Following his release, he'd given an interview to the Algerian independent *El Khabar*. Even the journalist's years of experience had not been enough to soften the rambling, incoherent quality of Ghafour's antiestablishment diatribe, but the interview *had* included one salient piece of information. During their shared time in prison, Ghafour claimed to have forged a close association with none other than Amari Saifi, the former head of the GSPC.

Normally, it would have been a meaningless detail, but in light of the recent wave of abductions in Pakistan—as well as Saifi's credible involvement—it had become the focus of the investigation, at least from the Agency's standpoint. Saifi had not escaped from prison. Nor had he served his full sentence, which could only mean that someone had arranged for his release. The hope was that Saifi had confided in his fellow prisoner, Kamil Ghafour. Admittedly, it was more than a long shot, but Ghafour was the only verifiable link to Saifi, and that made finding him a priority. The Algerian government had basically stonewalled the State Department's requests for additional information, which hadn't come as a surprise to anyone. Ghafour, like any convicted homegrown terrorist, was an embarrassment to them. Nevertheless, finding him had not been as difficult as it should have been, thanks to the Operations Directorate at Langley and a well-placed source in the Spanish embassy in Washington, D.C.

According to the source, Kamil Ghafour had entered Spain on a temporary visa with an accompanying work permit less than a month after being released from prison. Incredibly, his ties to the GIA had been missed by Spain's immigration officials, but the oversight didn't last long. Ghafour was soon found working on a building site in downtown Madrid, exactly as he'd claimed on his application. Deportation proceedings were immediately put into effect, but Ghafour's employer—another Algerian-born immigrant, who, since entering Spain twenty years earlier, had risen to a position of some wealth and influence—had called on his contacts to intervene. The result was something of an uneasy stalemate. Technically, Ghafour had served his time in Algeria, and since he wasn't wanted by any other country, especially his own, extradition wasn't an option. Even his worrisome interview with *El Khabar* hadn't been enough to get him kicked out of Spain. Still, his name had been placed on a list that went out to every Spanish consulate. In the event that Ghafour left the country, even for a day, he would not be permitted reentry. It was a simple solution, and one that had worked in the past.

It was through this list of "undesirables," as the briefing officer had put it, that Ghafour had been tracked down. From there, it was easy to trace him to the building site in Madrid. The problem lay in what to do next. The Spanish authorities had already made their ruling on Ghafour, and it had been determined in Washington that another official request for access would result in, at best, a long delay. The Spanish government's failed attempts to deport the former Algerian terrorist were proof enough of that. Simply put, the man's employer was connected in too many places, and the State Department couldn't be sure of getting to him quickly. This explained why Agency watchers had been trailing Ghafour in rotating shifts for the past week. Before leaving for Keflavík that morning, Harper had given Kealey a phone number and the address of a hotel where the watchers were based. Upon landing in Spain, their first task was to link up with the other operatives and establish a plan for getting to Ghafour, preferably without alerting the Spanish authorities.

Kealey had been rolling several ideas around in his head, but after much consideration, he'd settled on one in particular. Usually, the least confrontational method was the best course of action, and while there were never any guarantees, he suspected that Kamil Ghafour would react favorably to a straight cash offer. With this thought in mind, Kealey decided to call Langley once they reached the airport. It wouldn't take long to arrange the transfer, and with any luck, the money would be ready and waiting by the time they arrived in Spain.

A small movement to his left brought him back to reality. He glanced over but saw it was nothing; Naomi had merely shifted in her sleep. Watching her, Kealey felt the same warm feelings she always stirred in him, but also a growing sense of unease. While he was relieved beyond measure to see her again, he couldn't help but feel a deep pain over her apparent ambivalence toward their shared past, as well as a lingering concern over her strange behavior. She was up one minute, down the next. There didn't seem to be any middle ground, and her unpredictable behavior could only spell trouble once they were on the ground in Madrid.

Maybe it's just a temporary shift in her personality, he told himself, desperately searching for some kind of rational explanation. *Maybe she'll get back on track in Spain. Maybe she'll come back to you. Just give her some time, Ryan. . . .*

Catching himself, Kealey shook his head angrily. Deep down, he knew he was being naïve. He wanted to condone her actions, to fully accept her decision to resume working for the Agency, but he just couldn't bring himself to do it. It wouldn't be fair to her. Nor would it be fair to what he knew. In the months following the terrorist attack that had nearly claimed her life, he had personally cared for her at his home in Cape Elizabeth, Maine. She had spent part of the winter with him, and in that time, he'd come to understand how deep her issues actually ran. They certainly weren't the kind of problems that could be overcome by six months of training at Camp Peary. Still, he couldn't bring himself to give up on her. He'd made that promise to himself a long time ago, and he had no intention of breaking it now.

At the same time, he couldn't speak for the operatives they were going to meet in Spain. He couldn't make that decision for them, and if Naomi's behavior threatened to put them at risk, he'd have no choice but to intervene and pull her out. Before accepting the assignment, he had made one simple demand of Jonathan Harper: he wanted tactical command for the operation in Spain. The rest of it could be decided at a later date, but he insisted on running things in Madrid. Harper had readily agreed. Naomi had been told as much the next morning, with Kealey present, but she hadn't reacted in any noticeable way, and she hadn't mentioned it since. Kealey wondered if she'd taken it seriously, but in the end, it didn't really matter; he was in charge, and that was final. If he decided to pull her off, there wasn't a damn thing she could do about it. Then again, doing so would almost certainly mark the end of their relationship. And that was assuming, Kealey reminded himself moodily, there was even a relationship to salvage.

He turned back to the window and stared absently out at the rain. He decided to wait and see. He wanted to give her the chance, but if she didn't snap out of it soon, he'd have to make a hard, but necessary, decision. He had put her life ahead of thousands of others once before. He'd gotten away with it on that occasion, but he had no desire to push his luck. If she was going to see this through, she'd have to earn the right. It was just that simple, and just that hard.

CHAPTER 10

RAWALPINDI

When she blinked back to consciousness, Brynn Fitzgerald was momentarily confused as to what had happened. She could remember the first explosions, the sickening images of blood, smoke, and fire. She knew the driver had managed to get their vehicle turned around, but everything after that was a blank. Painfully turning her head to the right, she saw that the haze had started to clear, and she realized she was still in the vehicle. The front seats had been blown from their anchors and partially pushed back. She was lying on the floor, facedown. The driver's seat was jammed against her right shoulder, or maybe it was the other way round. Either way, it hurt to move, and there was a weight on her back that could only be Lee Patterson. She said his name a few times, raising her voice each time in the hope he was merely dazed, but he didn't respond.

Doing her best to push her way through the mental blocks of fear and confusion, Fitzgerald tried to figure out how serious her injuries were. Her limbs seemed to be moving well enough, but her chest felt tight, and it hurt to breathe. The pain was intense; it felt as if someone were pushing down on her chest with both hands, constraining her lungs. Her arms were pinned under her body, but she was able to feel around on her torso. There was a sharp pain on the left side, indicating that a few of her ribs were probably broken. Worst of all, no one was rushing to their assistance, which could only mean the attack had succeeded.

"Lee." Fitzgerald was taken aback by how weak her voice sounded. She coughed involuntarily, then cleared her throat. She could taste blood in her mouth, and that frightened her more than anything else. "Lee, can you hear me? Say something. Please, just say something."

There was still no response. A sudden flurry of voices outside the car jolted the secretary of state back to reality. She was hit by a wave of relief but then realized that the voices weren't speaking English. There was a banging on the door, then a strange noise that she couldn't decipher. It almost sounded as if something was being affixed to the exterior of the car, and if that was the case, it could only be one thing. She felt another sick wave of fear, but she just couldn't move; there was nothing to do but wait for the end.

The voices moved away as suddenly as they'd appeared. Fitzgerald could hear running feet and the screams of injured civilians. She was trying to figure out what to do next when her body was wracked by a fit of coughing. Then she realized that she hadn't made a sound; it was Patterson who'd been coughing on top of her. She could feel his chest rising and falling against her back, but his breathing was erratic and labored.

"Lee?" She tried to turn to face him, but the seat was wedged too tightly against her shoulder. It was almost impossible to keep the panic out of her voice. "How bad is it? Can you move?"

He muttered something she couldn't understand. There was a flash of searing light, followed by a loud bang. Fitzgerald blacked out again, but only for a second. Coming back to herself, she realized that the passenger-side door—the door closest to her feet—had been blown off its hinges. Although she could no longer hear out of her right ear, the desperate screams of pain and fear were suddenly louder. There was a sustained rattling noise, the sound of automatic gunfire, and some of the screams stopped abruptly. Fitzgerald felt the weight on her back shift without warning, Patterson's body sliding down her own. Then the weight was off completely, just as a pair of hands clamped round her ankles. She cried out and tried to kick the hands away, but it was no good. Arms were waiting for her as she was pulled roughly from the remains of the Suburban, and then she was dragged clear of the vehicle.

A pair of men hauled her across the road, supporting her with one arm on either side, their free hands gripping hers. As her feet scraped over the shattered glass that covered the asphalt, one of her shoes came loose. The splinters instantly tore through her nylons and into her foot. A scream rose in her throat, but she bit her lip and held it back in time, not wanting to give them the satisfaction. Turning her head to the right, she saw that Patterson was being moved by another pair of armed men. He was unconscious, his body limp, chin lowered to his chest. Once they were clear of the devastation, she was dropped into a painful heap on a patch of dead grass. Patterson was deposited a few feet away. The secretary of state looked back to the vehicle she'd just been pulled out of, and what she saw caused bile to rise in her throat.

The Suburban's engine compartment was a smoking ruin. The reinforced windshield was completely opaque, damaged by the force of the explosion, but Fitzgerald could see through the passenger-side window, which had completely blown out. Mike Petrina's head was partially caved in, covered in blood and lolling forward against the dash, which had been pushed into his chest. The man charged with her protection was clearly dead, and that was the worst blow yet. With Petrina at her side, Fitzgerald had never felt vulnerable; it had never occurred to her that something could happen as long as he was alive. He was just too capable. But now he was gone, and a man was walking toward her. . . .

The tall figure was dressed in what appeared to be a Pakistani army uniform, but his head was covered by a black balaclava. All Fitzgerald could see was his eyes, which were a flat shade of amber brown. He was holding a gun in his right hand, and as he drew near, he slowed by the prostrate form of an injured woman. She lifted a bloodied hand and said something that Fitzgerald couldn't hear, but she was clearly pleading for help. The man paused, looking down at her, then lifted the gun and fired once into her forehead. A fist-sized mass of bone, blood, and tissue spattered over the pavement. The man kept moving forward as if nothing had happened, impervious to what lay behind him, a nightmarish scene of burning vehicles, maimed people, and mangled bodies.

As horrendous as the sight was, Brynn Fitzgerald couldn't look away. Her mouth was hanging open, a scream frozen in her throat, but she couldn't tear her eyes from the man who had just killed an innocent woman in cold blood. She had just witnessed—and survived—a brutal attack, but it had happened so fast that it hadn't really hit her yet. None of it could compare to what she had just seen; the casual, routine way in which the man had carried out the act was simply overwhelming. Now the killer was walking toward her, *looking right through her,* and the gun was still in his hand. . . .

"Brynn." She swung her head to the right, gasping as a bolt of pain shot through her neck. Patterson had risen to his knees, and the two men behind him had their hands on his shoulders. Fitzgerald wasn't sure if they were keeping him down or holding him up; she was just relieved to see he had regained consciousness.

"Brynn, don't fight them," Patterson rasped. He was bleeding badly from a cut beneath his right eye, which was swollen shut, and more blood was streaming down from a wound on his scalp. His suit was torn and stained, but he didn't look scared in the least. "Help is on the way. A GPS signal went out to the backup team when the first rocket hit . . . The technology is standard issue for embassy vehicles. All the cars are fitted with it. Reinforcements will be here any minute."

"They won't arrive in time," a voice announced in perfect English. It was the man who'd just killed the injured woman. He had stopped a few feet away, and his gaze was alternating between them. "You have no chance of being rescued. You have no chance of escape. At this point, I'm afraid you only have one option, and that is to cooperate."

"What do you mean, 'cooperate'?" the ambassador demanded, his voice getting stronger and more indignant with each passing syllable. "Who the hell are you? Why are you doing this? What do you want?"

"Nothing from you," the man responded calmly. "In fact, we don't need you at all."

He nodded to one of the soldiers standing next to Patterson. The subordinate stepped back to allow for the length of his rifle, which he brought to his shoulder in one clean movement. The muzzle was aimed directly at the back of the ambassador's head.

"No!" Fitzgerald screamed. She got to her feet and staggered forward, but she was quickly restrained on either side. Her heart was pumping so hard, she thought it would burst. She didn't know exactly what was happening here, but she couldn't let her oldest, closest friend die right in front of her eyes. Not if she could stop it. "Don't hurt him! *Please!*"

The man with the handgun looked at her steadily for a long moment. Then, without warning, he peeled off the balaclava with his free hand.

"Oh my God," Fitzgerald breathed. She looked hard at the man's face, unwilling to believe her eyes. "I know you. . . ."

"Yes, I can see you do." Amari Saifi smiled gently; there was something about his voice and manner that was eerily pleasant. "Tell me, Dr. Fitzgerald . . . Why shouldn't we kill this man?"

"He's a senior member of the Foreign Service," she said, thinking frantically, "and he's very wealthy. If it's money you want, he could be useful to you. If you intend to keep me alive, it will be . . . You'll have two hostages instead of one. Killing him doesn't help you." Her voice had been rising steadily, but it couldn't be helped; she could no longer restrain her panic. "Don't you see that? *It doesn't help you to kill him!*"

"It doesn't necessarily hurt us, either, and we only came for you." Having made his instructions clear, Saifi nodded to the man with the rifle.

Fitzgerald howled in helpless rage and tried to pull away from her captors. At the same time, Patterson opened his mouth to speak. He didn't manage a single word. There was a sharp crack as the 7.62mm round tore through his face, leaving a gaping wound in place of his left cheek. There was a strange moment where everything seemed to freeze, after which his lifeless body pitched forward onto the grass.

Fitzgerald just stared in horror for a few seconds. Then it hit her like a solid blow to the chest, and she dropped to her knees, a low, sick moan rising up in her throat. She was in shock, completely numb, and she missed what happened next: the rapid approach of an unmarked van from the north, where the road was still clear; the sound of distant sirens and the steady blat of helicopter blades; the Algerian's rapid commands carrying over the din. However, despite her semiconscious state, she couldn't miss the needle that was jabbed forcefully into her right arm. The plunger went down, and the needle came out. Then the dark swarmed in, swallowing her in an endless black sea.

CHAPTER 11

WASHINGTON, D.C.

It was just after 7:20 AM Eastern Standard Time as the elevator slowed to a halt on the basement level of the West Wing. Once the doors slid open, Jonathan Harper stepped out and hung a right, making his way past a Secret Service agent and several members of the National Security Council secretariat. The men and women of the secretariat were the primary occupants of the White House Situation Room, which was actually a 5000-square-foot warren of interconnected rooms. The vast underground complex—sometimes referred to, in-explicably, as "the woodshed"—also incorporated the NSC watch center. Harper only glanced at the harried faces as he walked past, but it was clear they were operating in a state of suspended disbelief. The deputy DCI felt much the same; he was still trying to get his mind around what had transpired in Pakistan less than an hour earlier.

He'd gotten the first call from the watch officer at Langley at 6:25. He'd been at home, eating breakfast, when the secure line buzzed in the next room. Less than ten minutes later, he was dressed and on his way out the door, but he'd barely slid into the backseat of the waiting Town Car when his BlackBerry started to vibrate. It was the White House senior duty officer, or SDO, informing him that an emergency meeting had been called by the president and was set to begin in twenty minutes' time.

Before he had been nominated for the post of deputy executive director, Harper had served as the CIA's deputy director of operations (DDO). Back then his name had been classified, withheld from the media, but his current role did not allow for such ambiguities. The attempt on his life eight months earlier had only heightened the media's interest in him, and for this reason, he and his wife had been forced to sell their brownstone on historic General's Row, just south of Dupont Circle. After a brief search, they'd settled on a five-bedroom town house on Embassy Row. While the house itself was everything they'd been looking for, it made for a slightly longer drive to 1600 Pennsylvania Avenue. He'd used the time in the car to get hold of his primary advisors, who'd filled him in on what they knew. Unfortunately, it wasn't much, and now he had to share that fact with the president.

He was admitted to the conference room. Like the rest of the West Wing basement, the room had been extensively remodeled in 2006. The mahogany walls had been largely replaced with a specially designed, sound-absorbent fabric, and sensors built into the ceiling alerted the Secret Service to the presence of activated cell phones, which were prohibited for reasons of security. It all combined to make for a very quiet space, but never more so than today. The faces around the long mahogany table were understandably grim, but they were all recognizable, at least to anyone with a passing interest in the U.S. government.

Flanking the president was Emily Susskind, the recently confirmed director of the FBI; also, her deputy, Harry Judd; and Kenneth Bale, the director of National Intelligence. To Bale's left was Robert Andrews, the ample, dark-haired director of Central Intelligence. He nodded a curt hello when he caught his subordinate's eye. The other side of the table was occupied by the undersecretary for political affairs, Elliot Greengrass; Jeremy Thayer, the national security advisor; and Stan Chavis, the president's chief of staff.

There was one other person in the room, seated next to DCI Andrews. He appeared more shaken than the other officials around the table, which was understandable. As assistant secretary for the Bureau of Diplomatic Security and director of the Office of Foreign Missions, Gavin Dowd was responsible for the day-to-day operations of the DSS, as well as the protection of numerous State Department officials, including Brynn Fitzgerald. If blame was to be dispensed at this meeting, the sixty-year-old former prosecutor would likely receive the lion's share.

"Jonathan," the president said from the head of the table. David Brenneman usually looked at least a decade younger than his fifty-four years. His short, wavy hair still held more brown than silver, and it was no secret that his open, honest features had assisted him greatly over the course of his political career. On this particular morning, though, he looked every inch his age. Harper took that as a bad sign, as the day had hardly begun. "Pull up a chair. We were just about to get started."

There was only one chair to be had, but Harper didn't point this out as he sat across from Dowd. "That's fine, sir. Please, don't let me hold you up any longer."

"Very well." The president nodded and turned to Andrews. "Bob, if you could bring everyone up to speed."

"Yes, sir." The DCI used a remote to power up the NEC plasma televisions strategically placed around the room. After a few seconds, the presidential seal dissolved, and the first of several grisly images appeared. A few people winced, including Dowd, but no one looked away as Andrews began the briefing.

"Mr. President, ladies and gentlemen. As you can probably guess, what you see here is the aftermath of the attack on Secretary Fitzgerald's motorcade. These digital photographs were taken less than twenty minutes ago. For those of you who've never been to Pakistan, Airport Road is several miles north of Chaklala Air Base, approximately halfway between Islamabad and Rawalpindi. It's a fairly common route between the presidential palace and the air base. The agent who took these shots was part of the twelve-man reserve team that responded to the distress call. As most of you know, the signal is automatically broadcast once a tagged vehicle in the motorcade is incapacitated. In this case, the secretary of state's detail leader, Mike Petrina, had time to relay an additional request for assistance. Unfortunately, the reserve team was unable to respond in time. Special Agent Petrina was killed before he could get the secretary of state clear of the area, along with six other members of the protective detail."

Andrews paused and cleared his throat. "I'm afraid that's not the worst of it. It's my unhappy duty to report that Ambassador Patterson did not survive the attack. He was killed by a single gunshot wound to the head, which, according to eyewitnesses, was inflicted at point-blank range. These same witnesses saw armed men leaving the scene with a woman matching Secretary Fitzgerald's description. That was about two minutes before the first police units responded. She has not been accounted for, and at this point, I think we can safely assume that she has been kidnapped."

The room was completely silent. Everyone knew what had taken place, but until this moment, it hadn't really sunk in. Not for most of them, and nothing made it hit home like hearing the words aloud. Harper was slightly surprised that Gavin Dowd hadn't been asked to provide the initial assessment—it was his bureau, after all, that was responsible for losing Fitzgerald—but that was probably the exact reason Brenneman had settled on Andrews: he wanted a concise, unbiased account. It was Bale, the director of National Intelligence, who finally broke the silence.

"Do we have any idea how the secretary's route was compromised?"

"Not at this time," Andrews said simply.

"I take it, we're still waiting on a claim of responsibility," Chavis said.

"That's correct," the DCI replied. "We can probably expect a claim to be made within the hour. That will give us a better picture of who we're dealing with, as well as what kind of demands they'll eventually make."

"But won't we get the demands when the claim is made? Isn't that the way it usually works?"

"Not necessarily," Harry Judd put in. He looked over at Stan Chavis, who had posed the question. "In the case of a kidnapping, it's not unusual for days or even weeks to go by before a ransom demand is made."

"I understand that," the chief of staff said dryly. "But then again, this is not a typical abduction. Time is not on their side, Harry. Whoever is responsible for this must know that we will bring the full weight of the government to bear in tracking them down."

"With all due respect, Stan, you couldn't be more wrong." Ignoring the cold look his words earned him, Andrews went on. "Let me clarify. We *will* do everything we can to get the secretary back, but they—whoever 'they' are—have the clear advantage here. They have all the time in the world. Pakistan is their turf, not ours. With enough money and the right support network, the people who carried this off can hide indefinitely. They don't have to reveal themselves, and if they're patient and careful, they won't make the mistakes that get most people caught."

"On that note, what's happening right now?" Brenneman asked. He looked down the length of the table. "Gavin, what are you hearing from your people on the ground?"

"Sir, I spoke with the head of the reserve team less than fifteen minutes ago," Dowd said. His voice was shaky, but he seemed to be in control. "They arrived shortly after the Pakistani police, and so far, they seem to be getting all the cooperation they need. They've secured the scene, but it's still unclear exactly what's going to happen with the evidence. By that, I mean it's unclear where it will be taken, including the vehicles that were damaged and destroyed in the attack. Wherever it goes, though, our people *will* have access. I've been assured of that by the head of Inter-Services Intelligence, and I think we can take him at his word."

Dowd paused to check his notes. "When the incident occurred, there were a number of checkpoints already set up in the area, owing to heightened security for Secretary Fitzgerald's visit. Since her disappearance was verified, my people have been working with the Pakistanis to firm up the perimeter. Additionally, they've—"

"*Firm up the perimeter?*" Emily Susskind shot an angry look down the length of the table. "That's crap, Gavin. There's no way to secure that kind of urban area, especially not with an hour's notice. It's dense, highly populated, and there are roads all over the place. Hundreds of roads . . . too many to set up blocks on all of them."

"Look, I'm just telling you what I know," Dowd replied defensively. Normally, he would have taken offense to the challenge, particularly one made by the head of another agency. Given the circumstances, though, it was hard for him to sound anything other than defeated. "They've already expanded the perimeter twice, based on the amount of time that's elapsed. In all honesty, it's not enough, but it's hard to get things accomplished when something like this takes place on foreign soil." He pushed out a short, shaky breath, then ran a weary hand over his face. "Look, we're dealing with a number of serious problems here, and that's besides the obvious. The Pakistanis are not on good terms with us at the moment, and—"

"Stop right there," Brenneman said from the head of the table. His expression was hard to read, but the anger was plain in his quietly menacing voice. "Gavin, are you suggesting that my position with regard to the dispute over Kashmir—the fact that I won't interfere in the Israeli arms sale to India—is somehow related to Secretary Fitzgerald's abduction? That it somehow precipitated this event?"

"Sir, not at all," Dowd said hurriedly, his round face going very pale. "That is not what I meant. I'm merely pointing out that we have to take the current tensions between their government and ours into account. We can't afford not to. The Pakistanis may not move as fast as we would like them to, and chances are, they won't be as accommodating when it comes to giving our people access."

"Actually, that's a valid point, sir," Susskind put in, her voice returning to a more reasonable level. She shifted her steely blue gaze toward the commander in chief. "I mean, look at what's been happening over the past few weeks. They've completely stonewalled us with respect to our missing tourists. We're talking about twelve law-abiding Americans, people with valid visas who just disappeared into thin air, and they still haven't let us put a team on the ground."

"To make matters worse, we've just lost the single most important diplomat in the U.S. government, so breaking the ice is only going to get harder," Harper weighed in. "And our ambassador is dead, so he's no good to us, either. Those losses are only going to make it harder to establish a working relationship. At this point, we have to act fast, but we also have to tread carefully if we're going to get anything done. That's what diplomacy is all about, and we can't afford to forget that. We'll do more harm than good if we storm in there and start making demands."

With this contribution out of the way, the focus shifted toward the next speaker, but Harper felt the president's lingering attention. He knew he'd been blunt, and he couldn't help but wonder if he'd overstepped his bounds.

"Sir, if I could make a suggestion . . . ?"

Harper looked at the man who'd addressed the president. Owing to the untimely death of the former secretary and Fitzgerald's subsequent promotion, the post of deputy secretary was currently vacant. That made Elliot Greengrass the second-ranking official at the State Department. The deputy DCI knew Greengrass to be thoughtful, competent—traits he'd demonstrated in his previous roles with the NSC and as the U.S. ambassador to Greece, a position he'd held from 1997 to 2001. Nevertheless, it was unclear how effective the fifty-year-old diplomat would be in the current situation, given his lack of experience on the Asian continent.

"Of course, Elliot," Brenneman said. "By all means, let's hear it."

"Sir, I think I should travel to Islamabad to meet with President Musharraf immediately. We'll work to keep it low-key, but we really need a diplomatic presence on the ground. And by that, I mean we need an envoy prepared to stay in Pakistan for the duration."

The president considered for a moment, then nodded his consent. "I agree. Putting an envoy in place will send a few messages. First, it will show that we're not afraid to wade back in with both feet, and second, that we intend to play a very active role in the investigation.

"And that falls to you, Emily," Brenneman said, shifting his gaze once more. The forty-two-year-old Susskind was, by a slim margin, the youngest person in the room. She was also a Princeton grad, a mother of two, the seventh director of the FBI, and the first woman to hold the title. Her propensity for blunt speech frequently put her at odds with the president and his senior advisors, as did her left-of-center politics, but everyone in the room respected her opinion, as well as her considerable influence on the Hill.

"As I understand it," the president continued, "the Bureau has, shall we say, a *limited* presence in Pakistan."

"Unfortunately, that's putting it lightly, sir. We maintain small offices at the consulates in Lahore, Peshawar, and Karachi, but they're negligible in terms of manpower. Even the main hub at the embassy in Islamabad is minimally staffed . . . We have less than fifty agents in the entire country, and that's after we expanded our legal attaché program in '99."

"Well, we need to change that, and sooner rather than later." Brenneman set down his pen and studied the FBI director. "Obviously, I've already spoken to President Musharraf. He's assured me that his government is committed to finding whoever was responsible, as well as to the safe recovery of Secretary Fitzgerald. In keeping with this promise, he's agreed to allow a team of investigators into the country. They'll be given everything they need as soon as they can get there."

Susskind was visibly surprised. "After all the walls he's put up recently? He changed his mind that fast?"

The president nodded. "As far as he's concerned, the severity of this incident takes precedence over any diplomatic squabbling, and it has nothing to do with our missing tourists. That's a separate issue entirely. According to him, that is." Brenneman frowned, his forehead creasing thoughtfully. "Personally, I'm not so sure. Anyway, our team will be given full authority to conduct an extensive extraterritorial investigation. In other words, Emily, send your best, because they're not coming home until the job is done."

"I understand, Mr. President." Susskind was already jotting notes on a legal pad. "I'll get you the names by midday."

"That's not good enough. By that time they need to be in the air."

"Yes, sir . . . I'll make it happen."

"Good," Brenneman said. "Next, I want to talk about possible suspects. I realize we're in the early stages here, but a number of agencies have been looking at one man in particular for the last couple weeks. His name came up in relation to our missing tourists, but given the similarities between those incidents and the abduction of Secretary Fitzgerald, I think he's worth mentioning. Jeremy, if you wouldn't mind."

Thayer nodded and got to his feet. He left the room for a moment, then returned with a stack of briefing folders. The folders were distributed quickly, and the national security advisor retook his seat.

"Ladies and gentlemen, what you're about to see—for those of you who haven't been made privy to this information—is highly classified. It is not, I repeat, *not* to be circulated freely within your respective agencies. As it stands . . ."

Tuning Thayer out, Harper flipped open the folder. What he saw was the State Department's file on Amari Saifi. It was the same file he'd helped compile with help from people at State, Langley, and the National Counterterrorism Center in McLean, Virginia. Scanning the documents inside, he saw nothing new, and he would have already been alerted if anything substantial had changed. As a result, his thoughts began to drift as Thayer droned on and on. Before long, he found himself thinking about the way he'd left things with Kealey in Oraefi.

It still bothered him, which wasn't entirely a bad thing. In fact, it came as something of a relief to the deputy DCI. It meant he hadn't resigned himself to the indiscriminate use of the people who worked for him. The people who *used* to work for him, he reminded himself.

Ryan Kealey's five-year relationship with the CIA had always been hard to define, but there was one constant factor: his involvement always stemmed from some kind of national crisis, save for his first assignment in Syria. And he had always come through. He'd served as a full-time employee in the Operations Directorate for less than six months, none of them concurrently. Most of the time, he was listed as an independent contractor, but even that was rare. It was rare to see his name on paper, anyway. Plausible deniability, as always, was the key factor. Unfortunately, it was lost once a name popped up on any kind of official document, even on something as insignificant as an internal memorandum.

And that was the smallest threat to a field operative's anonymity. What had transpired in New York City ten months earlier had garnered worldwide attention, and once Kealey's role in that incident had been made public, he'd immediately acquired a certain degree of unwanted fame. The exposure had been mostly limited to his name and background, as there weren't many pictures of him floating around, but needless to say, his days of undercover work had come to a screeching halt. Still, it could have been worse. Kealey had wanted out, anyway, mostly because he wanted to devote himself to Naomi Kharmai's recovery, and Harper had let them go. Given the sacrifices they had made, it was the least he could do.

Only that was all in the past, and things had changed. Once it became clear that Amari Saifi had played a key role in the recent wave of abductions in Pakistan, the president had immediately asked for Kealey's help in tracking him down. Harper couldn't fault the president—Kealey's record spoke for itself, after all—but it did put Harper in the uncomfortable position of having to call his old friend out of retirement. Moreover, he had had to figure out a way to accomplish that task, which at the time had seemed just short of impossible.

Nevertheless, he had managed to do it. He didn't regret asking more of a man who'd already given so much. Nor did he regret the methods he'd used to lure Kealey back into the fold. The story he'd spun in Oraefi wasn't entirely a lie; Naomi Kharmai *had* trained extensively at the Farm and was more than capable in her new role as a field operative. Her instructors had all given her top marks, though to be fair, they didn't have the full story on their prized student. But to Harper, that was immaterial. He knew that Kealey's participation was entirely reliant on Kharmai's—that he was only doing it to watch out for her—but if that was what it took to get the younger man into the fold, then so be it.

In truth, he *was* deeply concerned about their underlying motivations, but as long as they were prepared to see it through, he was willing to set his reservations aside. He had set the wheels in motion, and that was that. If Saifi was, in fact, responsible for Secretary Fitzgerald's disappearance, the stakes had just been raised dramatically, and while Harper despised clichés, he had to admit that one was applicable here: drastic times called for drastic measures, and that meant taking advantage of every resource, no matter how it was acquired.

CHAPTER 12

WASHINGTON, D.C.

Twenty minutes after the briefing folders were handed out, the meeting came to a gradual close. The assembled officials got to their feet, following the president's lead, and started to file through the door. As Harper collected his materials, Brenneman caught his eye and indicated, with a quick, familiar gesture, that he wanted a word in private. The deputy DCI moved to the side to allow for traffic and watched as Brenneman murmured his way through a series of sidebars. Before long, Harper was the only one left; even Robert Andrews, his immediate superior, had been asked to leave the room. Either that or he'd been politely ushered out, which made more sense to the Agency's second-ranking official. While Andrews held the top spot, he wasn't a career intelligence officer, and the president had always placed a priority on experience.

Brenneman came around the table and extended a hand. "Thanks for waiting, John. I appreciate your patience." He shook his head slowly, as if the enormity of the situation was only just hitting him. "It's just unbelievable. The sheer audacity of these people. . . ."

"I know, sir, but we'll find her, and we'll bring her back." *Alive* was the key last word of that sentence. Unspoken, of course, but nevertheless, it seemed to hang in the air. "You have my word on it."

"And the people responsible?"

"We'll find them, too."

Brenneman nodded and glanced over his shoulder to the entrance of the conference room. A man in a dark suit was standing just inside the door, which was still open. His hands were in front of his body, one folded over the other, but his attention was clearly fixed on his principal. Harper had been alone with the president dozens of times, but Secret Service agents didn't differentiate between friend and foe; in their eyes, everyone was a potential threat. The constant paranoia was part of what made them so good at their work. "Sean, could you give us a minute, please?"

The agent hesitated, then nodded brusquely. "Of course, Mr. President." He murmured something into his sleeve and left the room. A moment later, the door closed with a gentle click.

Brenneman extended an arm toward the table. "Please, have a seat."

Harper picked out a chair. Once they were both seated, the commander in chief leaned forward and emitted a weary sigh. Nearly a minute passed in silence, and then he spoke without warning.

"John, how long have we known each other?"

The question caught the deputy DCI off guard, but he sensed it was serious. "About six years, I believe. You were the president-elect when we first met. It was a month or two before your inauguration."

"That's right." There was a meaningful pause. "In all that time, I've never seen you outside of Langley or this building. Do you realize that? I've never once spent more than a few minutes talking with you about anything other than national security. I've never met your wife. I have no idea where you live."

"Mr. President, I . . ." Harper wasn't sure where this was going, and nothing in his career had prepared him for this kind of conversation. "Sir, what exactly are you getting at?"

The other man smiled mildly. "John, for all the good you do at Langley, you are not a politician, so you may find this hard to understand. Especially since you work in such a sensitive environment. But here's the thing . . . You are one of the few people in government service who knows how to keep things quiet. We may not know each other very well, but I've told you a lot of things in confidence over the years, and I've yet to hear them anywhere else. In short, you've earned my trust, as well as my deep gratitude for your hard work in defending this country."

Harper nodded slowly; he was deeply surprised by the president's candor. "Sir, I don't know what to say. I'm pleased you feel that way, but it's my job. I would never divulge anything you tell me in confidence."

"I know that, and that's why I want to ask you something." Brenneman hesitated, then propped his elbows on top of the table and interlaced his fingers. "Remember, I'm looking for your honest opinion here. I won't accept anything less."

"Of course. It goes without saying."

"It has to do with Dowd's comments early in the briefing. About my stance on the India-Israel deal and how it may have . . . precipitated this event."

Harper was already shaking his head emphatically. "Mr. President, you are not responsible for what happened in Pakistan. Not for any of it."

"But if there's a chance I could get her back by opposing the deal, shouldn't I—"

"No." Harper waited for the other man to meet his eyes. "Sir, it's too late for that. If you renege now, you might as well negotiate directly with the terrorists, because that's how it's going to look."

"But that's not—"

"That's how the American people will see it," Harper repeated forcefully, "and that's exactly how it will be perceived around the world. You have to stay the course. At this point, it's your best option. Your only option, really."

"Stay the course," Brenneman repeated slowly. He closed his eyes, lowered his chin slightly, and began massaging his temples. "I feel like I've backed myself into a corner on this, John. There's no room to maneuver."

"I can understand why you feel that way, sir, but I repeat: this wasn't your doing, and my advice stands. Our best bet right now is to investigate as thoroughly as we can, follow up every lead, while at the same time preparing for the people who did this to make contact. Which they *will* do, and sooner rather than later."

The president nodded, looked up, and straightened his tie unconsciously. "I'm confident the investigation will proceed smoothly. I have a lot of faith in the FBI. Especially in Director Susskind."

Harper nodded. "That's understandable. She started out working violent crimes in New Jersey, and the Bureau has more experience with kidnapping cases than any other law enforcement agency in the world."

"Yes, they wrote the book on that particular subject, and they've had a lot of success with their extraterritorial work. Even in Pakistan, where it's not exactly easy to get an investigation off the ground. As you know, the Bureau was involved with the apprehension of both Ramzi Yousef in 1995 and Khalid Mohammed in 2003, so they have a proven track record in the area. At the same time, there are . . ." Brenneman hesitated as he searched for the right word. "There are *limits* as to what they can ask, as well as how they can ask it. And that's assuming they even manage to find Saifi."

"Sir, we can't link him to this yet," Harper cautioned. "He may top the list of suspects, but it's better to wait and see what the Bureau turns up before we start jumping to conclusions."

"I'll be immensely surprised if it turns out he wasn't involved. We know he took part in the incident two weeks ago."

"You're referring to the kidnapping on the Karakoram Highway."

"Yes," Brenneman confirmed. "Let's set aside the fact that he shouldn't even be a free man for a moment. He's perfected his modus operandi, it seems, and nothing about what happened today strikes me as the work of amateurs. At best, they were skilled professionals dressed in army uniforms. At worst . . ."

"They were actual Pakistani soldiers," Harper finished grimly. Eyewitness accounts had verified that Fitzgerald's abductors had been wearing in army fatigues. "And if that's the case, we have a very serious problem."

Brenneman didn't immediately respond. Instead, he stood and moved over to the far wall, where several 32-inch monitors were positioned next to each other. The volume had been muted on all three, but the identical images were already numbingly familiar. CNN had been running the tape on a continuous loop, and over the last half hour, the footage had been burned into the minds of millions of disbelieving Americans. Like many senior U.S. officials, the secretary of state only traveled with members of one network, known as "the pool," which shared coverage with its competitors under a long-standing agreement. The pool was rotated on a regular basis, and for Secretary Fitzgerald's first official trip, CNN had been next in line. The network had paid a devastating price for the privilege. Eight crew members had been killed in the attack on the secretary's motorcade, including Susan Watkins, a senior foreign correspondent and one of CNN's most recognizable anchors. The film taken after the incident had been shot by cameramen from the bureau office in Islamabad.

Finally, Brenneman addressed his subordinate's last point. He was still facing the monitors when he spoke. "John, do you think it's possible that the Pakistani government could be directly involved with this? On any level whatsoever?"

"It seems like a stretch, sir. They're extremely upset over your position on Israel's arms sale to India, I know, but Musharraf has too much to lose by engaging in something of this magnitude. I just don't think it's a possibility, despite the evidence we've seen so far."

"And what if you're wrong?" The president turned away from the monitors to face his subordinate. "You told me yourself how seriously Pakistan takes the dispute over Jammu and Kashmir. You emphasized the fact that they've fought a number of wars over that land. Kargil in '99 is only the latest example, and by no means is that the worst possible scenario. We're talking about a country with at least forty nuclear weapons here. Maybe the arms sale to India was just the tipping point. The final straw, so to speak."

"Sir, I just can't believe they'd risk something like this," Harper repeated, "but I think we should withhold judgment until the Bureau's team submits a preliminary report. Like I said, the Agency will be thoroughly involved as well."

"Which brings me to my next point," Brenneman said. "You just returned from overseas, correct?"

"Yes."

"I trust you managed to find your man."

"I did. And he's willing to help."

"Good." A genuine smile crossed the president's face, but it disappeared just as fast. The situation was much too dire for any real relief to take hold. "I'm reassured to know you have your best on this, John. I'm well aware of what Kealey has done for us, and I'm confident he'll be able to resolve this situation as well."

"I'm sure he will, sir, but he won't be working alone. Naomi Kharmai has also been tasked with this. You'll remember her from the incident in New York City last year, as well as the attempt on your life in 2007. She was instrumental in preventing both attacks."

"Yes." Brenneman nodded slowly. "She's a very capable young woman. I owe her a lot, as does the country, and I'm pleased to hear she's involved. But just so we're clear, I want to know exactly what their instructions are. Because I'm convinced that Amari Saifi is somehow involved with the abduction of Secretary Fitzgerald, and that's where I want you to focus your efforts."

"I understand, sir. And to answer your question, yes, finding Saifi is their primary objective."

Brenneman nodded his approval. "Have you talked to them since the attack?"

"No. I haven't had the chance yet. I'll make the call on the way to Langley."

"Good." The president's shoulders seemed to relax a little, as if some minor weight had been removed. Still, the burden that remained was clearly visible in his worried gaze. "I'm sure it's him, John. It fits his profile. He may be working alone; he may have backers in the Pakistani government. Either way, I want you to find him. Find him and you'll find her. I'm sure of it."

Harper got to his feet, sensing the meeting was over. "We'll do our best, Mr. President."

"Don't do your best." Brenneman met his eyes once more, and this time, his demeanor was adamant. "Just get it done. I'm counting on you, and so is she."

CHAPTER 13

MADRID, SPAIN

Like many countries in Western Europe—indeed, like most countries around the world—Spain had seen its fair share of terrorist activity over the years. Unlike many of its neighbors, though, the danger to Spain was largely born at home. For nearly fifty years, Euskadi Ta Askatasuna had been the country's most prominent terror organization. Better known abroad as ETA, its overriding aim was the establishment of an independent Basque state in the north, and the group presented a real and ongoing threat, having claimed more than eight hundred lives through shootings and bombings since its inception in 1959. Unfortunately, it wasn't the only threat to the Spanish government and a population of forty million. In recent years, the constantly reemerging, spreading network of al-Qaeda had claimed its stake on Spanish soil as well, just as it had in so many other places.

Tragic proof of al-Qaeda's presence in Spain had come on March 11, 2004, when the capital was rocked by the bombings of four commuter trains. The near-simultaneous blasts claimed the lives of 191 people and left another 1,200 wounded, and while the attack was initially attributed to ETA, it soon became clear that the work was not that of the Basque separatist movement. In the three-year investigation that followed the blasts, it also became clear just how elusive the threat could be, even in a country accustomed to waging the war on terror. When the highly publicized Madrid bombing trial finally began in February of 2007, the list of defendants included 15 Moroccans, 9 Spaniards, 2 Syrians, an Egyptian, an Algerian, and a Lebanese national, none of whom had conclusive ties to the Basque separatists. And yet, while al-Qaeda as a whole had been implicated thorough a veritable mountain of circumstantial evidence, there was nothing linking the key leadership to the perpetrators of the Madrid bombings. In fact, the origin of the plot largely remained a mystery to Spanish authorities.

Since his first assignment for the Agency nearly five years earlier, the slippery nature of the links between various terrorist groups was something that Ryan Kealey had come to appreciate. For several years after 9/11, terrorist activity—at least in the form of major attacks on civilian targets—had declined precipitously around the world. In Kealey's view, this period of inactivity had given security forces and intelligence agencies a completely false perception: the idea that they were winning the war, that the drop in attacks could be directly attributed to new and improved policies, as well as the improved dissemination of information.

In truth, the worldwide clampdown on terror groups and their financial backers *had* been successful, at least to a degree. The senior leadership of al-Qaeda had been largely cut off from its base of support, and the network's ability to pass on instructions had been severely hindered. Even the freezing of funds, most of which was instigated by the U.S. government, had helped to temporarily stem the tide. But what the intelligence agencies had missed—what even the Agency itself had overlooked—was, Kealey believed, the emergence of a new threat. Namely, the power of ideology. Radical Islam's hatred of the West was an incredibly unifying factor, more so than most Americans could ever understand. It was strong enough to turn an impressionable student, and it was strong enough to bring together fledgling terrorists from six countries. Terrorism was no longer a singular effort. It was a cooperative enterprise, and in many cases, the cooperation between the terrorists was much greater than that between the security forces and intelligence outfits of supposedly friendly governments. The war in Iraq had only made things worse, creating a deep philosophical and moral divide between the United States and nations the country had once enjoyed amicable relationships with.

Kealey had taken all of this into account when he'd first read the

Agency's file on Kamil Ghafour. Since then, he'd had plenty of time to mull over what he had learned. The previous day's bus ride to Keflavík International had been uneventful, and though the worsening weather had threatened to temporarily ground air traffic, the plane had left on time. After landing at Madrid Barajas, they'd taken a taxi directly to a hotel on the Gran Via, one of the city's most famous streets. Instead of going in, they'd shouldered their bags and walked for twenty minutes, checking for signs of surveillance. Kealey's primary concern was the Spanish authorities, who could have conceivably flagged the false passport he was traveling on. Kealey had been forced to travel from Keflavík to Madrid using his French passport, which bore the name of Joseph Briand. Naomi was better prepared, having acquired new false documentation through the Operations Directorate before she'd flown to Iceland.

After engaging in the standard surveillance detection run, they'd caught a second taxi to the Sofitel Madrid Plaza de España. Once they arrived, Kealey called the number Harper had given him in Oraefi. Several minutes later, one of the watchers, a man by the name of Ramirez, came down to meet them in the lobby. The room the team had appropriated was on the top floor, paid for by an Agency front, a small industrial company based in Lexington Park, Maryland. Inside the spacious, luxurious suite, he and Naomi were introduced to the lead members of all three surveillance teams. The senior operative, a woman named Marissa Pétain, had brought them up to speed on Ghafour's movements, after which they'd taken the elevator down to the lobby, then walked a few blocks over to get a firsthand look at the ground on which they'd be operating. Shortly thereafter, he and Naomi caught another taxi back to their hotel on the south side of the Plaza Mayor. Over a strained meal in the hotel's ground-floor restaurant, they'd made their arrangements for the following day. They agreed to meet at 7:00 AM in the lobby. From there, they would head over to the makeshift command center on the top floor of the watchers' hotel. Once the bill was settled, they had parted ways. That was the last time he'd seen her.

His fears about her mental state had been confirmed that very morning. He had gone down to the lobby at seven, the time they'd agreed upon, but she was nowhere in sight. After waiting for ten minutes, he'd gone up to her room to check on her, but she didn't answer the door. After a brief bout of indecision, Kealey took the elevator back down to the lobby, where he inquired at the front desk. All they could tell him was that she hadn't checked out, which wasn't much help.

Pétain had provided them each with a pay-and-go phone the previous day, but Naomi didn't pick up when he tried to call her. Once it became clear she wasn't going to show, he'd left for the second hotel without her. That had been seven hours earlier, and she had yet to make an appearance. As the hours crept past, her unexplained absence had hung in the air like a cloud, and Kealey knew that—despite his best efforts to conceal his tension—his concern with respect to her strange disappearance had been picked up by the other operatives. Now they were all on edge; the concern in their faces was impossible to miss. Kealey knew it wasn't a good sign. They had yet to make contact with Kamil Ghafour, and the operation was already off to a bad start.

Now, as he stood on the balcony overlooking the Plaza de España, Kealey tried once more to set Naomi's absence aside. There was too much riding on the next hour, and he couldn't afford the distraction. It was just after 3:20 in the afternoon, and the city below was starting to churn to life again. The lunch hour—or hours, as was more commonly the case in Spain—was drawing to a close. Kealey was wearing nothing more than a white T-shirt, lightweight khakis, and Nike cross-trainers, but the heat was still stifling. The fact that he'd flown directly to Madrid from Keflavík wasn't exactly helping matters, but it would have been hard to bear regardless. It had reached 95 degrees Fahrenheit by midmorning, and the mercury had topped 100 degrees by early afternoon. Worst of all, the air-conditioning in the hotel on Calle de los Jardines was subpar, at best, and the heat didn't seem to diminish at night. After a long day of travel, followed by a sleepless, sweaty night, Kealey had yet to see the appeal of the Spanish capital.

Removing his sunglasses, he rubbed his eyes, lifted a pair of binoculars, and used them to look out across the square. The Plaza de España didn't come close to topping the list of Madrid's tourist attractions, but it was still fairly impressive. Beyond a generous strip of bright green grass and a small pond stood an imposing stone statue of Miguel de Cervantes, the famed Spanish novelist, poet, and playwright. The sculpture, first started in 1925, took more than twenty-seven years to complete, and the results reflected the patience and skill of the various artists. Cervantes was portrayed in a seated position, gazing serenely down at the figments of his own imagination, Don Quixote, Sancho Panza, and Dulcinea, the beautiful peasant of Quixote's dreams. The smaller figures were immortalized in bronze, except for Dulcinea, who was rendered in stone. All of them were apparently unaware of the lavish attention their creator was bestowing upon them.

Kealey switched his view to the buildings north of the plaza. Nestled between the Torre de Madrid and the Edificio España, two of the tallest buildings in the city, were a number of less imposing structures. Most were packed tightly together, as one would expect, but there was a noticeable gap in the city skyline. The building that had formerly occupied the lot—a decrepit, four-story warehouse of red brick—had been brought down by controlled demolition two months earlier to make way for yet another skyscraper. Even from across the square and a number of narrow streets, Kealey could make out the chain-link fence surrounding the lot. A few trailers were positioned toward the north end of the building site, barely visible through a maze of iron columns and girders, all of which sat atop an enormous concrete pad. A number of cranes were located inside the fence, which seemed to have only two points of access. Both gates were large enough to allow vehicle access, though nothing much seemed to be happening at the moment. Several workers were scattered around the pad, but they weren't active. Most were sitting down with paper or plastic bags at hand, leading Kealey to assume they were still finishing up the lunch hour. He wondered which of the distant figures represented the man he wanted to talk to.

As Kealey surveyed the scene, he was startled by a sudden movement in his peripheral vision. He placed his left hand on the railing and turned to face the approaching figure. At the same time, he hooked a foot through the long strap of the bag at his feet. The bag, which bore the insignia of the Real Madrid football club, contained the money intended for Kamil Ghafour. Kealey had used Naomi's sat phone to make the request from Keflavík, and Harper had come through for him. One of the watchers had picked up the money from a locker at the Atocha train station the day before.

"Sorry." The woman who'd stepped up behind him started to laugh helplessly. "I didn't mean to scare you."

"No problem," Kealey said. He'd dismissed the incident, but she kept laughing. He stared at her for a long moment, clearly annoyed, and finally the laughter started to slow. "It's not that funny. And by the way, I don't like people sneaking up on me."

"Then I guess it is kind of funny," Marissa Pétain said, trying unsuccessfully to hold back another burst of laughter. She looked at his hand on the railing, then moved her gaze to the bag at his feet. She looked up and smirked. "My God, you're supposed to be some kind of superspy, and you didn't even hear me coming. I could have pushed you right over the balcony."

Kealey looked her over as he tried to decipher her thick accent. According to Harper, Pétain was a four-year veteran of the Clandestine Service. Before Kealey had taken over the previous day, she had been in overall command of the teams watching Kamil Ghafour in Madrid. She hadn't said anything to pique his concern, but Kealey couldn't help but wonder if she resented him for taking over her role in the operation. Apparently, the young operative had been based in the city for quite some time. He didn't really know anything about her, but what he knew so far, he could live without. She was opinionated, loud, and she didn't know when to keep her mouth shut. He didn't think it was intentional, but that didn't make her personality any easier to bear.

At the same time, there was something vaguely intriguing about her. Or at least about her name. It was clearly French, as was her accent, but an incident earlier in the day had caught Kealey's attention. She had called the front desk to ask a question, and much to his surprise, she'd lapsed effortlessly into Andalusian Spanish. It wasn't the fact that she spoke the language that caught him off guard; naturally, that would be expected of an operative stationed in Spain. It was her accent that he'd found surprising. It was near perfect. When she called down to the lobby, it was as if she'd completely shrugged off her French heritage in the space of a few seconds.

Still, Castilian was the official language on mainland Spain, and the receptionist would remember someone speaking with a different regional dialect. For this reason, Kealey couldn't help but wonder about Pétain's background. Was her Spanish limited in that respect? Had she keyed in on the *receptionist's* accent? Or had she just slipped up? It seemed like a small mistake, but given what they were about to do, the slightest error could result in disaster.

She was waiting for some kind of response. Kealey shook his head absently and nodded toward the room. "Any word from Naomi?"

Pétain's demeanor changed instantly, a serious expression sliding over her face. "Not yet. She's been gone a long time and, well . . ." She shrugged and looked away. "I know you want to wait for her, but our window of opportunity closes in less than an hour. We can push it back till tomorrow, if you like, but—"

"No," Kealey said, cutting her off. "We're going today." He ran a hand over his face and looked at his watch, a rugged Timex Expedition E-Tide. He'd picked it up a few months ago to replace his aging Wenger chronograph. "How long has it been since the teams checked in?"

"Ten minutes," Pétain replied. She didn't need to consult her own watch. "The timetable hasn't changed. As far as they're concerned, the building site is still the best place to make contact."

"I take it you agree?"

Pétain nodded, but the gesture was barely noticeable. It was something else that Kealey found annoying, though to be fair, she couldn't have known that. In this kind of situation, he wanted nothing less than clear yes-or-no answers.

He kept looking at her, and she finally got the message. "Yes, I think that's the best idea. Ghafour shares a flat with a number of people, so it would be hard to isolate him there. I think we have a better chance of catching him off guard at work. It's a good plan."

"And his employer? The one who caused all the trouble in the first place?"

"He's meeting with a group of developers in Seville, and he'll be gone through Tuesday. I verified that yesterday."

"Okay. Fair enough." Kealey nodded slowly. It was vital to approach Kamil Ghafour without his employer's knowledge. Given everything the man had done so far to protect Ghafour's immigration status, it was likely he'd go to any length to shield his employee from anyone who even remotely resembled the authorities.

Kealey lifted the duffel bag and slung it over his shoulder. Moving back through the open doors leading into the room, he paused to take a deep, appreciative breath. It was only slightly cooler inside, but once you topped the 100-degree mark, even a slight variation could seem like a world of difference. He was moving over to check with Ramirez, who was monitoring the radios, when the door to the hall swung open and Naomi walked in.

*   *   *

Kealey changed trajectory immediately and crossed the opulent room with three quick paces. He could tell that his anger was clearly visible, and on some level, he knew it was all a cover, that he was only trying to shield his relief. But as he drew closer, he slowed down, sensing that something wasn't quite right. She wouldn't meet his eyes, and she seemed distracted.

"Naomi, where the hell have you been? What are you . . . ?" He trailed off, then leaned in and studied her closer. "What's wrong with you?"

"Nothing." She brushed past him into the room. As she leaned down to murmur something at Ramirez's shoulder, Kealey watched intently, unsure of his next move. It was hard to tell what was going on with her. She hadn't been drinking: at least, he couldn't smell it on her breath, and her movements weren't raising any internal alarms. He could count the number of times he'd seen her tipsy on one hand, so for that reason alone, it didn't seem likely. Still, whatever he was seeing was definitely cause for concern. It was hard to pick out the little departures from her normal behavior, and if he hadn't lived with her for an extended period of time, he might well have missed them entirely.

"Naomi, can I talk to you for a second?"

She crossed her arms and stared at him for a full thirty seconds. Then she nodded and walked past him, out the door. Pétain and Ramirez followed her the whole way, with curious looks. Kealey trailed her into the hall and closed the door behind him, then faced her and cupped her elbow in his right hand, pulling her close. She looked up, and Kealey was shocked into silence. Her face was completely blank, no expression there at all, but that wasn't what caught his attention. It was her eyes, or more specifically, her pupils. They were nearly twice their normal size. He wondered how he could have missed it before. More importantly, how could *Harper* have missed it? A flurry of possible explanations began racing through his mind, nearly all of them bad, but he didn't have time to consider them now.

"What is it?" she asked. Her voice was nearly as dead as her gaze. "We're wasting time."

He shook his head in disbelief and gripped her arm a little harder. Not enough to hurt. Just enough to jolt her out of this strange, detached state. She blinked once, but otherwise, the touch didn't register.

"Naomi, what's going on with you?" he murmured forcefully, aware of the thin walls and the deafening silence inside the hotel room. He didn't have to be inside to know that Pétain and Ramirez were trying to listen in. "You've been missing since seven this morning. We were about to leave without you."

"Yeah, I know, and I'm sorry about that. But I'm here now, and I'm ready to go." He didn't respond, and a hint of irritation finally crossed her face. "Ryan, I already said I'm sorry. What more do you want? We went over everything last night. For hours on end," she reminded him. "Nothing has changed, so there's no problem. As far as I can tell, this couldn't be more straightforward."

"That doesn't make it any less risky," he shot back. "And it doesn't change what's going to happen if we fuck it up. Look . . ." He glanced down the hall to see if anyone was there. Satisfied, he turned back to her. "I just need to make sure. Are you good to go?"

She looked up and fastened her vacant green eyes on his. "Yes."

"Okay." In reality, nothing was okay with what he was seeing, but he needed to buy some time. With so much on the line, the last thing he wanted to do was make a rash decision. He thumped the door once with his hand, and Pétain pulled it open a split second later. "Tell Ramirez to start packing the gear. We're moving in five."

CHAPTER 14

MADRID

The alley behind the Sofitel Madrid Plaza de España was far from ideal. It was brightly lit, open, and clean. Four service doors led out to the space behind the ninety-seven-room luxury hotel, and a number of well-kept dumpsters were wedged against the clean cement walls. In other words, it was almost inviting, and anyone—a custodian, a lost guest, or even a waiter looking to catch a quick cigarette break—could have walked out at any time. Fortunately, none of the service doors were pushed open in the four minutes it took the van to arrive, and none of the city's less fortunate showed up to poke around in the garbage. As the side door slid open and they all climbed in, Kealey couldn't help but feel his spirits lift. It was an early stroke of luck, and if it held, they might still be able to pull this off.

Ramirez was the only person who hadn't entered the van through the sliding door on the right. Instead, he walked to the driver's-side door. It swung open, and the driver climbed out, leaving the keys in the ignition. Then he turned, walked down the alley, and melted into the mass of humanity on Calle de Tutor. The driver knew what needed to happen as well as anyone, but Kealey preferred to keep the 4-man teams intact. That way, everyone was sure to be on the same page. In his experience, even a short amount of time spent working with the same people could make a crucial difference, especially if they encountered a major hitch in the plan.

As the last door closed and the van lurched forward, Kealey dropped the bag from his shoulder and wedged it between his feet. In the time it took him to do that, Marissa Pétain had opened a plastic container near the front of the cargo area, which was bolted to the floor. She removed a weapon and handed it over, butt first, along with two spare clips. Her left eyebrow arched in a silent question, and Kealey nodded his approval: the gun was fine.

As Pétain handed Naomi a weapon and selected one for herself, Kealey locked the slide to the rear and examined the chamber, then the length of the barrel. The CZ 110 was a chunky handgun manufactured in the Czech Republic. It featured a strong but lightweight polymer frame, as well as a generous trigger guard. This particular model was chambered for 9mm rounds. He loaded a 13-round magazine, then let the upper receiver snap forward, chambering the first round. Looking over, he saw that Naomi was slipping a magazine into what looked like a Glock 26, and Pétain had selected an FN Forty-Nine. The weapons would do what was needed, if it came to that, but there was another reason these particular models had been selected. None were in standard use by any U.S. government agency, which would help deflect blame if the worst were to happen. Still, that was a last resort. Kealey was counting on the contents of the bag at his feet to get them the answers they needed.

As the Toyota van made its way through the dense afternoon traffic, Kealey looked over at Naomi. She was sitting upright, her face alert, but he couldn't forget the distracted look she'd been wearing ten minutes earlier, as well as what he had seen in her eyes. And that had been in a brightly lit hallway. He knew it didn't necessarily mean anything; for instance, eyedrops could cause temporary mydriasis, or dilation of the pupils. But so could a slew of pharmaceuticals, many of which were highly illegal. Kealey couldn't be sure what she was into. He didn't want to believe it was anything dangerous, but when he stopped to consider everything he'd seen over the past couple days, it was hard to ignore the truth. As the van swung a hard left onto Calle de San Leonardo de Dios, the suspension groaning in protest beneath their feet, he made a reluctant decision.

"Pétain?" The young operative looked over inquiringly. "I need you to go in there with me. Are you up for it?"

"What?" Naomi said, her head whipping around in surprise. "Ryan, I'm supposed to be—"

"Not anymore," he told her. He shifted his gaze back to Pétain. "Well?"

Pétain nodded and was about to respond, but Naomi got there first, her voice elevated and laced with anger. "Ryan, what the *hell* are you talking about? This is *my* assignment, not yours. Director Harper gave it to me personally, and you can't pull me off just because I showed up a few hours—"

"*Eight* hours, Naomi." He leveled her with a steady, uncompromising glare. "You were gone for eight hours. Nearly nine. You should consider yourself lucky. If Harper knew about what you pulled this morning, he'd want you on the first plane back, and your career would be all but over."

"We've been over this," Naomi tried again. Her hands were out, palms up, in an imploring gesture. Her eyes were wide with anger, but he could also detect a hint of desperation. It was something that Kealey hadn't seen before, and it made him uneasy; she had never begged him for anything. "I know what has to happen in there, and—"

"Forget it," Kealey interrupted. He didn't want to do this to her, but she wasn't giving him a choice. Besides, if he reversed course now, it would only undermine his authority. "You had your chance." He turned back to Pétain. "You know the drill?"

"Yes."

"Good. Just stay relaxed and follow my lead."

Pétain nodded again as the van slowed to a halt. A square hole measuring 12 by 9 inches had been cut out of the thin, custom-made metal partition that separated the cab from the rear of the vehicle. It was large enough to allow face-to-face communication between the passengers and the driver, but not so large as to allow people looking through the windshield to see the contents of the cargo area. Kealey shifted on the bench, moving close to the gap, and addressed Ramirez over the constant sputter of a police-band radio. "How are we looking?"

The swarthy, middle-aged operative scratched his chin and let out a short cough, but he didn't shift his gaze from the windshield. "There's a demonstration forming in the Puerta del Sol. Nearly a thousand people have shown up so far. They're students, mostly, protesting the upcoming summit in Barcelona. The CNP has five riot-control vans forming a loose perimeter. Nothing's happening so far, but they're keeping an eye on it, and they're about to commit another hundred officers to the scene. Two local cars are responding to an accident near the art museum . . . That's less than a quarter mile from here. That's about it. Why? You want to hold off?"

Kealey thought about it for a second. Typically, one of the first things he looked at when preparing to stage an operation on foreign soil was the local police presence. It was vital to know where the stations were located, which roads were most heavily patrolled, and how long it might take units to respond once they got the call. Usually, it wasn't that hard to get an idea of the local capabilities, but in Spain, things were more challenging. Particularly in the larger cities. He'd seen as much when they'd first landed at Madrid Barajas, the international hub located 15 kilometers north of the city center. The security inside the terminal had been impossible to miss. Dozens of officers with the National Police, otherwise known as the CNP, had been scattered throughout the building, along with soldiers in the Guardia Civil and private security guards. Outside the terminal, security and traffic control were handled by the local police, but their presence was just as imposing.

For Kealey, the skill, dedication, and sheer size of the Spanish police force were not factors to be taken lightly. However, the three teams assigned to Ghafour in Madrid had been keeping a constant watch on the building site north of the Plaza de España. It was determined right from the start that the site would be the best place to make contact, and part of their assignment had been to keep tabs on police movement in the area. Kealey had studied the logs in detail. Unfortunately, they hadn't presented him with a clear window; the patrols were reasonably light, but also constant. Still, he didn't think they would get a better opportunity than the one in front of them.

More to the point, they didn't have time to waste. The events of the previous day in Pakistan had thrown the missing tourist situation into a whole new light. He and Kharmai had learned what had happened at Keflavík International: every television inside the terminal had been tuned to CNN. Harper had called less than ten minutes later to give them the official version of what had transpired, and he'd also relayed the predominant stance in Washington. For once, Kealey happened to agree with the president's advisors. The fact that the secretary of state had been abducted in Pakistan—the same country in which 12 other Americans had recently vanished—could not be a coincidence. It seemed entirely possible—even likely—that Amari Saifi had played a part in the secretary of state's abduction, and although he had accepted Harper's proposal with reluctance, to say the least, Kealey was beginning to find himself drawn into the task of tracking down the Algerian terrorist. At the moment, the only way to do that was through Kamil Ghafour, so it was vital that everything ran smoothly once they were inside the gates. Kealey felt sure the man would accept the Agency's offer, but he couldn't operate solely on that assumption; he had to be ready for anything.

"We're not going to wait," he finally said, addressing Ramirez's last question. "I want to know what this guy has to say. Besides, the longer we push it back, the bigger the risk." All the watchers were traveling on false passports supplied by the Operations Directorate. There had been no direct contact with the embassy, and the Agency would deny any involvement if their cover was blown, as would the U.S. government. It was one of those situations where—despite having a vested interest—the administration was unwilling to put itself out on a limb, even to save the life of the secretary of state. Kealey had seen it all before, though that didn't make the self-serving politics any easier to stomach.

"Where do you want me?" asked Ramirez.

"Drive to the corner of the next street and look for a place to park. If you can't find one, and you probably won't be able to, circle the block until I get in touch. Either way, we'll walk up to the intersection, where this road meets San Bernardino. Worst comes to worst, you can pick us up en route. We'll get out here."

Ramirez nodded. "Good luck."

"Thanks." Kealey turned away from the hole in the sheet metal and shouldered the bag containing the money. After making sure the CZ 110 was secure at the small of his back, he pulled his T-shirt over the grip of the weapon. It didn't provide much camouflage, but it wasn't far to the gate, and the heavy pedestrian traffic in the area would help ensure their anonymity.

He looked over at Pétain. "Ready?"

"I'm ready."

Kealey turned to Naomi. "Stay here. Don't move an inch."

"You're wrong, Ryan." Naomi's gaze was still angry, but also adamant. "I don't know what you're thinking, but you're making a big mistake by cutting me out of this."

"I hope you're right," he said, fixing her with a meaningful look. "But this isn't the time to get into it." Kealey pulled open the sliding door and climbed out, Pétain following close on his heels. Seconds later, they disappeared into the crowd, and the van pulled away from the curb, joining the traffic streaming north on Calle de San Leonardo de Dios.

CHAPTER 15

MADRID

Ramirez had selected the spot well. Kealey realized as much as he moved down the sidewalk, Pétain trailing a few steps behind. The operative had dropped them 100 meters south of the gate leading into the building site, but more importantly, he'd picked an area where the road was completely shielded from the site. Not only by the 5-foot chain-link fence, but by a flimsy wooden fence. It meant the workers wouldn't have seen the vehicle that dropped them off. It was a small point, admittedly, but major operations had been blown on far less. Every intelligence agency around the world had suffered its fair share of embarrassments, including the CIA. Hopefully, today's work wouldn't fall into that category.

As they approached the east gate, Kealey saw with relief that it was already open. It would save them some time loitering outside, where they might be noticed by the wrong person. The second gate was on the other side of the site, where it opened onto a parallel street. A dump truck filled with stone was edging into traffic, and a number of workers in khakis, T-shirts, and hard hats were waiting to close the gate once the vehicle had made the turn.

The street wasn't especially busy, but noise seemed to be hitting them from all directions: the staccato sounds of rapid-fire Spanish, the groan of machinery on the other side of the fence, as well as the steady thump of rap music emanating from a passing Land Rover. To their left, an African street vendor plied his trade, his wares—bootlegged CDs and DVDs, for the most part—neatly lined up on a white cotton sheet spread over the cement. A few tourists stopped to gape at the blatant display of illegal merchandise, but the vendor ignored them, his wary eyes scanning the crowd for the smallest sign of an undercover police officer.

Kealey shifted his eyes from the scene and kept moving forward, Pétain a few feet to his rear. The strap of the bag was biting into his shoulder, and sweat was streaming down the back of his neck. Every inch of his skin was damp, his shirt soaked completely through.

A hand tightened around the back of his arm, pulling him out of his distracted state. He turned to face Marissa Pétain.

"What are you going to say?" she shouted over the roar of the dump truck and passing traffic. He frowned, pulling her close, and she caught the hint, lowering her voice as she put her mouth next to his ear. "They're not going to let us walk right in there, you know. How are you going to get us in?"

"I'm going to tell them the truth."

She stared at him for a long moment, her mouth hanging open. He didn't wait for her to snap out of it, instead hurrying forward, sliding past a tight knot of wayward tourists. Someone bumped him hard, nearly shoving him into the road, where cars were streaming by at a steady clip. He swore under his breath and kept going. He was angry with himself for letting the heat distract him. Pétain's question had slowed him down as well; he shouldn't have stopped to answer her. In truth, he would have preferred to leave her out of this altogether. She wouldn't be contributing much to the conversation; he just wanted her there to lower the tension, or at least keep it in check. Ghafour would be less suspicious, less confrontational, with a woman present. At least, that was the hope. According to the file, Ghafour had lost his father at an early age, and he'd grown up with his mother and four older sisters. That kind of upbringing would likely leave a lasting impression.

Kealey sprinted the last few feet as the gate swung shut. He reached it and grabbed the chain-link with his fingers. The man who was trying to pull it closed stopped and shot him a confused, slightly irritated look. "*¿Qué deseas?*"

"*Deseo hablar con un hombre que trabaje contigo,*" Kealey replied. "Kamil Ghafour."

The burly Spaniard froze and looked at him hard, his dark eyes unreadable beneath the plastic brim of his hard hat. *"¿Por qué?"*

"That's my business," Kealey continued in Spanish. Pétain stood next to him silently, nervously shifting from one foot to the other. "But he'll want to talk to me. Tell him I have something to give him. Something to offer."

The man shook his head, spat on the ground, and turned to walk away. Kealey called out, and when the man looked back, he lifted a crumpled fistful of Euros. The worker walked back cautiously and eyed the obvious bribe.

"One hundred Euros," Kealey said. "Fifty when you let me in, another fifty when you point him out."

The Spaniard hesitated, looked around slowly, then nodded his agreement. He lifted a finger, indicating they should wait, and walked off. Pétain started to speak, but Kealey silenced her with a quick gesture. "He'll be back," he told her. "Just give it a minute."

The construction worker reappeared in two. He opened the gate, waved them in, and handed them a couple of hard hats. They put them on and Kealey handed over the first fifty. The man held it up to the afternoon sun, as though verifying its authenticity. Satisfied, he turned and waved a heavily calloused hand, indicating they should follow. Kealey thought it strange that the man hadn't given Pétain so much as an appraising glance, but he quickly pushed aside the distracting thought.

They walked toward a series of trailers, following the deep impressions left by a heavy vehicle's tires. The ground was hard beneath their feet, red soil heaped to the right, the concrete pad to the left. The sound of an electric bolt gun filled the air, drowned out a moment later by the low, throaty rumble of a diesel crane.

After another 50 feet, the Spaniard stopped and pointed to the third trailer. "He's in there," he said in his native language. There was a hint of derision in his voice, and he paused again to spit on the ground. "The *maricón* doesn't get his hands dirty anymore, not since the police came. He sits inside, where it's cool, and does the paperwork."

Kealey looked around, trying to get a better sense of his surroundings. No one was paying them too much attention, and he didn't see the face he was looking for. As far as he could tell, the construction worker was telling the truth.

He handed over the second fifty, and the Spaniard grunted his approval. He shoved the money into the right pocket of his filthy khakis.
Then, finally, he shot a lecherous look at Pétain. She pretended not
to notice as she nudged the solid clay with her foot, her eyes stubbornly fixed on the trailer in the near distance. Finally, the man
snorted and lumbered off.

"Asshole," Pétain muttered. Once the worker was out of earshot,
she turned to Kealey and said, "So, what do you think?"

"I think he's in there. Most of these guys are natives. They'll put up
with an Algerian boss, if the money is right, but I doubt their goodwill
extends to a favored employee. Especially one born on foreign soil."

"That's how it looks," she agreed. "So what now?"

"Now we go in." Kealey moved forward suddenly, Pétain scram-
bling to keep up. As he crossed the uneven terrain, he couldn't help
but feel a tinge of doubt. There was no guarantee that Ghafour could
point them in the right direction, and just approaching him entailed
a huge risk. All he had to do was call out for his coworkers. They
might not care for him, but they would back him up if it came to that;
Kealey was sure of it. If summoned, they would arrive in a matter of
seconds, and the police wouldn't be far behind. Should that happen,
the whole operation would be blown wide open. The Agency would
suffer a major embarrassment, and they'd be no closer to finding
Amari Saifi. At the same time, they only had one shot at this—one
shot at getting Ghafour to talk. If he *did* know something, they had
to get it out of him. By any means necessary.

A low, pointed cough brought him back to reality. They had reached
the trailer, and Pétain was staring at him expectantly, flapping her
blouse in a fruitless attempt to dispel the suffocating heat.

"Okay," he said, after listening for noise inside the unit. He couldn't
hear a thing over the sound of the crane's engine and the high-pitched,
rattling whine of the bolt gun. Even here, more than 200 feet from
the street, the sound of traffic was incredibly noisy. He didn't continue
his thought; instead, he just banged twice on the door. Inside, there
was a slight squeak, as if someone had just risen from an old chair.
Kealey unzipped the duffel on his shoulder, thrust a hand inside, and
withdrew a bundle of notes. Seconds later, the door sprung open,
and a man stood before them. He looked confused at first, but a cautious expression soon slid over his face. "Who are you?" he asked in
fractured Spanish. "What do you want?"

Kealey had seen file photographs of the rail-thin Algerian. He knew he had the right man, but he decided to feign a little ignorance to keep things casual. "Are you Kamil Ghafour?" he asked in English.

Ghafour's shrewd brown eyes narrowed immediately. "Why?"

"I need to talk to you. I think you'll be interested in what I have to say."

"Are you the police?" he snapped. He extended a bony, threatening finger, then continued in English. "My status in this country is legal. I have documentation, and—"

"I'm not the police." Kealey held up the bundle of notes, and Ghafour's eyes locked onto the money immediately. Kealey was surprised when the man didn't visibly react. No smile, no greedy stare, no nervous lick of the lips . . . no gesture of any kind. Instead, his feral gaze slid sideways to Pétain, who was standing at the bottom of the wooden steps. "Who is she?"

"She's with me." Kealey tossed over the bundle, and Ghafour caught the money cleanly. "There's more where that came from. If you're interested, that is."

Ghafour looked at him a beat longer, then jerked his head to the rear. They followed him into the cool interior, and Pétain shut the door behind them. They removed their hard hats as the Algerian walked behind a cheap wooden desk. He turned to face them, but Kealey noticed that he didn't sit down, and alarm bells started ringing instantly. He scanned the top of the desk, but he didn't see any evidence of a weapon. That didn't mean anything, though; there could be a veritable arsenal in the drawers. Given the site manager's antigovernment stance and obvious disdain for authority, Kealey felt sure there was some kind of weapon hidden inside the room. Judging from Ghafour's stance, it was probably inside or behind the desk.

"So," Ghafour prompted, spreading his arms out to the side, as if to say, "Here I am . . . What do you want?"

Kealey lifted the duffel bag to eye level, then tossed it onto a ratty couch. "There's a lot of money in there. Twenty thousand Euros, to be exact. My gift to you."

Ghafour looked at the duffel once, but his eyes flicked back to Kealey instantly. "And what," he asked in a slightly amused voice, "would I have to do for all of that?"

Kealey didn't respond right away, although his eyes never left Ghafour's smiling face. The Algerian was short—five feet eight inches at the most—and he couldn't have weighed more than 130 pounds. He was the last person one would expect to find on a building site, and that was something else to consider. Had his employer hired him simply because of his nationality, or was Ghafour active again? Was the site manager involved with the GIA? The man had money and connections, Kealey reminded himself, and Ghafour had never renounced his ties to the Armed Islamic Group. Suddenly, the spark of doubt returned, but this time it was twice as intense. Maybe trying to pay him off had been the wrong play. Unfortunately, it was too late to change tactics now; they had no choice but to see it through and hope for the best.

"All I want is information," Kealey said, watching the other man carefully for a hint of where the weapon might be. The slightest shift of eyes could give it away, and he had to know. "Money for information, Kamil . . . Believe me, it's a fair trade. You were in prison for seven years, correct? In Algiers?"

Ghafour smirked, his thin lips twisting into something approximating a smile. "Yes, but you already knew that, didn't you?" The smile disappeared suddenly. "You're not the police, so who are you? MI5?"

"No."

"Where are you from? England? The States?"

Ghafour waited for a response. When it became clear one wasn't forthcoming, his smile grew wider. "That's it, isn't it? You're American. It's so obvious, when you know how to look . . . You seem familiar. What's your name?"

"That doesn't matter," Kealey heard himself say.

Pétain was shifting nervously beside him. She muttered something under her breath. Kealey didn't catch it at first, the air conditioner drowning out the words, but then she repeated it. *"Behind the files."*

Kealey's eyes dropped to the desk. To his left—Ghafour's right—a pile of files was stacked up to waist height. Kealey understood that Pétain had a view of what lay behind the folders, and a cold chill ran down his spine when he realized what she was trying to tell him.

Kamil Ghafour's gun was less than 2 feet from his right hand.

"You don't need to know who we are to enjoy the money, Kamil. All I want is a name. Who came to see Amari Saifi in prison? Who arranged to get him out?"

"Yes," Ghafour continued slowly. He spoke with a slight lisp. "You seem very familiar." It was as if he hadn't heard the questions. He extended his left hand and wagged a finger at the other man. "I've seen you somewhere before. I'm sure of it."

Kealey felt another chill. It could have just been the abrupt change in temperature, but either way, the man's relaxed, carefree attitude was putting him on edge. Pétain was completely immobile next to him; he could almost feel the tension radiating from her body. Clearly, she was just as uneasy as he was.

"You don't know me," he told Ghafour, adding a harder note to his voice. He doubted the Algerian had any idea who he really was. Earlier that morning he'd added some gray streaks to his hair, which made him look at least ten years older, and his eye color had been temporarily changed with a pair of green-tinted Clear View contacts. More importantly, he was still wearing the thick beard he'd grown over the past three months, which all but obscured the lower half of his face.

"I'll ask you once more, and then I'm taking the money and leaving," Kealey lied. "Who came to see Saifi in Algiers?"

Ghafour opened his mouth to respond, but before he could, someone began pounding hard on the metal door to the trailer. Kealey caught only part of what happened next: Pétain jumped at the sudden noise, her eyes darting to the left. At the same time, her right hand dropped to her hip, lifting the lower edge of her white cotton blouse. It was purely instinctive, and the FN Forty-Nine was revealed for only a split second, but that was all it took. Kealey sensed, more than saw, Ghafour's hand dart behind the cluster of files, and without thinking, he threw himself forward, reaching out for the other man's arm.

The gun discharged once as Kealey reached Ghafour, his left hand moving to knock the weapon aside. He reached out with his right to get hold of Ghafour's shirt at the neck, then used his forward momentum to propel them both into the wall of the trailer. The whole structure rocked with the impact as someone began to shout outside, calling for help in rapid-fire Spanish. Then Kealey and Ghafour were on the floor, wrestling for control of the gun. It went off again, the sound rattling off the thin metal walls of the trailer, then again before Kealey could pull it free of the other man's grasp. It wasn't until he got to his feet, struggling for breath, that he realized the third shot hadn't come from Ghafour's weapon.

He turned to face Marissa Pétain. Her feet were placed shoulder-width apart, and both hands were on her gun. It was extended at arm's length, and looking down, Kealey saw exactly where her round had gone. There was a small hole in the Algerian's upper left thigh. It didn't look too serious, but then, as Ghafour groaned and rolled to his right, the wound started to spurt.

"Oh, *fuck,*" Kealey said. His own weapon was still at the small of his back, so nothing had to happen there. He put the safety on Ghafour's 9mm and tossed it to Pétain. She managed to catch it as Kealey dropped to his knees and put both hands over the other man's wound, pushing down as hard as he could. Ghafour shrieked in pain, then let loose with a series of unintelligible curses. He flailed his arms wildly, trying to catch Kealey in the face, but he didn't have the leverage.

Ignoring the cries of pain, Kealey spoke to Pétain without turning to face her. "Make sure that fucking door is locked!" he shouted. After a second of frozen indecision, she burst into action, reaching the door with two quick paces.

She checked the handle quickly, then spun and said, "It's locked. It's already locked."

"Can they open it from outside?"

"No, I don't think so. Not without breaking it down. Oh, God, I didn't mean to . . . Ryan, what do you want me to—"

"Find me something to stop him from bleeding out. Gauze, tape . . . anything. Look for a first aid kit. *Hurry!*"

As Pétain began her frantic search, Kealey did his best to keep pressure on the wound. It was almost impossible; Ghafour was writhing around on the dirty floor, screaming at the top of his lungs. "Shut up!" Kealey screamed. "Stop moving around! I'm trying to save your life, asshole!"

Pétain, who'd been digging through a stand-alone closet in the corner, suddenly yelled, "I got it!" She stood up and sprinted the few feet between them, then dropped to her knees by Kealey's side. She struggled with the lid for a few seconds, and then the kit sprung open, its contents scattering over the floor. She scrambled to collect the gauze and tape, and Kealey—pushing as hard as he could on the wound with his left hand—reached out with his right to grab the tape.

He shot a look at Pétain and, over Ghafour's continued screams, yelled, "I need something heavier, something thicker than this gauze. Your shirt . . ."

She looked down at her blouse and caught his meaning immediately. She pulled it off as fast as she could, struggling to free her arms from the tight cotton sleeves. Once it was off—revealing a tank top underneath—she looked around the desk, found a utility knife, and began cutting strips of material. Each was approximately 2 feet in length and 6 inches wide. As she was working, Kealey was wrapping the gauze around Ghafour's spurting wound. Once he had taped it into place, Pétain handed over the first length of cloth, and Kealey used it to cover the gauze, tying a nonslip knot to one side of the small wound. Then he wadded up a second strip, placed it directly over the small hole in the Algerian's thigh, and secured it in place with a second strip of Pétain's blouse. This time he tied a nonslip knot directly over the wound.

Ghafour was still moaning in between ragged, shallow breaths. His screaming had stopped, which wasn't a good sign, but his eyes were wide open, and he was alert enough to respond to questions, which was all that mattered to Kealey. Retrieving a couple of cushions from the couch in the corner, he lifted the Algerian's feet and slid the cushions under. It worked to keep the man's legs well above the level of his heart, which would help to slow the bleeding. It was the best he could do without applying a tourniquet, but he wasn't willing to take that step just yet.

The adrenaline started to dissipate, and Kealey found he was suddenly exhausted; he had yet to catch his breath, and his limbs felt incredibly heavy. He suddenly realized he might have been hit. He checked quickly, his pulse pounding hard in his ears, but nothing seemed to be out of place. Looking over, he saw that Pétain was on the phone, telling Ramirez what had taken place in short, terse sentences. Kealey was relieved to see she was relaying the information quickly but calmly. He knew he needed to give the operative in the van some instructions, so he immediately began thinking along those lines. But then he looked down at his hands, and he lost track of his thoughts completely. His hands and arms were dripping with bright red arterial blood. Glancing over, he realized that the Algerian had already lost about a pint of the vital fluid, and while the pressure dressing would slow the bleeding, it wouldn't stop it completely. If Kealey was going to get the answers he needed, it would have to be soon.

Pétain looked over and caught his attention. "Ramirez wants to know what to do," she said urgently. "They don't—"

"Tell him to sit tight. There's nothing else he can do right now."

Pétain looked like she wanted to argue, but she pushed down her doubts and relayed the message. Seconds later, she snapped the phone shut and stared at him anxiously. "Ryan, do you hear that?"

Distracted by his efforts to slow the Algerian's rate of bleeding, Kealey had allowed the noise outside the trailer to fade into the background. Now he listened intently, and he caught her point immediately. Above the confused shouts of construction workers and the distant rumble of traffic, he heard a sound that changed everything: the two-tone scream of a police car's siren. The previous day, Kealey had seen a car flash past them using the same siren, and he realized the responding units belonged to the CNP, the National Police. Another siren joined in seconds later, completely drowning out the traffic on Calle de San Leonardo de Dios.

Kealey studied Ghafour for a few seconds. His face was pale and covered in sweat, and his eyelids were starting to droop. Sliding over, he quickly checked for a pulse, pressing two fingers hard against the man's clammy skin. The pulse was weak, but still there. Finding it didn't do much to relieve his concern, as the Algerian was clearly sliding into hypovolaemic shock. Kealey knew that unless he did something immediately, Ghafour would pass out, and there was a good chance he'd never regain consciousness.

Lifting his gaze, Kealey scoured the medical supplies scattered over the floor. Before long, he saw what he wanted. "Hand me that syringe," he said to Pétain. She looked uncertain for a second, but then she reached down and picked it up. She checked the markings quickly and handed it over.

"Epinephrine. Do you think it will work?"

"I don't know," he replied. He pulled the protective cover off the syringe and tried to block out the sound of rapidly approaching sirens. Judging by the speed with which the first cars had responded, they'd be completely surrounded in a matter of minutes. "But we have to keep him awake, and we need him to start talking. We're running out of time."

"You're wrong," Pétain said, her voice shaking with tension. She was standing at one of the small windows, using two fingers to separate the blinds. "We're *out* of time." She let go of the blinds, and they snapped shut with a slight metallic clatter. When she turned to face him, her face was pale and drawn. "The police are already at the gate, and it looks like they're coming in."

CHAPTER 16

SIALKOT, PAKISTAN

The house was perched atop a small hill in the Gujrat district of Sialkot, reachable only by a rutted driveway bordered on each side by patchy grassland. A number of sheep grazed in the open fields, which were separated from the road by a tangled row of scrawny trees. It was a quiet area just south of the Kashmiri foothills, small homes dotting the landscape. There were no natural wonders, nothing of interest for miles around. For this reason alone, few people would have noticed that the house was unusual for the area—indeed, for the country itself. It was like something out of the English countryside: thick stone walls that stood up to the hard northern winds, a garden trellis wrapped in jasmine and white orchids on one side, the building itself with a fine slate roof and double-glazed windows. The interior space was just as extraordinary. The living room featured a large stone fireplace, with exposed timber throughout and oil-fired central heating. The second-floor rooms stayed warm even in the coldest winter months, a rare benefit in the impoverished villages of northeastern Pakistan.

It had taken Said Qureshi many years to purchase the house. It was easily the most important thing in his life, other than his children, whom he hadn't seen in years. It also represented the only thing he had salvaged from his time in England: a love of British architecture. His family had immigrated to England when he was fifteen, and though it was hard to admit now, it had been the happiest time of his life. It was what he had secretly wanted from the time he could read and write—to leave Pakistan, to escape the squalor of Saddar Town, where he had spent his youth, and find something better in another land. And he had worked to make the best of the unexpected opportunity. He had shrugged off the callous remarks made by his classmates, most of which related to his skin color, and he'd devoted himself to his studies. His efforts had earned him a place at St. George's Medical School by the time he was twenty-one. Following graduation, he had worked for nearly a decade at Guy's Hospital in southeast London, where he specialized in cardiothoracic surgery. He had risen through the ranks with astonishing speed, despite the intense competition. It seemed as if he could do no wrong, until a failed surgery in 2004 resulted in the death of an eleven-year-old boy.

It was a small mistake, a nicked blood vessel they had caught too late, but that was all it took. Everything from that point forward had been a downhill slide. He could have argued that stress played a role, that his impending divorce, as well as the inevitable custody battle over his three children, had distracted him from his duties. He could have said that his drinking played a lesser role. There would have been penalties, but alcoholism was better than incompetence, and he might have been forgiven in time. But it wasn't the truth, and he wasn't one for making excuses. Instead, he quietly resigned his post—they had given him that option, at least—and moved to the Cornish coast a month later, taking up residence in a small cottage on the outskirts of St. Ives.

It was there that he had sought to rebuild his life. He had saved well over the years, a lesson learned from his impoverished youth, and although the divorce cost him a great deal, he was left with enough to start over. But earning a place in the hearts and minds of Cornwall's residents was nearly impossible, particularly for a foreigner. The community was close-knit and quick to lash out at unwelcome visitors, especially those seeking to make a home on the coast. Although he had hung on for nearly two years, trying to earn their trust, his practice simply wasn't bringing in enough patients. Finally, the bitterness began to sink in. Once he realized that he no longer cared about winning them over, he knew it was time to return to the only other home he had ever known.

That was in the winter of 2006. He could still remember the sense of personal failure that had consumed him when he first stepped off the British Airways plane in Islamabad, the realization that he had squandered the best—and perhaps only—opportunity of his life. Even now, years later, he deeply resented many of the choices and mistakes he'd made, but he had come to accept them. He had replicated his Cornish home in his native land, but otherwise, he had relegated England to the past. Admittedly, his life in Pakistan could have been worse. There was no shortage of patients in Sialkot. Many of them could not afford the state-run hospitals, so naturally, they turned to him for help. These were people who held his English medical degree in high regard. People who appreciated his lenient nature, reasonable rates, and kind manner, and he valued them in return. Sometimes he wondered if he would have been happier in Pakistan all along.

At least, that was how he had felt until the day he had met Benazir Mengal. Unlike Naveed Jilani, whom he had never met, Qureshi had not made the effort to form an alliance with the famed Pakistani general. In fact, it was the other way round. He had first encountered Mengal on a warm fall afternoon the previous year. Mengal had sent one of his men to collect him at Café 24 on the Kashmir Road, where Qureshi took his afternoon tea. He had been frightened at first, reluctant to leave without knowing the final destination. It was clear he wasn't going to be given a choice, though, and in the end he'd agreed. He was blindfolded and driven to a flat, where he was shown a young man, a soldier, from the look of it, who had been shot twice in the right arm. The wounds were superficial—no major arteries were hit, and neither bullet was still inside the limb—but it had still been a challenge to repair the damage, given the limited tools he was provided with. Mengal had watched with interest the entire time, and when Qureshi was done, the general had quietly congratulated him before slipping an envelope into his jacket pocket. It wasn't until he was back at the café that he opened the envelope to examine the contents. Inside he found 120,000 rupees—nearly $2000 American—and a handwritten note from Mengal, cordially thanking him for his services.

Over the next several months, Mengal called on him twice more. Qureshi was able to repair the damage on both occasions, and in the strained, anticipatory lull that followed the surgeries, the general began to open up. He told Qureshi of his service in the Northwestern Frontier Province, as well as hinting at his involvement with ISI, and he expressed sympathy when the doctor explained his misfortune in England. Qureshi had no idea what happened from that point forward, but his list of patients doubled virtually overnight. He assumed the general must have spread the word to people in high places. In any case, he was grateful, and he said as much the next time he encountered Mengal. He wasn't able to save the patient on that occasion—the bleeding was just too severe—but the general seemed to understand.

Qureshi never asked why these men weren't being treated by army surgeons, partly because the answer was clear. Whatever they were doing—whatever Mengal had involved them in—was not related to the military and, in all likelihood, was highly illegal. So Qureshi kept his mouth shut, and as the years passed, the relationship continued to bloom.

Night had fallen an hour earlier. A harsh wind sweeping down the foothills swayed the Chinar saplings outside and rattled the sturdy windows on the ground floor. Said Qureshi stood before a deep ceramic sink, his outline barely visible in the dim light from the hall. He lifted a scalpel from the steel tray by his elbow, then held it under the hot water, turning the light handle between his fingers in order to rinse the blade clean. He watched absently as blood swirled down the drain, but he wasn't really seeing it. Nor could he hear the elevated voices in the next room. All he could think about was the surgery he had just performed. More specifically, he was thinking about the person on whom he had worked.

Mengal's men had arrived earlier that evening, shortly after Qureshi had seen to his last patient of the day. From the moment he had opened the front door, Qureshi knew exactly who they had brought him. It had been all over the news, of course, but it was the look in their eyes that said it all. It was a shared look of desperation—not fear, but desperation—and when Qureshi had reached down to pull the blanket away from the woman's face, he had shared in their desperation, but also the fear. . . .

He replaced the scalpel on the sterile gauze and reached for a hemostat. As he subjected the surgical clamp to the scalding water, he saw that his hand was shaking. It was a delayed reaction, and the one thing he could take pride in. Throughout the procedure he had known the stakes. He had been all too aware that if she died, if she bled out on his table, ultimately, he would be blamed. Mengal's wrath would be nothing compared to that of the Americans if they discovered his involvement; he might as well have staged the attack himself. And yet, throughout the surgery, he had remained stoic. He had kept his composure. His hand had been steady the whole time, and if she died, he could console himself with the knowledge that he had done everything in his power to save her life.

It was a small comfort, but a comfort nonetheless.

From the next room came another shout, then the sound of a door banging shut. There were heavy footsteps in the hallway, and then he sensed a presence behind him. He turned to face the other man, who was half concealed in the shadows.

"Will the woman live?"

Qureshi lifted his hands in a noncommittal gesture. The general had spoken in Urdu, and he replied in kind. "It is too early to tell. I've done all I can. If her injuries were any more severe, she would not have survived the trip."

"Said, I am aware of how fortunate we are," Mengal responded tersely. "Tell me, will our luck continue to hold? Based on your experience, what do you believe?"

Qureshi shifted uneasily. "It is hard to say. *If* she is given the chance to rest, and *if* she is cared for by a skilled nurse, then . . . yes, she will pull through. The worst, I believe, is behind us now, but there are no guarantees, and there is still much to be done."

"I don't understand," Mengal said slowly. He was clearly speaking to himself. "My men described the entire attack. She was fine when they pulled her out of the vehicle. She was talking, struggling. . . ."

"She was bleeding internally. She is *still* bleeding internally. They should not have sedated her. Not all injuries are obvious, General. Sometimes it takes time for the symptoms to manifest."

"Bleeding internally?" Mengal's voice was sharp and accusing. "Why haven't you fixed it?"

Qureshi pushed down his rising impatience. Like so many soldiers who fought on the front lines, Benazir Mengal saw only the obvious signs of physical injury, the things he could fix immediately. The intricacies of the human body were completely lost on him.

"General, the woman has sustained severe injuries. The armor plating on her vehicle saved her from further injury, as did the fact that she was in the backseat, but she is still very fortunate to have survived. First, she suffered a pneumothorax of the left lung, most likely a result of blunt trauma. This means her lung was collapsed. I've already relieved the pressure and inserted a chest tube, but it must stay in for two days at the least, perhaps three. By that time, the excess air should be fully removed from the pleural cavity, and the tube can be removed safely."

Mengal's brow creased in annoyed confusion. "You said there was bleeding—"

"The bleeding," Qureshi continued, "is a result of a hemoperi-cardium, or tearing inside the membrane that surrounds the heart. That injury was also caused by blunt trauma, but it could be more se-vere than the pneumothorax. Perhaps much more severe. There is no way of knowing for certain until I operate."

"How did you determine the cause of the bleeding?"

"There was no puncture wound, admittedly, but all the signs of cardiac tamponade are present. She regained consciousness shortly after you arrived. I asked her to lie flat, but she said it only made the pain worse. She complained of discomfort in her chest, and the veins in her neck were slightly distended, indicating a backup of blood in the veins."

Qureshi paused, thinking about the best way to phrase it. "The heart, General, when surrounded by excess fluid, cannot beat effi-ciently. That is why she did not want to lie down. When her body was upright, the blood collected in the bottom of the pericardial sac, re-lieving the pressure. Her blood pressure was ninety over forty, low for a healthy woman in her late forties, and the EKG revealed J-waves, which are yet another indication of the injury I mentioned. She needs a pericardial window, and she needs it soon."

"To what purpose?"

Qureshi took note of the other man's voice, which had dropped to a dangerous murmur. Clearly, Mengal did not like being lectured to. Talking down to people was a habit common to many surgeons, and Qureshi knew he shared the affliction. He paused again to check his tone, then continued. "The window will relieve the pressure on the heart by removing the excess fluid. It is a relatively simple proce-dure, but I need an anesthesiologist to do it properly."

"You can't do it with Thorazine and a local anesthetic?"

Qureshi hesitated again, suddenly uncertain; perhaps this man knew more than he was letting on. "Technically, yes, but it is extremely risky. General, you went through a great deal of trouble to get this woman to me as quickly as possible. Why take a chance now? You want her alive, correct?"

"Yes." Mengal nodded slowly, absently scratching his beard with his left hand. "Yes, I do want her alive. And I agree with your assessment." He seemed to relax slightly. "As always, Doctor, you are correct. Who is best equipped to handle this?"

"I can handle it here, but I need help."

"Give me a name."

Qureshi thought for a moment, trying to disguise his rising panic. He was already well aware that he was involved in something beyond his control, and though he was desperately trying to push the thought aside, he knew he was now expendable. He had seen too much, learned too much, and whoever he brought into this situation would soon find themselves in the same position. He had no wish to subject an innocent person to that fate.

"General, I left my colleagues in England, and I have yet to seek out new ones here."

"I don't believe that's true, Said." Mengal took a menacing step forward, his short, blocky frame filling the doorway. "But if it is, then I will be forced to turn elsewhere for help. I could, with some effort, find the kind of man you need, but he may not want to work with you. He may prefer his own colleagues. Of course, that would negate the need for your participation."

The general paused to let this statement sink in, then continued in a voice as dry and hard as the wind sweeping across the Kashmiri foothills. "Said, I value your friendship. I believe we can work together for many years, but you must prove your loyalty now."

"Sir, I can't—"

"The name, Doctor. Give me the name of the man you want. I will find him for you."

"Craig. Randall Craig. He's a visiting professor from the University of Washington."

"How do you know him?"

"We used to work together. We've stayed in touch. You should be able to find him at a hospital in Lahore. Sheikh Zayed. Do you know it?"

"Yes. What about the supplies? Anesthesia, the machine, the monitoring systems . . . ?"

"I can find the supplies. They can be procured with relative ease in Sialkot, but I need Craig to make them work, and I need him soon. The woman's symptoms could become worse at any moment."

"Fine." Mengal nodded toward the kitchen, where several of his men were waiting. "They will stay and guard the house. Most will patrol outside, but two will remain outside the secretary's room at all times, even when you are treating her. Is that understood?"

"Yes, of course." Qureshi hesitated. "And the other one?"

"The Algerian?" Mengal offered a curious smile. "Why do you ask, Said?"

"He watches everything," Qureshi blurted out. It was something that had been on his mind from the moment they'd arrived, and he could no longer contain his fear. "He never stops smiling. It's as though he's waiting for something. He will kill her if you give him the chance . . . I can see it in his eyes. General, I don't want that to happen here. I don't want *her* here."

Qureshi caught himself and stopped suddenly, searching for some sign of anger in the older man's face. Mengal merely smiled again. "I understand your concern, Said, but he had the chance to take her life in Rawalpindi, and he didn't. He stands to benefit only if she lives, my friend. You have nothing to fear from him."

"But he will stay."

"Yes, he will." Mengal took another step forward, the smile fading. "And you will not. You must acquire the materials you need as soon as possible. Go to Sialkot. Find what you need. One of my men will accompany you. I will find this man Craig and bring him here. Once you fix what is wrong with the woman, we will leave you in peace. Agreed?"

"Yes, General." Qureshi did not believe a word of it, but he was in an impossible position. All he could do now was try to buy some time. "Agreed."

CHAPTER 17

MADRID

After dropping Kealey and Pétain at the building site, Ramirez had continued to circle around the block, just as Kealey had instructed. He had kept his eyes forward the entire time, and he had not tried to talk to Naomi, which—as far as she was concerned—was the only good thing about the whole situation. She still couldn't believe that Ryan had pulled her off in favor of Pétain, but at the same time, part of her wasn't surprised at all. Worse still, part of her said she deserved it.

She had tried to hold off from thinking about it, but now, alone with her thoughts in the back of the moving van, she couldn't help but wonder what he saw when he looked at her. Only one thing was certain. Whatever he saw, it wasn't good. There had been a time when she had enjoyed his genuine admiration and respect, but those days were obviously over. Now when she caught him looking at her, all she saw was concern or anger. Sometimes both. She involuntarily touched the scar on her face, which even a heavy application of make-up couldn't completely hide. She had grown accustomed to seeing the pity in other people's eyes, but she had yet to see it in Ryan's. The thought that his concern and anger might give way to something like that was almost unbearable, but she knew it was only a matter of time.

She slumped against the inner wall of the van and looked down at her hands. They were shaking slightly—not so much that anyone else would notice—but Naomi could feel the tremors shooting up through her forearms. Her legs were trembling, too. She'd taken her pills only five hours earlier, and her body was already demanding more. She closed her eyes as tight as she could and pushed down a wave of nausea, thinking about the little white tablets in her right pocket. The temptation was great, especially since she had more hidden in her bag at the hotel, but she didn't want to be stuck if they couldn't get back and she needed them later. She thought about asking Ramirez to slow down, but she didn't want to get him started. Besides, she could hear him talking urgently over his cell phone, and she didn't want to interrupt.

Suddenly, the van wrenched hard to the right, throwing her from the bench. She tumbled across the metal floor, flailing for something to hold on to, and then the vehicle squealed to a halt, propelling her into the metal partition. The air was knocked out of her lungs, so she lay still for a moment, trying to catch her breath. Dazed, she climbed to her feet and looked through the rectangular hole in the partition. The harsh words on the tip of her tongue dissipated when she saw the look on Ramirez's face.

"That was your man," he told her. "They're in a trailer toward the rear of the site, and they've got a serious problem. Ghafour is down. Pétain shot him."

Naomi pushed down the shock and thought as fast as she could, quickly considering, then discarding, any irrelevant questions. "Did they get anything out of him?"

"No. But he's still conscious . . . They're working on it."

"What did he tell you to do?"

"Stay here and wait for another call."

"What?" Naomi couldn't contain her surprise. "That's all he said?"

"That's it," Ramirez confirmed.

"That's bullshit! We've got to get them out of there. They don't have time to question him."

Ramirez's face turned hard, deep fissures creasing his forehead, his mouth turning down at the corners. "I agree, but that isn't our call. You heard the man . . . We stay where we are."

Naomi put her face up to the opening in the partition, cursing the metal divider, which partially obscured her view. She gazed through the windshield, trying to determine their exact location. It looked as if they were close to the gate, but it was the wrong one: they were on the west side of the construction site. "Look, let's just pull around the block once more. Then you can call and let them know. They'll be better off if they have our exact position."

Ramirez remained silent, thinking it through. He was clearly uneasy, but it was hard to argue with her logic. "Fine." He dropped the Toyota into drive and pulled back into traffic. Seconds later they had turned onto Calle de San Bernardino. Naomi was looking intently at an aerial view of the construction site and the surrounding roads when she heard Ramirez utter a low, hard curse. Then she heard the sirens. Ignoring the cold wave that swept through her body, she pressed her face back to the partition and looked through the windshield. Two CNP cruisers heading west were swinging a hard left onto San Leonardo de Dios.

"Oh, shit," Naomi breathed. "They've beaten us to it."

"Then that's it," Ramirez announced, his knuckles white around the steering wheel. He seemed resolute, but also strangely relieved. "They're on their own. There's nothing more we can do."

"No, keep going," Naomi commanded, thinking back to the aerial map. "Go to the next street, and take a right. We'll approach from the south."

"Are you out of your fucking mind?" Ramirez turned to stare at her, despite the speed at which they were moving down the busy road. "This op is blown. We have to pull out right—"

"Everything at the hotel is packed up, okay? We're not risking a thing. Make the call. Tell the team leaders to pull out, but we're circling around." Ramirez turned forward again and opened his mouth to argue, but Naomi spoke first, her voice low and cutting. "Ramirez, just do it. Do it now, or I'll personally tell Harper how fast you wanted to cut and run. Got it?"

"Fuck!" The operative slammed his hand against the wheel. Then he picked his phone up off the passenger seat and hit a button, muttering something under his breath. Naomi held her breath as the van passed the spot where the cruisers had turned. It all came down to the next intersection, but as they approached, Ramirez slowed for the turn. She let out her breath in a quiet sigh of relief. If they could get into position in time, Ryan might still have a chance of making it out in one piece.

* * *

Inside the trailer, Pétain was back at the window, peering anxiously through the gap in the blinds. Kamil Ghafour was seated on the floor, propped against the cheap wooden desk. Standing before him, Kealey searched his face. The man was pale and sweating profusely, but his eyes were open and clear. Kealey could tell the epinephrine had worked, but despite the pressure bandage he had applied to the Algerian's leg, the wound was still bleeding at a steady rate. Worse yet, the police were closing in. Kealey knew he could hold them off for a while, but if Ghafour died in the meantime, the whole situation would change dramatically, and not for the better.

Kealey knelt before the other man and stared directly into his eyes. "Kamil, can you hear me?"

The Algerian stared back blankly for a moment. Then his lips twitched, and he nodded his head weakly.

"Tell me you can hear me. I want to hear you say the words."

"Yes," Ghafour rasped. "I can hear you."

"Good. Now listen," Kealey said. He was striving to keep his voice low and deliberate, the better to get his point across. "You are dying, Kamil."

The words, which were delivered in a calm, rational tone, had little effect. Ghafour's eyes opened slightly wider, but otherwise he didn't react.

"I've applied a pressure bandage," Kealey continued, "but your femoral artery is partially severed. You are bleeding out. Unless you receive medical attention, you'll be dead in twenty minutes." Actually, it would be much sooner than that, but Kealey knew he had to give the other man hope.

"I need . . ." Ghafour lowered his head and coughed sharply, spittle and blood flying into his lap. "I need a doctor. Get me a doctor."

"Not until you answer my question. It's a simple question, Kamil. In fact, it couldn't be easier. You had the chance to come out of this a healthy, richer man, but you fucked that up. If you tell me what I need to know right now, you get to live, which is better than nothing. Now tell me . . . Who came to see Saifi in Algiers?"

Ghafour coughed again, and Pétain's worried voice filled the room. "Ryan, they're almost here. We've got to—"

"How many?" Kealey interrupted.

"Two. Just two."

"They have their guns out?"

"Yes. One handgun each. One is behind and to the left, covering the other . . . They know what they're doing."

"Okay. Shut those blinds. They'll bang on the door, but don't respond. They won't come in until they have backup and a better grasp on the situation. Whatever you do, don't say a word. Got it?"

"Got it."

As Pétain shut the blinds and stepped to one side of the door, her FN in two hands, down by her waist, Kealey prodded Ghafour again, his voice taking on a more urgent tone. "Come on, Kamil. You're running out of time. Tell me what I want to know."

Without warning, the Algerian raised his eyes and smiled broadly, revealing two even rows of bloody teeth. "I think you have it backwards," he gasped, a hint of fatalistic amusement coming through. "You're the one that's out of time. If those police officers don't kill you, they'll put you in jail for what you've done to me. I suggest you give yourself up." He laughed harshly, then coughed again, a trickle of blood running down the side of his mouth. "Maybe your friends at the CIA will be able to pull some strings, but I wouldn't count on it. From what I've heard, they don't reward failure."

Kealey stared at him for a moment, then spoke to Pétain without shifting his gaze. "Where's that knife?"

"Right here."

"Give it to me."

Ghafour's eyes narrowed in suspicion and curiosity, his gaze flicking back and forth between the two operatives. "What are you doing? What's that for?"

Kealey didn't respond as he stood and accepted the proffered utility knife. Ghafour asked the question again, raising his voice this time, but Kealey simply urged the blade out of the handle with his thumb, then dropped to his knees. Without saying a word, he grasped Ghafour's injured leg in his left hand, his grip tight around the bony part of the ankle. Then he hooked the blade under the fabric that covered the Algerian's wound. With two quick flicks of his wrist, the bandages were cut away. The small hole instantly started to spurt again, hot arterial blood arcing into the air.

Ghafour's eyes opened wide, and he began to scream and thrash around, just as he had when he'd first been shot. A second later, a fist pounded hard on the trailer door, and a voice called out a loud command.

"*¡Abran la puerta ahora mismo! ¡Salgan con las manos arriba!*"

Ignoring the police officer's instructions, Kealey shifted forward and pressed both hands over the Algerian's spurting wound.

"Answer the *fucking* question!" he shouted, his face less than a foot from Ghafour's. "Or I'll pull my hands away, I swear to God! Who came to see Saifi? What was his name?"

"*Mengal!*" Ghafour screamed. "His name was Mengal! Benazir Mengal!"

Kealey couldn't help but feel a weight lift from his shoulders; for the first time since they'd landed in Spain, he knew they were on the right track. "Who is he?"

"A Pakistani general," Ghafour gasped. His eyelids were starting to droop, and he had stopped sweating. Kealey knew dehydration was kicking in, but that was the least of the man's problems. "He's retired now, but he has many friends. They say he used to be ISI."

"What did Mengal want with Saifi?" Kealey demanded. He shifted his hands slightly on top of the wound to emphasize his point, and Ghafour looked on in horror as blood pumped through the other man's splayed fingers. "Why did he arrange to get him out of prison?"

"I don't know," Ghafour moaned. Kealey leaned forward; it was hard to hear the man's replies over the shouting outside. "I promise you, I have no idea. But Mengal was the only one who came to the jail."

"Okay," Kealey said. Without warning, he pulled his right arm back and slammed a fist into the Algerian's face. The man went instantly limp, and Kealey sat back on his haunches, trying to figure out his next move. As the adrenaline worked its way out of his system, reality began to kick in. With a sense of despair, he realized they were in an impossible situation. Ghafour would be dead in less than five minutes, perhaps as little as two. They had no way out of the trailer, and if Ramirez had any sense at all, he would have pulled the teams out the second Pétain called him with the bad news.

Thinking about Pétain, Kealey stood and turned to face her. He was surprised to find her on the phone, as he hadn't heard it ring. She had a finger in one ear to block out the shouted commands of the CNP officers, and she was nodding quickly, her eyes wide, sharp,

and completely alert. A moment later she said, "I got it," and hit the
END button. When she lowered the phone to her side, Kealey looked
at her inquiringly.

"That was Kharmai."

"What did she say?"

"She's going to try and get us out of here."

CHAPTER 18

MADRID

After they had pulled onto San Leonardo de Dios, Ramirez had managed to find a parking spot right on the road. The gate that Kealey and Pétain had first entered was about 40 meters in front of the van, and the street farther down was partially blocked off by a pair of CNP vehicles. The light racks on both were flashing blue, but the sirens were off. A number of pedestrians had gathered around, and Naomi knew it was only a matter of time before more police units arrived on the scene. The demonstration on the Puerta del Sol would slow the response time, but not by much. They had to move immediately.

Ramirez was saying something to her through the hole in the partition, and she shifted her attention toward him. "What did you say?"

"I said, 'What the hell is wrong with you?' I heard you talking to Pétain, and there's no way you're going in there, Kharmai. I'm not going to let you fuck up my career as well." He leaned forward to start the engine. "I'm done with this shit. We're out of here."

"No!" Kharmai adjusted her awkward stance, drew her Glock, and aimed it through the gap in the metal. The muzzle was level with the other operative's astonished face.

"What the fuck do you think you're doing?" he rasped, his dark eyes fixed on the end of the barrel.

Naomi shifted her aim slightly to the right. She steadied herself before she spoke, determined to make him believe. For this to work, there could be no doubt in his mind that she'd pull the trigger. "Ramirez, there's an alley just ahead on your right. I want you to start the van and pull it inside."

"Or what?"

"Or I fire through the windshield. There are still two officers in those cars up ahead. They're both behind the wheel. If I shoot, they'll be on us in less than a minute."

"You would do that? You would fuck us both?"

"Yes. If I have to, I will. Absolutely." She looked at him hard, hoping he couldn't see past her rigid, unyielding façade. Hoping her hands weren't shaking too much. Hoping he couldn't detect the cold flash of fear and nausea that had just swept through her body. "Start the van."

Ramirez shook his head in disbelief, but he did as he was told. The vehicle rumbled to life, and he dropped it into gear. Naomi kept her gun at arm's length until they were in the alley and parked. Then she turned and opened the sliding door. Closing it behind her, she circled the vehicle and approached the driver's-side door carefully from the rear, hoping he wouldn't try to back up in the confined space. There wasn't much room between the left side of the Toyota and the redbrick walls, and if he decided to make a run for it, she would almost certainly be crushed. She realized she should have taken the keys, but it was too late for that now.

Once she reached the open window, she aimed her gun in at Ramirez. She wasn't surprised in the least to see that he was holding a weapon as well, the muzzle aimed across his body, directly toward her head.

"What now?" he asked. His dark, unwavering eyes were fixed on hers. "You shoot me, I shoot you . . . We both end up dead. Is that what you want?"

"I don't want to kill you," she said. Her stomach felt as if it had been pulled out, shaken hard, then put back in. She could feel sweat on her face and beneath her T-shirt. It felt cold, despite the heat of the afternoon. In fact, it felt as if her entire body had just been submerged in a pool of freezing water. "Just get out and walk away. That's all I'm asking."

"That's it?"

"That's it."

Ramirez held her gaze for a moment longer, debating his options.

Then he nodded and pushed open the door. She stepped back and tracked him with her weapon as he walked to the end of the alley. He turned and gave her one last look before disappearing into the crowds sweeping by on the sidewalk.

Naomi instantly shoved the Glock under the waistband of her jeans, the grip flat against the right side of her stomach. Then she lifted the lower edge of her T-shirt to wipe the sweat from her face. A sudden wave of nausea caused her to bend at the waist. She kept one hand on the van's rear bumper for support and stayed that way for twenty seconds, trying to empty her stomach, but nothing came up. She shuddered, a low, involuntary moan rising up in her throat. Then she straightened and leaned against the rear doors, considering her next move, straining to think through the haze that enveloped her mind.

The sound of another siren broke her concentration. It was the last thing she wanted to hear, but she instantly factored it in. Turning her head to the right, she could tell the siren was coming from the same direction as the other cars. Thinking back to the maps they had studied the previous night, she recalled that the closest CNP station was to the north, which made sense, given what she was hearing. She lifted her cell phone and stared at it blankly. She knew that Ryan would be expecting her to call any minute with a plan for getting them out of there, but her brain wasn't working. What she needed was a way to distract the officers, to draw their attention away from the trailer. It wasn't much, but it was all she could do; Ryan and Pétain would just have to figure it out from there.

Taking a couple of steps away from the van, she quickly appraised her surroundings. The alley was empty except for a few battered dumpsters and a pile of empty boxes. Power lines ran the length of the wide corridor, the wooden poles wedged against the redbrick wall on either side. An advertisement for some type of Spanish beer was painted in bright colors on the uneven bricks to her right, just beneath the second-floor windows, most of which were open to the afternoon air. Farther down the alley, there was an open door, beyond which she could hear the sound of machinery and tinny music. There was a lot to take in, but nothing that could help her.

She tried to focus on the noise coming from the open doorway. It was on the left, about 10 meters in front of her. As she moved closer, the sounds became more distinct: music playing over a portable stereo, someone laughing, the steady *thunk thunk thunk* of an impact wrench. She thought back to what she had seen through the windshield when Ramirez swung the van into the alley. There had been a store of some kind on the right, and something else to the left . . . an auto-body repair shop. That was what she was hearing now, she realized—the sound of a mechanic working on a vehicle. What kind of vehicle, she didn't know, but that didn't matter. The noise seemed to draw her forward regardless.

She reached the doorway, edged closer, and peered into the shop. She pulled back instantly, her breath catching in her throat. There was a young man in coveralls right there, walking past the door. She was sure he had seen her, but the heavy footsteps seemed to recede, and after another twenty seconds, she looked in again. She didn't see anyone this time, but when she took a few cautious steps into the bay, she heard voices coming from another door to her left. That was the store, she realized; the mechanic must have gone inside for some reason, maybe to answer a customer's question, or perhaps to get a drink of water. Either way, she didn't have a lot of time; he could return at any minute.

Naomi moved farther into the bay and looked around quickly, her heart pumping hard, every nerve on edge. There were two partially dismantled vehicles in the garage, and both bay doors were closed, blocking out the view of the street. There were windows on the upper parts of both doors, but both were extremely dirty. No one could see in, and she couldn't see out. Shelves to her left were stocked with oil, dusty boxes of air filters, and bottles of antifreeze. On the other side of the door was a large metal toolbox, the kind with wheels and dozens of drawers.

She turned back toward the alley. Her eyes instantly fell on an object just inside the door. A number of objects, actually. Two metal tanks were chained together and resting on a hand trolley. She moved closer and studied both tanks, listening carefully for the sound of approaching footsteps. One tank came up to her waist. It was painted a pale shade of green, and there were two gauges sticking out from a brass valve at the top. A hose ran out from the valve, but she couldn't see where it went, as it was wrapped into a bulky mass on the other side of the cart. The second cylinder was unpainted and about two-thirds the size of the first. It also had two gauges, and a red hose ran out from the top. Looking closer, she realized the hoses were joined along their length with plastic ties, and both ran into some kind of metal fitting at the top. Most interesting of all were the markings on each tank. The larger read OXYGEN in bold letters. The smaller was marked ACETYLENE.

This was what she was looking for. Without hesitation, she moved behind the trolley, grabbed the handles, and dropped her weight forward. The tanks rocked back on the trolley, and she wheeled them around, carefully navigating the slight bump where the door frame met the asphalt. Soon she had the trolley out in the alley and next to the van. Letting go of the handles, she thought for a moment, then peered in through the driver's window, searching for the fuel gauge. She found it quickly and immediately realized that since the van wasn't running, the gauge wasn't any use to her. She debated starting it up to see how much fuel was in the tank, but then decided not to waste the time. Besides, it wasn't as if she could go and fill it up if it was low.

Moving back to the trolley, she carefully wheeled it next to the rear fender, then lowered it onto its handles. With a little effort, she managed to wedge the trolley behind the rear tire on the driver's side. Both tanks were now parallel to the ground, approximately 7 inches above the asphalt. Stepping back, Naomi appraised her work. She had no idea if her plan would work. The gauges seemed to indicate that the cylinders were nearly full, but she couldn't be sure of the end result. She had worked with all kinds of explosives at Camp Peary, but the training regimen had not included a lecture on the explosive properties of acetylene. Or oxygen, for that matter. Still, this was the only thing she had at hand, and she didn't have time to consider another course of action.

She examined the tanks once more, then hesitated, thinking about the Glock 9mm tucked into the top of her jeans. It occurred to her that the tanks would be well constructed, considering what they contained, and when she squeezed the trigger, she'd have to be as far away as possible. A 9mm round might not be powerful enough to penetrate both cylinders.

Jogging around to the other side of the van, she pulled open the door and climbed inside. Opening the lockbox bolted to the floor, she checked the inventory. There was one weapon left inside, a Para-Ordnance P14. She could tell from the size of the gun that it was chambered for .45 ACP cartridges, but she checked one of the fully loaded magazines to be sure. Satisfied, she pushed the magazine into the well and chambered a round. Then she climbed out of the van and shut the door. As she walked back toward the street, she pulled out her phone, hit the speed dial, and lifted it to her ear. Pétain answered a second later.

"I'm set on this end," Naomi said.

"What do you want us to do?"

"You're still inside the trailer, right?"

"Yes."

"Wait thirty seconds, then move. You might still have to deal with one or two, but that's better than half a dozen. Whatever you do, don't head for the gate you entered through. It looks like all the police cars are sitting on the east side of the site, so head for the opposite gate. Okay?"

"Got it. What will you—"

"I'll be in touch when I can," Naomi said, anticipating the question. "*If* I can. Just try to get clear. Did you get what you needed?"

"Yes, I think so."

"Then good luck."

Naomi hit the END button without waiting for a response. Slipping the phone back into her pocket, she did her best to conceal the P14 as she reached the street, holding it down behind her right thigh. She turned and looked back at the tanks, squinting into the afternoon sun. The van was sitting about 15 meters away, which meant it was much, much too close. Still, she had run out of room. If she kept walking, she would be out of the alley and back in plain view, where someone might catch sight of the gun and raise the alarm.

There was an overflowing dumpster to her left. Moving behind it, she dropped to one knee and raised the weapon with both hands. She aimed at the first cylinder, careful to expose as little of her body as possible. It was no good; her hands were shaking, and her breath was ragged. The nausea was worse than ever. She squeezed her eyes shut and forced herself to relax. Then she opened her eyes, took a deep, steadying breath, and squeezed the trigger.

The air inside the trailer was incredibly thick, both operatives waiting on edge for whatever Naomi was going to do. Kealey had already pulled off his T-shirt and used the damp cotton to wipe most of Ghafour's blood from his hands and arms. Looking around, he found a couple of discarded flannel shirts on the couch near the door—too warm for this kind of weather, too conspicuous, but they would have to suffice. He pulled one on and tossed the second to Pétain, whose eyes were locked on Ghafour's still form. She caught the shirt at the last possible second and looked over.

"What do you want me to do with this?"

"Put it on," he told her. "We'll wear the hard hats out of here. It won't help much, but a few seconds of confusion is better than nothing at all."

She nodded her consent and pulled on the oversized shirt. As she zipped up the front, she gestured to Ghafour and said, "What about him?"

Kealey glanced over, then returned his gaze to the door. "He's dead. How long has it been?"

He sensed more than saw Pétain look at her watch. "Forty seconds," she murmured. "Why haven't we heard anything?"

"Give her time. Just listen for movement out—"

The second part of his sentence was cut off by a distant boom. As the noise faded away, Kealey heard the officers shifting around outside. There was a babble of voices, then the sound of fast-moving feet. He realized that some of them must be moving back to the street in response to the explosion. Moving carefully, quietly, he stepped forward, separated the blinds, and looked outside. There were two officers left. Both were facing the street, their backs to the trailer. The others were running across the site, toward the east gate. Beyond the chain-link fence, Kealey could see a thick pall of smoke rising into the clear blue sky. It was a strange, disconcerting sight, but he recognized the diversion for what it was: the only thing that might get them out of there in one piece.

"Grab the money," he said.

"What?"

"*Get the fucking money,*" Kealey repeated. He crossed to the door as Pétain lifted the duffel bag off the couch, slinging it over her shoulder. She hung back as Kealey crouched beside the door, preparing himself for what was about to happen. "Going in three," he murmured. "Are you ready?"

"Ready."

Kealey put his hand on the door and began to count. When he hit three, he flung open the door and took in the scene, moving forward the whole time. Both officers started to turn at the noise. The first was about 3 feet from the door.

"¡Ayúdenos!" Kealey shouted. "That guy in there is crazy!"

The closest officer hesitated as he turned, his eyes looking past Kealey to the open door. It gave Kealey the split second he needed. His right foot shot out, catching the officer beneath the left knee. He started to go down as Kealey pushed off his right foot, shifting his weight to the left. It was a fast movement, but not fast enough. The second officer's right arm swung around with surprising speed, and Kealey had no choice. He fired once but didn't see where his round hit. The officer started to fall back as Pétain advanced, her gun drawn, and aimed . . .

Kealey turned back to the first officer. He was clutching his knee and groaning, his service weapon lying a few feet away in the dirt. Kealey leaned down and snatched it up, then shoved it into the deep right pocket of his work shirt. He removed his hard hat, tossed it aside, and turned to Pétain. She had already collected the other man's weapon; her FN Forty-Nine was still trained on the fallen officer, whose hands were raised in surrender. Looking closer, Kealey could see that his round had hit the man in the right side of his abdomen. As long as the wound was treated soon, it wouldn't be life-threatening.

"Let's go," Kealey said. Pétain nodded her assent, but he didn't see her acknowledge his words. His attention was focused on the west gate, the one Naomi had told them to use. Kealey could see right away that it wouldn't work; a number of construction workers were standing in their way, and their attention was riveted on what had just happened outside the trailer. A few looked like they wanted to interfere, but not one of them dared to advance. Kealey realized they had seen the whole thing. They had seen him attack, then shoot the officer. Apparently, none of the workers were willing to risk a similar fate.

He turned and started to run for the east gate, his feet pounding over the dry, uneven ground. He shouted over his shoulder for Pétain to follow, but she was already there, sprinting less than 3 feet to his rear.

"Kealey, what are you doing?" she panted between breaths. "This isn't the right—"

"You saw them," he shouted back at her. "This is the only way out."

"But the police are—"

"I know, but we don't have a choice. *Just keep moving!*"

CHAPTER 19

MADRID

When Naomi regained consciousness, the first thing she heard was the screams. Her entire world was pitch black, but the screams were incredibly sharp and distinct. It was almost as if hundreds of mouths were positioned on either side of her head, all of them howling directly into her ears. She tried to raise her hands to block out the awful sound, but her limbs didn't seem to be working correctly. One voice in particular was cutting through the cacophony, but she couldn't place it. She desperately wanted to see or hear something familiar, but everything around her was a meaningless blur.

A blur . . . That was a start, at least. Her eyes were open, and things were starting to come into focus. She was lying flat on her back. The tall shadows above her were moving fast, darting about in her peripheral vision. As she collected herself, the shadows began to take on distinct shapes. Before long they were silhouettes against the afternoon sun, and then they were people. Dozens of people running and screaming, running and screaming, standing and pointing . . .

She felt a hand on her arm, then two hands, warm skin touching her own, two fingers probing the right side of her neck. Searching for a pulse, she realized. The voice was taking shape, forming words, asking if she was all right. The rough hands moved behind her, sliding under her armpits, lifting her into a sitting position. She tried to protest, but all that came out was gibberish. Whoever it was clearly had no medical training; otherwise, he wouldn't have tried to move her at all.

"Easy, now." The person behind her was clearly American, speaking with a distinct Brooklyn accent. "Just take it easy. You're going to be fine."

"What happened?"

"You speak English." There was relief in the voice. *A tourist,* Naomi decided. "There was an explosion of some kind. A bomb, maybe. You were knocked out, but you're going to be fine. Just sit and wait for the ambulance. Don't move, okay?"

Naomi felt herself nod weakly. *What happened?* Did she really ask him that? *Why* had she asked that? She remembered squeezing the trigger, but everything that came after was a complete blank. Despite the confusion that clouded her mind, it was clear that she'd been much too close to the Toyota when she fired at the cylinders. Looking over, she saw, with surprise, that she had been thrown at least 10 feet from the mouth of the alley, perhaps more. She had known it from the start, but the space between the van and the street was just too short. If she hadn't been using the dumpster as cover, she probably would have been killed instantly. Still, she had done the best she could; the only question now was whether or not her diversion had worked.

Her thoughts shifted to Ryan. She could hear police officers shouting orders around her—she could tell they were officers by the measured authority in their raised voices—and she could hear additional sirens in the distance. The trouble was that she had no idea how long she'd been out. Additional units of the CNP would have responded quickly, along with the paramedics, but how fast? That was the question. Naomi decided she couldn't have been unconscious for more than a minute or two, which meant that if they were moving quickly, Ryan and Pétain should have already cleared the scene.

The American tourist had moved on to the next person. Naomi climbed unsteadily to her feet, then tested her limbs and performed a quick visual check of her body, or at least what she could see. Everything seemed to be working, but she knew it was early yet. Sometimes serious wounds didn't become obvious until the shock had passed, and she was still trying to get her bearings. She took a few uncertain steps as her vision cleared. Looking around, she saw that a number of people were lying in the street. Many were moving around, but others were completely immobile. Some were bleeding profusely.

Suddenly, it hit her that she was responsible for everything she was seeing. A wave of horror and guilt rose up in her chest, choking her as effectively as a pair of strong hands, but she pushed the emotions down as hard as she could, knowing it wouldn't help her to focus on them now. The dizziness started to clear as she stumbled north, skirting the injured pedestrians in her wake. She tried not to look at their faces. She didn't want to see, didn't want to account for what she had done. At least not until she could absorb it properly. Three police cars were positioned close to the intersection, barely 10 meters away from the chain-link fence that marked the eastern edge of the construction site. Shifting her eyes to the left, she watched as the gate swung open and two people stepped into view. Despite the work shirts they were wearing, Naomi instantly recognized Ryan Kealey and Marissa Pétain. As she looked on in disbelief, they turned left and started along the pavement, passing within 5 meters of the closest CNP cruiser.

Why did it take them so long? And why did they come out of the wrong gate? The anger welled up as she tracked them along the sidewalk. It didn't make sense; they should have been moving the second they heard the explosion. She watched as they cleared the cruisers, walking fast toward the intersection, then breathed a sigh of relief. They were going to make it.

Naomi kept moving forward and tried to relax, willing the tension out of her shoulders and back. All she had to do was trail at a safe distance; once they had walked a few blocks, she'd call Ryan and arrange a time and place to link up. Suddenly, she realized she no longer had the .45. She quickly checked her pockets, then her waist. The Glock 9mm was still tucked into the top of her jeans, but the .45 was definitely gone. After a moment's hesitation, she decided there was nothing she could do about it. She certainly couldn't go back and search for it, and she knew the Spanish police didn't have her fingerprints on file. The best thing she could do was keep moving, but as she quickened her pace, she realized that someone was shouting. A few people, in fact. Not behind her, but in front, close to where the police cars were parked.

Her eyes darted to the left, seeking out the source of the commotion. She quickly locked onto a small group of construction workers.

Half of them were trying to get the attention of the one officer who'd stayed with the vehicles, a slight man in his early twenties. He looked incredibly young and uncertain, but he was definitely listening to what they were saying. The other half were pointing down the sidewalk. Their accusing fingers were aimed directly at Kealey and Pétain. A split second later, the officer turned and cast a long look after them, his hand dropping down to his gun. . . .

Naomi started to run, a warning shout caught in her throat. She was too far away. They wouldn't hear her, and if they did, they wouldn't be able to react in time. She felt as if she was moving in slow motion, but she couldn't break free of the strange sensation. Her hand dipped to her waist, lifting her sweat-soaked T-shirt, finding the grip of the Glock . . .

She wrenched it free and tried to stop, her heels skidding across the pavement. The force of the blast had caused the windows of the second-story apartments to explode outward, raining glass down onto the street. Dimly aware of the crunching sensation beneath her feet, she raised the weapon but didn't take aim. The police officer's gun was out now, and he was shouting something at Kealey and Pétain. Both had turned to face the officer, and even at a distance, Naomi could see the caught-out-of-position look on Ryan's face, his hand hovering down by his side. The uncertainty was something she'd never seen before, and for a split second, it gave her pause.

But only for a second. Their eyes met a moment later, and she knew what she had to do. Taking a few more deliberate steps forward, she shifted her gaze and locked onto her target. The front sight was perfectly lined up with the rear. Her finger was resting lightly on the trigger . . . All she had to do was squeeze.

Kealey had heard the voices, felt Pétain's hand tighten around his arm in warning. He didn't need to look to know what had happened, and he knew that by turning around, he would only confirm whatever suspicions had been raised behind them. Still, he had no choice. He stopped walking and looked over his shoulder. In the same instant, he turned his body, set his feet, and let his right hand hang casually down by his side. The unsettling scenario became immediately apparent: the accusing faces of the construction workers, the fearful expressions of the civilians standing nearby, the scared but determined face of the young CNP officer in the foreground. He looked past the officer, aware of the gun coming up, the shouted command, but all he could see was Naomi's face. She was about 15 meters behind the policeman, and her Glock 9mm was already out and up. People were screaming and diving out of the way, but their shouts merged seamlessly with the cacophony of police sirens and the cries of the wounded.

Kealey knew he wouldn't be able to get his weapon out in time; he had waited too long. He locked eyes with Naomi, still ignoring the officer's shouts, and tried to communicate his thoughts to her. He couldn't be sure if she understood, or if she even knew he was trying to tell her something, but he didn't have time to think about it. She was already moving.

The moment she fired, the officer jerked, almost as if he'd been slapped on the back, then crumpled to the ground, his final expression marked by complete confusion. As he fell, his weapon discharged once, a reflex jerk on the trigger. Kealey heard the snap of the round as it passed a few feet overhead. Naomi was still moving forward, running faster now, her feet pounding over the debris-littered pavement. Her face was fixed in an unnerving expression, something between abject horror and utter resolve. . . .

Kealey couldn't help but stare as she approached, wondering what could possibly be going through her mind, but Pétain's voice jolted him back to reality. "We've got to move!" she urged, pulling frantically on his arm. Snapping out of it, Kealey stepped off the narrow sidewalk and into the street. Southbound traffic was tied up, hopelessly snarled, but the road was still relatively clear to the north. Inexplicably, one motorist had stepped out of his car to get a better look at what was happening. He was immobile, apparently unaware of the threat to his own safety. His entire body was rigid as he stared on in obvious shock. A few feet to his right, a small Ford Escort was still idling, exhaust rising up to join the pall of acrid smoke that still hung in the air. The driver's-side door was ajar.

Kealey considered training his gun on the man and shouting some kind of threat, but it wasn't necessary. He simply pushed him aside and climbed behind the wheel. The man didn't even protest, just fell to the ground and looked on in stunned disbelief. Pétain jumped into the passenger seat, and Naomi arrived on the run a few seconds later. Behind them, several shots rang out, pounding into the trunk of the car. One round penetrated the rear windshield, narrowly missing Naomi's head as she threw herself into the backseat. Keeping her body below window level, she reached back to close the door and screamed at Kealey to move, but he was already slamming the car into gear. The Escort jolted forward, then accelerated rapidly as he expertly shifted into second, his left foot working the clutch. The car scraped against another vehicle on the narrow road, swerving slightly, and the driver's-side mirror came off with a loud bang, arcing into the air before shattering on the pavement 20 feet behind them.

They were coming up on the intersection. The light was red, and a number of vehicles were waiting for it to turn. An erratic stream of cars was flowing east on Calle de San Bernardino, blocking their only escape route, but Kealey knew he didn't have a choice. Two CNP officers had already retrieved their vehicles and were coming up fast behind him.

"Get down!" he shouted as he turned the wheel hard to the right, bouncing the car up onto the sidewalk. Pedestrians dove out of the way as the Escort raced toward the intersection. The sidewalk wasn't especially crowded, but a few people weren't able to get out of the way in time, their bodies bouncing off the front of the vehicle. When they were almost through the light, Kealey flinched involuntarily and turned his face away from the driver's-side door. The inevitable impact came an instant later as an eastbound sedan caught the rear end of the Escort, spinning it around in the intersection, the glass exploding in the rear windows. Kealey heard the ear-wrenching crump of metal on metal as one car after another smashed into the back of the car that had plowed into them. Everything seemed to spin crazily for a few seconds, the surrounding buildings hurtling past his eyes, and then the car came to rest facing oncoming traffic, rocking slightly on its worn suspension. The engine had died, and Kealey instantly downshifted to first and turned the key, praying it would start up again.

Amazingly, it did. The engine caught for an instant, but then came to life. Kealey pushed the accelerator down and swerved back into the right lane, the damaged car surging forward, racing southeast toward the city center. The pileup behind them had blocked the police cars in pursuit, but it was only a temporary delay. More units were clearly on the way, as evidenced by the wailing sirens in the near distance.

Without taking his eyes off the road, Kealey asked, "Is everyone okay? Anyone hurt?"

"I'm fine," Pétain said, sounding strangely breathless. Looking over, Kealey saw that she was gingerly pulling the seat belt away from her chest; clearly, the collision had caught her completely off guard, and the belt had snapped taut across her body, forcing the air from her lungs.

"What about you, Naomi?"

"I'm okay," she said in a strange monotone. Kealey shot a look over his shoulder, alarmed by the tone of her voice, but she appeared unhurt, staring fixedly past him and through the windshield. He was relieved to find they had both been wearing seat belts. He had forgotten his, but somehow he'd managed to come through unscathed.

"Take the next left," Pétain urged as Kealey swung back around in his seat. "Calle de los Reyes."

"Is there a parking garage on that street? Somewhere with a little privacy?" Kealey asked.

"No, but a garage would have cameras, anyway," she reminded him. "We've got to dump this vehicle right now. The CNP will have the area sealed off in a matter of minutes."

Kealey nodded sharply; he was annoyed by the fact that he hadn't considered the cameras. Following her directions, he turned onto the narrow side street and found a parking spot alongside the curb. They all climbed out, ignoring the strange looks the battered vehicle was drawing. A number of sirens seemed to be converging on a point in the near distance, but Kealey decided they were mostly responding to the scene of the bombing on Calle de San Leonardo de Dios. None were close enough to indicate an imminent threat.

He turned to Pétain. "You still have your phone?"

She ran a hand over her right pocket and nodded in the affirmative. Thinking back to the maps he had studied that morning, Kealey checked his watch and said, "We'll meet at the botanical gardens off the Prado Road. Let's make it two hours from now. I'll call you in advance to give you a specific time and place." He didn't need to expound on this; the night before, they had each memorized the codes they would use in the event they were caught and forced to speak under duress. He felt sure they had slipped through the net, at least for the time being, but the precautionary steps were like rote to him, drilled in after years of operating illegally on foreign soil. There was no way he could discard them completely, not even under this kind of pressure. "Got it?"

Pétain nodded again. "Got it."

"What about me?" Naomi asked.

Kealey shot her an appraising look and frowned, deeply troubled by what he saw. She was still sweating profusely, and while her face was blank, her limbs were trembling violently. Her appearance alone was more than enough to attract attention, and that wouldn't work at all. The first thing they had to find was a public restroom, a place where she could clean herself up. Then they would have to set about finding a change of clothes.

"You're coming with me," he told her. He turned back to Pétain, but she was already moving away, slipping through the static crowd of pedestrians, many of whom had stopped to stare at the gray black cloud drifting past the towering skyline. Grasping Naomi's hand firmly in his, Kealey turned and started off in the opposite direction, wondering how Harper would react when he heard the news. They had acquired the name they needed from Ghafour, but somehow, Kealey didn't think that would be enough to justify the disaster that had just transpired. In fact, the situation could hardly be worse. At least one innocent man was dead, and now—despite the overall success of the operation—they were going to have to face the music. The only question was how bad it would end up being.

CHAPTER 20

WASHINGTON, D.C.

Jonathan Harper sat uneasily in the Oval Office, an untouched cup of coffee resting on the end table near his elbow. He'd been waiting for ten long minutes and wasn't expecting the president anytime soon. Director Andrews had been called out of the room a few minutes earlier, leaving Harper to dwell on what was coming next. Apart from a solemn Secret Service agent standing post at the door, he was alone. As he waited, he let his mind wander over what had transpired in Madrid less than three hours earlier. The president had been caught up in a press conference; otherwise, Harper knew he would have been expected at the White House earlier. He had used the unexpected delay to the best of his ability, working the information Kealey had given him through the system. The younger man had called him shortly after the disastrous encounter with Kamil Ghafour, and while the report as a whole was less than welcome, the name of Benazir Mengal seemed promising, at least based on what the Operations Directorate had dug up so far.

Reaching over for his coffee, Harper winced as a sharp pain shot through the left side of his chest. Knowing all too well what was about to happen, he leaned back in his seat, closed his eyes, and worked on controlling his breathing. He'd found that to be the hardest part; once he let it get away from him, it only compounded the other symptoms. The pain started to build, like his heart was being squeezed inside his chest. Then, after nearly a minute of pure agony, the edge wore off, and the pain began to subside.

"Sir?" Harper opened his eyes and looked up at the agent's worried face. The man had crossed the room to check on him. "Sir, are you all right? Should I get a doctor?"

"No." Harper managed a weak smile. "I'll be fine. It comes and goes . . . Trust me, I'm getting used to it."

The man looked uneasy. "Can I get you some water, at least?"

"Yes, that would be great. Thanks."

"No problem, sir." The agent crossed to another table to fill a glass from a chilled pitcher of water. He returned a moment later, still looking extremely concerned. Thanking him again, Harper drained half the glass, then dug out a clean handkerchief. He used it to wipe the cold sweat from his face, then leaned back in his seat and tried to relax. Over the next few minutes, his breathing returned to normal. As he'd just said, the pain came and went, but the other part wasn't true. He wasn't getting used to it. The attacks were a constant reminder of the bullet he'd taken eight months earlier. To be precise, he'd taken four, but one had done significantly more damage than the other three, and he'd been advised by his doctors that the effects of that particular wound would be long term. So far, he'd found that assessment to be entirely accurate.

He'd been prescribed medication for the pain, of course, but he did his best to use it as little as possible. He drank very little alcohol for exactly the same reason: he preferred to be in complete control at all times. Given the secrets he was charged with protecting, he thought it a prudent course of action. It was a decision he'd made more than twenty years earlier, when he'd first joined the Agency, and he'd never regretted it.

That wasn't to say he didn't harbor regrets. Twenty years in the intelligence business afforded one the time and opportunity to generate plenty of self-recrimination. One incident above all others haunted him day in and day out. As he considered this fact, he involuntarily touched his suit jacket, feeling for the scar tissue beneath the layers of clothing. He couldn't feel it, but he knew it was there. He could hardly forget. Eight months of relentless searching, Harper thought to himself, the anger welling up as it always did, and the Agency was still no closer to finding the identity of his would-be assassin. The woman who'd risked her freedom—indeed, her very life—to kill him.

The act itself was only part of the puzzle. The underlying question was how she had found him in the first place. Harper had his suspicions, but knew he'd never be able to prove his theory. The woman he suspected of leaking the information was his predecessor, a former congresswoman by the name of Rachel Ford. She had resigned under pressure from the White House shortly after the failed assassination attempt and, in doing so, had largely protected herself against prosecution. Simply put, she was an embarrassment to the Agency, as well as to the president, who'd nominated her to begin with. No one was in a hurry to give her an audience. For this reason, Harper suspected he'd never know the whole truth. It was something he had yet to come to terms with, and if he was entirely honest with himself, he doubted that he ever would.

The DDO, or deputy director of operations, was the individual charged with running the Agency's covert operations around the world. In its entirety, the Directorate of Operations, or DO, comprised less than 10 percent of the Agency's total workforce. Nevertheless, it was the CIA's most recognizable element. In short, the DO *was* the Agency, at least as far as the general public was concerned. It was the same directorate that all the movies and books were based on. Despite its notoriety, the DO was quite adept at concealing its ongoing operations from the public eye, and the identity of the department head was one of its most prized secrets. At least, it should have been. The knowledge that this information had slipped out on his watch was deeply unsettling to Jonathan Harper; indeed, he had nearly resigned over the incident. As it turned out, he'd been nominated for the second-ranking position at the Agency instead. The promotion—which had been confirmed by the Senate in record time—was largely based on Harper's adept handling of the attempted attack in New York City, as well as his role in limiting the fallout.

With this thought, Harper couldn't help but shake his head, a small, wry smile creeping over his face. It was the way things worked in the District, and despite his years of experience, the audacity of the players involved never ceased to amaze him. When it came right down to it, politics was nothing more than a game, albeit a game played on the world stage. That wasn't to say that the players in Washington were immoral, uncaring people, just that many of them frequently prized things other than the nation's welfare. It was human nature to covet, Harper knew, but that didn't make it any easier to bear. Or to witness, especially given what was at stake.

At that moment, the door leading in from the main corridor of the West Wing swung open, and the president stepped in. He was immediately followed by Robert Andrews, the director of Central Intelligence. Exchanging a brief nod with his immediate superior, Harper got to his feet and accepted Brenneman's proffered hand. Despite the circumstances, he wasn't surprised by the president's gracious behavior. He had never found Brenneman to be anything less than courteous and composed, regardless of the circumstances. Still, he knew it was forced, at least on this occasion. When he spoke, the man's voice confirmed as much. It was curt and carried a slight edge that hinted at his true level of anger and frustration.

"Take a seat, John," he said, without preamble. "Sorry to be so blunt, but if you don't mind, we'll get started right away. I'd like you to tell me what happened in Madrid. What went wrong? I thought we had this well in hand."

Harper couldn't help but hesitate, his eyes darting up to the ceiling, where the presidential seal was prominently displayed. He knew the Secret Service monitored the Oval Office with hidden cameras, a fact that never failed to bother him. "Excuse me, sir, but—"

"They've been turned off," Brenneman interrupted impatiently. "Back to my question, John. What went wrong in Spain?"

Satisfied, Harper leaned back. "It's hard to say, sir. Based on their initial surveillance, the teams we had in place decided that Ghafour was . . . better protected, more isolated than we first expected. There were very few ways to get to him, and it was determined that a straightforward approach—that is, a cash-for-information exchange— would offer the best chance for success. Especially given the time constraints."

"And whose decision was that?" Brenneman demanded. "Kealey's?"

"Yes, sir. He made the call."

The president leaned back, an impenetrable mask sliding over his face. "We'll get back to that later," he finally said. "For now, walk me through it. Explain what happened, from beginning to end. I need to know the specifics."

Realizing that Andrews had only offered up a preliminary briefing, Harper nodded and started in on a detailed explanation. He ran all the way through, starting from the time Pétain and her team had initiated surveillance on Ghafour, and ending with the aftermath of the improvised diversion on Calle de San Leonardo de Dios. To Harper's surprise, Brenneman didn't interrupt once, although his face tightened in anger or disapproval on several occasions.

When Harper was done, the president nodded slowly, thinking it through. "So in other words," he summed up, "all we took out of this was a single name. Is that correct?"

"Yes," Harper conceded, "but in truth, that was all we really expected. Remember, we were operating on the possibility that Kamil Ghafour might have no knowledge at all regarding these events. As far as I'm concerned, sir, we were fortunate to get *anything* useful out of him."

Andrews shot a warning look across the table, but Brenneman seemed to have missed the deputy director's uninvited candor. "I take it you've followed up on this man Mengal," he continued slowly. "What have you learned in that direction?"

"Well, Ghafour gave us the basics. Mengal retired as a general in the Pakistani army, and for a number of years, he served with Inter-Services Intelligence. That was a rumor we were able to quickly confirm. Obviously, we make an effort to keep tabs on people like that, and in Mengal's case, we've actually managed to amass quite a bit of information over the past twenty years. In particular, the contacts he developed over that time are worth noting."

"What do you mean by that?" Brenneman inquired. "Is there anything there to indicate why Mengal wanted to get Saifi out of prison? Or why he's working with him now, if that's the case?"

"There is no clear link between the two men," Harper conceded. "Mengal has ties to al-Qaeda, as does Saifi. That's one angle we're working, but that doesn't necessarily relate to this situation. The general has also forged links with the Afghan mujahideen, the North Koreans, the Iranians, and a number of Kashmiri rebels, many of whom once served under him in an official capacity. He may well have turned to the latter group if, in fact, he was involved in Secretary Fitzgerald's abduction."

"And that is starting to look more and more likely," Andrews put in. "The rebels could have easily provided the experience and firepower he needed to mount a successful attack on the bridge."

"That doesn't mean we can rule out the Pakistani Army's involvement," Brenneman reminded them, his voice taking on a cautionary tone. "As you said, Mengal spent more than twenty years in the service. His primary connection is to the army and the men he served with."

"That's a fair point, sir," Andrews said. "Again, we're pursuing all angles."

"What about Mengal's current location?" Brenneman asked. "Did Ghafour—"

"No, he didn't." The words were out before Harper could catch them. "Excuse me, sir. I didn't mean to interrupt."

"That's fine," Brenneman said, waving away the apology. "But do we have *any* indication of where Mengal might be? I mean, if he's disappeared into thin air, the name by itself won't do us much good."

"We're still pushing for a possible location," Harper admitted. He reached for his coffee. "The Agency is working hand in hand with the NSA and the National Geospatial-Intelligence Agency. A total of six KH-12 reconnaissance satellites have been retasked to pass over locations Mengal has been known to frequent over the past several years, including his personal residence outside of Islamabad. Unfortunately, the KH-12 does not have dwell capability, meaning it can't stay stationary over a given point on earth, and it moves in a low, fast orbit, so its value is limited in this situation."

"What about the 8X?"

Harper had expected the question. Before being elected to the highest office in the land, Brenneman had served five terms in the Senate, where he'd represented his home state of Massachusetts. In his fourth term, he'd served as the vice chair on the Select Committee on Intelligence, during which time he'd been instrumental in pushing for the development of the KH-12's successor. The 8X, a recon satellite developed by Lockheed Martin and first deployed in the spring of '99, possessed advanced optics that allowed it to travel at much higher altitudes while maintaining superior image resolution. It had infrared sensors, plus an adjustable dwell capability, which in this case wasn't strictly necessary, as it could be tasked to travel in geosynchronous orbit, or GEO. This meant that the orbital period of the satellite was exactly the same as the rotation period of the earth, allowing the 8X to essentially "hover" over one point on the planet.

The president knew all of this, just as he knew what dwell capability was. Everything Harper had said before was for the benefit of

Robert Andrews, whose expertise in the field of image intelligence, or IMINT, was decidedly limited.

"As you know, sir," Harper began, "the National Reconnaissance Office has only four 8X satellites in operation. Two more are undergoing repairs and won't be operational for another six to eight months. Given our limited resources, plus the low probability of finding Mengal through the use of image intelligence, the decision was made to keep them in GEO over areas of interest in Kashmir. It would be different if we had a firm location to lock onto, but since we don't . . ."

Harper didn't have to finish; he'd made his point clear, and Brenneman nodded his reluctant agreement. "Do we have assets on the ground?"

"Nothing worth bragging about," Andrews said. "Operating successfully in that area requires some very specific language skills, as well as a certain physical appearance. You need the whole package to pull it off, and people like that are hard to come by."

There was a slight pause; then Brenneman pushed forward. "But you do have some people who fit the requirements. Naomi Kharmai, for example. I assume she was brought into this, in part, at least, because she fits the criteria."

"Yes, sir," Harper said, shooting a quick look at Andrews. The DCI's face was remarkably composed; Harper couldn't tell if he'd mentioned anything about Kharmai's immediate past to the president.

Brenneman leaned back in his seat and ran a weary hand over his face. "Gentlemen," he said, "this . . . *situation* presents us with a unique problem. I've already met with Ambassador Vázquez. According to the Spanish government's initial figures, six people died as a direct result of this event, along with Kamil Ghafour. He was the sole enemy casualty; the rest were innocents. One was an officer with the CNP, the National Police. Another was a pregnant woman. She was killed in the blast on San Leonardo de Dios, along with a twelve-year-old child on his way home from a soccer game. Four more are critically injured."

The president paused for a moment to let that sink in. "It's a messy situation, and the problem is compounded by the fact that we—and by that, I mean the State Department—made an inquiry through official channels regarding Ghafour less than a week ago. The Spanish are curious about our possible involvement in this, and rightfully so. They're just testing the waters for now, but it's only going to get harder to deflect their interest as time goes by, especially if the body count continues to rise. Obviously, we cannot allow them to learn the truth."

Both Agency officials nodded, and Andrews voiced his agreement. Brenneman paused again, looking down at his hands.

"I understand the need for the actions your people took," he said. "The prospect of American intelligence officers being apprehended on foreign soil, especially while taking part in an operation of this magnitude, is simply unthinkable. It would undermine our ties to governments around the world, not to mention impugning my entire administration." He paused for a very long time, weighing his next words. "At the same time, what happened in Madrid today is completely unacceptable. *Completely* unacceptable. I don't know how to make that any more clear."

There was a long silence. Finally, Harper spoke up.

"Sir, I agree with everything you've said," he remarked, "and needless to say, disciplinary action will be taken against the people involved. Nevertheless, I feel that our people, Ryan Kealey and Naomi Kharmai in particular, remain vital to the successful outcome of this mission. The mission being, of course, the safe recovery of Secretary Fitzgerald."

Brenneman nodded slowly. "So you want them to stay on."

"Yes, sir," Harper responded, without delay. "I do."

"What do you think, Bob?" Brenneman asked, shifting his gaze. "Are you of the same opinion?"

Andrews debated for a long time, then nodded reluctantly. "Yes, sir, I am. Their combined track record speaks for itself. We can't afford to ignore their past success."

"Well, what about the ransom demands?" Brenneman asked after a moment, switching gears without warning. "Does that tell us anything more about the people who pulled this off?"

Both men considered that for a moment. A claim of responsibility for the abduction of Brynn Fitzgerald, as well as the abduction of 27 other hostages over the past several months, had arrived two hours earlier in the form of a VHS tape, which had been hand-delivered to the U.S. embassy in Islamabad. After an extensive interrogation—or at least as extensive as could be realistically expected in so short a time—it had been determined that the messenger was a blind cutout; essentially, he knew nothing of value. He couldn't even give an accurate description of the man who had paid him to deliver the tape. Still, he was being detained while the Pakistani authorities delved into his background.

The tape had been converted to streaming media, then sent to Langley via an encrypted file, where it was written onto a blank DVD. Brenneman had watched the recording in the Oval Office, along with Andrews, Harper, DNI Bale, and Stan Chavis. If nothing else, it was proof that Saifi had had a hand in everything that had taken place. It featured the Algerian terrorist standing before a white flag that bore the oval-shaped symbol of the Salafist Group for Call and Combat. Saifi's first demand had been quick and to the point: he wanted the release of 48 prisoners currently being held at Guantanamo Bay, all of whom were either Algerian-born or of Algerian extraction.

This hadn't come as a surprise to anyone. Neither had his second demand: a sum of fifty million U.S. dollars to be divided among forty accounts in banks known for their willingness and ability to block government inquiries. All of it was to be delivered within the next forty-eight hours, or Saifi would begin killing hostages. He had threatened to start with Fitzgerald, but Harper had immediately dismissed that part of the recording. The acting secretary was by far the Algerian's biggest bargaining chip, and there was no way Saifi would kill her until he had gotten what he wanted. On this point, they were all in complete agreement.

"Sir, there's nothing unexpected or unusual about Saifi's first two demands," Harper began. "Assuming Mengal isn't involved, Saifi could, theoretically, use the money to reestablish the GSPC, which hasn't been on anyone's radar for years. If Mengal *is* involved, then Saifi might still receive a portion of those funds. I doubt he really cares much about the prisoners . . . You'll recall that he hardly gave any instructions on where they were to be transferred, or how they were supposed to get there. He did, however, give extensive instructions on how the money was to be delivered. Saifi doesn't have a financial background, so obviously, he has someone advising him in that direction. More likely, Mengal—again, assuming he's involved— is the one calling the shots with respect to the second demand. He was a senior figure in ISI, so presumably, he would know how hard it is to wipe funds clean of electronic surveillance."

Brenneman considered that for a moment. "And what about the third demand?"

Harper hesitated. The third demand was the one that had thrown them all for a loop, mainly because it didn't fit in with what they knew about the Algerian terrorist. Before the tape ended, Saifi had demanded an immediate cessation to the forthcoming Indian-Israeli arms deal, pointing out that the sale of superior military technology to India would "infect the Indian people with the same grandiose, imperalistic dreams that have consumed the U.S. government for years." As with the money, Saifi had given specific instructions on how the cancelled deal was to be reported in the media. He'd picked out three major networks—DD National in India, PTV1 in Pakistan, and CNN in the United States—and insisted that the cancellation be reported on all three channels prior to July 18, the date the transaction was scheduled to go through.

"The third demand, sir, is not concurrent with what we know about Saifi's background. Nor does it make sense when one considers the aims of his group. In other words, it's completely out of character for him. But if Benazir Mengal *is* actually behind the whole thing, then it might make perfect sense. If that deal falls through, Pakistan will maintain the status quo, militarily speaking, and the Pakistani forces fighting in Kashmir will suddenly have a huge psychological advantage. We don't know much about Mengal just yet—I have people working on that right now—but we *do* know that he spent a decade with ISI in a senior role. If he still has some strange allegiance to his former service, I wouldn't put it past him to engineer something like this."

"Fair enough," the president said. He frowned for a moment, thinking it through. Then he looked up and appraised them both. "Gentlemen, I'd like you to take a hard look at that tape. We need to try to learn from it, and we also need to try and figure out why Saifi didn't use the secretary of state on the recording. That still doesn't make sense to me. But for now, let me return to the issue at hand, namely, what took place today in Madrid. The Spanish government is already asking some dangerous questions, and they've only just started looking. I have to know that there is nothing out there that could link us to this. If I'm going to deny it outright, I need to be sure it won't come back to us. That it won't come back to *me*."

"It won't, sir," Harper assured him. "That is the one thing you can be certain of. In the meantime, no one is standing still. The Bureau's team landed at Chaklala this morning, and they're already examining the vehicles destroyed in the ambush, as well as the site itself on Airport Road. With any luck, they'll have some preliminary observations by the end of the day. We can factor in whatever they come up with and go from there."

"Good," Brenneman said. He got to his feet, and the other men followed suit. "That's what I wanted to hear. Interagency cooperation on this matter is absolutely vital."

"Of course," Andrews said as he approached the door, Harper a few steps behind. "We're doing everything we can, sir."

"I'm glad to hear it." Brenneman paused just inside the door, which seemed to open of its own accord. He appraised them both in turn. "Gentlemen, I want hourly updates. Obviously, I want to see anything relating to the situation in Kashmir, but finding Secretary Fitzgerald remains our top priority. In order to do that, we need to find Mengal as soon as possible. As far as I'm concerned, nothing is more important than tracking him down. Is that clear?"

"Yes, sir," Andrews answered for both of them. "Perfectly clear."

CHAPTER 21

WASHINGTON, D.C. • LAHORE, PAKISTAN

Five minutes after the meeting was over, the two CIA officials left the building from a door on the south side of the West Wing. The air was oppressive: heavy, warm, and still. Mountainous black clouds positioned directly overhead seemed to promise rain, although the sun still broke through occasionally, spilling yellow light over the dark pavement. The surrounding trees seemed completely immobile, frozen in anticipation of the building storm. The two men began crossing the pavement toward the waiting Town Car, which was tucked in between a pair of black Chevy Suburbans. All three vehicles were running, and as Harper and Andrews approached, a number of security officers broke away from their idle discussions and climbed into the armored SUVs, preparing for the short drive back to Langley.

Andrews walked up to the Lincoln, and the driver's-side window slid down immediately. He spoke a few words to the driver, unbuttoned his suit coat, and handed it in through the window. Loosening his tie slightly, he turned and walked back to Harper.

"Hot as hell out here," he remarked, rolling his sleeves up over his thick forearms.

"Yeah, but it looks like rain, and we could use it."

"I hate this town in the summer," Andrews growled, looking up at the darkening sky. "The air is so damn thick . . . It's like trying to breathe underwater."

"August is just around the corner," Harper pointed out. "The worst is yet to come."

"My sentiments exactly," Andrews said. He seemed to brood for a moment before nodding curtly toward the east colonnade. "Come on. Let's take a walk. I need some air."

Having no real say in the matter, Harper ignored the verbal hypocrisy and fell in beside the DCI. They walked along the curved road until they reached the Jacqueline Kennedy Garden, which lay just south of the east colonnade. They entered the garden on the west side, following the redbrick walkway between strips of bright grass and beds of colorful flowers. Although the East Wing was visible through the vegetation, they were largely blocked from view by boxwood hedges and small trees. Harper knew that a number of marines and Secret Service agents were posted outside the building, but they remained out of sight. In short, they had complete privacy. They had walked for nearly five minutes before Andrews finally spoke.

"Did you know that Andrew Jackson planted some of these personally?" He gestured toward a cluster of small, well-kept magnolia trees. "A different time," he mused, more to himself than anything else. Still, Harper felt compelled to respond and muttered his agreement.

They continued in silence for a few minutes. Finally, Andrews paused beside a neatly trimmed hedge of American holly. He loosened his tie a little more, then wiped his brow with the back of his hand.

"John, nothing about this situation makes sense," he began, fixing his subordinate with a steady gaze. "The president made a good point in there. If they have her, why didn't they *show* her on the tape? That would have made a much greater impact than words alone, and let's face it: Brenneman might just pay them if it means keeping a tape like that out of the media. It's one thing to *know* she was kidnapped by terrorists, but it's another thing entirely to *see* it. It would be nothing short of a crippling psychological blow to the country."

"Maybe she's dead," Harper said quietly, gazing absently at a bed of pink tulips. "Maybe she was hurt in the accident and died once they got her away from the scene. Maybe that's why they can't show her."

Andrews winced. "Jesus, don't say that. I don't even want to consider the possibility."

"But it *is* possible, Bob. You saw the digital images, and you read the transcripts of the witness statements. The rocket that hit her vehicle did an enormous amount of damage. I mean, her driver was killed by the impact alone, as was her detail leader. The damage was mainly limited to the front of the vehicle, of course, and she was riding in back, but that doesn't mean much . . . There's still a good chance she was exposed to the shrapnel."

The deputy director paused thoughtfully. "On the other hand, if she *was* killed, they have no reason to keep that from us. They might as well take credit for it while the press coverage is still at its peak. That would at least pander to some of Saifi's supporters, which could help bring in some additional funding and arms, maybe even the backing of a rogue state. Besides, even without Fitzgerald, they still have plenty of hostages to ransom."

"I don't know about that." Andrews was skeptical. "We might pay him for Fitzgerald, but let's face it: we're not going to break with two decades of policy over twenty-seven civilians, especially since only twelve of them are ours to begin with."

"The Germans paid him," Harper pointed out. "When he took those hostages in Chad back in 2003, the government coughed up six million to get them back. You have to remember, Bob, Saifi has seen this work before. There's no reason for him to think it won't work again. At least, that's where I fall on the issue, and for the most part, my people agree."

"By 'people,' are you referring to Kealey and Kharmai?"

Harper caught note of the DCI's tone, which had suddenly hardened. "Yes," he conceded reluctantly. "Among others."

"Where are they now?"

"You know the woman initially tasked with heading up the teams over there?"

The DCI furrowed his brow, thinking back to his earlier briefings. "Something Pétain, isn't it?"

"That's right. Marissa Pétain. Apparently, she has family in the area. Her parents have a house on the coast. Cabo de Palos, near Cartagena."

Suddenly, the director's face lit up with recognition. "Her father is Javier Machado."

"Yes, sir."

"He was before my time, but I know his history. An accomplished case officer with an impeccable record, as I recall." He frowned slightly. "He had two daughters, I thought, both with the Agency."

"That's correct," Harper replied reluctantly, not wanting to get into that particular story at the moment. "Anyway, he's proving very cooperative, and that's where they are at the moment. Safest place for them, really. Until we can give them something useful on Mengal, there's no point in moving them around."

"And the rest of the watchers?"

"Most have already left the country. Their documentation and cover stories were good enough to get them out on commercial flights out of Madrid Barajas, even with the heightened security. We'll be moving the rest soon."

A long silence ensued, after which Andrews brought up the president's reaction to the events in Madrid. "He wasn't happy, John, but it could have been worse. I don't think he's had time to really consider what it will mean for us—and him—if the Spanish government learns what actually took place on the ground."

"Well, he doesn't have to worry. They're not going to find out."

"Are you sure about that?" Andrews pressed. "Can you guarantee they won't discover the truth?"

"You know I can't," Harper responded quietly.

Another long silence. "The president wants Kealey and Kharmai to stay on, John, so that's the way it will be," Andrews said. "For now, anyway. But they *will* answer for what happened today, and you'd better make sure they understand that they're walking a fine line. From what you've told me, as well as what I've read in their files, both have troubling incidents in their past. Frankly, their backgrounds don't inspire a great deal of confidence. The only reason they're involved at all is because you wanted it that way."

"I understand that. But as you told the president, you can't argue with what they've accomplished over the past couple of years."

"Yes," the DCI conceded reluctantly, "I did say that, and I meant it. But again, my patience is running short, along with my gratitude. Reel them in, John, or hand this assignment off to someone else. Even if it puts us further behind than we already are. We can't afford another mistake. Certainly nothing like what happened today."

Harper nodded and voiced his agreement, doing his best to appear reluctant. He didn't want Andrews to know that he was harboring similar concerns. In fact, his concerns were far worse, since he knew much more about both operatives than the director did. Still, he wasn't about to reveal the truth. The second he did, Kealey and Kharmai would be pulled out immediately, and they would lose their forward momentum. Like it or not, his best option was to let them see it through and hope for the best.

Andrews turned to begin making his way back to the cars, and Harper fell into step beside him. Thunder rumbled off in the distance, and the air seemed almost electric. As they walked, sprinkles started to spatter the path ahead, the first tangible sign of the forthcoming storm.

"One more thing," the DCI said. "I'd like to devote some additional resources to Kashmir. I'm talking about personnel, hardware . . . whatever we can spare. Before long, the president is going to shift his focus back to that situation, and when that happens, he's going to want some hard intel. You said six satellites were pulled from the NSA and the NGA to watch Mengal's known places of residence?"

"That's right. Six at last count. Obviously, they're being run out of the NRO." The National Reconnaissance Office was the primary government agency tasked with developing, building, and operating U.S. reconnaissance satellites. In the spring of '99, Harper had been seconded to the office, where he had served as a liaison officer for nearly a year. It had been a relatively boring, albeit enlightening, experience.

"How many of those satellites were diverted from the areas of troop movement in Kashmir? I realize we still have the four 8Xs over the area, but what about the KH-12s? How many were taken off?"

Harper hesitated, then said, "All of them."

Andrews shook his head in disbelief, but he was clearly resigned to the situation. "I don't like it. Retasking those satellites does nothing but limit our flow of information. I shouldn't have to rely on CNN for the latest developments. We're supposed to be ahead of the game, and right now we're playing catch-up.

"Still," he added, after a brief moment of internal debate, "that is a secondary result of the president's orders, so it's out of our hands. The way I see it, the only way we can get back on track is to find the general."

"That's how it looks," Harper agreed reluctantly.

"Then make it happen, John." Andrews paused to wipe his brow once more, then turned to face his deputy. "Make Kealey understand. Kharmai, too. They need to find Benazir Mengal, and they need to do it soon."

The Sheikh Zayed Postgraduate Medical Institute, so named for the famed sultan of Abu Dhabi, was one of several major hospitals in Lahore. It was a fairly well-administered facility, at least judging by the standards of the Islamic republic. When he'd first arrived in-country, Randall Craig had been surprised by the friendly, professional demeanor of the doctors and nurses who staffed the 286-bed hospital, though it had never occurred to him why this should be. He considered himself to be a reasonable person, a man open to cultures other than his own, but at the same time, he subconsciously harbored the same prejudices shared by so many of his fellow Americans. It wasn't a conscious bias; rather, it was something that lingered just below his active thoughts, a vague awareness of his own place in the world. A sense of entitlement, based on his nationality. There was a natural order to things, he had always suspected, and while he'd never stopped to really consider this point of view, it seemed to him that, for better or worse, the rank of nations was much like a food chain and that, as an American citizen, he was parked right at the top.

Regardless of whether this was actually the case, it was a comforting thought. Empowering, even. It was also a notion he found easy to reinforce in Pakistan, a country where the average citizen earned less than eight hundred American dollars every year. Of course, that sum went much further in the Islamic republic than it did in the States, but it was still a hard statistic to ignore. It was something that Craig had witnessed firsthand from the moment his flight had touched down in Rawalpindi. It never ceased to amaze him how the Pakistani people could make so much with so little. When he took in the poverty that surrounded him daily, he couldn't help but wonder how this country had managed to become a nuclear power.

Nevertheless, over the past couple of weeks, he had seriously considered cutting his work at Sheikh Zayed short. Ever since the announcement of the upcoming Israeli arms sale to the Indian government, the tension in the streets—particularly in the heart of Islamabad—had become nearly tangible. The abduction of Secretary Fitzgerald in Rawalpindi had brought things to a boiling point. In the

end, though, he'd decided against leaving. Pakistan and India had engaged in conflicts before, he reasoned, and it had never really
amounted to anything. Even the Kargil war in '99 could hardly be described as anything more than a cross-border skirmish. Hardly worth
fleeing the country over, he thought, especially since he was so close
to leaving, anyway. It had been ten months since he'd departed the
University of Washington for Sheikh Zayed on a yearlong visit, and he
was more than ready to get back. In truth, the first of September
couldn't come soon enough for Randall Craig.

He left the locker room on the ground floor shortly after eight in
the evening, pausing on the way out to examine his reflection over
the sink. A former girlfriend had once described his face as "kindly,"
though Craig had no idea what in the hell that meant. His lantern
lower jaw was completely concealed by a thick beard, which he'd
worn as long as he could remember, and despite a fair degree of worrisome searching, he had yet to find a trace of gray in his light brown
hair.

Overall, he was pleased with what he saw. At thirty-eight, he was
still carrying more muscle than fat on his six-foot, four-inch frame,
despite an appalling diet that consisted of two to three servings of
McDonald's a day. It was something he never remarked upon in the
presence of his patients, even though few of them—including the
very few who spoke fluent English—would have been able to decipher his strong Southern dialect, a remnant of a youth spent in the
soft, wooded hills of Etowah, Tennessee. The fast-food chain had recently opened a few restaurants in Lahore, and though the closest
was something of a drive from his apartment in New Garden Town, it
was well worth the trip. He simply couldn't abide the local cuisine,
which typically seemed to consist of overcooked rice and some kind
of rubbery, unidentifiable meat. Even the Pakistani version of
McDonald's was preferable to that.

Craig passed through the waiting area at a brisk pace, nodding to
a few of his colleagues as he approached the front entrance. Before
long he was making his way through the tightly packed parking area.
As he approached his vehicle, he was startled by the sound of squealing tires to his right. He stopped, then took a quick, unconscious
step back as a black van came to a sharp halt a few meters away. The
driver's-side door was flung open, and a young man jumped out. His
hair was askew, arms flapping out by his sides. He looked extremely

agitated, but despite his distracted state, he seemed to lock on Craig instantly.

"Doctor? Are you a doctor? I need help!" he shouted frantically. Half the words came out in fractured English, the rest in a language Craig recognized as Urdu. He'd made a genuine attempt to learn the various languages of Pakistan over the past ten months, but there were just too many. Urdu, Punjabi, Pashto, Balti . . . the list went on and on, and not one of them seemed to be common to all his patients. Despite his inner drive to succeed at all things, he could recognize a hopeless endeavor when he saw one. He'd finally given up back in January. As a result, he had no idea what the young man was saying. The only thing he caught was the word *doctor*.

"Yes," he said quickly, taking a few steps forward. "I'm a doctor." Thinking fast, he uttered one of the few phrases he knew in Urdu. *"Kyaa aapko angrezee aatee hai?"*

The man seemed to freeze, but only for a second. "Yes!" he shouted triumphantly. "I speak English!" It was almost as if he was just realizing he had the ability. "It's my brother. He's badly hurt. . . ." The man was babbling as he moved fast to the back of the van, reaching for the handle. "He was hit by a car. I saw it happen, but the car drove away before I could do anything. I didn't want to wait for the ambulance. Please, help me. . . ."

Craig moved forward instinctively, despite the warning bells going off in the back of his mind. If he'd thought it through a little longer, he would have realized that it didn't make sense. The emergency-room doors were on the other side of the lot and clearly marked. A person arriving with a patient would naturally try to get as close as possible to those doors before getting out of a vehicle. Unfortunately, the truth dawned much too late. As the rear door of the van swung up, Craig moved round the rear of the vehicle to get a better look. He froze when he saw that the cargo area was empty, except for a spare tire and a few ratty blankets.

Suddenly, he was wrapped up from behind. The same man who had drawn him in was now holding him in place, or at least trying to. It was a near-impossible task, given that he was much smaller and lighter than the man he was trying to control, but he was strong and determined. Craig shouted for help and started to struggle, but just as he was about to break free, the right side of his head exploded with pain. He had enough time to realize he'd been hit with something hard before the blackness moved in, his legs collapsing beneath him. He slumped forward, his limbs turning to water. He heard a hissed command in Urdu, then sensed a shadow darting in from the right, a person moving forward to break his fall. Then the dark tide swept over him, clouding out all thought, and the pain gave way to nothing at all.

CHAPTER 22

CARTAGENA, SPAIN

It was just after nine in the evening when Kealey woke with a start. Slowly but surely, his surroundings began to swim into focus. He lay still for a moment, trying to piece it together, and then it came back to him. Swinging his feet to the floor, he rubbed the sleep out of his eyes, aware of low voices drifting into the room. There was the sound of the wind as well, and as he stood and walked over to the open French doors, the brightly colored curtains rippled gently against the interior wall.

Stepping outside, he moved to the railing and put his hands on the waist-high bar of the balcony. Night had settled over the landscape, but small lights scattered round the perimeter helped illuminate the garden below. It was obviously well kept, a thick line of Spanish fir blocking the view of the road beyond. The trees were swaying in the cool, salty breeze moving in from the Mediterranean Sea, which wasn't more than a mile to the east. The towering pines were positioned just inside a black fence of wrought iron, where they framed a large square of grass. Although it was dark, the grass appeared as green as it would have during the day, the lawn luminescent in the clean white light.

A white aluminum table was centered on the grass, and two figures were seated there. One was a woman in her midfifties. Her dark, shoulder-length hair was touched with gray, but otherwise, she appeared far younger than her years. Her complexion was fair, her face remarkably free of wrinkles, and she was dressed in a pair of tan slacks and a green cotton cardigan.

The other person at the table was Marissa Pétain. Her dark brown hair was damp, shining wetly in the moonlight, and she was wearing a cream-colored blouse and a pair of wrinkled chinos. It was different clothing from what she'd arrived in; obviously, she'd taken the time to shower and change. The two women were talking quietly in French, but from where Kealey was standing, the conversation was barely audible. As he looked down at them, Pétain glanced up, as though sensing his presence. She smiled pensively and gave a little wave, but before Kealey could acknowledge the gesture, he heard a gentle tap behind him. He turned as the door opened slightly, a sliver of light creeping into the room.

"Kealey? ¿Estás despierto?"

"Yeah, I'm up. Come on in." The door opened a little wider, and a large man with dark features, unkempt eyebrows, and long, iron gray hair appeared in the doorway, his bulk drowning out the light in the hall. Born in Valencia in 1937, Javier Machado had graduated from the Autonomous University of Barcelona in 1960, before immigrating to the United States, where he'd earned a master's in economics at the University of Southern California, followed by a doctorate at Princeton. It was there that he'd been recruited by the CIA. He'd served as a case officer for more than thirty years, running agents in Mexico, Morocco, Algeria, Portugal, and France, among other places. According to Marissa Pétain, he'd spent the better part of that time trying to get out from under the shadow of his own father, Luis Méndez Machado, a famed poet who'd served a lengthy prison term for opposing the rule of Francisco Franco during the sixties.

Pétain had been unwilling to provide many specifics, but based on what she'd said in the car, Javier Machado had largely succeeded in this endeavor, having accrued a long list of intelligence coups during what could only be described as a stellar career. He had retired fifteen years earlier, after finishing up a stint as the CIA station chief in Lisbon.

Pétain had explained it all on the nerve-wracking six-hour trip from Madrid to Cabo de Palos. Although she seemed reluctant to speak of her father, Kealey had caught the reverence in her voice when she spoke his name. When they'd arrived earlier in the evening, Machado's eyes had lit up with complete adoration when he first caught sight of Pétain. He had embraced her fondly, as had his wife, Élise. On witnessing this warm reunion, Kealey felt vastly reassured. It was clear they had made the right move. He and Naomi were there with Pétain, which made all the difference. Machado had welcomed them into his home, apparently unswayed by what had taken place in Madrid, as well as by his visitors' role in that disastrous incident.

"Did you manage any sleep?" Machado asked. Kealey had noticed that the older man preferred to speak Spanish whenever possible, and he had made a conscious point to do the same.

"Yes, I did, thanks. Has Langley been in touch?" He had given Pétain the Globalstar sat phone once they'd arrived in Cartagena, and Kealey assumed she would have informed her father if Harper had called.

"No," the older man replied, shaking his head grimly. "Nothing yet. I think you are in some trouble, my friend."

"Tell me something I don't know," Kealey muttered. He crossed to the door and, keeping his voice low, asked, "What about Naomi?"

Machado shrugged uneasily, his frown deepening. "She has not come out of her room since you arrived. Élise tried to talk to her, but . . ." The Spaniard shrugged again and looked away. "It's your decision, but if you don't mind my saying so, I think you should leave it alone. She needs to work it out in her own time. Of course, it will not happen overnight. These things never do."

Kealey nodded slowly, a number of emotions racing through his mind, all of them bad. After procuring a second vehicle off the Prado Road in Madrid, they had begun making their way south to Cartagena, following Pétain's directions. The first reports had come over the radio quickly enough, but they had been sparse at best. For the most part, it was all guesswork, the kind of wild speculation employed by reporters around the world. As they turned off the E901 near Albacete, the reports began to firm up. It was then that Radio One had confirmed the worst: at least 4 people had been killed as a direct result of the bombing on Calle de San Leonardo de Dios, along with a two-year veteran of the CNP. Another 6 civilians were in critical condition at a local hospital, and two were not expected to live.

Kealey had been driving when the report came in, Pétain in the passenger seat, Naomi in back. When the announcer moved on to other news, Kealey could have sworn he heard a noise behind him— something between a groan and a choked sob—but he didn't look back. He simply couldn't bring himself to do it, because the truth was inescapable, and Naomi would know that better than anyone. She had set off the improvised device with the best of intentions, her goal being to help them escape the construction site. She had succeeded in this endeavor, but in doing so, she had committed an act that would haunt her forever.

To make matters worse, Kealey knew something that Pétain did not. Ten months earlier, Naomi Kharmai had taken two lives in an act of self-defense; at least, she had thought it was self-defense at the time. One of those people had turned out to be innocent. It was just one of the events that had contributed to her current state, but Kealey knew all too well how much it had changed her: he could see it every time he looked into her eyes. Now she had done something ten times worse. Kealey was trying not to think about it, but given her fragility prior to the day's events, he suspected that what had taken place in Madrid might prove to be her final undoing. The thought was hard to take, impossibly hard, in fact, since she had only been trying to help them escape, but he simply couldn't dislodge it from his mind.

Machado had said something, and Kealey snapped out of it, turning his attention back to the other man. "Sorry?"

"I asked if you would like a drink," the Spaniard repeated patiently, his hooded eyes giving nothing away. "You look as though you could use it."

Kealey nodded. "Yeah, I think I could. Mind if I take a shower first?" They'd arrived in Cartagena four hours earlier, and he'd fallen asleep without taking the time to get cleaned up. Now he realized that he probably looked as bad as he smelled.

"Not at all. Join me downstairs when you're finished."

"I'll be there."

Machado went out, and Kealey followed after gathering a few things from his bag. He had picked up new clothes and toiletries en route to Cabo de Palos. Pétain had done the same for her and Naomi. One of the operatives responsible for packing up the gear at the hotel had hung on to their bags and false identification, and was set to deliver it all the following morning.

On the way to the bathroom, Kealey slowed outside Naomi's door. He paused but, thinking better of it, didn't knock. He didn't want to intrude. As Machado had said, it would be better to let her broach the subject if and when she was ready. Of course, there were other things to consider, such as what he had seen in her eyes before they'd left the Sofitel Madrid to meet with Ghafour. He still didn't know how he was going to handle the whole situation, but obviously, he was going to have to make some hard decisions before moving forward with the op. He wasn't looking forward to that, but didn't see that he had a choice.

He took a long, hot shower, then dried off and returned to his room. After pulling on a navy T-shirt and a pair of dark jeans, he made his way downstairs, feeling considerably better. Javier Machado was sitting alone in the living room, the French doors open to the cool night air. A television tuned to CNN was flickering softly, the volume muted. The incident outside the construction site in Madrid was clearly the lead story, but Kealey had seen enough of the gruesome images flashing across the screen. Turning away, he moved to the doors and looked outside. Mother and daughter were visible at the garden table. They were still talking quietly, though they were too far away for Kealey to make sense of the words.

Machado gestured to a backlit alcove, where tumblers and various bottles of liquor were on display. "Help yourself, my friend. The cognac, sangria, and anisette are on the top shelf. Below you'll find sherry from Jerez, *pacharán* from Navarre . . . the very best that Spain has to offer."

"I don't suppose you have any beer."

Machado smiled wanly. "Americans . . . You're all the same. You have no taste for the finer things, but who am I to judge? You'll find it in the fridge. Kitchen is that way."

Kealey went into the kitchen and returned with an icy bottle of San Miguel, a local favorite. Taking a seat across from his host, he took a long pull, savoring the cool taste of the beer.

"Nothing like a cold drink after a long day," Machado remarked sagely. "Makes all the difference, doesn't it?"

"All the difference," Kealey agreed. He drank some more of the beer and looked around with genuine interest. The living room, much like the rest of the house, was lived in and comfortable. There was nothing sterile about it, which appealed to Kealey on a personal level; it reminded him of his old house in Cape Elizabeth. Rustic furnishings were scattered about, and warm light from a corner lamp illuminated a number of contemporary oils, including a large landscape that hung above the stone mantel. Of more interest to Kealey were the framed photographs standing directly beneath the painting. He'd glanced at them briefly before, but now he stood and walked over, beer in hand, to get a closer look.

"Ah yes," Machado said, standing to join him at the mantel. "The fruits of my misspent youth."

Kealey gestured at the first photograph, which was housed in a solid silver frame. "Do you mind?"

"Not at all." Kealey picked up the photograph and looked at it closely, a jolt of surprise passing through his body. The photograph depicted a beaming Machado standing beside a short, slender man in an army uniform. A very recognizable man. Kealey thought he must be mistaken, but when he glanced at his host, the modest smile on Machado's face seemed to confirm his first impression.

"This is you and Noriega?"

"That's right. Me and the general on the Panamanian coast, near Nata."

Kealey shook his head in disbelief, still staring at the photograph. "When was it taken?"

"The early months of 1984. March, perhaps, or maybe April. It's all a blur to me now."

"That would have been shortly before he fell out of favor with Reagan, right?"

"Right again," Machado replied, a note of approval in his voice. "He held presidential elections in Panama that October, the first in sixteen years. Of course, once he found out he wasn't going to win, he started manufacturing votes. You know what happened then, I'm sure . . . It was all downhill from there. The U.S. government actually backed him on paper until '88, but we—'we' being the Agency, of course—were making preparations to remove him well in advance."

Kealey nodded. Although he never actually claimed the title of president, Manuel Noriega had effectively ruled the Republic of Panama from 1983 to January 3, 1990, the date of his surrender to U.S. forces outside the embassy of the Holy See in Panama City. Although his reign over the country was relatively brief, many historians cited Noriega as one of the more remarkable leaders of the past half century. He'd gained favor and numerous promotions during the seventies by brutally crushing a number of peasant uprisings in western Panama. Having won his superiors' trust and respect, including that of his mentor, General Omar Torrijos, Noriega slowly began to engineer his rise to the top.

Throughout the late seventies and early eighties, Noriega worked to undermine his political opponents by any means necessary, and as the de facto leader of Panama, Omar Torrijos was a natural target. Although Noriega was never officially linked to the 1981 plane crash that killed Torrijos, few who knew the history of Panama's politics were in doubt of the general's culpability. A darker hint of Noriega's true nature was to come a few years later. In 1985, Dr. Hugo Spadafora— a resident of Costa Rica and one of Noriega's chief opponents outside the country—announced his intention to return to Panama. His goal was to actively oppose Noriega's regime by recruiting former *brigadistas* to his cause, the men and women he'd fought with in his earlier efforts to rid Nicaragua of the tyrannical dictator Anastasio Somoza. Spadafora held true to his word; he did, in fact, return to Panama, though he never had the chance to act on his ideals. He went missing on the day he returned, and later that evening, his decapitated body was found stuffed inside a U.S. post office bag. This gruesome discovery effectively silenced public outcries against Noriega from that point forward.

"Were you there when he was captured?" Kealey asked Machado.

"Yes. In fact, I flew back with him when he was extradited. I was there for all of it, even when two men from the State Department, Walker and Kozak, I think they were called, offered him two million dollars to go into exile. They had a luxury villa set up for him right here in Spain." Machado laughed quietly. "They showed him the pictures and everything. He refused the bribe, of course, because he knew he still had plenty of leverage. Remember, Noriega was an Agency asset from the early seventies right up until the time of his surrender. If he had wanted to, he could have made things very embarrassing for us. Later on, he did just that."

"Which only makes it more ironic that we turned against him," Kealey pointed out, "given our initial support for his regime, I mean."

"Yes," Machado said mildly. "The Agency does have a bad habit of backing the wrong horse. The same could be said of the U.S. government as a whole, I think. Saddam is the perfect example. He and Reagan were true *compañeros* during the Iraq-Iran war, the very best of friends, and look how that ended."

"Bin Laden could also be included in that group," Kealey murmured. "It's like we're doomed to repeat our mistakes."

"Perhaps, but that doesn't mean we should give up entirely. Back then, I believed that the Agency does its best to protect the interests of the American people. I *still* believe that."

"But you were born in Spain," Kealey protested, unable to suppress his curiosity. "You spent the first half of your life in this country. Why would you go to such lengths to protect U.S. interests? Why did you join the Agency in the first place?"

Machado shrugged. "Who knows? I was looking for adventure, I suppose. I was young at the time, much younger than you are now, in fact. It seemed like the thing to do, and besides, I was bored silly at Princeton. As to why I stayed on . . . Well, I can't honestly say. I've had plenty of time to think about it, though. A great deal of time to wonder what I could have done differently." A look of intense sadness crossed his face. "Believe me, young man, old age offers one plenty of time for regret."

Machado fell silent. Kealey felt like asking him what he meant by that, but then thought better of it. He handed back the framed photograph, and Machado replaced it carefully on the mantel. Then he walked over and retook his seat, Kealey following suit.

"And what about you, my friend?" the Spaniard asked quietly. He crossed his legs at the ankles, carefully swirling the contents of his glass. "I had a long talk with Marissa while you were sleeping. It seems that you've amassed quite a record at Langley yourself. And in a relatively short period of time, no less."

Kealey shrugged uneasily, unsure of how to respond to the gentle push for information. He had done his best to avoid the accolades his work had earned him. There were obvious reasons for his silence—he wasn't cleared to discuss 90 percent of what he did for the Agency—but there was more to it than that. Simply put, he was a private person by nature, and he preferred to remain in the shadows.

"You're reticent to speak of it," Machado said suddenly. He looked past Kealey, his gaze falling on the women outside. "Which makes sense, of course, but where Marissa is concerned, I have a personal interest. She is my only living child, and I love her dearly. I would do anything to ensure her safety. *Anything*," he repeated, his eyes flaring briefly. "Can you understand that?"

"Yes," Kealey said quietly, thinking about Naomi and how much she meant to him. "I understand that completely."

"Then you know how I would feel if anything happened to her. Much the same as you would feel if anything happened to the young woman upstairs, I imagine."

Kealey couldn't conceal his surprise and instantly went on edge. "What makes you say that?"

A small, knowing smile appeared on Machado's face, his black eyes glittering with the kind of insight that comes only with age and experience. "Forgive me, young man. Please excuse my direct manner, but it couldn't be more obvious. It's clear to anyone with half a brain that you love this woman." A small frown crossed his face, and he seemed to hesitate. "I wonder, though, if you are fully aware of just how badly she is damaged. That scar she bears is the least of it."

Kealey remained silent for a long time, unsure of how to respond. Part of him deeply resented this unexpected intrusion. He wanted to lash out, but that was an instinctive reaction, and he forced himself to set it aside. Thinking objectively, he slowly realized that no one was more qualified to dispense advice than the man sitting before him. No one had earned it more. He had read as much in Jonathan Harper's voice when they'd spoken earlier; the deputy director seemed to admire Machado enormously.

"I have a fair idea of what she's going through," he finally admitted, "but she won't open up. I don't know what to do. It's like you said earlier . . . If I push her, I'll probably just end up making things worse."

"That's a fair point," Machado said, nodding slowly, "but on the other hand, you need to know if she can go on, correct?"

"Yes."

"And I assume you achieved what you set out to do in Madrid."

"Yes."

"Then naturally, the Agency will want to put that information to some good use. If they call on you, and I assume they will, you'll need her help. But only if she *can* help. If she is focused on other things, she'll only slow you down, making it harder for you to accomplish your task."

"That makes sense, but—"

"You're going after the secretary of state, aren't you? You're going after Fitzgerald."

Kealey fell silent. He stared hard at the older man, trying to see past the wizened façade. "Did Marissa tell you that?"

"Yes, but she didn't have to." Machado drained his glass, stood, and moved to the open doors, gazing absently out at the women in the garden. His hands were clasped behind his back. "The Agency wouldn't have authorized your actions in Madrid unless the stakes were extremely high. In the present climate, the only thing that would warrant such drastic action is Secretary Fitzgerald's abduction. Do you have something to go on?"

"We have a name. Our people are running it now . . . We're waiting to hear back."

Machado sighed heavily; it was as if he was bearing the weight of the world on his shoulders. When he spoke, he did so without turning around. "If they send you in pursuit of this man, will Marissa be involved?"

The question caught Kealey off guard. "I don't know. That isn't up to me."

"But given your record, I'm sure you have a say in the matter," Machado persisted. He turned around, and Kealey saw that any trace of wry humor was gone; his face had assumed a business-like expression. Kealey couldn't help but feel that he was being sized up. "Kealey, I would greatly prefer to keep my daughter out of harm's way, but she is very good at her job. If you can't use Kharmai, you should consider taking Marissa in her place. She will not disappoint you."

Kealey hesitated, unsure of which part to respond to first. "I'm afraid I can't do that. There's a specific reason Naomi was brought into this. A few reasons, in fact, but one in particular."

"I can guess," Machado said. "The secretary was abducted in Pakistan, and setting aside the British accent, Kharmai is clearly of Asian descent. East Indian, if I were to hazard a guess."

"Exactly."

"And I assume she has some useful language skills."

"She speaks fluent Punjabi and some Urdu."

"Well, she seems to be the ideal choice, then. So you're on your way to Pakistan."

Kealey couldn't help but wonder how Machado was arriving at these assumptions, or if they were even assumptions at all. "It's a definite possibility," he conceded.

"I can help you." Javier Machado seemed suddenly eager, almost desperate, to offer his assistance. Even his posture was different. He was hunched forward in a strange way, and his stance seemed to emphasize the energy housed within his massive frame. It was a startling transformation, Kealey thought, given his calm, reassuring demeanor of a moment ago.

"I know a man in Lahore, a fixer of sorts," Machado continued. "He has many connections, and he can get you around without attracting attention. Anything you need, he can provide. And when it's time to leave, he can handle that as well. Should you find yourself backed into a corner, his services will be invaluable to you." The Spaniard let his voice drop a fraction of a decibel. "Perhaps more importantly, he knows everything there is to know about Benazir Mengal."

Kealey froze, unsure if he had heard correctly. "What did you say?"

"You heard me, young man. I can give you direct access to Benazir Mengal."

Kealey looked for his voice and managed to find it. "Have you shared this information with the Agency?"

"No," Machado said, his face turning suddenly hard, "and if you take this to them, I'll deny every word. I will work with you and you alone to find Mengal, provided you do one thing for me in return."

"And what would that be?"

"I want you to take my daughter with you." Machado leaned forward, his eyes flickering with a strange, unsettling light. "I want you to use her, but more importantly, I want you to bring her back alive. Let me be blunt, Kealey. I value her well-being more than you could possibly understand."

Kealey shook his head. "Even if I agree to this, there's no way I could—"

"Stop playing games. I know all there is to know about you and the things you've done. Remember, I worked at the Agency for thirty years. I may be out of the loop, but I still have a small degree of influence. Marissa didn't have to say a word, though she was good enough to fill in some blanks. I happen to know that if you want something, Jonathan Harper will make it happen, so there's no point in trying to play down your status." He paused to let his words hit their mark. "So . . . Do we have an agreement?"

Kealey stalled for a moment, pretending to think it through. Then he addressed the obvious point. "If your daughter's safety is really that important to you, then asking me to take her along seems pretty counterproductive. Whatever happens, there's going to be plenty of risk involved."

Machado smiled gently. "That's where you're wrong . . . Having her by your side is very much in my best interest. I have my reasons for asking this favor, of course, but I'm not going to share them with you. No offense, but you don't need to know more than what I've already said. At least not yet." He walked over to refill his drink. "As I mentioned earlier, I am well versed on your background, Kealey. I know that you were reluctant to take on your current task, and that Jonathan Harper effectively forced you into participating by dangling Naomi Kharmai in front of you."

There it was. Kealey sat back, stunned by the extent of the man's knowledge. He was too surprised to even be angry. *Who could have known that?* he wondered distractedly. He began running through the names in his head, but he could only come up with one. Other than Harper, who could have known? But why would Harper reveal that information, especially to Machado, who was supposed to be out of the loop? It didn't make sense. . . .

"I know you are anxious to put the Agency behind you," Machado continued gently, "and believe me, I want to help you do that. By finishing your assignment as fast as possible, you will only be helping yourself. Besides, what I said about Marissa was not a lie. She will, in fact, be very useful if you choose to bring her along. There are several reasons I want her with you, one of them being your record. You have a reputation for getting the job done, and I know that once you give me your word, you will do everything in your power to bring her back safely. As I mentioned earlier, her welfare is my only concern."

Kealey considered these words, dimly aware of a phone ringing off in the distance. "Assuming I accept your offer, what happens to Naomi?"

"She can stay here, of course. Or she can return to Langley. But if she stays, we will look after her well. You have my word. My wife is a former nurse, and she's very capable. Anything she needs, she gets. No exceptions."

Kealey sat back, thinking it over. His thoughts kept drifting back to Naomi's thousand-yard stare, the look she'd given him at the Sofitel Madrid. She was clearly into something, but that could be overcome. He knew how important her work was to her, and he honestly believed that in the end, it might prove to be her salvation, if she could find a way past the day's events.

On the other hand, if he sent her back to Langley in her current state, there was a good chance she would be forced out immediately, no questions asked. He simply couldn't do that to her, even though a small part of him was saying that might be the best thing.

"Okay," he finally said. "I agree to your terms. But I want Naomi to stay here."

Machado leaned back and let out a long, unsteady sigh; clearly, he was vastly relieved by Kealey's decision to accept his proposal. "You'll have to talk to her," he cautioned. "She might not take it well. You leaving her behind, I mean."

"That's the understatement of the year," Kealey said, "but don't worry. I'll give her a reason to go along with it."

"Good." Machado stood, as did Kealey, and offered his hand. Kealey accepted it reluctantly, still wondering what he was getting himself into. "I appreciate this more than you know. I'm sure my contact in Lahore will prove to be a valuable resource in finding Mengal. Just one other thing . . ."

"What?"

"This arrangement stays strictly between us," Machado said quietly. There was a hint of menace beneath his words, nothing pronounced, nothing overt, but just enough to trigger Kealey's internal alarm. "Not a word to Jonathan Harper. Not a word to my daughter . . . not a word to anyone. Make up any story you like, but it stays between us. *¿Entiende?*"

Kealey was about to reply when he sensed movement behind him. Turning, he found himself face-to-face with Marissa Pétain. She was staring at each of them in turn, a slight frown on her face, but Kealey didn't notice. His eyes were drawn to the bulky satellite phone in her right hand.

"It's Director Harper," she announced, breaking the awkward silence. She thrust out the phone, and Kealey accepted it without a word. He walked into the kitchen, feeling their eyes on his back the whole way. Then he closed the door behind him and lifted the phone to his ear.

"Yeah, I'm here, John. What do you have? Anything new on Mengal?"

"Plenty," the deputy DCI replied grimly, "but you're not going to like a word of it."

CHAPTER 23

CARTAGENA

Twenty minutes later, Kealey ended his conversation with Harper. He lowered the phone and stood there for a moment, thinking it through. Then he opened the door to the living room. Finding it empty, he walked past the couch and looked through the French doors, which were still open to the cool night air. Marissa Pétain was seated alone at the garden table. She was absently toying with the stem of her wineglass, apparently deep in thought. Kealey thought about leaving her to it, but she deserved to know what had been said, and he had questions of his own. Questions that couldn't wait until morning. Walking back to the kitchen, he popped the top off a fresh bottle of beer and went out to join her.

The evening air was cool on his face and arms, the slight breeze scented with flowers and fresh-cut grass. As he approached, she looked up quickly, clearly startled. When she saw it was him, she nearly came out of her seat. "Well?" she demanded. "What's happening?"

Kealey took a seat and placed the sat phone on the table. Then he started to explain, beginning with Benazir Mengal. The analysts in the Operations Directorate had worked with their counterparts at the Defense Intelligence Agency and the National Counterterrorism Center to build a complete profile of the former Pakistani general. What they had dug up was of considerable concern. His long-term association with Inter-Services Intelligence was a problem all by itself. To dissuade any one person from gaining too much power, military officers were never assigned to ISI for more than three years in their entire career. This standard had been put into place by Pervez Musharraf himself, but exceptions had clearly been made for Mengal, who'd spent nearly ten consecutive years as the head of Joint Intelligence North (JIN), the ISI section responsible for the disputed areas of Jammu and Kashmir. In that role, Mengal had worked closely with Kashmiri rebels—secretly, of course—in an attempt to track Indian troop movements, as well as to keep the conflict bubbling at a low boil.

And that was only the hard evidence. The rumors were equally insightful. According to a Pakistani major captured by Indian forces during the Kargil war, Mengal was personally responsible for the murder of a dozen Kashmiri rebels who'd been working as double agents for India's Special Frontier Force, an outfit created in 1959 with the assistance of the CIA. According to the major, who had narrowly survived the interrogation methods used by his captors, Benazir Mengal harbored no ill will toward the men he had killed in that incident; in fact, he'd been seen joking around with them prior to the executions. The way the Pakistani major had described it, Mengal was a man who had no special allegiance to his men or even to his country; he did what he did simply because he was extremely good at it.

Pétain listened carefully to Kealey's recitation, then leaned back in her chair. She blinked a few times, then pursed her lips thoughtfully, as though processing the information. Kealey watched her carefully, but he couldn't detect a hint of fear or hesitation, two things that would have caused him to reconsider his plans. She was simply thinking things through.

"That's an interesting point of view," she finally said, "but it begs the obvious question. If Mengal has no allegiance to anyone but himself, why is he mixed up in all of this? Why did he break Amari Saifi out of prison, and why did he orchestrate the abduction of Secretary Fitzgerald?"

"I've been wondering the same thing," Kealey replied. "But remember, this is just one man's opinion, and he shared it under duress. It may be the closest thing we have to a psychological profile, but it's far from conclusive. The only person who can really answer those questions is Mengal himself."

"Well, I suppose we'll just have to ask him. Has the DO had any luck in tracking down his known associates?"

"Yes. In fact, they've come up with an interesting theory. You know that the FBI flew an Evidence Recovery Team into Rawalpindi a couple of days ago, right?"

Pétain nodded. "They were sent in to start an extraterritorial investigation."

"Exactly. They've already completed a preliminary report, based on what they found in the remains of the vehicles, as well as their interviews with some of the witnesses. It was standard fare, for the most part, but they did construct a possible scenario that caught the Agency's interest. Apparently, a senior investigator with the NTSB accompanied the Bureau team to Pakistan." The National Transportation Safety Board is an independent federal agency tasked with investigating civil aviation accidents in the Unites States, as well as major accidents involving other modes of transportation. "Based on his initial assessment, the vehicle carrying Brynn Fitzgerald sustained damage severe enough to ensure serious injuries to *all* its occupants. As we already know, Fitzgerald's driver was killed in the attack, as was her detail leader."

"So, the investigator is saying that Fitzgerald was seriously injured in the attack?"

"He's saying it's possible, even likely. According to people who witnessed the ambush, Fitzgerald was carried away from the wreckage of her Suburban by two of her assailants. Not dragged, not escorted, but *carried*, indicating she may have been too hurt to walk on her own."

"So where does this leave us?"

"Obviously, they were trying to keep Fitzgerald alive," Kealey pointed out. "Otherwise, they would have shot her like they did Patterson. And if she was hurt in the attack . . ."

"Mengal would need to find someone to treat her," Pétain concluded. Her eyes widened in realization. "And he has plenty of connections. He would know the right man to turn to. A licensed doctor on his payroll, maybe, or a medic who used to serve under him."

"Exactly, and now we have a starting point. There's a man in Lahore who knows Benazir Mengal personally. If anyone can point us in the right direction, it's him."

Pétain frowned and stared at him warily. She was unsure of the story he was feeding her, Kealey realized. "Where did this 'man in La-hore' come from? I thought the Agency didn't have any reliable as-sets in Pakistan."

"That's what I thought, too, but Harper managed to dig someone up. I didn't push him on it."

Pétain seemed to accept this explanation, much to Kealey's relief. Harper had given him a list of possible candidates to check up on, in-cluding names and probable locations. All of them were based in Pak-istan, and the majority of Mengal's associates were located in Islamabad and the outlying area. As Pétain had just suggested, many of them were military-trained medics who'd once served under Men-gal, but with Javier Machado's offer of assistance, Kealey now had a more probable lead. As Machado had instructed, Kealey hadn't men-tioned anything about their arrangement to the deputy DCI. Harper had ordered him to take Kharmai and leave Pétain behind, but Kealey was going to do the exact opposite. He and Pétain would be able to fly once they recovered the passports they'd left at the Sofitel Madrid. One of the operatives tasked with watching Ghafour in Madrid had been instructed to drop off the documents in the morn-ing, then catch a flight back to the States. Kealey and Pétain would be going in a very different direction, and now was as good a time as any to tell her.

When he was done explaining it, she nodded her agreement. He was surprised at first by her willingness to accept his story at face value, but then he remembered that she had no reason to doubt him. After all, she knew nothing about the accord he had struck with her father.

"So what time are we leaving?" she asked.

"We have to wait for the courier, but once he arrives, we'll head straight for the airport and catch the first flight out. I don't want to waste any time."

"Fair enough." She fell silent for a moment, examining her empty glass. She pointed at his beer, which he'd almost finished. "Would you like another? It's early yet."

"Sure," Kealey said. As she stood up and went inside to fetch the drinks, he began working through a list of questions in his mind. He didn't know what Machado's angle was, but at the moment, Marissa Pétain was his best chance to figure it out.

* * *

They were on their fourth drink, and Kealey could see that it was starting to catch up to her. Over the last two hours, the conversation had been gradually shifting course, drifting away from work to more personal matters. He had been careful not to rush it, as he didn't want to seem too eager to change the subject. As far as he could tell, he had navigated the waters well. She was responding readily, and she wasn't acting overly defensive. At the same time, Pétain was not the open book he had thought she would be. She seemed reluctant to talk about her family, especially her father. Kealey couldn't help but think this was strange, given that she'd followed his career path so closely. There was something in her past, he kept thinking. *There's got to be something there.* . . .

She had just finished talking about her first assignment with the Operations Directorate, a surveillance op in Mexico City, when she suddenly paused and shifted uneasily in her seat. Sensing she was about to bring up something important, Kealey set down his beer and gave her his full attention.

"Ryan, I just want you to know . . ." She trailed off, fidgeting absently with a thin silver bracelet around her left wrist.

"Know what?"

"That I'm sorry about what happened today." She lowered her eyes, but it was a gesture of contrition, nothing more. She wasn't upset in the least. "I only meant to wound him. I didn't mean for it to turn out the way it did. What Kharmai had to do was . . . Well, that was because of me. I know apologizing doesn't change it. I know I can't even begin to make it right for her, but I don't know what else to say. I should tell her myself, I know, and I will, but I just . . ."

Kealey didn't fill the silence right away, as her words seemed to leave something out. Then it hit him: she hadn't expressed the slightest remorse for killing Kamil Ghafour.

Of course, it could be argued that she wasn't responsible for the man's death, since Ghafour might have lived with immediate medical attention. But Pétain had pulled the trigger, and as far as Kealey could tell, it didn't seem to be bothering her at all. It wasn't natural, and he felt a spark of concern; any way he cut it, he had to work with her for the foreseeable future, and he had to have some idea of her mindset.

"She went through something similar last year," Kealey found himself saying. "Naomi, I mean. She never really got over it. Truthfully, she shouldn't even be here."

"Maybe," Pétain said quietly, "but that was then, so I can't really speak to it. This is now, and I'm responsible."

Kealey looked up at the new tone in her voice. She avoided his gaze, looking into the trees. It was a long time before she spoke again.

"I didn't follow my father into the Agency, you know. I'm sure you must be thinking that, but it isn't true."

"So what was it? What made you join?"

Pétain pinched her full lower lip between her teeth, obviously wishing she could take back the words. But she had already said too much, and she seemed to know it. "It was my sister. I joined because of her."

"Your sister?" Kealey had looked at most of the photographs on display in the house. He hadn't seen any depicting a second daughter, and Machado hadn't mentioned her, either. Or if he had, it had been in an abstract kind of way. This was news to him, and his instincts were already telling him it was relevant. He leaned forward unconsciously, waiting for the rest of it.

"Her name was Caroline," Pétain continued awkwardly. "She was older than me by eighteen months. I was seventeen when she was recruited by the Operations Directorate. That was in the spring of '98."

Which made Marissa Pétain twenty-eight years old. Kealey would have pegged her as a few years younger than that, but her age made sense, given the fact that she had initially run the teams in Madrid. The Clandestine Service seemed to be getting younger every year, he thought wryly.

"She was an amazing person," Pétain was saying. Her eyes were misting over, but her voice was steady. "She would do anything for a friend, but she wasn't naïve. She was strong and independent. Smart, too. Incredibly smart, actually, but that was her way. She was just . . . really good at everything she tried. *Really* good." She let out a short, bitter laugh. "I know people always say that when somebody dies, but in Caroline's case, it was completely true. She studied political science at Georgetown, and after she graduated, the first thing she did was apply to the Agency. When she told us she'd been accepted to train at the Farm, my father was so *fucking* proud. . . ."

She choked on the last two words, then paused to wipe her sleeve across her eyes. Kealey was tempted to give her an out, but knew that he couldn't. He needed to hear the rest, no matter how difficult it was for her. He waited uncomfortably until she'd composed herself, and when she resumed speaking, her voice was low and strangely detached.

"It happened in Colombia, when she was on her first assignment. By the late nineties, the Medellín cartel had begun to fragment, along with its chief rival, the Cali cartel, and a number of organizations were rising up to take their place. The North Valley cartel was one of the bigger threats, and a number of American agencies—including the DEA and the CIA—were concerned by their lack of knowledge in that department. So the decision was made to send someone in on the lower end of things, just to get an idea of what they were up to."

She fell silent for a minute, lost in her own little world. "I suppose the NVC felt it had something to prove," she mused. "After all, it was the first real attempt to infiltrate the organization, so they had to make a statement, if only to dissuade another attempt. From their point of view, it probably made perfect business sense."

Kealey had heard enough to get the picture. "Marissa, you don't—"

"No," she said, holding up a hand to stop him. Her voice was calm but firm. "I want you to know. You've heard this much, so you might as well hear the rest."

She took a deep breath, then drank the rest of her wine in one fast swallow. Kealey waited patiently, trying to disguise his rising unease. He suddenly wanted her to stop where she was, to leave it alone, but he knew that she wouldn't. She wasn't the type to run from a painful experience; he could see that now. Clearly, he'd misjudged her right from the start.

"They killed her, of course, but that wasn't the worst part. I was a junior at Marquette at the time. I had just finished out the semester, so I decided to fly home for a couple of weeks. My parents met me at the airport, and when we got home . . ." She paused, bracing herself. "There were photographs inside the house. Someone had broken in and plastered pictures everywhere. On the walls, the refrigerator . . . They even hid a few so we'd find them later by accident."

"Pictures of your sister?" Kealey asked quietly.

"Yeah," Pétain sniffed. A few tears were working their way down her face, but she didn't seem to notice. "And not just after, either. They took pictures the whole time they were torturing her. They made a video, too. They left that playing on the VCR. We could hear her screaming when my father opened the door . . . It was like she was right there, inside the house."

"Jesus Christ," Kealey said softly. It was most depraved thing he had ever heard, and it fit right in with what he knew about the Colombian cartels. At the same time, it answered all of his questions. Machado's intense desire to shield his remaining daughter from harm made perfect sense now, as did Pétain's lack of remorse for the death of Kamil Ghafour. After what she'd been forced to endure, the lives of men like Ghafour must have meant very little to her. Kealey couldn't help but wonder how she'd made it through the Agency's intensive screening process. Her background alone should have raised enough red flags to keep her out, though he reminded himself that her father could have pulled some very long strings on her behalf.

"So now you know," she said, pushing her glass away. She looked at him steadily, and Kealey saw that the tears had already dried on her cheeks. He supposed she'd had plenty of time to grieve over the past decade, and it didn't take a genius to see that her grief had evolved into something far more dangerous. "Caroline's death changed everything. My mother handled it as well as anyone could, but my father was devastated. He aged ten years the minute he walked into that house, and he's never been the same."

"And what about you?" Kealey asked quietly. "How did you deal with it?"

"Me?" She looked at him evenly, her body completely still. "I joined the Agency."

She stood and collected her empty glass. "I know what this was about, Ryan," she said, catching him by surprise. He knew protesting would get him nowhere, so he simply sat back and waited. "This whole conversation. You came out here to learn something about me."

She paused for a moment, just watching him. "I can't say I blame you . . . It's important to know who you're working with. But now that it's all out in the open, I guess I should ask if you've changed your mind. So, do you still want my help?"

He looked up and studied her face for a long moment. As far as he could tell, she was completely indifferent. He could answer either way, and she would accept it completely.

"You'd better get some sleep," he finally said. "We've got an early start in the morning."

She smiled and turned to go inside. She'd only taken a few steps when Kealey called out, and she turned to face him.

"Marissa." He hesitated, but he had to ask it. He had to know. "The people who killed your sister . . ."

She shook her head, but she was still smiling, and there was a strange light in her dark brown eyes. "They never caught them, but I know who they are." She seemed incredibly poised, once again in complete control. "The Agency, for all of its faults, does not abandon its own. The men who were responsible were lackeys at the time. Now they're among the most powerful figures in the business, but that doesn't mean a thing. Not in the long run."

"They can't hide forever, is that it?"

Kealey instantly regretted the words. They sounded patronizing, and that wasn't like him at all. It didn't seem to make a difference, though, as her smile didn't falter.

"That's it exactly," Pétain said. "And the end may be coming sooner than they think."

With that, she turned and melted into the darkness. Kealey watched her go, and for some reason, he believed her completely.

CHAPTER 24

SIALKOT · CARTAGENA

The light was searing and shockingly bright, even through the opaque, fluttering shields of his eyelids. It burned into his brain, lighting the gray matter, illuminating every neuron, axon, and synapse between. The light joined the dull ache behind his right ear, the twin sources of pain coalescing, bundling right in the middle, preparing to radiate. The pain was intense, clouding out all thought. Dizzying, crushing, mobile waves of pain, and he hadn't even opened his eyes yet . . .

Randall Craig stirred, and his eyes snapped open. He pushed away the agonizing thump in his head, trying to think it through. An impossible task right from the outset . . . Christ, it hurt. He sat up, looked around, blinking away the confusion. The light wasn't as bad now, and it was warmer than he'd thought at first. Not fluorescent light, so it wasn't an office or warehouse. He was in a house, he realized, his impression confirmed by the comfortable surroundings. A scarred desk, built of sturdy oak and stacked with paper; a chair covered in cracked faux leather; small watercolors on two of the walls. A home office, maybe, but there was a bed. He was sitting on it now, a narrow bed with brass railings at the head and feet. Sitting up a little more, he swung his feet to the floor. The movement caused his head to thump savagely.

"Motherfucker," he groaned. He dropped his head forward, leaning over his knees, trying to stretch the pain at the back of his head.

It was too centered; he needed to move it around a little. He clamped his eyes shut and reached back, gingerly feeling the lump. It was big, but his hand came away clean. He looked back at the pillow and didn't see blood. He hadn't been consciously afraid, but something came off his chest regardless: the absence of blood was vastly reassuring. "Motherfucker . . ."

No blood, and his head was starting to clear. He tried to focus on those positive signs, wondering what they had hit him with. It was all coming back now; the little flashes of memory were starting to cooperate, the images lining up in the right way, forming a picture. He had been walking out to his car . . . He could remember the van, the frightened face of the young man. He could remember the pang of doubt, the little spark of uncertainty, but he'd stepped into it anyway, drawn in by the man's tangible fear. *Stupid, stupid, stupid.* Twelve American tourists kidnapped in the north, the secretary of state ambushed in Rawalpindi, abducted in plain sight of dozens of witnesses . . . He should have had his guard up. Should have been thinking. He started to shake his head before realizing his mistake, the pain thumping back into place. It was okay if he didn't move too much, but it was still there, like the worst part of a migraine. The part right before the peak and the slow ride down. He wanted to shake his head, the self-disgust like a living part of him. Should have been thinking . . .

He had to think now; he knew that much. *Okay.* He stood up, fighting back the nausea, and checked his watch instinctively. It was gone. He frowned; that didn't make sense right there. Why would they take his watch? It was a cheap, plastic piece of shit, worthless unless . . .

Unless they wanted to isolate him, to bar him from the outside world. He nodded to himself, ignoring the pain this time. He was pleased with his realization. There were no windows in the room. He had no idea what time it was; it could have been day or night. If they were trying to cut him off, they had done a damn good job.

He wondered how long he'd been out. What had they hit him with? Something hard, but the skin wasn't broken, so what was it? He shook his head sharply, ignoring the pain once more, frustrated with his wavering train of thought. Why had they taken him? That was the important question. There had to be a reason, but he just couldn't get to it. He was nobody special. He didn't have any famous relatives, and he wasn't connected to anyone with any real power. Basically, he was just another foreigner, and yet, he knew that the same could be said of the dozen tourists who'd gone missing over the past several months.

This had to be somehow related. But they had disappeared far to the north, Craig reminded himself, and from what he had read, they had been taken in groups in isolated areas. If he had been kidnapped by the same organization, why would they change their mode of operation so drastically? There was also Fitzgerald, of course, but he had absolutely no connection to the secretary of state, so that didn't make sense, either. What was it? What was the connection? He had to think. . . .

He pushed it aside; there would be plenty of time for that later. First things first. He had to know where he was. There was only one door. He walked over, his legs shaky beneath him, and checked it. Locked. He was tempted to pound on it. He wanted to call for help but knew it wouldn't get him anywhere. Instead, he turned and looked at the desk. There was a lot of paper. It was strewn about, obviously a work area. There had to be something there. A name, an address . . . something.

He checked the drawers first. Two hardcover books: an ancient copy of the Koran and a recent edition of *Gray's Anatomy,* both in English. *Strange to find the Koran in English,* he thought, but that was assuming he was still in Pakistan. There were a few other medical books, some written in English, others in Urdu. Otherwise, the drawers were empty. Frustrated, he sat down on the bed to think it through. He was still sitting there, trying to ignore the throbbing pain in his head, when he heard a sound at the door. Startled, he stood up, unconsciously bracing himself as the key scraped in the lock, and the door swung in on its hinges. . . .

More than 4,000 miles to the west, Naomi Kharmai sat on the floor in the small bedroom on the second floor. The room was pitch-black, warm, and quiet. She sat in the corner on the far side of the bed, her back pressed into the spot where the walls formed a right angle, her arms wrapped round her knees. The house was completely still; no one had moved for more than an hour. She was looking down, her eyes not quite closed. She was staring into the black emptiness, immobile, unseeing.

She had shed her tears, and though she had tried, she could not summon more. She was exhausted, but she could not sleep. The faces were too clear in her mind. Some were imprinted from the news coverage, the blurred, disbelieving features of the people out on the street. Their stunned eyes and gaping mouths. The others she had conjured herself, her guilty conscience summoning the faces of its own accord. Imagined faces, imagined lives, but as real in her mind as they would ever be. The happy face of a young woman, glowing with the thought of a child on the way, her first. The innocent face of a twelve-year-old boy, a child walking home after a football match. The wizened face of a widow in her sixties. All of them dead, stripped away before their time. Three others dead. Countless injured.

She was responsible. Not responsible in some abstract manner of speaking, like the general who authorizes the bombing of a target in some distant country or the executioner who pushes the plunger in the death chamber, but actually, physically responsible. She had killed 6 people, and for what? She just didn't know. She could never justify it, that much was certain. On the whole, the DCI was pleased; the Agency had been spared public humiliation, spared the need to explain the arrest of at least two operatives on foreign soil. Overall, the president was pleased; his administration had narrowly ducked an international incident, the kind that cropped up on a regular basis. The kind that would be forgiven in six months regardless.

For this, she had taken innocent lives. For this, she had killed a pregnant woman and a twelve-year-old child.

Naomi felt sick. Sick of her life and the things she had done. Sick of herself.

She had waited as long as she could. Groping blindly for the jeans she'd been wearing earlier, she dug into the pockets, finding the plastic Baggie by feel. She pulled out three of the tiny white pills, hesitated, then swallowed them dry. Her third dose in as many hours, too much, even for her.

She tipped her head back against the wall and waited for sleep or dawn, whichever came first.

CHAPTER 25

SIALKOT

Craig followed the armed guard down the narrow, musty hall, the walls crowding in on either side. A second man followed a few steps to the rear. He was also armed, and Craig had seen the wary, alert look on his face when he first stepped out of the room. Clearly, they expected him to fight or run, which he found interesting in a detached sort of way. Back in high school, Craig had read about the 1974 kidnapping of Patty Hearst, his chosen topic for a required book report. He knew about Stockholm syndrome and thought it was a bunch of bullshit—he just couldn't imagine empathizing with someone who'd kidnapped him—but now, walking between his captors, he wondered about the percentages. He wondered how many people tried to fight.

How many tried to escape.

He had considered it briefly, the instant the door first swung open, but he changed his mind when he saw the gun. Craig had spent his youth in the wooded hills of Tennessee. The place was a haven for Heston's acolytes, the kind of people who thought the NRA was a government agency. He had fired all kinds of weapons, dozens of handguns, shotguns, and rifles. He had never served in the military, and he'd never fired an automatic weapon, but he could recognize the simple lethality of the submachine gun the man cradled in front of his body, and he knew better than to make a rash, unplanned move.

The gun made him wary, but it didn't make him meek; he had expressed his anger with the stone-faced guard, who had simply repeated his first words: "Get up and follow me." Craig had tried arguing, getting nowhere, until he realized that the guard's English was probably limited to that one phrase. Finally, he decided to follow their instructions. Obviously, they had taken him for a reason; arguing wasn't going to get him released, and it might just get him killed. Better to wait and see.

They descended a staircase, their feet beating a soft rhythm on the threadbare runner, then turned into a second hall. They passed a living room off to the left. Craig glanced into the room, saw no one, and kept moving forward. The first guard tapped lightly on the door, received a response, and pushed it open. Looking at Craig, he tipped his head to the right, indicating that he should enter. Craig hesitated for a moment, then stepped forward, past the guard, and into the room. It was then that he got the shock of a lifetime, his eyes falling on the man seated at the kitchen table.

"Said?" He heard the name come out of his mouth, knew it was right, but he still couldn't believe it. *Said Qureshi, here?* It had been years since he'd seen the man. How the hell was *he* mixed up in all of this?

The Pakistani doctor stood and greeted Craig with a slow, sad nod of his head. His mannerisms were polite but grim; clearly, he wanted to apologize for what had happened but was afraid to do so. "Randall."

Craig wasn't sure what to ask first. He looked to the other person in the room, a squat, stocky man with a full head of wiry black hair. He was leaning against the oven, neat in a tailored dress shirt, dark slacks, and a pair of thick-soled boots. The boots looked vaguely military, like something that might belong to an old soldier. And that was what the man looked like, Craig realized. A soldier. But not just any soldier. His gaze was calm and commanding, and there was a considerable intelligence behind the dark brown eyes. *A man with a good mind and a laborer's build,* Craig decided. As he looked on, the Pakistani pushed away from the oven with his hips, walked forward, and stopped. He did not offer a hand.

"Randall Craig?"

"Yes . . . ?"

"Do you know who I am?"

Craig studied the older man for a half a minute, thinking back to newscasts and faces he'd seen on the street. Doctors he'd met at various clinics around the country. Members of the secretariat he'd met on a brief visit to Aiwan-e-Sadr, the presidential palace in Islamabad. Nothing was coming to mind. "No."

The older man stared at him for another few seconds, then nodded in satisfaction. "You've been brought here against your will," he stated in cultured English. His voice was gravelly, rough, but somehow distinguished; he reminded Craig of a professor he'd once had at Vanderbilt, a brilliant man with a lifelong two-pack-a-day habit. Ironically, the year Craig had graduated from medical school, the professor had been on the short list of nominees for the Nobel Prize in Medicine. "For that, I apologize. Believe me, you would not be here if it wasn't important."

Craig started to ask a question, glanced at Qureshi, and thought for a minute. "Who are you?" he finally asked, steering his words to the older man.

"My name is not important. Believe me, in the long run, it is better for you if you do not know."

Craig nodded, not buying a word of it. *Believe me* . . . He'd used that phrase twice in a row. Craig had lowered his defenses for a second on seeing Qureshi, but now they rolled back into place, like a steel shutter sliding down the front of a street-level store. "What the hell am I doing here?"

"We need your help," the older man said simply. "Said has agreed to perform an operation for us. He requires your assistance. We need you to help him—that part, I regret to say, is not an option—but once you are done, you will be released. You have my word on it."

Craig looked at Qureshi, watching for some sign. The man looked nervous but composed, as though he were biding his time. *Good man,* Craig thought. *Wait for the right time. Wait for your chance.*

He knew the Pakistani doctor well. They had met during a weeklong seminar at the University of Chicago, and they had hit it off over a long weekend on the town. A year later, in 1995, they'd ended up working together at the University of Washington, Qureshi on the tail end of a yearlong visit. Qureshi, Craig had learned in one of Seattle's most raucous bars, was quick to flaunt some of Islam's more stringent rules, but he was a good man and an excellent doctor. They had made a strange pair, Craig knew, the Tennessee farm boy turned anesthesiologist and the small, mild-mannered Pakistani, but their friendship had flourished in the face of their colleagues' skepticism, even if it had not survived Qureshi's move back to London.

Through the usual channels, Craig had heard of Qureshi's minor disgrace at Guy's Hospital. There had been rumors of drinking and medical malpractice, but Craig had never taken them seriously; anything could happen during a surgical procedure, and often did. There was a good chance that Qureshi was not even responsible for the incident that had killed his career and a young boy on the same table. In short, he knew Said Qureshi as well as he knew any man, and there was no way he could be mixed up in all of this. At least, not of his own volition.

Craig looked back at the older man, his skepticism obvious. "You'll release me if I help you? Just like that?"

The man nodded solemnly, his thick, square hands clasped over his ample midsection. "You have my word," he said again.

Which didn't mean shit to Randall Craig. If this man was behind the kidnappings in the north and the attack on Brynn Fitzgerald's motorcade—and Craig was fully convinced that he was—then the man was a killer. There was no way he would release two people who'd seen his face.

Still, there was no point in resisting. Not yet, anyway. Better to let them see what they wanted to see, namely, complete and total submission.

Craig let his shoulders drop a fraction of an inch in defeat, a resigned expression sliding over his face. He looked at Qureshi and thought he caught a glimpse of defiance in his old friend's eyes. He didn't have to ask why he was there. If Qureshi was going to undertake a serious procedure—and it had to be serious to go to this amount of trouble—he would need someone to put his patient under.

"What's the situation?" asked Craig.

Qureshi let out a shaky sigh and looked away. Finally, he looked back, his composure restored. "It's better if I show you."

He stood and turned to a second door leading out of the kitchen. He opened it, stepped out. Craig looked at the older man, who nodded and indicated for him to follow. Craig crossed the tile, his apprehension growing; something about Qureshi's last expression was sticking with him. He felt a little shaky himself as he followed the small Pakistani through the living room. They skirted a dusty grand piano and entered another hall. Craig had not seen the outside of the house, but he could tell it was large, judging by the sheer number of rooms they had passed through. It also had a vaguely British feel to it, something he couldn't quite put his finger on.

Turning right now, passing a dark room the size of a coat closet, Craig glanced to the right and saw the outline of a ceramic sink and a tray full of instruments. His stomach tightened inexplicably. He had seen far worse than a tray full of sterilized instruments in his thirty-eight years, but something about the way it was sitting there in the dark made him feel distinctly uncomfortable. It was like an omen of some kind, a sign of bad things to come.

There were two guards outside the door, both standing ramrod straight, both holding stubby black submachine guns. Qureshi eased between them and opened the door, then stepped into the room. Craig followed, sensing the stocky Pakistani was a few steps to his rear. He stopped just inside the threshold, more out of surprise than anything else.

The room was large and square. Unlike the rest of the house, which was warmly lit, the surgical suite was thrown into stark relief by harsh fluorescent lights that ran the length and width of the plaster ceiling. The floor was a light blue tile with cement-based grout, easy to clean and maintain. The instruments common to all surgical theaters were clearly visible: a portable Medtronic defibrillator; an aging Hewlett-Packard EKG, the monitor sitting nearby; a transport ventilator with a cracked plastic shell. There was also an array of tools that anyone on the street could identify: an IV pole with 2-inch swivel casters, blood pressure cuffs, a box of surgical gloves. There was a scrub sink directly opposite the door and, to the left, a piece of machinery that Craig recognized immediately. He guessed that it had been purchased specifically for this procedure; if Qureshi had frequent need of an anesthesiologist, he would also have access to one, and he wouldn't have needed Craig.

His appraising eye took note of the quality—judging by the array of medical supply stickers that lined the base, it was a refurbished model—but he had used the Drager before, and as long as it worked, it would get the job done. The Drager Narkomed 4 had been one of the better anesthesia machines available when it first hit the market back in the late nineties. Now it was considered hopelessly outdated, at least in the States. In Pakistan, it still represented the best of modern medicine.

Craig could have dealt with far worse. Over the past ten months, he had learned how to make do with substandard equipment, and the Drager was anything but. The surgical table was off to the right, a simple, stainless-steel contraption with a circular base and hydraulic hand cranks. Twin Burton lamps were mounted over the table, a total of eight bulbs lighting the patient below.

The patient . . .

Qureshi was standing at the head of the table, partially blocking Craig's view. He walked forward, took a single step to the left, and looked down. He saw the woman's face and experienced that brief moment of recognition. Then came the split second of complete inaction before his instincts took over. He took a fast step back, his hands coming up to ward off the sight.

"Oh, fuck," Craig heard himself say. His eyes went wide, and he took another quick step back, his right arm pointing accusingly at the table, as if he were the first to figure it out. "Jesus Christ, do you know who that is?" *A stupid question,* he realized a split second later, but he continued, anyway. "That's the fuckin' . . ."

Qureshi was pulling him off to the side, pushing him into a chair. It was a considerable effort, given his small frame. The older Pakistani was standing next to the door, subtly blocking the only exit. Craig heard himself protesting, swearing, but he couldn't seem to stop. His mind was moving in a million directions at once, and part of him was saying, *You knew what you'd find when you walked in.* He ignored that part, reminding himself that he *couldn't* have known. . . .

"That's Fitzgerald," he blurted out. He was still pointing the accusing finger. "That's the goddamn secretary of state. The whole world is out looking for her, Said, right now, as we speak. What the hell have you done?" He whirled on Qureshi, shaking his head, his whole body trembling. "What the hell have you done? I can't. . . ."

"You will," someone said. The hard voice came from the door. Craig looked over, eyes wild. Qureshi said nothing, just looked at the floor. "You can and you will," Mengal reminded them. "She is your patient. You are both responsible, and you will fix what is wrong with her."

"No way," Craig mumbled. "No fucking way. I'm not going to—"

Mengal was already crossing the floor, coming up from the rear. His left hand moved in a blur, snatching the hair at the base of Craig's neck. His right hand came up, and he shoved the muzzle of a snub-nosed .38 into the right side of the doctor's temple. Craig froze at the touch of the gun, his mind sharpening, narrowing with the nearness of death.

"You listen to me," Mengal hissed, his words cutting the cool, quiet air in the suite. Qureshi froze along with Craig; on the table, Brynn Fitzgerald remained motionless. She had barely stirred in thirty hours. "You will do what you were brought here to do. You will save this woman's life. If you don't, I promise you now, you *will* share the grave you dig for her."

He shoved Craig's head forward, releasing his grip at the same time. The pain was intense, so close to his earlier injury, but Craig was oblivious. He was too stunned to even react. The woman's face was stuck in his mind, pale, calm, so unnaturally still . . . He just sat there, trying to see a way out of it.

The footsteps were fading behind him. He heard voices, a harsh, rapid exchange of Urdu. For the moment, he and Qureshi were alone in the room. Qureshi crouched before him, so their eyes were level. His expression was one of limitless sorrow.

"You gave them my name," Craig said in a monotone. It was hard to know how he meant it. "You told them where to find me."

Qureshi shook his head, but it wasn't quite a denial.

"Who is he?"

"His name is Mengal," the Pakistani murmured. "Benazir Mengal. He was a general in the Pakistani Army. He's killed many people, and he's behind everything that's been in the news. The disappearance of those climbers on the Karakoram, the ambush of Fitzgerald's vehicle . . . everything."

"What about me, Said? Why am I here?"

Another hesitation. "You have to understand," Qureshi began weakly, "I wasn't given a choice. They were going to—"

"What's wrong with her?" Craig cut in. His face was red, his tone suddenly harsh. He was embarrassed, Qureshi realized, ashamed that he'd allowed Mengal to get on top of him. Ashamed that he'd been bullied into submission.

"Blunt force trauma sustained in the attack on her car. She had a partial pneumothorax of the left lung, but I've already put in a chest tube. That was the lesser injury."

"So . . . ?"

"So she needs a pericardial window," Qureshi said quietly, "and she needs it soon. Preferably within the hour."

Craig had only briefly surveyed the equipment in the room, but he didn't have to look to know that Qureshi didn't have access to a digital EMI. "You don't have a—"

Qureshi waved it away, slightly annoyed. "It's a physiologic diagnosis . . . I don't need a CT scan to see the obvious." He quickly went over his earlier observations: the abnormal blood pressure reading, the J-waves on the EKG, the specific complaints Fitzgerald had made when she was still lucid. "She's sedated at the moment, but I need you to put her under all the way. I have everything you need. We can start as soon as you're ready."

"How do you—"

"I wrote the list out myself, and Mengal sent his people to pick up the items. It's all here, ready and waiting. I've checked everything personally."

Craig nodded slowly. He could see that Qureshi had sold him out, had provided them with his name, but he couldn't summon the anger he should have felt. They would have put pressure on him, and while he wasn't a coward, Qureshi wasn't the kind of man to fight back. At least, not unless he was facing imminent death. Craig couldn't blame him for what he'd done.

Craig looked up, directly into the other man's deceptively placid eyes. "They want her for propaganda value, Said. In the end, they'll probably kill her. And if they're willing to kill her, we don't stand a chance. You must know that."

"Yes, I do." Qureshi seemed to hesitate. "But I can help her, and for that reason alone, I have to do as they ask. I can't walk away from that responsibility."

Craig didn't alter his steady gaze, just gave a short, understanding nod. "So you're going to operate. Then what?"

Qureshi smiled in a resigned kind of way, but he never broke eye contact. "I'm not a fighter, but I won't make it easy. I don't want to die, but they are all over the house, the grounds, and one of them . . ."

"Yeah?" Craig was intrigued; Qureshi had gone away for a few seconds there, an expression of pure, unadulterated fear crossing his dark face. "One of them what?"

Qureshi shuddered and said, "One of them is the devil himself."

CHAPTER 26

CARTAGENA

Dawn was slipping steadily over the landscape, ocher-colored light pouring into the room on the second floor of the house. Lying on his back in bed, still fully dressed, Kealey stared out the window, his view limited to the tops of the dark firs that shielded the house from the road. He had been awake for most of the night, unable to sleep. His mind was too occupied with all that had happened. His disconcerting conversation with Javier Machado was weighing heavily on him, as were Marissa Pétain's startling revelations regarding the death of her older sister. There was a lot of history there, much of it wrapped up in the Agency, and while Kealey had heard the facts, he was worried about each person's underlying motivations. For Pétain, it seemed pretty straightforward. She wanted revenge for what had happened to her sister in Colombia. Machado's goals were not nearly as clear, which troubled him deeply.

Marissa Pétain's desire for revenge was something that Kealey could understand. He'd heard it said that revenge didn't accomplish anything, that in the end, it only made the pain more acute. He didn't believe that. Revenge was not a pure motivation, but when applied to a specific task or goal, it could provide one with the strength and clarity of mind needed to accomplish almost anything. Kealey knew this was true because he had gone through it himself, and in Pétain, he saw that same kind of focused intensity. She wanted the Colombians, but to get a crack at them, she would have to prove herself.

That was what she was doing now, Kealey suspected: carving a niche for herself in the DO, waiting for the right time and the seniority she would need to initiate another move against the North Valley cartel. Kealey didn't think she'd have to wait long. Diego Sanchez-Montoya, one of the principal leaders of the NVC, had been a mainstay on the FBI's most wanted list for years. The Agency would get a lot of mileage out of a successful undercover operation in Colombia, especially if it managed to bring Sanchez-Montoya down.

Javier Machado, on the other hand, was completely unreadable. Why was he so intent on keeping his daughter with Kealey? They had never met before, so why the strange degree of trust? And how did he know about Benazir Mengal? The answer to the third question seemed obvious: Pétain had brought her father into the loop the previous day, while Kealey was sleeping. But how did Machado *know* Mengal? And who was this man in Lahore? Kealey just couldn't be sure. As troubling as the whole situation was, though, and as much as it deserved his attention, he couldn't focus on it. He was far more concerned by what had happened in Madrid. More specifically, he was worried about what Naomi had done, as well as the effect it was clearly having on her.

He had wanted to speak to her the night before, after Pétain had gone to bed, but he just couldn't bring himself to knock on her door. He'd told himself that it was too late, that their conversation would likely dissolve into an argument, which would wake everyone up, but that wasn't the truth. The truth was that he didn't know what to say to her. Before he'd been drawn into the Agency by Jonathan Harper, Kealey had served in the army for eight years. In all that time, he had never killed a noncombatant. He knew that might not be strictly true. He'd fought in Bosnia, Kosovo, and the Gulf, and some of those battles had taken place in heavily populated urban areas. It was possible that one of his rounds might have gone astray, but he didn't know of a specific incident, and he felt reasonably sure that the rounds he'd fired had hit their intended targets and nothing else.

Naomi, on the other hand, knew exactly what she had done; there was just no escaping it. She had killed 6 innocent people in one fell swoop. Not intentionally, of course—in fact, her actions had been purely selfless—but Kealey knew that didn't make a difference. At least, it wouldn't make a difference to her. It didn't help matters that she had killed another innocent person ten months earlier. Kealey didn't have to remember how hard that had been for her, because he could see it every time he looked at her. She was still trying to come to terms with what she had done, and that had been *one* person. . . .

And now this.

He rolled off the bed, got to his feet, and padded into the adjoining bathroom. He turned on the shower and climbed in without waiting for the water to heat up. Three minutes later he was out and reaching for a towel. He wiped some steam from the mirror and looked at his face, wondering about the beard. He'd been growing it out for months now. It wasn't exceptionally long, falling a few inches beneath his chin, but it served to conceal his age and the shape of his face. He thought about keeping it, knowing it would help him to blend in when he and Pétain landed in Pakistan.

But he wouldn't be able to pass as a native, anyway, and they still had to get out of Spain. The beard, he realized, would be remembered by witnesses in Madrid, noted on the incident report, and included in the sketches the CNP would have undoubtedly drawn up and distributed to the airports. Better to take it off.

Once he'd shaved and rinsed off his face, he went back to the bedroom and dressed, pulling on a pair of dark jeans and a charcoal T-shirt. Stepping into the hall, he paused for a moment, gauging the sounds of the house. It was early yet—just after eight—but he could hear clanking dishes coming from the bottom of the stairs, as well as the sound of running water. Walking down the hall, he paused outside Naomi's door. That was where the sound was coming from, he decided; she must be in the shower.

He hesitated, thinking about it. Then he tried the handle. The door was locked, but it was a simple lock; he could pick it in twenty seconds. If he wanted to.

Did he want to? He thought back to the look she'd given him at the hotel in Madrid. Back to what he had seen in her eyes. She had been so distracted, but it was more than the post-traumatic stress he knew she was dealing with. The PTSD wasn't a secret; he'd known about that for a long time, and so had the psychiatrists at Langley. It wasn't the kind of thing she could hide. What he had seen at the hotel was something else entirely, and he had to know where it was coming from, even though he'd decided to leave her behind.

It was just that simple: he had to know.

Having made his decision, he turned to walk back to his room, thinking about what he could use to pop the lock. He had taken two steps when he paused, then turned and went back to the door. His own door had done that the night before, he remembered, sticking when he'd tried to open it. It could have been something as simple as a slightly warped frame, but if it was like that on his, then maybe . . .

He was right. Her door came open with a little bump of his shoulder, and he was in.

The bathroom door was closed, the sound of running water louder inside the bedroom. She'd removed her clothes before going into the bathroom; her underwear was lying outside the door, along with a plain white blouse and a pair of dark pants. Pétain had picked up the outfit for her en route to Cartagena; Naomi must have changed into it the day before, while he had been sleeping in the next room. Ignoring the small pile, Kealey went round the side of the bed and found what he was looking for: the clothes she'd been wearing in Madrid.

The shower was still running as he picked up her jeans. They were stiff with dried sweat, the denim covered with concrete dust and spots of dried blood. He checked the pockets quickly. There was a tube of cherry-flavored ChapStick in the left pocket, along with a few Euro coins and a receipt from a coffee shop. In the right pocket he found a plastic Baggie. He pulled it out and found it empty except for half a tablet. He tipped it out of the Baggie, held it between his thumb and forefinger, and examined it closely. Had it been whole, it would have been about the size of the nail on his little finger. It was white with numbers on one side: a four over a three and what might have been another three. He didn't recognize it.

Feeling a sudden draft, he looked up. Naomi was standing in the doorway to the bathroom, a white towel wrapped around her too-thin body. Her jet-black hair was damp, clear drops sparkling on her bare shoulders. The shower was still running behind her.

"I heard a noise," she said. Her dark green eyes were flashing, and her stance was confrontational; she was ready to fight. "What are you—"

She broke off, seeing the Baggie in his hand. He was caught, but so was she, and he wasn't about to apologize. Lifting the tablet so she could see it, he said, "What is this? Codeine?"

She folded her arms across her chest, her face working. "That's none of your business."

He flared instantly, taking a quick, menacing step forward. "Naomi, you—"

"It's morphine." She took a step back and looked away, her mouth tightening. Her eyes were dry, but as Kealey watched, her face changed, her expression shifting from mild anger to complete despair in the blink of an eye. And just like that, it was gone again. It shook him to the core, but the transformation happened so fast, he couldn't be sure he had seen it at all.

"Where did you get them?" he asked quietly, holding the remains of the last tablet down by his side. "Were they prescribed?"

She nodded slowly without looking at him, but it wasn't a yes; she was simply considering the question. Wondering if she should lie, maybe. "Why does that matter?"

"It matters, Naomi. If you—"

"No," she said, her voice barely audible. "They weren't prescribed. I got them from a friend in Washington. She's a physician."

"Some friend." The anger was still there, but he was trying to think past it, trying to weigh the implications. "Does Harper know?"

She looked up reluctantly, meeting his eyes. "I don't know."

"He knows." Kealey felt his hands curling into fists, the muscles tightening in his arms. It was a completely involuntary reaction; he just couldn't control the anger rising inside of him. "He fucking knew the whole time, and he sent you, anyway. Tell me I'm wrong."

She shook her head, but he was right, and they both knew it.

"How bad is it?" He held up the tablet. "How many of these a day?"

"I don't know. Between ten and fifteen. Sometimes I don't . . ."

He waited, but she wasn't going to finish. "What's the dosage?"

"Twenty milligrams each."

"So . . . what? Two hundred milligrams a day? Two hundred twenty-five?"

"Yeah, I guess." She was leaning against the door frame, her rail-thin arms still crossed over her chest. She was mumbling her responses at the floor. Kealey didn't know if she was ashamed, embarrassed, or just sorry that she'd been caught. It was probably a combination of all three.

"Naomi . . ." He waited for her to lift her head, but the silence seemed to stretch on forever. "You can't keep this up."

She finally looked up, and he saw that the combative attitude was gone. Tears were streaming down her face, running over the pale, jagged scar on her right cheek. She lifted a hand to touch it, then subtly shifted her body to the right, turning the scar away from him. She'd been doing this since the day she was first released from the Agency's private facility in Loudoun County, Virginia, and it stung him deeply every time. He didn't think she knew she was doing it, which only made it harder to watch.

"What are you going to do?" she asked.

"I don't know." And he really didn't. He knew how important the Agency was to her, but he couldn't let her continue in this state. He was tempted to throw the question back at her—*What would you do in my shoes, Naomi?*—but that would have been too easy. He had been trained to set aside his feelings in order to make hard, fast decisions, and in this case, the decision was already made. What had just transpired only served to reinforce it.

"I'm not going to say anything," he said quietly, "but you've got to fix this. I know you want to work, but if you keep going the way you're going, it's going to end badly. You're going to get yourself or somebody else killed, and if that—"

He didn't catch his mistake until the words were out of his mouth, but he caught every part of what happened next. Her face crumpled, and her shoulders seemed to jerk forward slightly, as though she'd been punched in the stomach.

"Oh, Christ." He was instantly contrite. "Naomi, I didn't mean that. I wasn't talking about what happened in Madrid. You couldn't have known it would turn out the way it—"

He was wasting his breath; she had already turned in retreat. The bathroom door closed behind her, with a solid thump, and he heard the lock snap into place. He couldn't get to her now; she was lost in her own little world, and Kealey knew that he wasn't welcome.

He looked at the pill in his hand, his mind a complete blank. A thought came: he should crush it, destroy it, remove the temptation. Instead, he tossed it onto the bedspread, turned, and left the room.

CHAPTER 27

SIALKOT

Randall Craig stood in the harshly lit surgical suite. The room was almost completely silent, but he was aware of Said Qureshi's tense, economical movements over by the scrub sink. He was also aware of the unnaturally still form of Benazir Mengal, who was leaning against the counter a few feet away. As Craig stared down at one of the most recognizable faces in the world, he was reminded of a patient he had once worked on, a minor celebrity and self-proclaimed socialite. To his knowledge, it was the only time he had treated a person of public interest, but that was different. *This* was different. Brynn Fitzgerald was much more than a glossy teen with a cult following and too much of her parents' money; simply put, she was one of the most important people in the U.S. government. In the hundreds of procedures he'd attended, he had been able to maintain the necessary air of cool, calm detachment. Complete professionalism. He had always been proud of this fact, but not overtly proud; it was simply part of his job. Now he felt his composure deserting him. He was sweating beneath the scrubs that Qureshi had provided him with, and his hands felt hot and damp beneath a tight layer of latex; the surgical gloves felt like oven mitts, alien to his hands.

He was consumed by the possibility of failure. Looking down at her, he didn't see another patient; he saw the woman whose face had graced the covers of *Newsweek, Time,* and *Harper's,* all inside a three-month period. He saw a regular fixture on CNN, MSNBC, and

FOX News. He saw the most powerful woman in the United States, and he was terrified by what he might do to her. All it would take was one mistake, one little slip, one minor allergy they didn't know about, and she would be gone forever, killed at the hands of a Tennessee farm boy. . . .

"Randall?" Craig's head shot up, and he turned to face Said Qureshi. The Pakistani doctor was looking at him with an expression of uncertainty. "Are you all right?"

Craig tried to shake it off, feeling Mengal's intense, suspicious stare. "I'm fine."

Qureshi walked over with a tray full of sterilized instruments. Setting it down, he reached up and adjusted the arm on one of the Burton Genie lamps, positioning the four bulbs directly over Fitzgerald's upper abdomen. Snapping his mask into place, he looked up and met Craig's eyes. "Are you ready?"

Craig nodded slowly. He and Qureshi had not had the chance to decide exactly what they were going to do when the operation was over. He suspected that the Pakistani would fight for his life, as he'd indicated earlier, but no matter how Craig looked at it, he just couldn't ignore the overwhelming odds they were facing. There were at least 8 armed men on the property, according to Qureshi, and more stationed at the end of the drive. He suspected—and Craig believed he was right—that there were more armed guards positioned at either end of the main road, which was located 150 meters south of the house. If Mengal's background was any indication, Qureshi had said, the men who worked for him were ex-soldiers, probably drawn from the ranks of the SSG, the Special Services Group. The SSG was Pakistan's answer to the Green Berets, and while trained to a lesser standard, they were still extremely proficient, particularly on their own ground.

Craig knew that fighting them would only get him killed, but he wasn't going to lie down, either. It just wasn't his way, and besides, he felt he owed something to Brynn Fitzgerald and the people who'd been kidnapped on the KKH. A few of them were fellow Americans, after all, and his national identity was something that Craig held very close to his heart. If he could stand up for them, he would. But first, he had a job to do.

"I'm ready," he said, his voice firm. He glanced at the bank of monitors. The blood pressure cuff was already on Fitzgerald's right arm. The catheter was in place in her left arm, and on her left forefinger, a portable pulse oximeter was clipped into place. This was used to monitor the amount of oxygen in her blood; if it dropped below 95 percent during the procedure, they'd have to increase the flow.

Qureshi had explained what he'd been doing prior to Craig's arrival. He'd been administering 5 milligrams of Midazolam every thirty to forty minutes to keep Fitzgerald calm and compliant, and so far, it seemed to be working. The cardiac monitoring they were using only allowed for six tracings—not as good as the twelve tracings a better EKG would have provided, but it would have to suffice. Otherwise, everything looked good. Craig had everything he needed: the anesthesia machine itself; an endotracheal tube, 20 millimeters in length, already smeared with Xylocaine jelly to ease insertion into the trachea; a laryngoscope with a No. 3 blade, which would be used to check the airway prior to intubation; and the drugs that would put her under for the duration of the surgery.

The drugs, of course, were the most important element, and he had them all at hand. Fentanyl, an opioid analgesic eighty times more potent than morphine, would be used as the primary sedative, followed immediately by vecuronium, a paralytic compound. Both were contained in 12ml disposable syringes. Approximately thirty seconds after administering the vecuronium, Craig would intubate Fitzgerald. At that point, all he had to do was monitor her vitals. Qureshi would take care of the rest.

A pericardial window was a fairly simple procedure, but like any surgical procedure, there were always risks. To keep those risks to a minimum, they would do everything in a predetermined order, following the established protocols. Surgery was much like a court decision; everything hinged on precedence. If something had worked in the past, it would likely be used in the future. The pneumothorax was a minor inconvenience, but Qureshi had handled it well; Craig had already noted the quality of the work. He was pleased to see that the lesser injury had already been taken care of, because waiting to start on the window clearly wasn't an option. According to Qureshi, her blood pressure had dropped dramatically over the past several hours.

Now, as Craig screwed the syringe of fentanyl into the port in Fitzgerald's left arm, he checked the monitors and saw that her BP was eighty-three over forty, indicating that the blood filling the peri-cardial sac was beginning to put a great deal of pressure on her heart, decreasing its ability to pump blood to other parts of the body. Qureshi had been right when he'd remarked on the urgency of the situation. If they were to walk away now, Fitzgerald would probably go into cardiogenic shock in the next few hours.

Once the syringe of fentanyl was secure, he pushed down the plunger, marking the time and dosage. Unscrewing the empty syringe, he replaced it with the vecuronium, then did the same thing. Unscrewing it, he watched and waited. Once twenty-five seconds had elapsed, he touched Fitzgerald's eyelids. Nothing happened; she didn't react at all.

Looking up at Qureshi, Craig nodded once, then moved quickly to the head of the table. Standing behind Fitzgerald, he reached for the endotracheal tube, grabbing it with his right hand. Adjusting her head slightly, tipping it back, he opened her slack mouth and inserted the tube. He reached out with his left hand for the laryngoscope, which—like the endotracheal tube, or ETT—was smeared with lubricating jelly. Using the lighted mirror on the end to ascertain his progress, he moved the epiglottis out of the way, then slid the plastic tube down her trachea, stopping a few centimeters short of the point where the trachea split into the lungs. When he was done, approximately 4 inches of the tube protruded from her mouth, the end marked by a connection point. To this, he attached the clear plastic tubes that were already connected to the ventilator. Then he taped the ETT into place. Checking the monitors, he saw that the numbers were falling into an acceptable range.

"That's it," he said, stepping back from the table. Mengal had already moved in and was practically leaning over Fitzgerald, but Craig ignored him; his words were intended for Qureshi alone. "She's all yours."

Qureshi nodded and shot a practiced glance at the monitors. Then he approached the table. Fitzgerald was wearing a loose-fitting surgical blouse. The material was already pushed up to the lower curve of her breasts to expose her abdomen, which Craig had needed to see while putting her under. The rate of abdominal rise and fall was a good indication of the patient's response to the intravenous drugs he'd administered.

With practiced speed, Qureshi applied Betadine to the exposed abdomen with a few disposable swabs, turning Fitzgerald's skin a sickly shade of orange red. That done, he draped sterile towels over most of the area, leaving only a small patch of skin exposed. As the surgeon's fingers danced over the stainless-steel tray, searching for the appropriate tool, Craig tried to ignore what he was feeling inside. He tried to remind himself that at the end of the day, Brynn Fitzgerald was just another patient, a person in need of medical attention, but it just wasn't working. It didn't matter how he looked at it, because he couldn't get his mind around her title. He couldn't forget about all those magazine covers, about the dozens of times he'd seen her on the news. He just couldn't forget. . . .

Qureshi had found the scalpel he needed, a long blade with a rounded head, mounted in a sturdy titanium No. 4 handle. Craig couldn't help but wince as the Pakistani lifted the scalpel in his right hand, the razor-sharp steel flashing under the Burton lamps. He automatically adopted the palmar grip, which was ideal for larger, deeper cuts. Using the fingers of his left hand, he probed for the base of Fitzgerald's sternum, then lowered the long blade to her skin, preparing to make the subxiphoid incision.

A few seconds later it was done. There was little blood, but Craig had seen this done often enough that the absence of blood no longer surprised him. Qureshi used a pair of retractors to spread the 2-inch incision, then locked them into place. The next part was the worst, at least for Craig, and he had to turn away as Qureshi picked up a 16-gauge needle. To Craig, the surgical instrument looked like a long roofing nail, much like the kind he'd used when working construction in his teens. He'd never been able to dismiss the mental comparison.

He was still looking away as Qureshi slid the tip of the needle into the small incision. Then, moving his arm slowly but steadily forward, the Pakistani pushed it in, angling the point up into Brynn Fitzgerald's heart.

CHAPTER 28

CARTAGENA

It was just after two in the afternoon as Kealey stepped outside, holding Naomi's Globalstar sat phone and a glass of iced tea. The sky was a clear, brilliant blue, not a cloud in sight, and it was extremely hot, at least 90 degrees Fahrenheit and climbing. The second he closed the French doors behind him, he could feel the heat enveloping him, the air so heavy it seemed to cling to his exposed skin. He could hear the traffic moving on the other side of the trees, but it wasn't too bad at this time of day. As he crossed the grass, moving past the aluminum table, toward the trees, he looked back at the house, his eyes flickering up to the second-floor balcony. No one was there. Satisfied, he punched in the number to Jonathan Harper's office, adjusted the antennae, and lifted the phone to his ear, waiting for the satellite above to make the connection.

One of the watchers from Madrid—the last member of Pétain's team who was still in-country—had just left, having dropped off their bags and passports, all of which they'd left at the hotel the previous day. Kealey had gone through all of it, and everything seemed to be in order. He would have preferred to wait for new passports, not wanting to use the same ones they'd flown in with, but he and Pétain didn't have time to wait. The day before, Amari Saifi had made his ransom demands public through a videotape sent to al-Jazeera's headquarters in Doha. Now the whole world knew what the U.S. government had discovered barely twenty-four hours earlier, and so far, the fallout had been nothing short of catastrophic. Harper had said as much the night before, and Kealey, clicking through the various news channels that morning, had seen what he was talking about. The media speculation had been wild to begin with, but now, with this new development, almost nothing else was touched on. Even the burgeoning conflict between India and Pakistan wasn't enough to derail the networks' intense focus on the abduction of Brynn Fitzgerald, as well as the murky background of the man who had just eclipsed Osama bin Laden as the world's most famous terrorist.

Lee Patterson, the U.S. ambassador to Pakistan, had been buried the day before at Arlington National Cemetery, with full military honors. According to MSNBC, Patterson had served as a navy officer for six years before resigning his commission to join the Foreign Service. More than 600 people had attended his funeral, including several well-known businessmen, a former secretary of state, and the president of the United States, David Brenneman. The anchor went on to recap the ambush on Airport Road, noting the fact that the FBI was currently conducting an extensive extraterritorial investigation in Rawalpindi.

Much to Kealey's relief, there was no mention of the name Benazir Mengal. Although he'd informed Harper of Mengal's ties to the Algerian only the day before, Saifi's name had been in circulation at the Agency for nearly two weeks, plenty of time for it to leak. Kealey was surprised it had taken this long to come out, but with the release of the tape, it was unavoidable. A quick check of the other news channels had been enough to confirm that Mengal's involvement had yet to be revealed in the media. *Possible* involvement, Kealey reminded himself. He had yet to discover hard proof that Mengal had participated in Fitzgerald's abduction, but he felt sure he was on the right track. With any luck, he'd know for sure in less than twenty-four hours.

Of all the major networks, only CNN had made an effort to report on the escalating situation in Kashmir. The network had dispatched Christiane Amanpour, its chief international correspondent, to Udhampur, where she was reporting from the Indian Army's Northern Command headquarters. Kealey only caught the tail end of her report, but it was clear that the situation was escalating to the point of no return. More than 50,000 troops were now amassed in the region, in addition to an unknown number of Kashmiri insurgents, the vast majority of whom were affiliated with Pakistan's Inter-Services Intelligence. Shots had already been exchanged, and it looked as though India was preparing for a prolonged conflict, having moved supplies and additional support personnel into the region. The Indian Navy had also instigated a blockade of several strategic Pakistani ports, prompting Musharraf to appeal once more for U.S. intervention. The White House had yet to issue a statement, but it didn't look as though Brenneman was prepared to reverse his stance.

A voice in Kealey's ear snapped him back to reality. He recited an eight-digit number, asked for Harper, and was put on hold. Five seconds later, the deputy DCI picked up the phone.

"John, it's Ryan."

"Where are you?" Harper sounded like he was still half-asleep, but then Kealey remembered it was just after eight in the morning at Langley. If it wasn't for the current situation, Harper wouldn't have been there so early. "What's happening?"

"We're still at the house," Kealey said. He shot a glance at his watch. "Our flight leaves at five this evening, so we'll be out of here soon."

"When do you land?"

"Tomorrow at one."

"One in the afternoon?"

"Yeah."

"Okay. Let me tell you what's happening on this end. We've got a team en route to Pakistan. Obviously, they weren't invited, so they're traveling under false identities. I have a number for you to call once you're on the ground."

"Give it to me."

Harper recited a long string of numbers, which Kealey committed to memory. He didn't bother to tell Harper that he wouldn't be making the call, at least not until he'd met with Machado's man in Lahore.

"Your goal," the deputy DCI was saying, "is to link up and start running through the list. Get eyes on all of them. Remember, these are known associates of the general, all with medical backgrounds, so we have no way of knowing which of them, if any, were brought in to work on Fitzgerald."

"John, we don't even know if she *is* being worked on," Kealey reminded him. "All we have to go on in that direction is what the NTSB investigator put down in his statement. His *preliminary* statement."

"We have the witness statements as well," Harper said, "and there's something else I forgot to mention yesterday. We got a look at the autopsy results on Lee Patterson. The official cause of death was the gunshot wound to the head, but there was evidence of serious internal injuries, all of which were sustained when the RPG hit the car. The medical examiner said he probably would have died even if they hadn't shot him. So, in other words, it seems pretty clear that Fitzgerald was also injured in the attack, perhaps critically." He seemed to sense the younger man's doubt in the ongoing silence. "Ryan, this is the closest thing to proof we're going to get."

"Maybe," Kealey said, "but assuming you're right, Mengal wouldn't take her to someone in the city. He'd want her in a rural area, someplace where he could set up a good perimeter. That way he'd have time to move her quickly if it looked like he needed to."

"Well, that's why we have to look at each and every one of these people. There are only four names on the list, so with six people, including you and Kharmai, you should have enough manpower to get it done in a couple of days."

Kealey felt the anger stirring inside with the mention of Naomi's name, but he pushed it down. He was 90 percent certain that Harper knew about her addiction to morphine, yet he'd dangled her in front of him, anyway, just to draw him into the hunt for Amari Saifi. By letting her participate in the surveillance of and approach to Kamil Ghafour, Harper had risked the lives of every operative involved. Kealey wasn't about to forget or forgive what he had done, but now was not the time to confront him. That would come later, once this whole mess was sorted out, and he was back in the States.

He didn't bother to tell Harper that he was leaving Naomi behind. He and Pétain would stick out in Pakistan, especially given the ongoing tensions between Musharraf and Brenneman, but that couldn't be helped. Pétain would turn heads regardless, but her remarkably pale skin, which she'd obviously inherited from her French mother, would only increase their visibility on the ground. Worse still, neither of them spoke the local languages. In that respect, Naomi would have proved invaluable, but Kealey had made his decision. Besides, he needed to take Pétain if he was going to get the access that Machado had promised.

"Who are you sending?" Kealey asked, struggling to keep the anger out of his voice.

"You only know two of them, Walland and Owen. The rest were selected mostly for their physical characteristics—dark hair, dark skin, you know the drill—but they've all worked in Asia. Unfortunately, none have ever operated in Pakistan, but you know that we have limited resources in the area. Plenty of informants on the payroll, of course, especially in the north, where the Taliban are dug in, but no one we can use on this. We can't risk local law enforcement getting an anonymous tip. If they come down on you, the fallout will be ten times worse than it was in Madrid. We simply can't afford to get caught."

"You're sending Owen?" Kealey was surprised. Paul Owen was a lieutenant colonel in the U.S. Army. He'd served as Kealey's commanding officer when they were both stationed at Fort Bragg with the 3rd Special Forces Group. A few years later, Owen had been reassigned to the 1st SFOD-D, better known to the general public as Delta Force. They had worked together the previous year in Iraq. Kealey remembered the operation well; it had ended with Owen swearing he'd never speak to him again. "How did he get involved?"

"We've used him on a few things before, as you know, and he's always worked out for us, so I made a few calls. It helped that he was in Afghanistan already, so it was a short hop. He's in-country now, and the rest should be landing over the next ten to twelve hours."

"Does he know I'm on the way?"

"Yes, and he's willing to go along with it. You and Kharmai can work on your own if that makes it easier. You can give control of the other three to Owen."

"Fine. What about weapons?"

Harper let out an audible sigh. "You're not hearing me, Ryan. All you're doing is trying to learn which of these people, if any, are working with Mengal. If you get too close and he has spotters, which he will, the first thing he'll do is call his contacts at ISI. If that happens and they come after you, you can't afford to be carrying a weapon."

"I can't afford not to," Kealey said angrily. "If they catch us, they're not going to assume we're fucking tourists, John. You know what they'll do to get a confession, and once they have it, they'll use it to put the clamps on Brenneman."

"That's why you can't get caught. Look, if they figure out what's going on, you won't be able to fight your way out of it, anyway. They'll send every man they can spare after you, and the people they *don't* send will be watching the airports and the border crossings. Having a weapon on you won't make a bit of difference."

"Fine." Kealey was done arguing, but only because he could see it wasn't getting him anywhere. Nothing—not even Harper's half-assed rationalizations—could change the fact that he'd be looking for a weapon the second his feet touched Pakistani soil. "What happens if we find something?"

"You call it in, and I'll take it from there."

"John, you can't—"

"This is the way it's going to happen, Ryan," Harper said, his voice turning hard. "There is a political element to this that we have to consider. I know you don't give a shit about things like that, but it matters. If you find something, we have to make it look like it came through the Bureau ERT. Brenneman has already spoken to Emily Susskind about it, and she's agreed. The Bureau will go along to get along, but we have to be sure that either Mengal, Saifi, Fitzgerald, or the other hostages are present. Preferably all of them. Once we know that they are, the White House will leak it, and Musharraf won't have any other choice but to cooperate. So do it my way, okay?"

Kealey fought down another surge of anger. Part of him was wondering why he was going forward with this at all. Knowing now what he did about Naomi, he was tempted to call a halt to the whole thing. After all, he'd only come this far in an effort to watch out for her. He could tell Harper to go fuck himself, go inside, get Naomi, and fly her back to the States. Maybe he could convince her to come back to Cape Elizabeth. It wouldn't be easy, but with time, she might be able to beat her addiction. He *knew* she could, and all he had to do was convince her to leave with him. . . .

But at the same time, he was in too deep to back out now, and something had changed. Before, all he'd wanted was to keep her out of harm's way. Now, having failed miserably in that task, he was set on finding Mengal and Saifi. He wanted them to pay for what they had done in Rawalpindi. He wanted them to suffer for what Naomi had been forced to do, and for what she was going through now. Most of all, he wanted to find Fitzgerald and bring her back. He wanted to find the other hostages as well. If he could do all that, then maybe it would lessen Naomi's guilt. Maybe, in time, she would feel that some had died so that others might live. It wasn't much to hope for, but better than nothing. Besides, at the moment, it was all he had to offer her.

"Okay," he finally said. "I'll do it your way, John. I hope to God we find something."

"So do I," Harper said. His tone was more congenial now that he thought he'd won. There was a slight, uncomfortable pause. "What about Naomi? How is she holding up?"

"Fine," Kealey lied. His knuckles were white around the plastic housing of the phone; it was taking every ounce of his self-control not to unload his inner rage on the other man. "I think she's still trying to sort it out in her mind."

"Is she good to go?"

"Yeah. Just leave it to me."

Harper gave a few more instructions, asked a couple of questions, then ended the call. Kealey lowered the phone and tapped it lightly against his leg, staring into the dark green mass of the trees. He stood there in the sunshine for a moment, sipping his watery tea, thinking about what he had just heard. It was clear that the whole situation was descending into a political nightmare. Brenneman was trying to balance two conflicting goals. He was trying to find Fitzgerald and appease Pervez Musharraf at the same time, and Kealey had seen enough political wrangling to know that it wouldn't work. The problem was that Brenneman had burned his bridges by refusing to help Musharraf prevent the Israel-India arms deal, and now he was seeing the consequences of that decision.

Kealey still wasn't sure why Musharraf had agreed to let the Bureau ERT into the country, especially given his earlier opposition to the idea. Perhaps he'd still been trying to curry favor with Brenneman at the time, hoping for a last-minute intervention. Or perhaps he was trying to be the bigger man, at least in terms of world opinion. Either way, Kealey knew he would be quick to take advantage if CIA operatives were discovered operating illegally in his country. Kealey and the others would be paraded in front of the cameras, and any hope of finding Fitzgerald—or the other hostages—would go down the drain. Under such circumstances, Musharraf would be insured against just about any outcome, even the discovery of Fitzgerald's body.

Kealey didn't care about politics, but he'd served as an army officer long enough to understand them. He agreed with Harper's assessment of the situation, but that didn't change the way he was
going to approach the operation. He was going to find a weapon
once he was on the ground, and if he could manage it, he'd arm the
others as well. If Machado had been telling the truth about his man's
link to Benazir Mengal, they'd be able to avoid pulling surveillance
on multiple targets, anyway. Instead, they'd have a direct line to the
man they were looking for, which would help eliminate some of the
risk.

A noise behind him caused him to turn. Marissa Pétain was standing on the patio, one hand on the door handle. She was wearing a
pair of sleek cotton pants that ended at midcalf, wedge heels, and a
lavender blouse, the sleeves rolled up to her elbows. She had an incredibly feminine figure, Kealey couldn't help but notice: generous
hips, a narrow waist, and toned, slender arms. Despite the hot sun
beating down, her face was noticeably pale, but not in a bad way. Her
pallor was clearly natural, and it suited her, as it seemed to lend extra
color and a strange vitality to her dark brown eyes and pale pink lips.
Her shimmering chestnut hair, which fell to the middle of her back,
was probably her best feature. It framed her face perfectly, and for a
moment, Kealey couldn't help but stare. It was the first time he'd noticed how beautiful she really was. Beautiful in an elegant, effortless
kind of way. Beautiful like Katie had been.

Katie. He didn't often think of her, but not because he didn't want
to. It was just so damn hard. He'd never actively repressed the mem-
ories, but he didn't encourage them, either. She was the first woman
he'd ever really loved. It had been difficult enough to get past her
loss at the time, and he had no desire to experience that depth of despair on a regular basis. Even now, nearly two years after her death,
he still felt her absence. Not all the time, but when it did hit him, it
hit him hard. Something as simple as cooking a meal she had once
enjoyed could bring it all back. When he felt her loss to that degree,
he usually preferred to visit places that reminded him of her, places
they had seen together, rather than her grave. He didn't know why
he did this, but he'd never examined it too closely. Losing her had
been the worst thing that had ever happened to him, even harder
than losing Naomi to her inner demons, and he didn't want to en-

dure that hell a second time. He supposed that was part of the reason he was so intent on keeping Naomi out of harm's way, not that
he'd managed to do it.

Pétain's mouth was turned up at the corners, and Kealey realized
he still hadn't spoken. He tried to think of something to say, but
nothing was coming. Clearing his throat, he looked away, feeling incredibly awkward. Sensing his embarrassment, she jumped in to save
him. "I just wanted to let you know that the car is here."

Kealey nodded. Javier Machado had arranged for a vehicle they
could use to drive to the airport. Machado had told him to leave it in
the long-term parking lot, and someone—the owner, Kealey guessed—
would collect it in a couple of days. Pétain thought the embassy had
arranged for the car. "Are you ready to go?" he asked her.

"Absolutely." She hesitated. "What about Kharmai? Did you—"

"I don't want to bother her. I think she's sleeping, anyway."

She looked doubtful. "Ryan, I think you should—"

"Don't worry about it," he said sharply. "When she wakes up, we'll
be gone, and she can do what she wants. If she wants to fly back to
Washington, she can. If she wants to stay here, so be it. It's up to her.
All I know is that she isn't coming with us."

Pétain hesitated, then closed the door behind her. She walked
over until they were just a few feet apart. Then she folded her arms
across her chest and looked at him, her gaze curious, slightly reticent, but also intent. "Ryan, what happened to her?" she asked quietly.

"What do you mean?"

"You know what I mean. I'm not talking about Madrid. I'm talking
about New York. I know she was there when the attack took place. I
know what Vanderveen did to her, but . . . It just seems like there's
something else. Something everyone's missed, except for you,
maybe."

"She didn't go through enough as it is?" Kealey asked tightly. She
was probing, and he didn't have the patience to deal with it. "Is that
what you're saying?"

"No." Pétain wasn't retreating. "It just seems that—"

"Well, that's what it sounds like you're saying," he snapped. "Let
me tell you something, Marissa. What happened to her is none of
your business. I'm sure you've read the file, and you probably re-

member the media coverage. The networks never managed to identify her, but there were plenty of witnesses, and they all had something to say. So you know what she went through, and you know what Vanderveen did to her. If you know all of that, why are you bringing it up? What are you asking me?"

"It just seems like there's something more," she said in a low voice.

"There isn't. Believe me, you know everything there is to know."

"Okay," she said, though it was clear she didn't buy a word of it. "I'm sorry I brought it up."

"Yeah, okay," Kealey said distractedly. He pushed a hand through his hair and tried to relax. He reminded himself that she'd only been asking an innocent question, and he still had to work with her, perhaps for a long time. Besides, the strained conversation with Harper was the root cause of his bad mood; Pétain didn't have anything to do with it.

"Look, I'm sorry I bit your head off," he said by way of apology. "It's just a touchy subject."

"I can see that." She gave him a tentative, apologetic smile. "I'm sorry I said anything, really. I don't mean to be nosy. I just wanted to know." She paused. "Look, I'm going to stick the bags in the car. I'll see you out there."

He looked her up and down and shook his head. "You'd better change first. You can't be wearing that when we land in Lahore."

She looked down at her outfit, frowning; Kealey could see that she didn't understand. "You need to cover up," he told her. "Pick a plain cotton top, something dark, and keep the sleeves down. Lose the jewelry, too. Flat heels and jeans or khakis. Do you have a scarf? Something to cover your hair?"

"I think so. My father worked out of the embassy in Islamabad for two years in the late eighties. He brought me back some souvenirs, including a head scarf. It should be around here somewhere."

"Find it," Kealey said. "You're going to need it. The idea is to attract as little attention as possible once we're on the ground. We'll talk about the rest on the way to the airport."

"Okay." She turned to walk away, and he watched her go. She was almost to the doors when she stopped and turned once more.

"Oh, and Ryan?"

"Yeah?"

She gave a half smile, her eyes sparkling, and said, "You look a thousand times better without the beard."

It was the last thing he expected to hear, and it caught him completely off guard. He collected himself and muttered his thanks, but she had already turned away. Then she was gone, the door closing softly behind her.

Once Pétain was inside, Kealey let out a long, slow breath, feeling the tension drain from his shoulders. She had struck too close to home, closer than she probably realized. For the most part, he'd been telling the truth. What had happened the year before with Vanderveen *had* been extremely traumatic for Naomi, but it was the other thing that had caused the most problems. The fact that she had killed an innocent person had never come to light; not even Harper knew the truth. Kealey had done everything he could to cover it up, and Naomi had reluctantly gone along with it.

He suspected that the cover-up was the hardest part for her: not that she had pulled the trigger, but that she had lied about it. The cover-up probably made it more like murder than the case of mistaken identity it had actually been, Kealey suddenly realized, at least in her mind. And in the end, that was what it came down to; what she thought, and how she felt about it, was all that really mattered.

With this thought in mind, he found himself looking up at the second floor, seeking out her window. There was nothing there. She must be sleeping again, he decided. He found himself moving over, scanning the rest of the windows. In the last one, he thought he saw a silhouette. It was hard to tell with the glare from the afternoon sun, but it looked as though someone was standing there, staring down at him. Then, without warning, the figure was gone.

Kealey stood there for a moment, thinking about it. Then he crossed the lawn, heading toward the house, wondering what the following day would bring. For the most part, it was all up in the air. Only one thing was certain: in less than twenty hours, they were going to be in hostile territory. No matter what happened next, the stakes were about to rise dramatically, and there could be no room for error.

CHAPTER 29

SIALKOT

Randall Craig stood beneath a broad, aging acacia to the rear of the house, smoking one of Said Qureshi's English cigarettes. The procedure had gone as well as could be expected, and some of his tension was starting to fade. The nicotine was definitely helping with that, he thought, though the fear was as strong as ever. Before, he had been primarily concerned with saving the secretary of state's life. Now that he had helped Qureshi to accomplish that task, he found his thoughts returning to the strongest, most basic of all human instincts.

Namely, self-preservation.

The urge to run was intense. His legs were as taut as compressed springs, and the adrenaline was pumping through his veins like gasoline; he felt as if he could fly across the gently sloping field and lose himself in the bracken before the guards could react. It was just past ten on a moonless night, and the stars overhead were largely blocked from view by fast-moving clouds, billowing black clumps against the charcoal sky. Across the distant fields, where the terrain rose into the gentle Kashmiri foothills, he could see a column of lights snaking along a winding road. Dozens, if not hundreds, of lights. The sound of diesel engines was a distant, constant rumble. Qureshi had told him they were in Sialkot, and that the city was home to a major Pakistani army base. He guessed that the vehicles were moving toward the battlefields to the north. Before long, they would switch to infrared to conceal their locations, to guard against the IAF bombers patrolling the skies over the Kashmir Valley.

Craig let his gaze drift over the fields, weighing the possibilities. Deep down, he knew it wouldn't work; it was at least 200 feet to the nearest line of trees, and he would have to cross a waist-high fence of tightly strung wire to get there. He was standing at the end of the garden, as far away from the guards as he thought he could get without rousing their suspicion. There were two of them, he knew, and both were armed. Not with the stubby submachine guns the interior guards were carrying, but with long-barreled rifles. He didn't doubt for a second that both weapons were mounted with night-vision scopes; if he tried to run, he wouldn't get more than 20 meters. It was too much to chance. He was willing to take a risk when he made a break for freedom, but only a calculated risk; he wasn't prepared to throw his life away. Not if there was a better alternative.

As he stared down the sloping hill, searching in vain for clumps of vegetation that might provide him with enough cover to reach the fence, he felt a presence behind him. Turning suddenly, he was startled to see a man standing less than 10 feet to his rear. His features were not discernable in the low light, but he was tall, and his head was wrapped in some kind of cloth. Not a turban exactly, but something similar . . . a kaffiyeh, maybe. As Craig stared at him, the man took a few steps forward, his teeth flashing white in a brilliant, friendly smile.

"Dr. Craig?" The man drew closer, and Craig could see that he was dressed in long, flowing robes, quite unlike the slacks and shirts that Mengal and his guards had been wearing. The man, with his long, hawkish nose, thick black beard, and piercing hazel eyes, looked more suited to the desert than the Kashmiri foothills of northern Pakistan. Stranger still were his Western-style running shoes, the toes of which protruded from the bottom edge of his robes. "Forgive me, I didn't mean to startle you. I only wanted to congratulate you on your fine work this evening. The secretary owes you her life."

The man spoke with an accent that Craig could not place; it was completely different from anything he'd heard before, though his English was word perfect. The man was moving closer now, standing *too* close, and he seemed to radiate a kind of commanding energy. Craig felt a spark of revelation, accompanied by a little fear. He suddenly realized who this was. He had to be the man Qureshi had mentioned earlier, the man he knew only as the Algerian. What was it he had said . . . ?

One of them is the devil himself.

"Doctor, do you know who I am?"

Craig took a shifting step back and shook his head. "No."

The Algerian moved forward again; he was so close that Craig could smell his breath. He caught a hint of the same mint tea he had been offered earlier. "Are you sure?" the man persisted. A strange half smile was wedged into place on his gaunt, weathered face. "You've never seen me before?"

Craig couldn't think through the terror that seized him, but he was certain he'd never seen this face before. He felt a sudden anger cutting through the fear, and this time he summoned his strength, took an aggressive step forward, and squared his shoulders.

"I said I haven't," he snarled, jabbing a finger into the man's chest. "You speak English, don't you?"

"Yes, I do." Amari Saifi smiled mildly, apparently unswayed by the pointless show of defiance. "A benefit of my army service. In fact, I once trained with some of your countrymen, though I suppose you'd find that hard to believe."

A sudden noise caught Craig's attention, and he turned to look up at the house. A Mitsubishi box truck had pulled up to the side of the trellis, and a number of guards were walking out to meet it, the exterior lights coming on. As Craig watched, a man opened the doors to the rear, climbed up, and began handing items down to the waiting hands. Craig recognized most of the equipment immediately: a pair of portable halogen lamps, a collapsible aluminum tripod, a bulky black case that might have contained a camera.

The Algerian, following his eyes, turned to examine the scene. Another slow smile spread over his face. "So," he said, sounding pleased. "It would appear we're almost ready. We just have to wait for our star to recover. Another fifteen or sixteen hours, perhaps. I find it so hard to be patient after all this time. Don't you agree?"

"What are you talking about? What do you mean, your 'star'?"

"Fitzgerald, of course." The man turned his calm gaze on Craig and smiled again. "An unwilling star, perhaps, but a star nonetheless, and she is only the main attraction."

"What do you mean?" Craig repeated, but he didn't really need to ask. Somewhere, deep down, he already knew.

Saifi put a hand on his shoulder and smiled. This time there was nothing friendly about it. "Doctor, you didn't think you were brought here for just one reason, did you? You've performed admirably so far, but your work is far from done. You're going to be famous, my friend . . . more famous than you ever dreamed possible."

It hit him then, what was going to happen. It was everything he'd seen in the news over the past few years, the grainy images out of Iraq, Afghanistan, and Karachi, a city less than 900 miles from his current location. It was what had happened to Daniel Pearl and so many others, and though he'd never seen the footage, he could see and hear it all in his mind: the masked men standing on either side of an Islamic flag; the resigned look in the eyes of the victim; the voice reading out the demands that would never be met; the blade coming down in a sweeping, glittering arc. . . .

The decision to act was not a conscious one, but he found himself moving forward, reaching out for the Algerian's throat, eyes fixed on the sensitive bundle of nerves beneath the chin. He heard the shouts rising up from the back of the house, the sound of legs swishing through the damp, knee-high grass on the hill, but it was all meaningless background noise; he was entirely focused on killing the man in front of him. The Algerian moved to the left and raised an arm to ward off the attack, but he didn't fight back, and Craig—having missed with his first strike—turned to mount a second attack. He launched himself forward, head down, and felt his shoulder connect with the man's midsection, the air coming out of the Algerian's lungs in a great rush. He felt a moment of profound satisfaction before the first of the soldiers arrived. Suddenly, his head exploded with pain, a heavy blow landing exactly where he'd been hit before, and he slumped to the ground.

Despite the overwhelming odds he was facing, he tried to hold on, knowing this might be his last chance to resist. It just wasn't working; the black sea was moving in with incredible speed, and the last thing he heard before he lost consciousness was the sound of the Algerian's laughter. To Craig's ears, it sounded like a harsh, grating tear, as if the laughter itself was ripping a hole in the still night air.

And then he was gone.

CHAPTER 30

LAHORE

The flight had been rough, particularly the seven-hour stretch between Rome and Tashkent, the plane rocked hard by a high-pressure front building over the Black Sea. From his seat near the back of the plane, Kealey had been in a position to see Pétain jump up from her seat on numerous occasions, practically sprinting to the bathroom each time. On each occasion, she'd returned to her seat looking decidedly queasy, her face even paler than usual, one hand pressed over her mouth as if to suppress what might come up. Normally, Kealey might have been amused by her slightly theatrical gestures, but he couldn't help but notice the attention she was drawing from the other passengers. Each time she got up to run to the front of the plane, he wanted to drag her back by the hair. They weren't even in harm's way yet, and she was already doing things that people would remember. He would have preferred to leave her behind, of course, but that wasn't anything new; he'd felt that way from the moment Machado had made his proposal.

The proposal. That was what Kealey kept coming back to. Information and a direct link to Benazir Mengal for . . . well, for *what?* What the hell did Machado want? Kealey just couldn't figure it out, and it was driving him crazy. He couldn't see how bringing Marissa Pétain to Pakistan would benefit her father. There had to be some ulterior motive; after all, Machado was one of the Agency's most celebrated operatives, at least within the small circle of people who knew about the things he'd done in his thirty years with the DO. What was the man's angle?

Kealey was still thinking about it as the plane—a UZB Airbus A310-300—landed with a slight jolt, slowed, and began taxiing toward the main building. After a few minutes, the plane stopped moving, and the seat belt light blinked off. As the passengers sprang out of their seats to dig for their cell phones, Kealey remained seated. He preferred to wait for the other passengers to disembark before leaving the plane himself, just as he preferred to wait for everyone else to board before doing so himself. It had nothing to do with tradecraft; he simply hated waiting in lines. Especially lines that weren't going anywhere.

Once the last passenger walked down the aisle, Kealey stood and collected his carry-on. It contained nothing more than a change of clothes and a paperback novel, but it was better to have a carry-on than nothing at all, particularly on a long flight. It was one of the things that other passengers expected to see, and in the post-9/11 world, people—especially air travelers—had become remarkably aware of their surroundings. Not all of them, but certainly enough to justify the extra precaution.

Making his way through the Jetway, he entered the cool expanse of the terminal. Pétain was nowhere to be found, so—taking a guess—he located the nearest women's restroom and stood where he could see who was coming and going. Before long she emerged, spotted him, and walked over. As she approached, Kealey could see that her legs were still shaky, her face pale.

"That was the worst flight of my life," she groaned, adjusting the strap of her carry-on. Before they'd left Cartagena, she'd changed into beige linen pants, a black pin-tuck blouse, and plain white tennis shoes. Her face was framed by a brightly colored head scarf, the gauzelike material patterned in shades of violet and blue. The scarf she'd managed to dig up was more colorful than Kealey would have liked, but better than nothing at all, and they'd be able to pick up something less noticeable before long. Thankfully, the loose-fitting blouse did little to flatter her shape. Kealey was still wearing the charcoal T-shirt and dark jeans he'd put on nearly eighteen hours earlier.

"I kept thinking my stomach was empty," Pétain was saying, "but then it would hit me again. I have no idea what was coming up . . . I just hope it wasn't important, whatever it was. . . ."

They were making their way toward the baggage claim. Like their carry-on luggage, the bags they had checked were filled with the usual clothes and toiletries; they contained nothing that couldn't be left behind in an emergency. The things he and Pétain needed— money and passports—would be on their bodies at all times. It was the same for the rest of the team. Paul Owen, the Delta colonel seconded to the Agency for this particular operation, had already managed to secure a sat phone for Kealey's use. According to Harper, the phone was waiting in a locker at the railway station, just east of central Lahore. The key to the locker was taped behind the toilet in a stall at the local Pizza Hut. The restaurant was located off Shahrah-i-Quaid-i-Azam, a few kilometers southwest of the station. It would take a little running around to get the phone, but Kealey would have expected nothing less. Success, as always, hinged on precaution; it was the same for each and every operation. He wasn't going to pick the phone up for a while, anyway; he wanted to meet with Machado's fixer first.

The public telephone outside the main terminal, just past the taxi stand, Machado had said. *He'll call at 1:20 pm, provided your flight arrives on time. If you don't answer, he'll continue calling at twenty-minute intervals. Once you pick up, he'll provide you with additional instructions.*

Kealey could remember the Spaniard's precise words, but that wasn't the problem. It wasn't what Machado had said that was bothering him, but what he *hadn't* said. He'd never offered an explanation for his unusual terms, and he hadn't volunteered how he knew Mengal to begin with. Something was very wrong with the whole scenario. Kealey knew that now, and he was torn. Part of him was saying that he should do the right thing: that he should go to the restaurant, collect the key, collect the phone, and make the call to Owen. From there, they could begin running surveillance on Mengal's known associates.

At the same time, part of him was saying that Machado was not the kind of man to fuck around, that once he gave it, his word was good. Kealey couldn't explain it, but somehow, he knew that if he did what was asked of him, Machado would hold up his end of the bargain. He felt sure that Machado could get them closer than surveillance could, and more importantly, it would happen much faster. As for the rest of it, Kealey agreed with Harper; once he found Benazir

Mengal, he'd find Fitzgerald. The only question was what kind of shape he would find her in.

The afternoon air outside the terminal was heavy and damp, the sky like a grayscale image: flat, somber, and absent of anything bright. *Perfect weather for a funeral,* Kealey thought. He turned right after leaving the building, then started to walk, weaving his way through the small crowd of travelers, Pétain by his side. They had walked half the length of the terminal, passing a number of taxi stands and bus shelters, before Kealey stopped in his tracks, looking around in confusion. Catching his expression, Pétain said, "What's wrong?"

He was still looking around. "I think we must have passed them."

"Passed what?"

"The pay phones. We're supposed to get a call from the man we're going to meet." Kealey checked his watch. "He should be calling right now."

"Harper told you that?"

"Yes." Pétain still thought that this lead had come through the Agency; she had no idea that her father had set it up, and Kealey wasn't about to tell her the truth. He was about to say something else when he heard a phone ringing.

"Over there," Pétain said, pointing toward the building. A few pay phones were lined up against the exterior wall, partially hidden behind a cluster of abandoned luggage carts, all of which were dented and scarred from years of wear and tear. A pale, balding, grossly overweight man in blue Adidas warm-ups had one of the phones pressed to his ear, and he was staring at the phone that was ringing. Clearly, he was thinking about picking it up, but before he could, Kealey jogged over, snatched up the phone, and turned his back to the other man.

"Hello?"

"Is this Kealey?"

"Yes, that's right."

Kealey took note of the heavily accented voice and let his mind play over the possibilities. The accent didn't mean much, at least not by itself. The Agency employed hundreds of foreign-born citizens, some of whom held high-ranking positions in the Operations Directorate. The man on the other end of the line might be an Agency operative, but somehow, Kealey doubted it. For one thing, if he *was* actively employed by the CIA, Harper would have brought him into the operation directly; there would have been no need for Machado's secret offer of assistance.

And there was something else to consider. Javier Machado had been retired for fifteen years—too long to still have reliable contacts in the Agency. Kealey was willing to bet that the man on the other end of the line was an agent, someone Machado had used to generate intelligence and recruit other agents when he had been posted to Islamabad. Machado had never said as much, but it was clear to Kealey that the older man had spent some time in Pakistan; otherwise, he wouldn't have had the connection in the first place. Besides, Pétain had told him as much the day before. When he had asked her about the head scarf, she had revealed more than she'd probably planned, including the fact that her father had spent time in the Pakistani capital.

"What about the daughter?" the man asked, as if reading Kealey's mind. "Machado's daughter. Is she with you?"

Kealey looked at Pétain, who was staring at him expectantly, hands propped on her hips. "Yes."

"Good. Do you have money?"

"Yes." Kealey had stopped in the arrival hall at the airport to change a few hundred dollars into rupees. "Where am I going?"

"Find a taxi and have the driver take you to the Queen's Way Hotel. Don't check in . . . Just walk south through the bazaar. When you reach the first road, take a left and head east. Eventually, you'll pass a telephone exchange on your right, and then you'll see a restaurant, the Bundu Khan. Go inside and ask for Nawaz, one of the servers. He will give you instructions from there."

Kealey resisted the urge to lose his temper, reminding himself that he'd be taking similar precautions if he were in the other man's shoes. At the same time, the fixer had to know that time was an issue.

"You understand that this is time sensitive, right? We don't have all day to—"

"I understand perfectly." The voice was clipped, impatient. "If you want to get to Mengal quickly, you will do as I say. These precautions are for my benefit, not yours."

"Fine." Kealey glanced up and saw that Pétain was fidgeting, clearly anxious to know what was going on. "We're moving now."

The other man ended the call without a word. Kealey dropped

the phone back onto the hook, grabbed Pétain's elbow, and began guiding her toward the curb. There was a line of taxis, and the vehicles were facing the other direction; he'd forgotten that they drove on the left in Pakistan. There was a short line of people waiting at the taxi stand, but it looked like the queue was moving quickly; they wouldn't have to wait more than a couple of minutes.

There was no one around to overhear them, so as they walked toward the taxi stand, Kealey repeated what the fixer had said. When he was done, Pétain looked uncertain.

"You said it was Harper who dug this guy up?" she asked.

"No, I said his name came through the Agency. Harper didn't have anything to do with it, other than passing the name on to us."

"But you don't *know* his name," Pétain said. Kealey looked at her, momentarily caught off guard. "Or if you do, it's news to me. You haven't mentioned it once."

"Didn't I? His name is Khan," Kealey said, saying the first name that popped into his head. *Where the hell did I hear that?* he wondered briefly. Then it came to him; A. Q. Khan was the renowned scientist and metallurgical engineer who had almost single-handedly turned Pakistan into a nuclear power back in 1976. Kealey remembered seeing the name in *Newsweek*. "We're going to meet him now."

"Can we trust him?"

Kealey debated the question, and when he looked at her, his smile was gone. "I don't see that we have a choice."

CHAPTER 31

PUNJAB PROVINCE, PAKISTAN

The house that belonged to the first target sat on the other side of a large square in the small town of Sharakpur Sharif. The square was strewn with unsteady-looking wooden structures, all of which were loaded with racks of clothing, cell phones, televisions, head scarves, fruits and vegetables, and just about anything else a person might wish to purchase. A number of potential customers were browsing the stands, while a man with white eyebrows as thick as his beard swept the pavement with a whisk broom, oblivious to the people moving around him. Metal pylons erupted around a camera-shaped ad for Fuji Film, another for Kodak, and a cluster of fading eucalyptus trees. Fortunately, the open space was not crowded; from his seat near a small tea stand, the American had an acceptable view of the squat, whitewashed, two-story house that sat on the south-eastern edge of the square.

As he sat watching the house, the American took a sip from his bottle of water and checked his watch. He was not surprised to see he had been in place for just over thirty minutes. He had moved his position around the square four times over the past two hours. It felt like he had been sitting there much longer than half an hour, and he knew how long he might still have to wait. Still, he was used to the long periods of inactivity that came with fieldwork, just as he was always prepared for the sudden burst of activity—as well as the danger—that might present itself at any moment. Such was the nature of his profession, and Lieutenant Colonel Paul Owen was a man well suited to his line of work.

At the reasonably young age of forty-two, Owen had the gaunt face and tired eyes of a man years older, a man who might have recently undergone some tragic personal event, such as recurrent cancer or the loss of a child. In reality, these physical attributes were an indirect result of his chosen occupation. More specifically, they were brought on by the things he had seen in places like Afghanistan, Iraq, and Sarajevo, where he had worked in conjunction with SFOR, the multinational peacekeeping force dispatched to Bosnia-Herzegovina in the mid-to-late nineties. During his twenty years of army service, Owen had been exposed to countless horrors, including rape, murder, and genocide, but he'd also had the privilege of commanding—in his opinion, at least—the finest soldiers in the world. It had been a difficult trade-off to make, but he had never regretted his choice of profession.

That wasn't to say he didn't regret some of the associations he had forged in that time. For several years, Ryan Kealey had been one of the men under Owen's command—first at Fort Carson, Colorado, where they both served with the 10th Special Forces Group—then at Fort Bragg, where they served with the 3rd SFG. At first, Owen had been impressed with Kealey's ability to lead troops and make fast, effective tactical decisions, both in training and in combat. For this reason, he had pushed to put the young first lieutenant on the fast track for promotion, but before his efforts could yield results, Kealey had made the first of two grievous errors, effectively ending his own career before it could really get started.

The first incident occurred in Sarajevo, during the last few months of the Bosnian War. In September of 1995, Kealey had been implicated in the murder of a Serbian warlord, a man by the name of Stojanovic, who had raped and killed a thirteen-year-old girl. The particulars of the case were not a factor. It didn't matter that Stojanovic had gotten what he'd deserved, and it didn't matter that the case against Kealey was circumstantial at best; it only mattered that the entire incident threatened to make an already volatile situation worse. Perhaps more importantly, if it had come to light, it would have reflected poorly on the U.S. Army and the troops it had committed to the NATO multinational force. As a result, Kealey was not subjected to a court-martial. Instead, he was eased out in the fall of

2001, but not before a disastrous operation in Syria that nearly cost him his life, not to mention the tattered remains of his career. Nevertheless, Kealey remained a highly trained operator, and it wasn't long before he found a new home at the CIA, an agency he had already worked for on multiple occasions.

Owen had also been recruited by the Agency for a few covert operations around the world, most notably in Somalia, where he had played a minor role in the Battle of Mogadishu and the events leading up to that disastrous conflict. Following Kealey's dismissal from the army, they had operated together on several occasions: Kealey as an independent contractor of sorts, Owen as an active-duty officer on TDY (temporary duty) assignment to the Agency. The first two operations had come off without a hitch, but it was the third, a meeting with a former general of the Republican Guard in Iraq the previous year, that had decisively changed the Delta colonel's opinion of his former subordinate, and not in a positive way.

Owen had been watching the house for two hours, shifting position every twenty minutes or so. Three other operatives, Mark Walland included, were watching the house as well; Walland was on a mobile route throughout the square, while the other two were in static positions on the other side of the house. The building belonged to Tahira Bukhari, a twenty-four-year-old Pakistani who had just returned from the United States, where she'd been training at the University of Virginia's School of Nursing. What had brought Bukhari to the forefront of the investigation was her father, an army officer who had served with Benazir Mengal for nearly fifteen years.

In effect, Colonel Amir Fariq Bukhari had served as Mengal's aide-de-camp for the duration of his career. During that time, he'd amassed nearly three hundred thousand dollars, which he'd left to his daughter prior to his death in 2005. The source of the money, which was presently sitting in Tahira Bukhari's Citibank account, could not be traced, though the general assumption at Langley was that her father had come into the money through Mengal's illicit activities, which included cross-border smuggling and illegal arms sales to Kashmiri militants. That kind of money could create a lasting loyalty, and if Bukhari knew where it had come from, it was reasoned, then she might be the person for Mengal to turn to. The only obstacle was her training; if Fitzgerald's injuries were, in fact, life threatening, a licensed nurse would be able to do only so much. Nevertheless, the

decision was made at Langley to add Bukhari to the list, which explained why Owen and the rest of the team were watching her house.

Owen's cell phone began ringing on the cast-iron table. He snatched
it up, hit the TALK button, and lifted it to his ear. "What's happening?"

It was Walland. "She's on the move. She just left the house and
turned left. It looks like she's going to stay on foot . . . .She's heading
north right now."

"Okay. Call Massi and Manik and let them know. We're switching
to alternate comms."

"Will do."

"Who's driving?" Owen asked. The CIA station chief in Islamabad
had already procured a car for them, an old Toyota four-door sedan,
in addition to supplying the Motorola earpieces and lip mics they
would use to communicate while on the move. He had also provided
cell phones of the pay-and-go variety, which rendered them all but
untraceable. He had supplied it all gladly and would have done more
without being prompted by Langley. During their brief discussion the
previous day, it had become clear to Owen that the station chief and
Lee Patterson, the late ambassador to Pakistan, had been good
friends.

"Massi will wait by the car . . . We can call him up if she hails a
taxi."

Owen nodded to himself; they were already fairly certain that
Bukhari didn't own a car, but they couldn't afford to take the risk.
Like in many Pakistani towns and cities, it was easier to get around in
Sharakpur Sharif in taxis and rickshaws than in one's own vehicle.
Bukhari had left the house once before since they'd started the surveillance. She'd only walked down to the café for a pastry and a cup
of coffee, but it was enough time to get a positive ID. Given the fact
that they still had three other people to look at, they couldn't afford
to waste time following the wrong person, and they certainly couldn't
risk letting her slip through the coverage.

Owen stood, nodded his thanks to the proprietor of the tea stand,
and began making his way through the throngs of shoppers. He
mulled things over as he walked, listening to the traffic coming over
his earpiece. Personally, he didn't think that Bukhari was involved.
For one thing, her house was in a clamorous residential area, and
Sharakpur Sharif was a fairly small town. A foreigner being brought in

on a stretcher would definitely earn her some unwanted attention, so it seemed unlikely.

At the same time, Owen wasn't going to leave anything to chance. It was the reason he had lobbied so hard for this assignment, despite the fact that he had to work with Kealey. Unlike many of the other prominent figures in the U.S. government, Brynn Fitzgerald commanded his deep respect. In part, he thought, it was probably because she wasn't really a politician. The vast majority of her years in government service had been spent behind the scenes, which was something that Owen could definitely relate to. At the same time, she had made an irrefutable difference. In short, she was one of the few people in Washington for whom Owen would gladly risk his life.

The crowd ahead began to clear; the road was just beyond. There was a sputter of radio traffic, and Owen quickly adjusted his flesh-colored earpiece.

"Owen, this is Walland . . . What's your twenty?"

"Just coming into the main road from the east," Owen murmured. It was one of the first things he had learned about communicating over a radio net; people had a tendency to talk too loud, which rendered the words inaudible on the other end. It was a common problem, especially in a firefight, when clear communication over the net could mean the difference between life and death. That didn't mean that he was always disciplined when it came to radio procedure. U.S. Special Forces operators were a different breed. They operated outside the lines, and unlike the regular army, they tended to refer to each other by name, as opposed to rank. In an operational detachment, it wasn't unusual for a staff sergeant to refer to a first sergeant by his first name, just as it wasn't unusual for operators to leave out the unnecessary radio jargon, such as adding "over" at the end of every transmission. In a small, cohesive unit, all that did was slow things down.

"She's approaching from your right," said Mark Walland, a former army ranger and a four-year veteran of the Special Activities Division, the paramilitary branch of the CIA. "You want to take point?"

Walland was asking if Owen wanted to take a position forward of Bukhari. The trick to good surveillance was to form a sort of mobile, shifting perimeter around the target. Sometimes a specific operator might stay 20 to 30 feet ahead of the target; other times, he might drop back and take up the rear. One man stayed back with the car at all times, in case the target caught on or otherwise moved unexpectedly.

"You right behind her, Walland?"

"Ten meters back, same side of the street."

"What about you, Manik?"

"I'm on the other side, moving parallel." The speaker was Husain Manik, an eight-year veteran of the Operations Directorate. A native of the Maldive Islands, Manik had immigrated to the States at the age of twenty-four. He'd joined the Agency after earning his master's in electrical engineering at MIT. Owen had yet to figure out why the man was stuck on surveillance, unless he spent most of that time developing new tools for the watchers. Perhaps he wanted to see what his tools were used for in the field, or perhaps he just fit the physical profile needed for this particular job. Either way, he seemed to know his business, and Owen was glad to have him along.

"Okay, drop back, Manik. Walland, cross the street and get in front of her. Get over there quick . . . Let her see you moving. I'll move in behind, and you can shift to Manik's current position, Mark. Got it?"

Both men reported back in the affirmative. Owen was watching carefully as he approached the sidewalk, checking and discarding each passing face. Bukhari came into view, and he caught her profile for a few brief seconds: a large nose, sallow skin, a full face, with rosy red lips turned down at the corners. She wasn't wearing a head scarf, and her clothes were very American: jeans, a short-sleeve T-shirt, and Nike running shoes. She was wearing earbuds and had what looked like an iPhone in a carrier clipped to her belt. *If only her father could see her now*, Owen thought, biting back a smile. Her style of dress only seemed to reinforce his earlier thoughts, and the iPhone clinched it; anyone this in love with U.S. culture wasn't likely to be involved with the abduction of one of America's most beloved public figures. More to the point, Bukhari was young, and she had just completed a difficult program at a very prestigious school. It would be a lot to risk for a man she barely knew.

Owen stepped onto the sidewalk, moved slowly until Bukhari had built a lead of about 10 meters, and then let the crowd carry him forward. Momentarily taking his eyes off the target, he lifted his cell phone, looked at the screen, and frowned involuntarily. Once again, he found himself wondering why the hell Kealey had yet to make contact. There was no excuse for it; according to his latest information, Kealey and Naomi Kharmai should have landed several hours earlier.

Goddamnit, Ryan, Owen thought angrily as he slipped the phone back into his pocket, returning his gaze to Tahira Bukhari. *If you fuck this up, I'll fuck you up, and that's a promise.*

In Cartagena, Naomi woke to the sound of rain falling outside her second-story window. She shifted her feet to the floor and rubbed the sleep out of her eyes. Then she stood and walked into the adjoining bathroom. Splashing her face with cold water, she looked up and examined her reflection in the mirror above the sink. She looked terrible, but that was only to be expected, and it could have been worse. *Should have been worse*, she thought. Her hair was askew, and the skin around her red-rimmed eyes was puffy and bruised, which was strange, considering how hard she'd slept. Staring into the mirror, she traced her scar with her forefinger, following it down from her right cheekbone to the hinge of her jaw. Not for the first time, she found herself thinking that she deserved the disfiguring mark.

Drying her face on a hand towel, she wandered back into the bedroom, pulled on a robe, then walked over to the balcony. Stepping outside, she took in a deep breath of the clean morning air, then felt a sudden surge of overwhelming guilt.

What am I doing? she thought to herself, a wave of depression washing over her. *I don't deserve this. I shouldn't even be here. I should be dead like the others. Dead like the people I killed.*

Hot tears sprang to her eyes, but she didn't make an effort to wipe them away. Instead, she turned and went inside, glancing at the bedside clock on her way to the hall. Freezing in her tracks, she did a double take, her mouth falling open. She wiped her eyes to make sure the numbers weren't blurred, but they stayed the same. The clock said 7:00 AM, which meant that she'd been asleep for nearly . . . nineteen hours.

Nineteen hours? She briefly wondered how that was possible, but she already knew the answer. Her eyes darted to her bag, which was lying at the foot of the bed. On receiving it the day before, she'd found that her pills were still buried inside. She didn't know if Ryan had checked the bag, but she didn't think he had; if he'd found them, he wouldn't have let her keep them. She could dimly remember taking a few of them, shortly after he'd confronted her the previous day. A handful, maybe, but it must have been some handful, she realized, to keep her under for nineteen hours.

Reaching the door, she undid the latch, pulled it open, and stepped into the hall. As she made her way downstairs, she could hear noise in the kitchen, and she entered the room a moment later. Élise Machado was standing at the counter, still in her bedclothes, pouring grinds into the top of a coffee machine. She smiled at Naomi, then caught the younger woman's expression and frowned, a concerned look coming over her face.

"What's wrong?" she asked. "Has something happened?"

"Where's Ryan? Where's your daughter?"

"They're gone. They left yesterday." Élise looked confused. "I thought you knew. . . ."

Naomi was stunned. What was going on here? "What do you mean, 'they left'?" she sputtered, grabbing the door frame for support. "Where did they go?"

The older woman shook her head apologetically, obviously unsettled by Naomi's reaction. "I really don't know. They didn't say much . . . just said good-bye and left in the car my husband gave them."

"And where is he?" Naomi managed. "Your husband, I mean?"

"He went out to collect something. He said he'd be back in a few hours. Why?"

Naomi shook her head in disbelief. How could Ryan do this? Why would he just leave without telling her? More to the point, why had he taken Pétain, and where were they going?

After looking around blankly for a few seconds, she thought of another question. "What about my phone? Did Ryan take it with him?"

"You mean that bulky black thing? The one with the antennae?"

"Yes. Did he take it?"

Élise seemed to think for a moment, then slowly shook her head. "No, I don't think so, but I can't be sure."

Naomi closed her eyes and shook her head. Catching the gesture, Élise asked if anything was wrong.

"No," Naomi replied, but she could tell her voice was distant, not her own. "I'm fine. I'm . . . going upstairs to take a shower. I'll be back in a little bit."

Élise nodded uncertainly. She offered a tentative smile, then gestured toward the dripping machine. "Would you like some coffee first?"

"No," Naomi replied sharply. Catching herself, she tried for a more conciliatory tone. "I mean, no, thank you. I'm sorry. I just . . ."

She turned abruptly, not bothering to finish her sentence, leaving Élise Machado staring after her. She stalked down the hall and began climbing the stairs. Halfway up, she paused, placing a hand on the rail to steady herself. Then she pressed the other to her forehead, closing her eyes. She felt light-headed all of a sudden, as if all the energy had been drained from her body. She assumed it was partly due to the pills she had taken the day before, but part of it, she knew, was also anger. Blinding, deep-seated anger of a kind she rarely experienced. It was suddenly clear what had taken place. Harper must have called with additional background on Benazir Mengal, and instead of telling her, instead of trying to wake her up, Ryan had snuck off with Pétain to follow it up himself. Clearly, he had taken it upon himself to push her out of the search for Fitzgerald and the other hostages.

Clearly, he had decided she was no longer capable.

And the worst part of all, Naomi realized, was that he was probably right.

Once she was back in her room, she straightened the covers on the bed, then lay down on her back, staring up at the ceiling. For nearly an hour, she did nothing more than lie there—staring up, listening to the rain, waiting for some kind of insight. Finally, the tears came. She didn't try to stop them, and she didn't make a sound the whole time, even as they formed a puddle behind her head, then soaked into the bedspread. She wasn't thinking about anything, and she didn't have to prompt them; the tears simply came of their own accord. It was almost as if her body was purging itself of everything that had happened. Everything from Madrid to New York City the year before, but she knew it would take a lot more than one moment of weakness to fully release the guilt that was weighing her down. In fact, she couldn't think of a single solution; there was just no way she could ever forgive herself for the things she had done.

At the same time, she knew she could not continue down the path she was on. She had always thought of herself as a strong person, but the past ten months had shown her just how weak she could be. She could see that now. She had tried to numb her sorrow and guilt instead of facing it head-on, and it just wasn't going to work anymore. For the first time since she'd arrived in Spain, Naomi realized just how badly she wanted to find Fitzgerald and the other hostages. She didn't know if doing so would earn her some kind of reprieve from her past actions, but it was the best—and only—option she could see. At the very least, finding them would mean doing the right thing, and that was reason enough; it had been a long time since she could claim even that much.

After lying there for another twenty minutes, she sat up, her gaze falling on the foot of the bed. Getting to her feet, she went to the end of the bed and knelt by her bag. Unzipping it, she dug out the Baggie containing the last of her pills.

She was almost entranced by the tiny white tablets; they seemed to call out to her. The pull was so hard to resist, but it had always been that way. When she'd first been prescribed the morphine, she had genuinely needed it. The pain on the right side of her face had been intense, which was understandable, given the severity of the wound. It had been so bad that the doctors had initially anticipated minor nerve damage. In time they were proven wrong, but no one had ever questioned the serious nature of the injury. As the weeks went by, her physician began reducing the dosage, but Naomi had not been able to adjust as quickly; she'd needed the pills just as much as she had at the start. Eventually, he'd cut her off completely, and she'd been forced to find outside channels. An old friend had reluctantly come through for her and would continue to do so if Naomi asked her. For now, she still had two dozen of the little white pills, more than enough to keep her going until she got back to the States.

And she could still go back, she knew. She could leave now if she wanted. She could catch a taxi to the airport, fly back to Washington, and go back to hating herself and her life, just as she'd been doing for the past ten months. Or she could put a halt to the slide right now.

Only if she did, if she made the decision to stop things now, she had to be sure. Because by doing the right thing, she'd be entering her own personal hell for at least the next four to five days, and maybe much longer.

Clutching the Baggie in her right fist, she took a deep breath and steeled her resolve. Then she went into the bathroom and tipped the

Baggie upside down over the bowl. Her breathing quickened as each pill plopped into the water, but she forced herself to keep going, her limbs trembling with the mental effort it took to destroy her synthetic relief, her only real retreat from reality. When the Baggie was completely empty, she flushed the toilet, her stomach clenching as the swirling water carried them all away.

Lowering the lid, she sat down, propped her elbows on her knees, and lowered her face into her waiting hands. She had a vague idea of what was coming over the next twenty-four to forty-eight hours. The next two days would mark the worst of it, but she had made her decision. Besides, she no longer had a choice; the pills were gone, so she had to see it through.

Shifting gears, she started to think about her next move. The first thing was to get in touch with Harper, and she had to do it before the withdrawal symptoms came on. Harper wasn't an idiot, and it was just as Ryan had suspected; the deputy DCI knew damn well what she was into, and he would be able to tell—even over the phone—if she was off the morphine.

Naomi wasn't an idiot, either. She knew that Harper had placed her in Ryan's path to draw him back, to get him involved in the op. She had been unwilling to admit this earlier, even to herself, but now she was done pretending. At the same time, she knew that she could contribute, that she was much, much more than a simple pawn. She didn't know where Kealey had gone, but her gut was telling her he was en route to Pakistan, if he wasn't already there. In that place, her help would prove invaluable. She spoke fluent Punjabi and passable Urdu, she knew the culture and customs, and she could blend into the local population. Ryan may not know it now, but he needed her, and despite the anger she was currently feeling, she would forgive him for the shit he had pulled the previous day if it meant she could be involved. She had to do it; she knew that now. Not for him, and not for the people who'd died at her hand, but for herself.

A sound from the next room startled her from her reverie. She lifted her head, listening hard, then jumped up and ran into the bedroom. Dashing out to the balcony, she looked down and saw Javier Machado's E-type Jaguar rolling up the driveway, to the right of the garden.

Moving back to the bed, she threw off her robe and began to

dress quickly. Despite what the immediate future held for her, she felt suddenly energized. Machado would know where her encrypted sat phone was, and once she had it, she could call Harper and get things moving. For the first time in nearly a year, she felt sure about what she was doing, and that felt better than she would have ever believed.

CHAPTER 32

LANGLEY, VIRGINIA

It was just after 8:00 in the morning as Harper walked into the DCI's office on the seventh floor of the Old Headquarters Building. The OHB was part of the sprawling campus that made up the CIA's headquarters in Langley, Virginia, home to the Memorial Wall and to an impressive library with 26,000 volumes, which, unfortunately for the general public, was open only to Agency employees. There was a day-care center on the ground floor, along with a cafeteria and a small gymnasium. In short, the OHB had all the amenities of most modern U.S. corporations. Like the employees of those corporations, however, the people who worked for the Agency rarely had time to enjoy such luxuries. This was especially true in times of crisis, and the Agency—along with the rest of the U.S. intelligence apparatus—had been running on crisis mode for four days, ever since the abduction of the secretary of state in Rawalpindi.

This being the case, it was fitting that the director looked as tired as the people who worked for him, Harper thought. Robert Andrews was seated behind his heavy, hand-carved desk, his sleeves rolled up, a telephone receiver wedged between his ear and shoulder. He was looking over a sheaf of documents as he talked, and, glancing up for an instant, waved Harper into a seat. A few minutes later, he ended the call with a series of terse instructions, then slammed the receiver down and glared at his deputy.

"So," he began, his fingers drumming out an uneven rhythm on his desk, "what's the situation? What's going on in Pakistan?"

Harper sighed inwardly as he considered where to begin. He'd received Kharmai's call at home nearly six hours earlier, at 2:15 in the morning. Once he was awake enough to hear what she was saying, he'd jumped out of bed and moved into his study, where he proceeded to get all the facts from her. The general situation appeared pretty clear; Kealey had disobeyed a direct order by taking Pétain to Islamabad instead of Kharmai. And that was assuming he'd even flown into Islamabad, as instructed; at this point, he could be anywhere. To make matters worse, he had yet to make contact with Owen and the rest of his team.

Harper relayed all of this to Andrews. The full explanation took about five minutes, during which time the director didn't utter a word. When Harper was done, Andrews ran a hand over his face, then cast a long glance out the west-facing windows.

"Why hasn't Kealey made contact?" he finally asked, shifting his gaze back to Harper.

Harper shrugged. "There's no way to know. Maybe he picked up some surveillance when he arrived. Maybe he shook it, and he's waiting to make sure he's clean. It could be anything."

"And why did he leave Kharmai behind? Why take Pétain? From what I've read, it seems that Kharmai would be far more valuable in that situation."

"That's a fair assessment. As far as I can tell, Pétain is more of a liability to operational security than an asset, at least in this situation. I don't know why he brought her."

Andrews mulled over that for a moment, then nodded his agreement. It was one of the things that Harper had noticed about the DCI. Since taking the reins of the Agency two and a half years prior, Andrews had mellowed substantially. There had been a time when he'd been quick to express his dissatisfaction with the pace of the Agency and the endless dissemination of information that intelligence work required, but he had since learned to control his temper. In the end, the man's change in demeanor didn't really affect day-to-day operations, thought it certainly made for a more relaxed work environment, at least in normal circumstances. Of course, the current situation was anything but, and the public dissemination of Amari Saifi's demands had only made things worse.

"I know the basics about her father, but Pétain is a mystery to me. There has to be some reason Kealey would want her along, though . . . What's her background?"

Harper had anticipated this question, and he'd taken the time to read up on the young operative. "Marissa Pétain was born in 1981 in Paris, the second child of Javier Machado and Élise Pétain. Her father was stationed at our embassy at the time, but Élise and her daughters stayed in France when Machado was transferred to Rabat in '84. Pétain attended the American School of Paris from '85 to '99, during which time she became fluent in German, Italian, and Russian. She also has English, Spanish, and French, thanks to her parents. After graduation, she was accepted to Marquette. She immigrated to the States in '99, by which time her father had already retired from the Agency. Pétain did a BS in information systems at Marquette, then went on to earn master's degrees in mathematics and psychology . . . She picked up both of those at the University of North Carolina at Chapel Hill."

Andrews frowned. "You mentioned the second daughter. She was with the Agency as well, wasn't she?"

Harper sighed again, aloud this time. Then he went on to explain the rest, telling the director the same thing that Pétain had told Kealey less than two days earlier. When Harper was done, Andrews appeared to be slightly stunned.

"How did she get through the front doors, John?" he asked, spreading his hands in a questioning gesture. "Given that her sister was killed on assignment in Colombia, not to mention the incident with the pictures and the videotape, she should have been screened out during the psych exams, don't you think?"

"Maybe," Harper admitted, "but she had the qualities we were looking for, and you can't deny her credentials. She seemed to be a perfect fit for us, especially for the DO, and besides, her family history with the Agency wasn't all negative."

"You're referring to Machado."

"Yes. I'm sure you know about him and Noriega . . . I mean, the man was a legend. Javier Machado is one of our most decorated operatives, past or present."

Andrews nodded slowly. "Yes, I know about Machado. I'm just saying we should have taken a harder look at Pétain before taking her on. You have to admit, John, it sounds like the woman has a ton of baggage."

"I'm not saying she doesn't, but she's extremely motivated. In fact, she's in line for something big later in the year." Harper paused, realizing it would be doubly hard to get that particular op approved, given Pétain's leading role in it, the area in which it would be conducted, and Andrew's obvious skepticism with respect to the young operative's state of mind. But that could all be figured out at a later date.

"Anyway," Harper continued, "here's the point. She's a capable operative, but she doesn't belong in Pakistan, and we're still not sure why Kealey brought her along. I'm afraid we only have one recourse for the time being, and that's to sit and wait. Eventually, he'll have to make contact."

"And what about the rest of the team?" Andrews demanded. He thumped a hand on his desk, a flash of the old temper coming through. "Are they just supposed to sit around and wait for him?"

"Of course not. Owen has been in constant contact for the past thirty hours. They've already managed to rule out two of the names on the list, and they're moving on to the third, a veterinarian living in Faisalabad."

"A vet?" An incredulous look crossed the DCI's face. "You must be joking. Mengal would never entrust Fitzgerald's life to a veterinarian. She's too valuable to him."

"Maybe he doesn't have a choice. Maybe we've overestimated his reach . . . Perhaps his contacts aren't as extensive as we initially thought. In any case, the vet came up as a possible candidate, so he has to be checked."

Andrews let out a long breath through pursed lips, then leaned back in his black leather chair. "What about Kharmai?"

Harper shifted his weight in his seat, but he wasn't stalling; he'd already thought this through. "I want her in Pakistan. At the very least, she's an extra pair of eyes. Owen could use her in Faisalabad, at least until Kealey checks in. Then we can go from there."

"Actually, I'd like her to stay where she is," Andrews said, throwing Harper off track. "Something's come up, and we can't risk moving her until we know where it's going."

The deputy director straightened in his seat, suddenly alert. "What do you mean? What's going on?"

"I received a call from Stan Chavis late last night," Andrews explained, referencing the president's chief of staff. "He told me that the Spanish ambassador has requested a meeting with the president. Apparently, the investigation of the bombing in Madrid has already turned up some evidence. The CNP has recovered a handgun that was dropped at the scene, and they've managed to get some usable prints."

"That doesn't matter," Harper said dismissively. "Naomi was the only one who handled that weapon without gloves, and they don't have her prints on file."

"Maybe not, but that's not all. They've also managed to get their hands on a video recording, which was taken at the scene of the bombing."

"Oh, Jesus Christ," Harper muttered, rubbing a hand across his face. "What kind of tape? What does it show?"

"The ambassador didn't say. Anyway, I'd order Kealey and Pétain to stay put as well, but since they can't be found, just get word to Kharmai. Hopefully, it's nothing, but we have to take the proper precautions."

"I'll let her know," Harper said grimly. "Anything else?"

"Yeah. Chavis wants us there for the meeting, which means that the president wants us there. It's set for three this afternoon."

"I'll be there."

"We'll ride together," Andrews said. "We need to prepare for the worst."

"Which is?" Harper asked. He had a good idea of what "the worst" entailed, but he wanted to hear the other man's thoughts on the matter.

"The worst," Andrews remarked glumly, "is that they're holding something back to catch Brenneman on his heels. The worst is that Kealey and Pétain never made it to the airport. The worst is that the Spanish have them in custody, even as we speak."

"Christ," Harper murmured. He hadn't thought of that; in his mind, the worst possible scenario was that the Spanish had made a positive ID on one of the operatives who'd taken part in Madrid. "You think that's possible?"

Andrews shrugged. "I doubt it. I don't think they would sit on that kind of development for twelve minutes, let alone twelve hours. At the same time, we have to be ready. They know *something* . . . That's the main thing. Otherwise, they wouldn't have gone to these lengths to get an audience with the president."

"Okay," Harper said, drawing up a list in his mind of steps that had to be taken. He was already thinking about deniability. "I'll start putting together a list of plausible scenarios and our possible response to each. We already have protocols in place, but with something of this magnitude . . ."

"I know," Andrews said, his tone despondent. "We've got six dead civilians in Madrid, John, along with Kamil Ghafour, whom we just happened to inquire about a week before his death. We can't afford to be tied to this. We'll let the ambassador say his piece, but we need to be ready for anything."

"It all depends on what they have. If the footage is less than conclusive, we might be able to wiggle out of it."

"But if it *is* conclusive . . ."

Harper nodded his understanding. Andrews didn't have to finish his sentence, because his meaning was clear. Whatever else happened, the incident would not touch the president. Stan Chavis would make sure of that. But that was long term, and Harper pushed the thought away, choosing instead to focus on the immediate situation. The upcoming meeting would not be pretty. All hell was about to break loose regardless, but if the Spanish had incontrovertible evidence that the CIA had played a role in the Madrid bombing and the death of Kamil Ghafour, then the fallout would stain the Agency for years to come. They simply couldn't allow the truth to come to light.

"See what you can do, John," Andrews said. Harper took his cue and stood, just as the DCI's phone began to ring. "Find us a way out. If one of your people was caught on video, you know what has to happen. As for the meeting with Vázquez, Diane will call you when it's time to leave."

Harper nodded and left the room. On his way through the anteroom, Diane Neal, the DCI's long-standing secretary, said good-bye and lifted a hand in a little wave, but Harper was oblivious. As he walked the short distance back to his own office, his legs felt heavy, a weight settling onto his shoulders. His head was spinning with the possible consequences of what he had just heard. Although the Spanish ambassador's precise agenda remained a mystery, Harper knew that he wouldn't have sought the meeting with Brenneman without the express approval of his government. In other words, the Spanish government clearly had some kind of damaging evidence on its hands, and that could only mean one thing: at least one of the people involved in Madrid was facing a very long vacation in a non-extradition country, immediately preceded by complete separation from the Central Intelligence Agency.

The truth was staring him right in the face, and as much as he wanted to, Harper couldn't ignore it. Somebody's career was about to come to a very decisive end, and if the Agency couldn't sidestep the Spanish government's allegations, then Harper—along with most, if not all, of the senior staff—would be following that unfortunate person right out the door.

CHAPTER 33

WASHINGTON, D.C.

The cool, still air inside the Oval Office was laced with nervous tension, despite the warm light seeping in through the colonnade windows that overlooked the South Lawn. It might have been a perfect summer day for everyone else in Washington, Harper thought bleakly, but not for the people in the president's inner sanctum. He could feel the tension, which was almost tangible, and he could see it in the faces of the three other men in the room. Brenneman and Andrews were seated on the other side of a low-lying coffee table, deep in quiet discussion, while Lawrence Hayden, the head of European and Eurasian Affairs at the State Department, stood to one side of the president's desk, muttering into the phone he was holding.

Stan Chavis, who had stepped out a few minutes earlier to handle a minor emergency, had suggested Hayden's presence. Harper did not particularly care for the abrupt, socially challenged chief of staff, but on this point, he happened to think the man was right. Hayden, a twenty-year veteran of the Foreign Service, had served as the U.S. ambassador to Spain from 2004 to 2007, his last foreign posting before he'd been tapped to head up the European bureau at State. During his brief stint as ambassador, he'd forged close relationships with a number of high-ranking Spanish officials, including José Zapatero, the current prime minister. Given the volatile subject matter of the upcoming meeting with the Spanish ambassador, Hayden was the perfect person to help deflect the forthcoming accusations, as well as to help minimize the fallout when the meeting was over, if it became clear that damage control was needed.

Harper still had no idea what evidence the Spanish government had in its possession, and the possibility Andrews had brought up earlier in the afternoon was still weighing on him heavily. He had yet to hear from Kealey or Pétain. As far as he knew, they could be anywhere, including a Spanish jail. He doubted it somehow; it seemed likely that news of their arrest would have reached Langley through the American embassy in Madrid, but until he knew for sure they had made it to Pakistan, he could not rule anything out. His last communication with Paul Owen had been forty-five minutes earlier, and the news had not been positive: The surveillance just wasn't yielding anything useful. After ending that disappointing call, Harper had received the summons from the DCI's office, informing him that the car was ready to depart for the White House.

He and Andrews had spent the thirty-minute ride brainstorming and strategizing. They'd agreed on a variety of possible responses, but it was too early to settle on one in particular. It all depended on the severity of the charges that were levied against the Agency, as well as the quality of the evidence that was going to be presented. Clearly, the ambassador would have to show cause for requesting the meeting in the first place, so they were going to see at least a few of the cards the Spanish were holding, but Harper knew that Vázquez might hold something back, just to see if he could catch them in a lie. He had warned Andrews of this possibility, and Andrews, in turn, had warned the president.

Brenneman had not taken the news well. He had demanded to know why they had learned nothing useful about the extent of the evidence, and he'd wanted to know how the team in Madrid could have been caught on tape to begin with. Unfortunately, Harper had nothing to contribute in that regard; in fact, he had been wondering the same thing. Before Kealey and Kharmai had landed in Spain, Pétain's team had performed an extensive canvas of the area in which they would be operating. They had looked at the hotel they were staying in, as well as the construction site on Calle de San Leonardo de Dios and everything in between. They'd checked for traffic cameras, police kiosks, and surveillance cameras positioned outside the neighboring stores. They'd noted the areas of coverage provided by the cameras inside the hotel lobby, and they'd mapped out the best ways to avoid them while moving through the building. In short, they had covered every angle to the best of their ability, but somehow, somewhere, they had missed something crucial, and in a few minutes' time, Harper was going to find out what they had overlooked.

At that moment, Hayden replaced the receiver in its cradle with slightly more force than necessary, then exhaled heavily. Brenneman and Andrews paused in their conversation, and both men cast an expectant look at the assistant secretary of state.

"James has no idea what's going on," he reported wearily. Edward James was the U.S. ambassador to Spain. He'd taken over the job in the fall of 2007, shortly after Hayden had been promoted and brought back to Washington, and he had yet to make an impression. "He can't get in to see anyone at the Congressional Palace, and the foreign minister isn't taking his calls. Essentially, he's been frozen out for the past eight hours."

"What does that mean?" Brenneman asked, looking from Andrews to Hayden for an explanation.

The assistant secretary let out a short sigh, one hand massaging his bearded chin. "Basically, sir, it's not good. It means that whatever they have is pretty much set in stone. It's nothing we're going to be able to deny . . . If they weren't sure, they'd be probing for more, just as we are. They're going to try to catch us off guard."

"So what do you recommend?" Brenneman asked.

Hayden grimaced and shook his head. "I hate to say it, sir, but it sounds like they've got the goods. I recommend we shift our focus to limiting the impact of our involvement, as opposed to denying it outright, which will only draw more attention to the situation. Maybe we can get the Spanish to hush it up in exchange for some kind of perk. Our trade agreements are up for review in a few months, so maybe we can get something moving in that direction."

Brenneman nodded slowly as he mulled over the assistant secretary of state's advice. Then he shifted his gaze to the DCI, who was already shaking his head emphatically. "What do you think, Bob?"

"Sir, I'm afraid I have to disagree." Andrews nodded respectfully in Hayden's direction. "I'm sorry, Larry, but I don't think we can afford to admit to this. I mean, we're talking about six dead civilians here. If we accept the blame, we'll be looking at a diplomatic catastrophe. It'll be worse than the incident in China."

The room fell silent for a moment. Andrews didn't need to refer-

ence a specific time or place, because they all knew what he was referring to. Everyone in the room recalled that prolonged diplomatic
battle, which had begun when a U.S. Navy EP-3E collided with a Chinese fighter jet over the island province of Hainan in 2001. The surveillance plane managed to land safely on Hainan, but the Chinese
pilot was killed in the midair collision. A serious diplomatic spat had
ensued as the State Department began to negotiate quietly for the
return of the plane and its crew of 24. Eleven tense days passed before the crew was released from Chinese custody, and the plane itself
was not returned for three months. When it *was* finally returned, it
was dismantled and flown back on a cargo plane, even though in-
spectors had deemed it capable of flight. The reason for this was simple: the Chinese government, in an effort to save face following the
release of the U.S. crew, had decided that the plane could not be allowed to leave under its own power, as that would have been seen
around the world as a national humiliation and a clear victory for the
U.S. government.

However, that incident, as bad as it was at the time, had eventually
blown over. The situation they were facing now was far more serious.
Six Spanish nationals were dead, and they had not been killed in an
accident. Furthermore, the U.S. government had been forced to admit
its culpability when the EP-3E had gone down in China, but so far,
Brenneman's administration had remained mute with respect to the
bombing in Madrid and the death of Kamil Ghafour. Worse still, the CIA
was involved, which would automatically guarantee a prolonged media
blitz if the truth came out. The severity of the situation could not be
overstated. If the Spanish had incontrovertible proof of what had really happened, bilateral ties between the U.S. and Spain wouldn't just
be damaged. They might well be severed entirely, and everyone in
the room knew that could not be allowed to happen.

The president, having taken a moment to consider the director's
words, looked over at Harper. "John? What are your thoughts?"

Harper cleared his throat gently. "Sir, I agree with Director Andrews. It doesn't matter if they have pictures of our people walking
into Langley. They can have all the proof in the world that we played
a role in Madrid, but we can't admit to it. We just can't afford to."

Brenneman nodded slowly. "I agree," he said at length. "At this
point, I don't think we can risk admitting that we were responsible.
That said, I want to hear what Vázquez has to say. Maybe they don't—"

The president was cut off by a tap at the door. A few seconds later, Stan Chavis entered the room. "Ambassador Vázquez has just arrived," he informed them gravely.

Brenneman got to his feet, the other men following suit. Taking a second to straighten his tie, the president nodded to Chavis and said, "Show him in, Stan, and ask Claire to hold my calls for the next twenty minutes. Let's get this over with."

Harper had never met Miguel Ruiz Vázquez, the Spanish ambassador to the United States, but he had heard the name, and he'd read through a brief biography on the ride in from Langley. At sixty-two, Vázquez was a diplomat whose career had spanned forty years, which, in a country like Spain, was an achievement all by itself. He had survived the brutal regime of Francisco Franco, then the political restructuring that came about with the restoration of the kingdom in 1978 under King Juan Carlos I. During that time he had risen steadily through the ranks of the Foreign Ministry, holding senior-level posts in Brazil, Greece, and Luxembourg, where he learned to speak reasonable French. Over the course of his foreign service, he had also managed to earn advanced degrees in law and management from the Autonomous University of Madrid. The second degree, in particular, had served him well in Washington, where he presided over a staff of 170 at the Spanish embassy on Pennsylvania Avenue, just a short distance from the White House itself.

The main thing that stuck out in Harper's mind, though, was the ambassador's reputation, which was that of a shrewd political operator. This wasn't surprising in a man who'd accomplished as much as Vázquez had, but nevertheless, it was a worrying fact. At the very least, it meant he would not be easily intimidated. If he had the evidence to support his government's claims, he would not hesitate to deliver a very forthright message to the president, regardless of his surroundings.

This fact was weighing heavily on Harper's mind as Claire Bouchard, the president's secretary, showed Vázquez into the room. Everyone was standing as the ambassador crossed the presidential rug and accepted Brenneman's proffered hand.

"Miguel, it's good to see you again," Brenneman said, with a warm, apparently genuine smile. Harper had always been impressed by the man's courteous nature, which rarely seemed to slip. He had always wondered if it was real or just a façade, but now, recalling the president's words of just a few minutes earlier, he could see just how skilled an actor David Brenneman actually was. He was greeting the Spanish official like an old friend, even as he was preparing to lie right to his face.

"Thank you, Mr. President," Vázquez replied, bobbing his head politely, "and thank you for taking the time to see me. I realize this is a difficult time for you and your country. I understand that the leaders of my country have already contacted you to express their concern and outrage over the abduction of Secretary Fitzgerald in Pakistan, but please allow me to convey my personal condolences. My family and I are praying for her safe recovery, as are the people of Spain."

The president accepted the expected words with a slight inclination of his head, then grasped the other man's hand in both of his own. "Thank you, Mr. Ambassador. I appreciate that, and I'm grateful for your support and that of your government. It means a great deal, not only to me, but to everyone here."

Releasing the other man's hand, Brenneman began making the introductions. Vázquez cordially shook each man's hand, his face revealing nothing at all. When Harper's turn came, the deputy director thought he saw something flash across the ambassador's face, an expression that fell somewhere between distaste and contempt, but given the situation and their surroundings, Harper had no choice but to let it slide.

Gesturing to the numerous chairs in front of his desk, Brenneman invited them all to sit. The president took the seat closest to his desk, on the south side of the room. Vázquez sat to his immediate right, and Lawrence Hayden took the next seat down. Andrews, Harper, and Chavis picked out chairs on the other side of the coffee table, the chief of staff selecting the seat closest to the president. As they were settling in, a Navy steward entered the room with coffee, cream, and sugar on a silver tray. He left the tray on the table, along with cups for everyone present. Then he left the room, closing the door quietly behind him.

For a moment, no one spoke as Stan Chavis began pouring the coffee. Then the ambassador turned to Brenneman. As he did so, he placed both hands on top of the file he was holding in his lap.

"Mr. President," he began cordially, "I believe you know why my government requested this meeting."

"Actually," Hayden said quickly, trying to shift Vázquez's attention away from the president, "the reason for this meeting has not been made entirely clear, Mr. Ambassador. As you can probably guess, we tried to contact certain people through the usual diplomatic channels in an effort to learn more, but we've had a difficult time accessing certain members of your government over the past eight hours. Perhaps you could tell us why this is the case."

"I'm afraid I can't speak to that," Vázquez replied mildly, one hand lightly tapping the top of the file. "Unfortunately, I'm somewhat out of the loop myself. I'm sure you understand that things have been very hectic over the past couple of days."

No one believed that for a second, but the unwritten rules of diplomacy did not allow them to question the statement. An uncomfortable silence fell over the room, and then Vázquez continued, aiming his words once more at the president.

"Mr. President, I believe you're familiar with the recent events in Madrid. I'm referring, of course, to the bombing two days ago that claimed the lives of six innocent people. Indirectly, that incident also resulted in the death of an Algerian national by the name of Kamil Ahmed Ghafour. Ghafour, as you may or may not know, was not killed in the bombing, but in a related shooting incident just minutes before. Both events occurred on the same street in downtown Madrid."

Brenneman nodded slowly, ignoring the cup that Chavis placed before him. "I'm familiar with the situation. As you probably know, I've already contacted the king and Prime Minister Zapatero to express my condolences."

"Then you probably also know," the ambassador continued, acknowledging the president's words with another bob of his head, "that less than a week prior to this incident, the U.S. State Department submitted an official request to the Foreign Ministry in Madrid. In this request, they asked that Ghafour be made available for an interview regarding his association with a man named Amari Saifi, another Algerian national and a prominent member of the Salafist Group for Call and Combat, otherwise known as the GSCP."

Once again, Hayden jumped in. "Yes, that's correct. We had reason to believe that Saifi was responsible for the recent abductions of twelve U.S. tourists in Pakistan. As I'm sure you know, that initial theory was right on the mark. I assume you've seen the tape."

Vázquez nodded slowly, though the question was clearly rhetorical. He *had* seen the tape that al-Jazeera had first aired two days ago, and he was now fully aware—along with everyone else in the civilized world—that Amari Saifi had been implicit not only in the earlier kidnappings, but also in the abduction of the secretary herself. He had known this would probably come up, but given the evidence he was holding in his lap, he was not about to go on the defensive.

"In retrospect," he finally conceded, "we probably should have made a greater effort to accommodate your earlier request. But wouldn't you agree, Secretary Hayden, that this entire episode strikes one as quite a coincidence?"

"What, exactly, are you referring to?" Stan Chavis asked tightly.

"I would have thought that was clear, Mr. Chavis." Vázquez stared directly across the table, not backing down an inch. "I'm referring to the exquisitely short gap between the State Department's request to meet with Ghafour and his rather untimely death in Madrid."

Brenneman cleared his throat gently. "Miguel, I can see where you're going with this, but you're a career diplomat. You know how this works, and I don't have to tell you that you're treading on dangerous ground. If you're insinuating what I think you are, you're making a grave mistake. Making that kind of accusation without proof would not be in your best interest, or in the interests of your government, for that matter."

The Spanish ambassador's eyes widened slightly, and he raised one hand, palm out, in a conciliatory gesture. "Mr. President, I did not mean to level any kind of accusation, and please forgive me if I left that impression. I merely wish to emphasize the unusual timing. That both incidents should occur so close together seems to strain credulity."

Hayden opened his mouth to speak, but Vázquez raised his hand once more. "Please, Mr. Hayden, bear with me a moment. I think you'll be interested in what I'm about to say."

Settling back in his chair, the ambassador looked at them each in turn. "As you can probably imagine," he said, "the bombing on Calle de San Leonardo de Dios immediately prompted a large-scale investigation. Personnel and material resources from a number of our agencies, including the National Police and the Guardia Civil, were dispatched to the scene to begin searching for evidence. What they found was very surprising. You see, the explosion was not caused by a conventional explosive, such as dynamite or TNT, or by a plastic explosive, such as Semtex—a favorite of the Basque separatists—or C4. The explosion was caused by the detonation of two tanks, one of which contained acetylene. The other contained oxygen. According to the preliminary report issued by the CNP, both tanks were either full or close to it, which would account for the extensive property damage and loss of life."

"Acetylene?" Brenneman murmured. He shook his head slowly. "That seems . . . unlikely."

"I can assure you, Mr. President, it's true." Vázquez seemed pleased that the president had spoken, Harper noticed uneasily. Personally, he wished that Brenneman would stop talking completely; every word that came out of his mouth was something that might potentially incriminate him later. Besides, that was the reason for Hayden's presence. If anyone was going to go out on a limb, it should have been him.

"Fortunately, it didn't take long to trace the source of the tanks," Vázquez continued. "Both were removed—stolen, actually—from a vehicle repair shop less than twenty meters from the site of the explosion. The owner was quickly able to verify that the tanks were missing. Apparently, he'd had trouble with theft before—unfortunately, there is considerable demand for black market tools in Madrid— and after the last incident, which occurred two months prior to the bombing, he installed a closed-circuit TV in the repair bays. Obviously, this turned out to be a major break in the investigation."

Vázquez opened the folder on his lap. Removing the first of several eight-by-tens, he handed the photograph to the president. Brenneman examined it briefly, his face giving nothing away. Shaking his head slightly, he passed the photo to his left. The DCI studied it briefly, then gave it to Harper. The image had obviously been cleaned up, but it hadn't been forged. Harper knew it was real because the person he was looking at was none other than Naomi Kharmai. In the photograph, she was standing in the middle of the first bay, looking around, as if deciding what to do next. A moment later, Andrews handed him another photograph. The time stamp in the upper left-hand corner indicated that it had been taken less than five seconds after the first. This image showed Kharmai wheeling a hand truck out of the shop. Two tanks—one green, one unpainted—were strapped to the hand truck.

"As you can see," Vázquez was saying, "these images are less than perfect. First, the tape had to be compressed, to improve the quality.

Then the still images were extracted from the tape itself. Obviously, it's difficult to print a usable image when the source is lower than print quality, but our technicians did their best. The result isn't ideal, but the woman's face is clearly visible in each shot. That's the main point I wish to impress."

Removing a third image from his folder, the ambassador passed it to Brenneman. When it reached Harper, he studied it briefly. He could immediately see that it had been taken at the airport, from a ceiling-mounted camera. The image clearly depicted the same woman in the first two photographs.

"This image," Vázquez said, once he was sure they had all seen it, "was captured at Madrid Barajas International Airport one day prior to the bombing. According to customs, the woman you see here was traveling on a U.S. passport issued to one Sarinder Kaur Nagra. I'm sure we can all agree that all three of the images depict the same person. If there is any doubt in your minds, however, I can show you data provided by our facial-recognition software, which conclusively matched the face in all three photographs."

No one had spoken as the ambassador had made his presentation, but Harper could no longer remain silent. "Mr. Ambassador, it's gratifying to see that your government has made such remarkable progress in its investigation, but why, exactly, are you bringing this to our attention?"

"I would have thought that was obvious, Mr. Harper. This woman has an American passport; therefore, she's a U.S. citizen. We would like the FBI to locate her, take her into custody, and begin extradition proceedings."

The room fell silent. After what seemed like an eternity, Harper asked, "Is there anything else you can tell us with respect to the investigation?"

Vázquez nodded curtly; clearly, he'd been expecting the question. Removing a final photograph from his folder, he handed it to the president. Brenneman looked at it for what seemed like a very long time, his eyes narrowing, his jaw visibly tightening. By the time the photo was passed to Harper, he already knew what he was going to see.

"This final image," Vázquez said quietly, "was printed in *Time* magazine ten months ago. The photograph was taken by a fast-thinking tourist during the failed terrorist attack in New York City last September, and as you can see, the content speaks for itself."

Harper had seen the image a thousand times, but he forced himself to study it once more. The photograph, which had been taken outside the Renaissance Hotel in Times Square, depicted William Vanderveen, the soldier turned traitor who had once served under Ryan Kealey, and Naomi Kharmai. In the photograph, Vanderveen was using Kharmai as a human shield, his right hand holding a knife to her throat. In the foreground, a man was pointing a gun in Vanderveen's direction. Ryan Kealey's back was to the camera; the only part of his face that was visible was the right hinge of his jaw.

Kharmai's face, on the other hand, was only too clear. In the picture, her hands were up and pulling against the restraining arm wrapped round her throat. Her mouth was wide open, frozen in a silent scream, but it was her eyes that had made the picture famous. They were filled with sheer terror, the kind of pure, unadulterated fear that was rarely caught on film. Harper despised the picture for obvious reasons, but he had to admit that it was a powerful image. He felt sick every time he looked at it.

"The woman in this photograph," Vázquez was saying, "is clearly the same woman who carried out the bombing in Madrid. Interestingly enough, the name Sarinder Nagra cannot be found in any U.S. periodicals dating back to September, which strikes me as extremely unusual, given the considerable fame of this photograph. It seems as if Ms. Nagra would have been interviewed by every major network, newspaper, and magazine in the country. After all, the accompanying article states that she survived the attack, after which she received medical treatment at an undisclosed location in Virginia. That last part is a direct quote, by the way."

Vázquez paused and looked at them each in turn. "Needless to say, my government is going to keep working until this woman is brought to justice. The magnitude of this incident does not allow us to look the other way. Therefore, I feel compelled to ask the obvious question."

There was a short, tense silence, and then Andrews said, "Forgive me, Mr. Ambassador, but perhaps it isn't so obvious. What, exactly, are you asking?"

Vázquez leaned over the table and put a finger on one of the eight-by-tens, which had made its way back to him. Then he looked up at the DCI and asked, "Is this woman employed by the CIA?"

Andrews stared directly across the table, meeting the other man's eyes. "No, she isn't."

"Is she employed by any state or federal agency?" Vázquez asked.

"No," Brenneman said, shaking his head emphatically. "Absolutely not. I can tell you right now, unequivocally, that she has no affiliation with the U.S. government whatsoever."

Vázquez nodded and leaned back in his chair, apparently satisfied. "Then I assume my government can count on your cooperation in this matter. It shouldn't be too hard for the FBI to track her down, and once they do, we can begin extradition proceedings."

Hayden hesitated, then said, "That seems a bit premature." He tapped the photograph that showed Kharmai wheeling the hand truck out of the auto-repair shop. "You can't prove that this woman detonated the bomb."

"At the very least, she's an accomplice," Vázquez pointed out, "and she must be held accountable. If she is willing to help the police piece together what actually happened, it might go easier for her. Either way, for this matter to be fully resolved, she must stand trial."

"We don't even know if she's a U.S. citizen or permanent resident," Hayden remarked cautiously. "The passport she was traveling on might have been forged. That's a problem we've been dealing a lot with lately. If she's well funded, with the right kinds of connections, she might be beyond our reach."

"With all due respect, Mr. Hayden, I find that hard to believe. It takes great skill and a number of tools, many of which are hard to find, to forge a credible passport. Very few people can do it successfully. It would likely take the combined efforts of an experienced group of people to do it right, such as the forgery department of a major intelligence agency."

Vázquez paused for a beat to cast a long look in Harper's direction, driving the unsubtle hint home. "We've back-checked passenger lists for all commercial flights leaving Spain over the past two days, and we have yet to find the name Sarinder Nagra. Unfortunately, that doesn't mean much. She could have crossed into France or Portugal with relative ease. Personally, I suspect she's already back in the States. If that is indeed the case, you must decide what happens next."

Vázquez turned to Brenneman. "Mr. President, I trust that you will do what is best in this situation. My superiors value the relationship between our two countries very highly indeed, and we would like nothing more than to continue working in a positive direction. However, this woman could be perceived as a serious stumbling block. If she is not apprehended soon, I'm afraid it could cause a considerable strain on our current ties. Naturally, it would also impede any forward progress."

A brief silence fell over the room. Before the president could respond, Lawrence Hayden stepped in to offer the usual diplomatic platitudes. "Mr. Ambassador, safeguarding the relationship between our two countries is one of this administration's highest priorities. I can assure you that the FBI and a number of other federal agencies will be . . ."

Harper didn't hear anything after that. In his mind, he saw a door closing on the young operative, and he felt a sense of deep, genuine regret. He would fight for her, but in the end, it wouldn't make a difference. Naomi Kharmai's career at the Central Intelligence Agency had just come to a very unfortunate, all-too-sudden end.

The discussion ended a few minutes later, and the ambassador left without delay, which surprised no one. Everything that had to be said was out in the open, and there was little point in prolonging the awkward pleasantries. Surprisingly, given what had just transpired, the meeting did not stretch on. Brenneman kept them for as long as it took to make his wishes clear, if not his orders. He didn't issue any specific instructions on how to handle Kharmai, for instance, but then, he didn't really need to, and by keeping things vague, he was able to distance himself from the whole situation. Hayden left without a word, hung a right at the end of the main corridor, and disappeared from sight. Harper waited directly outside the Oval Office, along with a group of staffers who were waiting for an audience with the president. When Andrews stepped out a moment later, having been briefly detained by Brenneman, Harper tilted his head toward the Roosevelt Room, which was still vacant. Andrews, catching the hint, walked in after him.

"What do you think?" Harper asked, once the door was closed.

Andrews, who was standing with his hands on his hips, shrugged and exhaled forcefully. "They definitely know that we were involved in Madrid."

"That's the impression I got as well. They can't prove that she's with the Agency, though, or Vázquez would have said as much."

"He's an arrogant little prick," Andrews said, scowling.

"I agree, but that doesn't change a thing," Harper pointed out. "He may be a prick, but he happens to be holding all the cards."

"That's an exaggeration, but I see your point. We've got to move fast on this. What do you suggest?"

"We need to be careful getting her out," Harper said absently. "Maybe Machado can help us with that. Portugal's probably the best bet. That's a very porous border, and it offers the best chance for success. Morocco's another possibility. There's a lot of border security on the southern tip of Spain, but it's entirely focused on keeping people out. She might be able to slip out that way."

Andrews considered the options for a minute, then said, "I agree. Get Machado involved. See what he recommends, and then get back to me. The president is going to want an update soon, and we better have something to tell him."

"Fine. I'll get on it."

CHAPTER 34

NORTHERN PAKISTAN

Kealey stared out the rear window of the fast-moving sedan. The scenery passed by in a dull, meaningless blur, the trees and buildings shrouded in gray, muted by the building storm to the east. As the Subaru clattered over a parallel set of railroad tracks, Kealey stretched his neck from side to side, trying to relieve the aching pain in his shoulders. The fifteen-hour flight had been bad enough, but there had been no time to stop and catch their breath. They had left the airport three hours earlier, and they'd been moving nonstop. After receiving the call outside the terminal, he and Pétain had followed the contact's instructions to the letter. They had navigated the clamorous din of the Anarkali Bazaar; the throngs of impatient, unapologetic pedestrians in Bank Square; and the surprising after-lunch rush at the Bundu Khan, which, according to a whispered aside from Pétain, was the last place a prominent American journalist kidnapped the previous year had been seen alive.

That scrap of information, which she'd mentioned merely in passing, had been bothering Kealey for the past couple of hours. He had already noticed the suspicious, unfriendly glances that he and Pétain had been met with for much of their brief stay in the Islamic republic. He was reminded of a short trip he'd taken to South Korea back in '93, shortly after he'd been commissioned in the U.S. Army. He'd been walking through Seoul, dressed in civilian clothes and minding his own business, when an elderly woman had started screeching at him and shaking her fist, her face contorted. Not knowing what else to do, he'd simply walked away. When he got back to Fort Carson, he'd mentioned the incident to his company commander, who'd spent some time in Korea, but the man had simply shrugged and changed the subject.

It was just part of the region's torn history, Kealey had decided. There was still some widespread antagonism toward the United States in South Korea, much of it based on the fact that the United States had never completely withdrawn its troops following the end of the Korean War, the "end," in this case, being the uneasy cease-fire that was settled upon in '53. To date, the United States still had over 30,000 troops on the Korean peninsula.

But that situation, at least in Kealey's mind, was very different. The Koreans had a legitimate gripe, he thought, and the incident with the old woman was the only time he'd encountered any tangible anti-American feelings in the Far East. In Pakistan, he could feel the hostility everywhere. He didn't know how much of it was related to the political tensions between Brenneman, Musharraf, and their respective governments, but he couldn't deny its presence.

Feeling a movement on the warm leather seat beside him, he turned to look at Marissa Pétain. He couldn't see her face, as she was staring out the opposite window, but he could see the tension in her shoulders and could tell that she was having the same troubling thoughts he was. In fact, Kealey realized, it was probably worse for her, as she had even less information than he did. At least he knew who had prompted this little excursion, though knowing wasn't doing much to relieve his anxiety. He wondered how Pétain would react if he were to tell her they were only here because of her father's connections.

Kealey shifted his gaze to the front. The man driving was the same man who'd picked them up at the restaurant. The server, Nawaz, had taken them through the kitchen and out the back door. No one in the kitchen had given them a second look. The driver had been waiting in the narrow alley, an unregistered taxi parked nearby. He'd introduced himself as Abdul, which Kealey had dismissed immediately. "Abdul" was the equivalent of "John Smith" in the States, a completely meaningless name, and likely false. *Abdul will take you to the man you're supposed to meet,* Nawaz had murmured in Kealey's ear. *He is close to the man who sent you here. You can trust him.*

Abdul's face was visible in the rearview mirror, and Kealey studied it for a fraction of a second. For the most part, it was completely forgettable: greasy black hair; a large, hooked nose; complacent brown eyes; and thin lips. There was, however, one thing that caught Kealey's attention. The man's face was not that of an inner-city taxi driver, but that of a man who'd spent a great deal of time in a hostile, unforgiving climate. His skin was etched with hard lines and appeared as coarse as sandpaper. At that moment, his eyes darted up to the rearview mirror, but Kealey didn't bother to look away. They locked eyes for a few seconds, neither of them giving anything away, and then Abdul returned his gaze to the road ahead.

The storm was approaching fast from the east, and the driver slowed as they headed into the worsening weather. After they'd first set out from the Bundu Khan, he'd followed a fast, erratic route through the city center, obviously searching for signs of surveillance. After an hour, he'd left the city via Allama Iqbal Road, which happened to bear the same name as the airport. They flashed through rural, rolling green countryside, passing farms and a number of sparsely populated towns. Twenty minutes later, he braked sharply and swung the car onto a narrow road. Trees crowded in on either side as they rolled slowly down the road, wet leaves brushing against the windows. They emerged on the other side, and Abdul brought the car to a gradual halt, the ancient brakes squealing in protest.

"Where are we?" Pétain asked, shifting to the left so she could look out the windshield. "What are we doing here?"

"I have to look around before I call the next man in," the Pakistani said, ignoring her question. "Wait with the car until I call you forward."

Removing the keys from the ignition, Abdul got out, shut the door behind him, and started walking across a gravel parking lot. On the far side of the lot was an electrical substation, the giant transformers ringed by a 10-foot chain-link fence. Kealey followed suit, and once he was out of the car, he looked after Abdul, taking in the surroundings carefully. There were no other cars in the parking area, and no other sign of life. That gave him reason for pause, but he kept looking, taking it all in. There was a broad green field on the other side of the substation, and past that he could see the roofs of several houses and a short brick smokestack, all of it blurred by the driving rain.

Pétain had exited the vehicle. Coming around the side, she moved close, shivered inexplicably, and stared after Abdul. "What do you think?" she asked quietly, her words almost lost in the sound of the storm.

Kealey shook his head, trying to see all the angles. Suddenly, he wished he'd gotten in touch with Owen before linking up with Machado's man. The Spaniard had seemed straightforward and genuine enough when he'd offered to help, but now, on hostile ground with no real means to defend himself, Kealey was starting to wish he'd reconsidered the whole thing.

"I don't know," he finally said in response to her question, "but it's like I said before . . . We don't really have a choice. We aren't setting the rules here . . . They are."

Abdul had reached a gate in the chain-link fence. As they watched from a distance, he seemed to open it without any real trouble, leaving Kealey to wonder if it had been locked to begin with. Then he slipped inside the perimeter. He passed under an A-frame structure, moved around one of the bulky gray transformers, and was gone from sight. Two minutes later, he reappeared at the gate and gestured for them to follow.

Neither of them moved for a few seconds, and then Kealey started across the parking lot. Behind him, Pétain hurried to catch up. When they reached the gate, Abdul tilted his head inside and said, "He's waiting for you."

"That's it?" Pétain asked, a perplexed expression crossing her face. Kealey couldn't help but wonder what she had been expecting.

"That's it," the Pakistani said, his face an impassive mask. "I will wait here until you're done. It shouldn't take long."

"Fine," Kealey said. He put a hand on Pétain's back and pushed her gently through the opening, but she resisted and dug her heels in, firing another series of questions back in Abdul's direction.

"Who are we meeting?" she asked, raising her voice to be heard above the driving rain. "What's his name? How is he connected to Mengal?"

"Stop," Kealey said through clenched teeth, pushing her forward a little more firmly. "We'll find out soon enough. Just keep moving."

She relented, went through the gate, and fell into step beside him, shooting one last look over her shoulder at the stoic driver. "I don't trust him," she muttered.

"Join the club."

"I'm serious, Ryan. Something isn't right with this whole—"

He stopped and grabbed her arm, turning her to face him. Shooting a quick glance at the gate, he saw that Abdul was already walking back toward the car. Coming back to Pétain, he found her staring up at him. Her eyes were wide and expectant, and her dark hair was plastered to her forehead, long strands clinging to her pale cheeks.

"Marissa, listen to me," he said in a low voice. "I happen to agree with you. I don't want to be here, either, and I don't feel great about this scenario. But it's worth the risk. This guy, whoever he is, can give us Mengal's exact location, and we need that info. We can't afford to waste any more time. We can't afford to screw things up, either, so do me a favor, okay? Try to relax, and stop asking questions. All that's going to do is put this guy on edge, and that's the last thing we need."

She didn't reply for a long moment, looking up at him silently, rainwater streaming down her face. Then, finally, she nodded her consent.

"Good," Kealey said, "and thank you. Believe me, this will all be over soon. I'm as ready to leave as you are."

"Well," she said as they continued walking through the maze of transformers, "that all depends, doesn't it?"

"On what?"

"On whether or not we're going someplace nicer."

Kealey smiled and shook his head, impressed despite himself. Pétain was showing remarkable poise. They were walking through a thunderstorm, soaking wet, operating illegally in a foreign country without backup of any kind, and still, she was making jokes. That was something to admire, he decided, but he pushed the thought away as they passed an elevated structure bearing a circuit switcher. A figure, slightly blurred by the rain, was standing in the middle of the gravel walkway to the right, just in front of the small control building.

"I guess that's him," Pétain whispered needlessly. They walked forward, Kealey taking note of the man's appearance. He was wearing a long raincoat, which fell just short of his knees, and a black knit cap beneath the coat's oversized hood. The knit cap was a strange choice, Kealey thought, given the oppressive heat. The man's slacks were tucked into the tops of his rubber boots, revealing just a swath of black fabric between the coat and the boots, both of which were olive drab in color.

As they approached, he lifted his head and smiled out from beneath the hood. Through a gray curtain of rain, Kealey had an impression of pale green eyes, a thick black mustache, and a bulbous nose. Then the man pulled off the hood and studied them both in turn. Kealey saw that his first impression had been correct, but now he saw something else: like their driver, this man had obviously been exposed to the elements for months, if not years, at a time, his face as rough and battered as a chunk of worn granite.

"Welcome to Pakistan," he said, looking at them both in turn. "I apologize for the lengthy, somewhat circuitous trip, but thank you for indulging me."

"Who are you?" Kealey asked.

"My name is not important, but for the purposes of our brief association, you may call me Fahim."

"Fahim?" Pétain murmured. She leaned in to make herself heard over the driving rain and the incessant thunder. "I thought you said his name was Khan."

Kealey ignored her, choosing instead to focus on what he had just heard, as well as what he could learn from it. Fahim's English was remarkable; it was word perfect and tinged with a slight British accent. He had clearly spent a prolonged period of time in England, probably at one of the better universities, such as Cambridge, Oxford, or King's College in London. At the same time, his physical appearance seemed to speak to a very different kind of existence. Kealey was struck by the obvious paradox, but he shook off his curiosity, remembering why they were in the Islamic republic to begin with.

"So where is he?" he asked finally. "Where's Mengal? We need to—"

"Forgive me for interrupting, but there is one small matter we need to discuss before we get to business," Fahim interjected. He raised a hand, palm out, as if to plead for their patience. "Mr. Kealey, my associate has informed me that you stopped to make a purchase in the Anarkali Bazaar. Is that correct? And before you answer, let me remind you that you were followed the entire time."

Kealey hesitated, then reached behind his back and under his shirt. A worn leather sheath was secured at the small of his back, hooked onto his belt and positioned horizontally. Finding the wooden grip of the 6-inch knife with his hand, he pulled it out and held it up in a nonthreatening manner.

Fahim smiled mildly. "Toss it over here, please."

Kealey obliged, the knife falling onto the gravel 5 feet in front of the other man. He walked over, picked it up, and examined the blade.

"Not much good, is it?" he said. "Still, I suppose it's the best you could do on such short notice. I thought this was supposed to be a friendly meeting, Mr. Kealey, arranged by one of our common associates. I wonder why you felt the need to arm yourself."

"Your driver was armed," Kealey pointed out calmly, "and I expect you are as well. You know how this works."

"Yes," Fahim said, "I *do* know." He turned and threw the knife with an overarm motion. It went over the fence and disappeared into a clump of bushes. When he turned back to face them, he was holding a gun in his right hand.

"Oh no," Pétain whispered. Kealey wanted to look over, but he couldn't shift his gaze from the gun in the other man's hand. He should have expected it, he thought bitterly, but he hadn't really considered the possibility of a trap. Clearly, Machado's man had gone over to the other side. Perhaps he even worked for Mengal directly. It didn't really matter, Kealey thought. Not anymore. He felt rooted in place, completely helpless, and he realized, with a sense of complete self-loathing, that he had made a terrible mistake in coming to this place. "Ryan, what are we going to . . ."

The rest of Pétain's question was lost in the driving rain. She repeated it, louder this time, but Kealey couldn't concentrate on the words. He was still focused on the other man, who was now walking toward them. When he was 5 feet away, he stopped, reached into the deep left pocket of his raincoat, and pulled out a pair of handcuffs.

He tossed them over to Kealey, who managed to catch them. Gesturing to Pétain, Fahim said, "Cuff her. One hand only, to that transformer over there."

He gestured to a large gray box, which was positioned to Kealey's left. Pétain looked over, then snapped back to Fahim and screamed, "What are you doing? Why are you doing this, you bastard? You're supposed to be helping us!"

The man didn't react. Turning to Kealey, Pétain gripped his arm and whispered urgently, "We've got to run. He's going to kill us both. You know we can't—"

"He's not going to kill us," Kealey said, his mind suddenly clearing. He felt intensely ashamed that he'd frozen, if only for a few seconds, but he couldn't think about that now. In truth, he should never have let things get this far to begin with, but there would be plenty of time to focus on his numerous mistakes later if—and only if—they managed to survive the encounter. For now, he had to stay sharp and look for an opportunity. They might only get one, he knew, and he'd have to move fast to make the most of it. "He wouldn't bother locking you up if he wanted us dead. Something else is happening here."

"*What?*" Pétain demanded. "What could possibly be happening? This wasn't supposed to—"

"Stop talking," Fahim commanded, his voice carrying over the sound of the surging rain. "We don't have a lot of time. Get over there and cuff her now."

Kealey hesitated, then grabbed Pétain's arm and began pulling her toward the transformer, the cuffs in his left hand banging against his thigh with each step. She was struggling, but not too hard. Kealey couldn't figure out why, at first, and then it hit him; she was too confused to put up a real fight. As they neared the transformer, though, she pulled away violently, obviously trying to catch him off guard.

Kealey barely managed to keep his tenuous grasp around her wrist. Realizing she was about to break loose, he swung her hard against the metal access door. As she bounced off, her breath coming out in a rush, he caught her on the rebound. Slamming her back against the door, he pressed the outer part of his right forearm across her upper chest. Moving fast, he used his weight to pin her in place. She began to struggle violently, screaming for him to stop, but Kealey started to talk in fast, low tones, and she gradually stopped struggling. Then, panting for breath, she lifted her wild, questioning eyes to his.

"You've got to stop," Kealey said forcefully, once he was sure he had her attention. His face was just a few inches from hers. "I know you're scared, but this isn't helping. I can't focus if you're distracting me. Just try to stay calm, okay? I'm going to get us out of this."

She stayed silent for a few seconds, breathing hard. Then she looked away briefly. When her eyes came back to his, Kealey saw that she was calm, but only just, and she was clearly desperate for answers.

"Ryan, what are you going to do?" she whispered urgently. "Why is this happening? I thought this guy was on our side. That's what you told me . . . that he was here to help us."

"I don't know what's going on, but I'm going to figure it out." He removed his forearm from her chest and took a couple steps back. "Here, give me your hand."

She hesitated for what seemed like an eternity. Finally, she held up her left arm. Taking hold of her forearm, Kealey closed one of the cuffs around her wrist, then secured the other to the curved handle in the access door. As the second cuff ratcheted into place, Pétain closed her eyes and shook her head slightly, as if in denial of what was happening.

Looking down at her, Kealey was tempted to offer some words of comfort. He wanted to tell her it was going to be okay, that he wouldn't let anything happen to her, but they would have been empty promises, and he'd already made enough of those in his lifetime. Instead, he simply turned to face their supposed contact.

It didn't look as if Fahim had moved. He was still standing in the center of the gravel footpath, the long raincoat flapping around his legs. A satellite phone was now pressed to his left ear, but the gun was still in his right hand, aimed vaguely in Kealey's direction.

As he approached, Kealey heard a few snatches of conversation, but nothing that made sense to him. When he was about 7 feet away, the other man altered his aim, leveling the muzzle with Kealey's chest. Kealey didn't react visibly, but his muscles tightened, his breath coming faster, as he stared down the barrel of the semiautomatic. Fahim muttered a few more words, then lowered the receiver slightly, pressing it to his shoulder. Looking up, he said something that caught Kealey completely off guard.

"He wants to talk to you."

For a few seconds, Kealey was left speechless, his mind racing to catch up with this strange development. "Who?" he finally asked, raising his voice to be heard. "Who the fuck are you talking to? Is that Mengal?"

The other man didn't reply. Instead, he simply tossed over the phone. Kealey managed to catch it, and once he verified that it was still on, he lifted it to his ear. "Who is this?" he demanded, shouting over the sound of the driving rain. "What do you want?"

"I want you to listen," Javier Machado said. His deep, cultured voice was as clear as a bell, despite the thousands of miles that separated them. "I want you to listen well, Kealey, because make no mistake, at least one life—and not necessarily yours—depends on what you do next."

CHAPTER 35

NORTHERN PAKISTAN

"You son of a bitch," Kealey whispered. He was only dimly aware of his surroundings. Fahim was standing nearby, the gun leveled in his direction, and the rain was streaming down his face, but everything else had faded away. Just one thing was stuck in his mind, and that was that he had missed something big. He was frantically trying to figure it out, but nothing was coming to mind, and the anger was threatening to drown out his rational thoughts. "What the fuck do you think you're doing? I swear to God, I'm going to—"

"I told you to listen," Machado snapped over the line. "Where is Marissa? Can she hear you?"

Kealey looked over, but he already knew the answer. Pétain was only about 20 feet away, huddled against the transformer to which she was handcuffed, but even at that short distance, the driving rain and the thunder pounding overhead were enough to obscure anything less than a shout. "No, she can't hear us."

"Good." Machado's tone seemed to ease a little. "But we're not going to take any chances. If you refer to me by name, you will not leave Pakistan alive. Is that understood?"

"Yes," Kealey hissed, unable to hide his anger.

"Good," Machado repeated. "Now, listen to me. Despite how this looks, I did not mislead you. Fahim, as you may have already guessed, was one of my Afghan agents when I was stationed in Pakistan. He was the first man I recruited in-country. He is very reliable, and he can lead you directly to Benazir Mengal. Everything I told you before was true."

"Then why all the bullshit? Why is your daughter handcuffed to—?"

"¡Cállate!" Machado shouted. "I told you not to use my name!"

Kealey hadn't done so, not in so many words, but he understood what the Spaniard was driving at. "She can't—"

"Stop talking," Machado said calmly. Kealey couldn't help but lock on to the sudden shift in his tone. The man's emotions were all over the place, but Kealey could detect an underlying, unmistakable tone of pure guilt. It was as if the Spaniard had done something wrong, something besides the obvious. Or was about to, Kealey thought.

"I'm going to instruct Fahim to help you," Machado was saying. "He is part of a larger network, a group he formed—with my help, of course—in 1988. At that time, they were primarily concerned with transporting funds and weapons to the mujahideen during the Soviet-Afghan war. Now, they're more concerned with . . . Well, let's just call it private enterprise."

Kealey saw it immediately. "They're smugglers." Then he saw the other part. "And Mengal is their primary competition."

"Exactly," Machado said. "So you see, it's in his interest to help you. His men are watching Mengal right now, and he will take you to that location once you have carried out your end of the bargain."

"And what is my end of the bargain?"

There was a quick intake of breath on the other end of the line, and then a long pause. Kealey sensed that the older man was steeling his resolve. When he finally spoke, his voice was laced with guilt and despair, but that did nothing to lessen the shock of the words.

"I need you to shoot my daughter."

For a long moment, Kealey couldn't reply. It was hard to believe he had heard correctly, because the words just didn't make sense. On some level, he knew they combined to form a perfectly grammatical sentence, but the overall meaning, the very implication, was just too far-fetched to believe. Somehow, he had walked into something he didn't fully understand.

Finally, he managed to find his voice. "I don't understand. You want me to . . . kill Marissa?"

"*No!*" Machado blurted. With that single word, Kealey heard all the certainty, strength, and confidence drop out of his voice. He hurriedly regained control, but the younger man had caught the slip, and he was already thinking about how he could use it to his advantage. "God, no. I only need you to . . ."

"To what?"

"To injure her. To take her out of the field," Machado said. There was a long pause. "Kealey, there is more to this than I can really—"

"No," Kealey said.

There was an uncertain hesitation on the other end of the line. "What do you mean no? What are you talking about?"

"I won't do it. I won't shoot her. You must be out of your fucking mind."

Kealey heard a long, weary sigh, and then Machado spoke in a voice devoid of emotion. "You don't understand. I knew you wouldn't understand, but it needs to be done. It's the only way."

"The only way to *what?*" Kealey demanded, his frustration rising to match his anger and confusion. "Why are you asking me to do this?"

"You wouldn't understand."

"Then explain it."

The pause lasted much longer this time, and when Machado finally spoke, Kealey was caught off guard, his attention divided between Fahim, the gun in his hand, and the blurred form of Marissa Pétain in the near distance. "You know about Caroline? Did Marissa tell you about her?"

"Yes, she told me what happened."

"Then you know how she died. You know what the Colombians did to her."

"They tortured her," Kealey said uneasily.

"No," Machado said. "You're wrong."

"What?" Kealey was confused; he remembered every word of what Pétain had told him in Cartagena, and while she hadn't delved into the details of her sister's death, she had made the graphic nature of the incident reasonably clear. "I thought—"

"You're wrong," Machado repeated quietly. "You see, it's a matter of degree. They didn't just torture her, Ryan. They started with her toes, so she wouldn't try to run. Once they had them off, they began removing her fingers. Do you understand what I'm telling you? Do you understand the severity of what I'm saying? They took her apart piece by piece. That is not torture. That is something else entirely."

Machado stopped talking, and Kealey decided to venture a few words. "Look, I can understand how you—"

"They gave her a mirror," Machado continued. His voice was unnaturally calm and casual. "Did Marissa tell you that? They gave my firstborn child a mirror so she could see what they had done to her. Once they had taken her fingers, she obviously couldn't hold it up for herself, so they did it for her. Very courteous people, the Colombians, and very thorough." Machado let out a low, mirthless laugh. "You can say what you like about them, but they *are* devoted to their work, and they certainly like to be recognized for it."

And to that, Kealey had no response. Suddenly, it was clear to him just how far gone Javier Machado actually was. His daughter's death—not to mention the nightmare he'd walked into when he'd opened his front door eight years earlier—had clearly pushed him over the edge, and there was no bringing him back. The only thing Kealey could do now was try to talk him out of the bizarre demand he had levied a few moments ago, but for that to happen, he had to know how Pétain figured into the story.

When he asked the question, though, Machado merely offered a short, hollow laugh. It was a deeply unsettling sound, and Kealey had to pull the phone away from his ear just to get away from it. "You still don't get it, do you, Kealey? Marissa joined the Agency because of Caroline. I'm sure she told you that."

"Yes, she did."

"Did she tell you that I did everything I could to stop her from joining? That I used every ounce of my influence to keep her away from Langley?"

"No," Kealey said. He remembered thinking the exact opposite, that Machado had used his pull to get her *into* the Agency. "She didn't mention that."

"And why do you think she did that? Why do you think she ignored me when I pleaded with her to reconsider? Why do you think she ignored Élise when she begged her to stay in Spain?"

"I don't know."

"Because she wanted revenge. She wanted to find the people who killed Caroline, and she wanted them to suffer. And now she's just a few months away from getting her wish."

Kealey went suddenly cold. "What are you talking about?"

Machado laughed again, but it was a bitter, angry gesture. "Didn't

Harper tell you? Of course he didn't . . . That isn't his way. One hand never knows what the other is doing. That's how it is at the Agency, though . . . I only wish I had known that sooner."

"What do you mean?"

"Two months ago, Marissa was selected to participate in an upcoming op in Colombia. And by 'participate,' I mean she *is* the op. Once she lands in Bogotá, she's on her own. No control, at least not in-country, and no support from the embassy. Nothing but biweekly reports to Langley. The target is the NVC, otherwise known as the North Valley cartel."

"The same cartel that killed her sister," Kealey murmured. He was speaking more to himself than anything else, but Machado had heard him over the line.

"Exactly. The same people who butchered my Caroline. Marissa is going after the same bastards, but it's not going to work, Kealey. She has minimal experience working undercover and almost no experience working without a team. They'll weed her out in no time, and when that happens . . ."

Kealey let the silence linger as he thought it through. Perhaps Machado wasn't as mentally unstable as he'd initially thought. But then again, what he was asking was just . . .

As if sensing the younger man's second thoughts, the Spaniard hurried to fill the dead air. "You know as well as I do that they'll kill her. I've tried everything. I've tried arguing with her, threatening her, and I've tried pulling some strings at the Agency to keep her away from this. Nothing has worked . . . Not even Élise can talk her out of it, and Harper seems intent on sending her. The Agency is desperate to get a foothold in Colombia. But if, for some reason, she wasn't physically able to go into the field . . ."

"Then Harper would have no choice but to scrap the op," Kealey concluded. He didn't know what to think about what he had just heard, but for the first time, he had a glimmer of understanding. He had to admit that in some ways, what Machado was proposing made perfect sense. At the same time, there was nothing rational or even sane about what the older man was asking him to do. "At the very least, he'd find someone else to send."

"Exactly," Machado said. He sounded resigned and despondent, but also resolute. "This is the last thing I want, Kealey, believe me, but it's for the best. She will still be able to stay at Langley. She has exceptional skills in other areas, and she's a brilliant girl. Much too smart to be wasted on an operation like this. It is destined to fail . . . Believe me, I know. I spent some time in Medellín when I was with the DO. I know what it will take to infiltrate the cartels, and one person with limited experience is not the answer. If she goes, she'll be dead inside a week. I guarantee it."

Kealey looked over at Pétain, who was standing in front of the transformer, her left wrist cuffed to the access door. Her head scarf had come loose and was blowing across the gravel footpath. Her pale face was blurred by the rain, but he could tell that she was staring in his direction, waiting for some kind of sign. As he watched her, something clicked in his mind, and he made his decision.

"I understand what you're saying," he said slowly, "and you're probably right about what will happen if she goes, but you're going to have to figure out another way to stop her. I'm not going to do it, Machado. If you have to call off our arrangement, then so be it, but I won't do it. She deserves a chance to take those fuckers down, and I'm not going to take that away from her. I *can't* take that away from her."

There was a long, tense pause, and then the Spaniard came back on, his voice tight and insistent. "Kealey, perhaps I didn't make myself clear. This isn't a choice. You can't decide one way or another. You're going to do it, and that's final."

"Hey," Kealey snapped, his hand tightening around the phone. He had tried letting the man down easy; this was something else entirely. "Fuck you. I don't have to do a fucking thing you tell me. Who the hell do you think you are? Now, listen—"

"No, you listen. In case you've forgotten, I want to remind you of something. When you flew to Pakistan, you left someone behind."

Kealey closed his eyes and bit back his instinctive response. Suddenly, it was all clear, but he tried not to let his emotions cloud his judgment. There was no way that Machado would go that far . . . would he? "Naomi."

"That's correct. I talked to your employer a few hours ago, and he's brought me back into the fold, in a manner of speaking. He asked me to help get her out of the country. In other words, she's with me for the foreseeable future."

"You wouldn't hurt her," Kealey said. He was fairly confident that he was right. He had misjudged the older man in Spain, but he didn't think he'd gotten it that wrong. "You spent thirty years in the DO. She's one of us, Machado. If you hurt her, you'll be throwing away everything you ever did with the Agency, not to mention the fact that they'll track you down in a heartbeat."

"What is your point, Kealey? Perhaps I didn't make myself clear when we last spoke. I'm seventy-two years old, and the doctors are not optimistic when it comes to my health. I have very little to look forward to. Marissa is my youngest daughter and my only living child. She is *everything* to me, and I would do anything to keep her out of harm's way."

"Machado, if you—"

"*Anything,*" the Spaniard repeated, "even if that means sacrificing your girlfriend. For eight years, Kealey, I've had to choke on the memory of what the Agency did to my daughter. *Eight years!*" His voice was trembling with rage and something else that Kealey couldn't identify.

"I understand that, but—"

"No, it is something you can never understand. I will not let it happen again," the Spaniard continued. His voice had dropped into a frightening monotone, a fact that had not escaped the younger man's attention. "And I don't care what I have to do to stop it. Not anymore."

"Listen, Naomi has nothing to do with this. You have to let her go."

"I wouldn't have to kill her, mind you." The older man was already working it out, Kealey realized, figuring out the best way to pull it off. "She'd simply . . . disappear."

"People would know what you did, Machado," Kealey said. He tried to sound sure of what he was saying, but he couldn't entirely disguise his rising panic. The man sounded completely sincere; clearly, he was not moved by the fact that Naomi was as innocent as his daughter. "*I* would know."

"Maybe, but you'd never be able to prove it. You know the record I have at Langley, and the investigation alone would keep Marissa tied up in congressional hearings for the next eighteen months. That would serve my purposes just as well."

"You sick fuck," Kealey said. It was all he could manage; he just couldn't believe what he was hearing, and he couldn't pretend any longer. "You sick fucking bastard. Why me? Why not your man Fahim, or whatever the hell his name really is? Why can't he do it? Why didn't you turn to him in the first place?"

"I thought you might ask that, but the answer is simple, Kealey. Fahim is a good man, but his loyalty has its boundaries. You were in the right place at the right time. Marissa is an active operative with the CIA, a covert employee of the U.S. government. Were he to pull the trigger, the Agency would track him to the end of the earth. They would never stop looking."

There was a brief pause, and then Machado continued. "You, on the other hand, are known for your somewhat . . . unorthodox methods. You've survived some very controversial incidents over the course of your career, and you'll survive this. Given your admirable record, the worst they'll do is kick you out. Besides, you need something from me, and I need something from you. Believe me, I will keep my end of the bargain."

"It's no fucking bargain," Kealey snapped. "Not from my point of view."

"Yes, it is," Machado insisted. "Think of Fitzgerald. If you do this, you'll be saving her life. You'll be a hero to every American man and woman, and to many others around the world. And in the long run, you'll be doing the right thing for Marissa as well."

"That isn't for you to decide. She's a grown woman. You don't have the right to decide her future, and neither do I. If I go through with this, I'll be taking away the one thing she wants most in the world. Have you thought of that? Have you even considered what she wants? What's best for her?"

"Enough," Machado snapped. Kealey knew he'd hit a nerve, but it was too little, too late. "It's time for you to make a decision. Now, what will it be? And just remember, at this particular moment, I'm less than twenty feet from your little friend. Her life is in my hands."

Kealey restrained his instinctive reply, but only just. "How do I know you'll let her go when it's done?"

"You don't. But I have no desire to hurt her. The only way that will happen is if you want it to."

"Fuck you," Kealey spat. He shut off the phone and tossed it back to Fahim without warning. The Afghan caught it awkwardly. Ten seconds later it started to ring, and Fahim lifted it to his ear. He spoke a few words, listened, then spoke again and ended the connection. Walking over, he reversed his grip on the gun and held it out to Kealey at arm's length.

Kealey wrapped his hand around the warm plastic grip. He could tell from the weight that the Makarov 9mm pistol was fully loaded, but he pushed the slide back a couple of centimeters, anyway. When he saw the brassy glint of the chambered round, he released the slide. Then he took a few steps back and raised the weapon. When the muzzle was level with the other man's face, he said, "What's to stop me from shooting you right now?"

The Afghan appeared unconcerned, his swarthy face fixed in a neutral expression. "I expect you already know the answer to that," he said calmly.

Kealey shook his head in frustration, but the man had called his bluff. He flashed on Naomi, the way he'd seen her the previous day: leaning against the door frame of her borrowed bedroom, clear droplets of water on her shoulders and tears in her eyes, her skinny arms wrapped round her lean, undernourished body.

He was torn by the image in his mind, just as he was torn when he was in her presence. It was clear that she wanted nothing to do with him, but he couldn't abandon her. He'd heard everything he needed to hear in Javier Machado's voice. In Kealey's mind, there was no doubt that the Spaniard would carry out his threat, but either way, he wasn't prepared to risk double-crossing the former case officer. There was just too much to lose if he was wrong.

And that left just one alternative.

His legs felt like concrete blocks as he crossed the gravel, his feet sinking into the loose, rain-soaked pebbles. He couldn't believe it had come to this; in a thousand years, he never would have made the connection. He just didn't see how he could have known what Machado was up to. Pétain's participation in the upcoming op was highly classified information, and there was no way he could have known about it, mainly because he didn't have to. Even with that piece of information, though, he didn't think he would have been able to spot Machado's true intentions in Cartagena. There were just too many links to follow, and his attention had been focused on other things, all of which took precedence over Marissa Pétain's family history.

In the end, though, Kealey knew that these thoughts were meaningless. There was no point in deluding himself. He could try to rationalize it for as long as he wanted to, but nothing would change the fact that he had missed some crucial developments, and now Pétain was going to pay for his mistakes.

As he crossed the last few feet through the driving rain, Pétain started to speak, clearly anxious to learn what had happened. Then she saw the gun in his hand. She met his eyes, and she must have seen the truth behind them, because her face went completely white, and her knees seemed to buckle. She wrapped her hand around the handle of the access door for support, but she managed to stay on her feet.

"What are you doing, Ryan?" Her voice carried a slight tinge of hope, but only a tinge; on some level, she already knew what was going to happen. "Why did he give you the gun?"

"Marissa," he began woodenly, "I have to do something. You won't understand now, but in time, I—"

"Why did he give you the gun?" she said, cutting him off. Her voice was rising with each word, climbing into hysteria. She was stalling, that much was clear, but she was also desperate for answers, even at this late stage of the game. "Who was that on the phone?"

There was a bright flash of lightning overhead. The thunder followed a split second later, the sound like that of a tire shredding at high speed on the interstate. As the noise ripped over the gray black sky, parts of Kealey's words were drowned out, but he didn't notice. They were all platitudes, anyway, and they wouldn't change a thing. He felt sick for even saying them, but he had to say something, and nothing worthwhile was coming to mind.

"I have to, Marissa. I know you don't understand, but I can't get around it. Believe me, I tried. . . ."

"What do you mean, *'you tried'*?" she screamed. "This is my life you're talking about! Who was on the phone? Who told you to do this?"

"Marissa, I can't—"

"Who was on the goddamn phone, Ryan?" She was struggling now and crying freely as she tried to pull away from the handle. It wasn't going to happen; she was secured too well, but she kept trying regardless, fighting for all she was worth. *"Who was it, you bastard? Why do they want me dead? What did I do to them?"*

"They don't—" Kealey stopped himself before he could say the rest. Clearly, she hadn't heard him before. He wasn't going to kill her, but if she thought he was going to, it might make the next part easier. "Close your eyes, Marissa. Turn around, close your eyes, and face the door. It won't hurt, I promise."

"You can't do this," she moaned, tears mingling with the rainwater on her face. The fight had drained out of her without warning, leaving behind the empty hope for some kind of last-minute salvation. "You can't do this."

"I have to," he said, the words catching in his throat. *Christ,* he thought bitterly, *how did it come to this? Goddamn you for making me do this, Machado. Goddamn you.* "Now do as I say. Face the door, and close your eyes."

Her legs gave out, and she dropped to her knees, her face clearing of all expression. Her eyes were wide and vacant as she stared ahead, shaking her head slowly from side to side. Kealey couldn't help but wonder what she was seeing in that strange moment. Was it her whole life flashing before her eyes? Or was she simply wondering how it had come to this, as he was?

"Marissa," he said gently, prompting her.

After what seemed like an endless pause, she slowly turned, her knees making a curved groove in the wet gravel that bordered the transformer. Resting her forehead against the steel access door, she began mumbling something under her breath. Moving closer, his footsteps masked by the sound of the storm, Kealey leaned in. As he braced himself to do what Machado had ordered, the gun like a lead weight in his hand, he couldn't help but overhear what she was saying, and the words caused him to freeze in his tracks.

She was praying. Not for redemption, not for absolution, but for her parents' forgiveness. She was praying that they might understand—that in time, they might forgive her for causing them so much pain.

Hearing this, Kealey stepped back and took a deep, shaky breath. At that moment, he wanted nothing more than to kill Javier Machado: to put a gun to his head, pull the trigger, and send him to a hell more real than the one he had created for himself. For a split second, he considered abandoning the whole thing and telling Pétain the truth: that her own father was entirely responsible for what she was going through now. That he would rather see her crippled and safe behind a desk than living her own life, risks and all.

But then Naomi's face reappeared in his mind, and he remembered the Spaniard's grim, resolute tone when he had issued his threat. Kealey knew that the man had deluded himself into thinking that this was the only way to protect his daughter, and that meant he'd do anything to accomplish his goal. As long as Pétain was walking, Naomi wasn't safe, and that was all it took to convince him he had to act. That was what it came down to accomplish his goal. Kealey could see the irony; both he and Machado were intent on doing the wrong thing to keep the people they cared about "safe," which was a relative term for both of them. At the same time, he just couldn't see an alternative.

Pétain was still mumbling to herself, her prayers interspersed with deep, gut-wrenching sobs. Taking a deep, steadying breath, Kealey moved forward quickly. He couldn't think about it anymore; he just wanted it over with. In one fast movement, he pinned her to the door with his left forearm, his right hand moving between her legs. Before she could realize what was happening, he glanced down to get his bearings, jammed the muzzle of the Makarov into the back of her left knee, and prepared himself to pull the trigger. . . .

And nothing happened. All he had to do was squeeze, but . . .

He was hesitating. *Why?* he wondered. *Why am I waiting?* In his peripheral vision, he saw Fahim moving across the gravel, following the footpath to the right. With the dark, shapeless raincoat and the hood pulled over his head, he looked almost unreal, like a ghost drifting through an unmarked graveyard. But he *was* real, Kealey reminded himself, and he was waiting. Presumably, he was moving to get a better look at what was happening. Pétain was still frozen with fear, but that wouldn't last; Kealey knew he was running out of time. He had to act. Steadying himself, he wedged the gun harder against the back of her knee, willing himself to pull the trigger.

CHAPTER 36

FAISALABAD

Paul Owen and the rest of the 4-man team had been in place for most of the day, having arrived in Faisalabad early that morning. The Bukhari woman in Sharakpur Sharif had failed to pan out. In the twenty-four hours they had spent watching her, she'd left her apartment twice. On both occasions, she'd done nothing more than walk to a local café for coffee and baklava. She hadn't spoken to anyone other than the clerk, and they had been unable to spot any watchers around her building. What clinched it for Owen, though, was not the woman's movements, but her general demeanor. She was casual, unhurried, and entirely too relaxed to be involved on any level whatsoever. He had dismissed her two minutes after he'd seen her on the street, but they had stayed on her just to be sure. Finally, at ten the previous evening, he'd decided to strike her from the list, and they'd moved on to the vet.

They had been in the city for less than twenty-four hours, but Owen felt sure that their current target was just as innocent as the previous one. The veterinarian had left his home at six that morning, walking the half mile to his office on Circular Road, just south of the river. He had not left the building since, and the two men watching his house—Husain Manik and Mark Walland—had reported nothing unusual. When the storm had hit an hour earlier, his wife had emerged briefly to pull down some clothes from a line in the back garden, but otherwise, nothing was happening.

Owen sighed wearily as he leaned back in his chair. He was sitting in a crowded café, next to one of the large windows looking out to the street. Through the rain-streaked glass, he had a clear line of sight to the front of the vet's office. The office was housed in an unremarkable two-story building constructed of granite and limestone. There was plenty of foot traffic going in and coming out of the building, but there was nothing suspicious in that, and Owen had seen nothing to indicate that the man had countersurveillance in place. He felt reasonably sure that it was business as usual inside the building, which meant they were wasting crucial time pursuing yet another useless lead.

He shook his head angrily as he snatched his bottle of Orangina off the table. He'd been in place too long already; it was time to move. Making his way through the clamorous seating area, he stepped outside and hung a right. As he made his way east, weaving his way through the heavy pedestrian traffic, he thought back to the list of Mengal's possible associates. They had crossed two names off the list, which left two more to go. Owen wasn't holding out much hope for any of them.

All of the targets had verifiable links to Benazir Mengal, but despite that fact, Owen couldn't help but feel that they were on the wrong track. The next few days would prove as much, he was sure, but this was one situation in which he'd be glad to be proven wrong. It had been four days since Fitzgerald's abduction, and he could feel the time sliding away. With each passing day, she became more of a risk to her captors. Eventually, they would figure that out and decide to cut their losses, if they hadn't done so already. Owen wanted nothing more than to stop that from happening, but he needed somewhere to start—something to work with. Otherwise, he was just as helpless as everyone else.

The unproductive time they'd spent in Pakistan was only part of the reason for his bad mood. Kealey was supposed to have checked in the previous day, and he had yet to make contact. Through Jonathan Harper, Owen had learned about Kealey's actions in Spain—that he had ignored his instructions by leaving Kharmai behind and taking Pétain instead. He had then proceeded to ignore his orders on landing in Pakistan, and that was assuming he'd even arrived to begin with. None of it surprised Owen; he had worked with Kealey long enough to know that the man had an irritating habit of going his own

way, but in the present situation, that kind of behavior was simply un-
tenable. Too much was on the line for Kealey to make up the rules as
he went, as was his usual mode of operation.

Owen was still thinking about it and getting angrier as he entered
the Qaisery Gate, the main entrance to the eight markets. A number of
people were huddled beneath the weathered concrete arch, obviously
seeking refuge from the relentless rain. The humid air was redolent
with cheap cologne and cigarette smoke, conversations echoing off
the frescoed walls. Beyond the arch, steam drifted up from the warm,
wet road. Owen was debating whether to take up another position
on Circular Road or switch positions with Massi, who was watching the
back of the vet's office, when his cell phone vibrated in his right pocket.
Pulling it out, he hit the TALK button and pressed the phone to his ear.
"Yeah?"

"Owen?"

The Delta colonel gripped the phone tighter when he heard who
it was. "Kealey, is that you? Where the fuck have you been? I needed
you here yesterday. I'm trying to get this done with three—"

"Where are you?"

Owen took a deep, calming breath and tried to restrain his temper, knowing it wouldn't help matters to let it out now. "Faisalabad,"
he said tightly. "Where are *you?*"

Kealey didn't bother to answer the question. "Can you talk?"

Owen didn't even need to look around. There were people everywhere. He couldn't take a step in any direction without bumping
into somebody. As he started edging his way through the crowd,
preparing to leave the gate on the south side, he said, "No, not really."

"Then just listen," Kealey said. His voice was low and edgy, and
filled with something that Owen couldn't quite place. Frustration,
maybe? Or was it guilt? But neither possibility really made sense . . . It
had to be something else.

"I'm somewhere east of Lahore," Kealey was saying, "and I need
you to get there ASAP. How soon can you move?"

Owen thought about it as he paused next to a vendor selling halal
beef, chicken, and fried potatoes, his stand covered by a broad blue
umbrella. "Forty minutes, give or take. What do you have?"

"Nothing yet, but it's just a matter of time."

Owen stopped walking and looked at the phone, trying to figure out the younger man's angle. "I don't understand. Why do you want me to move if you don't have—"

"Look, I'll explain later. Just get your people to Lahore as fast as you can."

"Fine. Where do we link up?"

"I don't know yet . . . I'll call you back when I figure it out. Have you talked to Harper?"

Owen barely managed to catch the question, as something in the background was overlapping the younger man's speech. To Owen's ear, the nearly constant, high-pitched noise sounded a lot like someone screaming, but he quickly dismissed the thought, knowing it had to be something else. "Yeah, I talked to him earlier. He's not happy."

"Fuck him," Kealey snapped. "I don't give a shit how he feels. He's got a lot to answer for when we get back. In the meantime, I need you to get your people moving. I'll meet you on the other end shortly."

"What about Pétain?"

There was a hesitation on the other end of the line. "Don't worry about her," Kealey finally said. "Just get moving. I'll call you back."

Owen started to ask another question, but the line was already dead. He swore viciously under his breath, prompting a sharp look from the halal vendor, but as he turned to head back through the gate, his anger started to dissipate. Instead, he found himself consumed by a deep-seated concern. As he began punching Walland's number in on his phone, he couldn't stop thinking about what he'd heard in the background on Kealey's end of the conversation. He had decided the sound couldn't possibly be that of someone screaming, but given Kealey's strange tone and his curt, strained reference to Marissa Pétain, Owen was no longer sure.

Either way, he *was* certain that the information Kealey had learned—or was about to learn—had come at a steep price. The only question was how steep, but that, along with his many other questions, would be answered soon enough. For now, he had other things to focus on, not the least of which was getting to Lahore as soon as possible.

After ending the call with Owen, Kealey lowered the phone and looked down at the man he knew as Fahim. The Afghan was pale. His eyes were squeezed tightly shut, and despite the rain, Kealey could tell he was sweating. It wasn't a serious injury, but from the place-ment alone, the CIA operative could tell that he was in a great deal of pain. After he had pulled the gun away from Pétain's knee, Kealey had fired a single shot into the Afghan's leg, more to disable him than anything else. The round had gouged a considerable chunk of flesh from the outer part of his thigh. For the moment, that was all Kealey wanted. For this man, the real pain had yet to begin.

He had not been able to pull the trigger on Marissa Pétain. He didn't understand it, because it should have been easy. In fact, it should have been beyond easy. After all, she meant nothing to him, whereas Naomi meant . . . well, *everything*. He didn't know why he had turned the gun on Fahim instead. He didn't understand how he could have betrayed his own emotions—his own gut instincts—to that degree. It had not been a conscious decision, and to make matters worse, he believed everything Machado had said. On some level, Kealey knew what he had done, and he knew what it meant. By sparing Pétain, he had probably just condemned Naomi to death, but that was some-thing outside his current realm of acceptance. He didn't even need to push the thought away, because he could not fully appreciate its true meaning, just as he could not appreciate the consequences of his actions. It wasn't the kind of thing he could bear to deal with. Not now. Not in this place, and maybe not ever.

As if reading his thoughts, the Afghan looked up at him. He was clutching his wounded leg, and his face was tight with pain. "You fool," he managed to hiss through clenched teeth. "Do you know what's going to happen now? Do you know what you've done?"

"Nothing compared to what I'm about to do," Kealey assured him coldly. He could ask himself those questions, but he wasn't about to take them from someone else, especially the man he had just put down. His fear for Naomi was already hitting him hard, and he knew it was just a matter of time before it completely crippled him. For the moment, though, he knew he had to maintain his composure—to set it aside. Otherwise, everything he had done so far would have been for nothing.

Pétain was still handcuffed to the transformer; Kealey could see her from the corner of his eye. Her legs—still intact—were curled up under her body, and her right hand was clutching her left arm, which was still pulled over her head. Kealey could feel her eyes on him, but he didn't shift his gaze from the man lying at his feet. He crouched down so their faces were almost level.

"Listen to me, Fahim," he began, straining to keep his voice even. Straining to force Naomi's face out of his mind. Straining to believe she might still make it through, despite the fact that he had just betrayed her in the worst way possible. "Let me tell you what's going to happen. Nothing has changed; helping me is still in your best interest. You're going to supply me with everything you have. In Cartagena, Machado told me you have an exact location for Benazir Mengal. Is that true?"

"Yes."

"What else do you have?"

"Everything. Weapons, ammunition, surveillance shots . . . We've been watching him for days."

"And are your people still watching him?"

"Yes."

"I'm going to make another call, and then I'm going to give you the phone. You're going to start pulling them out. I want them gone by the time my people get there, and I mean gone. I don't want them within five miles of that house. Then you're going to call your driver. Is he still out there?" Kealey gestured toward the other side of the substation, which was blocked by a number of large transformers.

The Afghan nodded tightly. "Good," Kealey said. "You're going to tell him to lie facedown on the road and stay that way until we come out. Tell him that if I see a gun in his hand when we walk out there, or if he isn't flat on his face, he's a dead man. Do you understand?"

"Why would I do all of that?" The Afghan's voice was flat and resigned, despite the obvious pain of his wound. In spite of himself, Kealey could not help but admire the man's resilience, but it didn't change how he felt. He would make all the promises he needed to for now, but eventually, he was going to kill everyone who had forced him into this position, including the man he had just shot. "You're going to kill me, anyway," Fahim observed.

How clever you are, Kealey thought, a dark tide sweeping over his mind. He was quietly impressed by the Afghan's foresight, but he could not let that show.

"You're wrong," he said, trying to sound reassuring. "I'm not going to kill you. But even if you're right, you have nothing to lose. If you cooperate, I might let you live, but if you don't help me, then I no longer have any use for you." Kealey paused to let the full weight of that statement sink in. "So what's it going to be? Yes or no?"

It seemed to take a long time, but finally the Afghan nodded, grimacing with the pain in his leg. "Yes. I can get what you need."

"Good," Kealey said. "Now, where is Benazir Mengal?"

The Afghan started talking immediately, and less than a minute later, Kealey was punching in Jonathan Harper's direct line. The deputy DCI answered immediately.

"John, it's me. Listen, I—"

"Where the hell have you been?" Harper said. His voice was laced with fury he was beyond trying to control. "You were supposed to—"

Kealey cut him off with a few harsh words of his own, then launched into the story. It took a few minutes, but Harper gradually began to understand what he was being told. Once that happened, he stopped trying to interrupt and listened, with escalating disbelief, as Kealey explained what had just taken place. He remained silent until the younger man was done, and by that time, he had forgotten why he was angry to begin with.

CHAPTER 37

WASHINGTON, D.C. • NORTHERN PAKISTAN

It was just after eight in the morning, and Harper was standing in the West Wing, just outside the Oval Office. He'd excused himself to take Kealey's call, and he was still trying to get over what he'd just heard. If it had come from anyone else, he would not have believed it. It seemed too far-fetched to be possible. But at the same time, part of him was not surprised to hear how far Javier Machado had gone to protect his only living child. He knew something of the Spaniard's background, and he had been with the Agency—albeit in a lesser position—when Caroline Pétain had died in Colombia. It was something that Harper couldn't fully understand, as he and his wife did not have children. Still, he knew how he would feel if something were to happen to Julie, and he could imagine that losing a child would be ten times worse. Maybe twenty times worse, and the way Caroline had died . . . Well, it didn't get much worse than that. Clearly, her death had affected Javier Machado more than anyone had ever suspected, including those closest to him, namely, his own family.

Lifting the phone, Harper called Diane Neal, the director's secretary, and had her patch him through to the station chief in Madrid. Without going into specifics, he explained the situation quickly, and the station chief agreed to dispatch two of his people to Machado's house in Cartagena. Harper thanked him and ended the call. Then he tried to call Machado direct. Unsurprisingly, the man didn't pick up, and neither did Naomi when Harper tried her sat phone.

Harper tried to think of something else he could do, but he had exhausted his options. He had done his best to reassure Kealey during their brief, tense conversation, but it hadn't really worked; they both knew Machado's background in operations, and they both knew he would have planned this out extensively. The embassy personnel would almost certainly find an empty house when they arrived in Cartagena, but they had to be sure. He wondered how he would ever be able to tell Pétain what her father had done; part of him hoped that Kealey would take care of it for him.

Checking his watch, he turned, opened the door, and stepped into the Oval Office. Brenneman, Andrews, DNI Bale, and Stan Chavis were engaged in quiet discussion around the coffee table, and they all looked up as Harper approached.

"What was that about?" Andrews asked.

"We've got a lead on Mengal," Harper replied. He didn't bother relaying the rest of it; right now, they didn't need the whole story. Besides, they wouldn't have been able to sit through it. Not after what he'd just told them. All four men shot up in their seats, giving him their full attention. "It looks like he might be in northern Pakistan, in a town called Sialkot."

"What about Brynn?" the president instantly asked, momentarily forgetting how high Fitzgerald ranked in comparison to Harper, Hayden, and even Andrews. Normally, he would never have used her first name in their presence.

"At this point, it appears that Secretary Fitzgerald is probably in the same location," Harper said, and he watched as all four men breathed a shared sigh of relief.

Brenneman sprang to his feet, and the others followed suit, although they had nowhere to go. "What do you mean, 'probably'? What makes you say that, and where did you get this information?"

Harper quickly relayed everything Kealey had just told him, limiting his words to what they needed to know. He finished by explaining that a considerable number of guards were stationed outside the house in Sialkot, which elevated the probability that Fitzgerald was being held inside the building.

"But we don't know for sure," Andrews clarified, once Harper was done. "We can't verify that she's on-site."

"No," Harper admitted. "But we can't know for sure until we're inside."

"You're suggesting we raid the house?" Brenneman asked skeptically.

"No," Harper replied. "At least, I don't think we should do that yet. But I do believe we need to have reliable eyes on the target until we're ready to move decisively. Sir, as I mentioned before, we have four 8X satellites over the region. We can easily shift one away from the area of fighting to cover this part of the Punjab. We have a number of well-trained paramilitary officers in the area, including Ryan Kealey, and with satellite coverage, we have nothing to lose by setting up surveillance on the residence. Even if Mengal moves unexpectedly, we'll be able to track him. He'll have nowhere to go."

"These people you have in the area . . . ," Chavis began slowly. "Are they armed?"

Harper hesitated, but only for a second. "No, they aren't. But that's a problem we can fix easily enough, once the president clears this course of action."

"How many men are we talking about?" Brenneman asked. "How many do we have in the area?"

"Five men, including Kealey, and one woman," Harper replied. "Of those six, two are current or former members of Delta, and one is a former army ranger, a captain with the 82nd Airborne. Another, Aaron Massi, served as a combat controller in the air force."

"Still, that's six against a force of eight to twelve, plus another unknown number of guards inside the house," Andrews remarked. He shook his head uneasily. "It's a risk. There could be a lot of unknowns in that equation, and if the surveillance is blown . . ."

"Alerting the Pakistani government would be even riskier," Harper pointed out. "I've been thinking this through over the past couple of days, debating how it might play out if we actually got a lead on Fitzgerald's location. And I have to tell you, I think it would be a mistake to go through official channels. Mengal still has a lot of friends in high places. If we ask Musharraf to move on this and word gets out to the wrong man, which it will, Mengal will kill the secretary of state and leave before we can even get into position."

"Jesus," Brenneman said shakily, his face turning pale. He retook his seat, and after a moment, everyone else did the same. Looking over to Harper, he asked, "How long do we have to decide on a course of action?"

Harper wondered why the president had used the word "we." In the end, it was his decision and his alone; everyone else was just there to advise. Harper wondered if Brenneman was already attempting to spread the blame around, at least subconsciously. Harper knew it didn't really matter either way; if the president took his advice and the surveillance was blown, Harper would almost certainly be out of a job, as would Andrews and Hayden. Chavis would probably survive the fallout, but not because of his position. He and the president shared a personal friendship that dated back to their college years at Georgetown, and that, more than anything else, would insulate the chief of staff if the worst were to happen.

"Sir, there is no time to waste," the deputy DCI cautioned. "Mengal won't want to stay in one place for long. He'll be moving around as much as he can, but it would be pointless to launch a rescue operation until we have reliable surveillance in place. Once we have eyes on the building, we can strike in a matter of hours, if that is what you decide to do."

"But with satellite coverage, we don't need to—"

"Sir, forgive me for interrupting, but IMINT isn't enough. We need men on the ground."

Brenneman let out a weary sigh, then lowered his head in thought. After a minute, he looked up and said, "What happens next? I mean, what do you need to do right now, assuming I agree with your proposal?"

"With your permission, I'd like to head over to the NRO. We need to get an 8X over Sialkot as soon as possible. A call from you to the director would help greatly in that regard, sir. Once that's done, we can establish things here. By that, I mean we can set up downstairs in the Situation Room."

"I'll call him before you get there," Brenneman said. He seemed to think for a few seconds more. "John, I want you to draw up a plan to recover Secretary Fitzgerald. As of now, we're proceeding with the understanding that the Pakistani government will *not* be alerted in advance. That may change before I authorize anything, but for now, that's the plan. Start getting your people in place."

"Yes, sir," Harper said. The president looked at Andrews, just to make sure they were all on the same page, and the DCI acknowledged the order.

"Sir," Bale cautioned, "if you do this, the diplomatic fallout—"

"Will be worth it," Brenneman said, finishing Bale's sentence. He fixed the director of National Intelligence with a stern glare. "If Musharraf had control over the subversive elements in his country, Ken, we wouldn't be in this position to begin with. We might only have one chance to get her back, and I'm not going to let it slip through our fingers."

Bale nodded, and the president shifted his gaze to include them all. "We're going to find her and bring her home, gentlemen, by any means necessary. Is that clear?"

Everyone murmured their agreement. The president stood, and everyone followed suit.

"Good. Let's go to work," said Brenneman.

Kealey had been staring out the window for the last half hour, but the passing scenery meant nothing to him. He was entirely fixed on the images running through his mind. All he could see was Naomi, and it was killing him. He still couldn't believe he had misjudged Javier Machado that badly, and he wondered if the man was actually capable of doing what he had threatened to do. His background said that he wasn't. People with that kind of temperament didn't last long in the Operations Directorate, and that was assuming they even managed to get through the doors in the first place. Machado had spent thirty years in the DO, and his career had been marked by a long string of accomplishments. Simply stated, he was one of the best operatives the Agency had ever seen, and by extension, that made him a consummate professional. If that had been the only factor involved, Kealey would have felt sure that he was bluffing—that he had no intention of really hurting Naomi.

But it *wasn't* that simple. Machado's actions were clearly based on an emotional element that Kealey couldn't fully appreciate. When Pétain had told him about her sister's gruesome death in Colombia, Kealey had been shocked by the sick nature of the crime, as well as what had come after. But he hadn't really considered how much that must have affected the people Caroline had left behind, namely, her immediate family. The pain of that event would have been bad in the beginning—Kealey knew that much, because he had once suffered a similar loss—but over time, the initial impact of that tragedy had clearly evolved in Pétain and Machado. In the former, it had fostered a desire for revenge; in the latter, it had fostered something else. Something far more dangerous. A willingness to go to great lengths—any lengths, perhaps, if he was serious about the threat he had made—to protect his only surviving child.

Kealey had been turning it over in his mind since they'd left the substation three hours earlier. He had used the time to brief Owen over the phone and move his people into position, but he'd still had hours—hard, painful, prolonged hours—to think about what had happened. He was no closer to an answer now than he had been then. He still didn't know how he could have seen the truth in time. He wasn't even certain what *truth* he was supposed to have seen. Was Machado simply acting out of a twisted desire to shield his daughter from harm? Or was he just trying to control her life by any means necessary? Kealey tried to push the distinction aside, as it didn't really matter either way. What *did* matter was how he had reacted when it all came unglued, and he still didn't know if he'd done the right thing. Other than following Machado's instructions, what else could he have he done? *Was* there anything else he could have done? Any real alternative? He didn't think so, but there was no way of knowing, and the uncertainty was slowly but steadily wearing him down.

"Here," Fahim said from the front seat. Kealey shifted his attention to the front. He silently rebuked himself for letting his mind wander, but he didn't really have to worry about their prisoner. Kealey had used the man's own handcuffs to secure him to the passenger-side door. Pétain was driving, and Kealey was seated behind the Afghan. He had the only gun in the car, and the flimsy seats in the Subaru would not stop a bullet. Kealey had made their prisoner abundantly aware of both these facts, and apart from the occasional groan of pain, he had remained silent throughout the journey. "This is the road you need to take."

Pétain looked over her shoulder at Kealey, and he nodded his approval. He suddenly realized that she hadn't said a word since they'd left the substation, and he wondered what might be going through her mind. Could she have overheard either of his conversations with Machado and Harper? If she had, it would certainly explain her silence.

She took the exit, and Kealey said, "Slow down." To Fahim, he said, "Where is it?"

"Just a few kilometers." The car went over a bump, and the Afghan let out a guttural moan. Clearly, the pain from his gunshot wound was starting to intensify. "The car should be over this next hill. A white Toyota. It will be parked on the shoulder."

"Okay. Pull over here, Marissa."

She pulled over without a word. Kealey got out, went to the driver's-side window, and asked her to get in the back. He gave her the gun, then slid behind the wheel. She climbed in back a moment later. Next, he called Owen, who picked up after a couple of rings.

"Where are you?" Kealey asked. He already had a good idea; he just wanted the specifics. Shortly after Fahim had arranged for his people to drop off the equipment, Kealey had directed Owen and his people to an overwatch position, from which point they could monitor any unwanted activity around the site. They had moved into position two hours earlier, and the last time they had checked in, everything had looked good.

"In the tree line south of the car. Two guys dropped it off an hour ago."

"How does it look?"

"As clean as can be expected."

"What does that mean?"

"It means you need to reconsider, Ryan. We don't know anything about these people, and we have no way to cover you. That car could be loaded with explosives. It could blow the minute you—"

"They didn't have time to do that," Kealey pointed out, knowing full well that the other man was right. Fahim's people had had plenty of time to set up any kind of ambush they wanted. "And you know as well as I do that we need what's in that trunk. They want their guy back . . . I don't think they're going to try anything."

"Ryan . . ." Owen was clearly frustrated. "What's it going to take to convince you that this is a bad idea? There's got to be better ways of—"

"We don't have time, Paul. You know I'm right. Just do it my way, okay?"

"Fine. It's your neck. We'll be watching."

"Good. Stay where you are. I'm three minutes out."

Kealey ended the call, then looked at the man in the passenger seat. "For your sake, I hope you're playing this straight."

"It will be there," the Afghan assured him. Kealey looked into his eyes for a moment, searching for some sign of a hidden agenda, but after a second, he gave up and looked away. The man was completely

unreadable. *Besides,* Kealey thought, with a deep sense of bitter regret, *it's not like I know how to read people. Even if he is lying, I'd
never be able to see it. Just look at Machado. I sure as hell got that
one wrong, didn't I?*

He started the car and continued down the road. He drove slowly,
noting that there was hardly any vehicular traffic. His eyes were scanning every hidden path in the trees, every open field, and every ditch
in sight, searching for the smallest sign of a forthcoming ambush.
Even as he did so, he knew full well that if it was coming, he would
never see it. Turning to Pétain, he saw that she had the gun trained
on the back of the Afghan's seat.

"Drop down," he told her. "Get as low in the seat as you can, and
keep your head below the window. Don't move that muzzle an inch.
When I get out, if you see or hear anything that doesn't sound
right—I mean anything at all—you pull the trigger, okay?"

She nodded and slunk back down in the seat. Looking over at
Fahim, Kealey said, "There's fourteen rounds left in that gun, and if
anything goes wrong, you're going to catch all of them in the back.
Bearing that in mind, are you sure you don't want me to call your
friends and make sure they understand the situation? Because if
there's any confusion, we should clear it up right now."

The Afghan shook his head. He was dripping sweat, and his face
was twisted with pain. It was really starting to hit him now. "No," he
gasped. "You don't need to call them. They won't try anything. I
promise you."

The Subaru crested a small hill, and there was the car, parked off
on the shoulder. Kealey pulled in behind it, then got out. He approached the rear of the waiting car at a fast walk, fully aware that he
was completely exposed. His mouth was dry, and his heart was beating hard as he felt behind the left rear tire for the keys. He found
them as expected, and he quickly opened the trunk. Despite what
he'd just said to Owen, he half expected some kind of explosion,
though if there *was* a bomb in the trunk, he knew he would never
see or hear a thing. It would be over before he even registered the
flash.

But there was nothing. The trunk was filled with nothing but a
half dozen canvas holdalls. He started unzipping them quickly, checking the contents.

He found the surveillance photographs first. He looked through them quickly and saw what appeared to be armed men standing out-side an English country home. He didn't know why the house struck him as British in design, but it certainly didn't resemble any of the predominant architecture in Pakistan, despite the country's history of British colonialism. He kept flipping through the photographs, but nothing really jumped out at him. The most useful item he found was a hand-drawn map of the surgeon's house and the surrounding grounds. The map was marked with a series of insertion points, indi-cating the best angle of approach. Fahim's men had maintained sur-veillance for a number of days without showing out, which could have meant a number of things. Perhaps the vast majority—or at least the primary figures—had fought with the mujahideen in Afghanistan, or perhaps Machado had trained some of them personally all those years ago. Kealey suspected it was a little of both.

He set the photographs back in the holdall, then began checking the weapons. There were four rifles with accompanying scopes, pre-loaded magazines, night-vision equipment, and a number of pistols. The weapons, he saw, were high grade: a SIG 550; two HK G36 as-sault rifles; and a Bofors AK5B, a 7.62mm rifle adapted for use by mil-itary snipers. He also found a couple of sturdy combat knives. Moving as fast as he could, Kealey field-stripped one of the G36s. He was intensely aware of how close the road was: the asphalt was just a few feet to his right. A car had yet to pass, but it was just a matter of time. Once he had the weapon apart, he saw that all the necessary components were there. Putting it together, he dry-fired it once and heard a satisfying click.

Good enough. Kealey shouldered two of the holdalls and brought them back to the Subaru. Opening the trunk, he tossed them in, then went back for the rest. Once all the gear was transferred, he closed the trunk on both cars, then climbed behind the wheel of the Subaru, which was still running.

"Everything okay?" Pétain asked. Looking back, Kealey saw that she was still slumped down in the backseat. She looked edgy but composed. He shot a quick look at her right hand and saw that the gun was steady. That told him everything he needed to know.

"Everything's fine. It's all there." He pulled onto the road and kept driving, watching his rearview mirror carefully. He half expected to see people running out of the trees for the Toyota, but he couldn't spot any movement.

Ten minutes later, he called Owen. "What's happening?"

"A car just pulled up," the Delta colonel reported. "One guy is getting out . . . He's walking to the car. Hang on a second." Kealey waited for five, and then Owen came back on. "Okay, the car is pulling away. He's too far behind to catch up to you, and Massi didn't spot any additional vehicles on the road ahead. Looks like we're clear."

"Good." Kealey couldn't help but breathe a quiet sigh of relief. A million things could have gone wrong with the plan he'd hastily devised, but it looked like they had managed to pull it off. The opposition had acted in good faith, which was a rare enough thing. Kealey decided that Fahim was as important to the organization as he'd initially suspected, and that was probably why they hadn't been ambushed. "I'll meet you in Sialkot in forty-five minutes."

"Got it. What about the equipment?"

"I've got all of it. Looks okay."

"Then I guess we're in business."

"Yeah, it looks that way. I'll talk to you soon."

Thirty minutes later, Kealey eased off the gas, then turned the Subaru onto a rutted dirt path. They passed between two immense stone pillars, rolled down a steep incline, and after a couple of minutes, the trees gave way. There was a large, murky pond off to the left, dragonflies drifting lazily over the dappled surface; to the right, there was nothing but a green, open field. Once they were past the pond, he pulled off to the side of the road. Kealey had marked the route carefully; now he called Owen to relay his exact location. After consulting his map, Owen said he could be there in fifteen minutes. Everything was running right on schedule.

There was nothing to do but wait, so Kealey got out to stretch his legs. Fahim had passed out a short while earlier and was no threat to anyone, even without the handcuffs, which he was still wearing. The hole in his thigh was still leaking, but an improvised pressure bandage—which Pétain had fashioned using strips torn from the Afghan's raincoat—had done its part to limit the blood loss. Besides, Kealey wasn't interested in the man's comfort. All that mattered was keeping him alive long enough to find Fitzgerald and get her out of the country. Kealey was checking the contents of the canvas holdalls more thoroughly when he sensed Pétain by his side. He looked up and saw that she was watching him steadily.

He waited for her to speak. "What happens now?" she finally asked.

"I need you to watch him," Kealey said, gesturing to the unconscious man in the front of the car. "He might have held something back, so we can't let him go until we can verify that the targets are at this surgeon's house in Sialkot. You might not be able to let him go until morning. You'll have to fly out separately regardless."

She absorbed this silently. "And if they're not? In Sialkot, I mean?"

"Then you're going to need to convince him to come clean." He looked into her eyes. On this point, he had to be sure. "It might take a lot of convincing. Can you do that? If you have to, I mean?"

"Yes, I can." She said it without hesitation, Kealey noticed. In fact, she didn't even blink. He felt sure that she would do whatever it took, and that was enough. On that point, at least, he felt he could still trust his instincts. "Will he live that long?" Pétain asked.

"I hope so. We might need him."

Pétain seemed to consider this for a few seconds. "Ryan . . ."

Here it comes, he thought. He still didn't know how he was going to handle this part, though it had certainly crossed his mind over the last couple of hours.

"I don't know what happened back there," Pétain began slowly. "At the substation, I mean, but I want to . . . well, thank you for what you did."

"What?" It took a second for that to sink in, as it was the last thing he expected to hear. He shook his head and looked at her in disbelief. "Marissa, what are you talking about? I almost shot you."

"Yes, but you had to, right?" It wasn't really a question, but she hesitated before going on. "I mean, I don't know *why* you had to, but you wouldn't have even considered it unless you had no other choice. I know that, Ryan. I know about you . . . Everyone in Operations knows about you." She blushed a little with this admission, but somehow, it took nothing away from her demeanor, which was completely controlled. "I couldn't hear what you were saying, but whoever you were talking to . . . Well, they clearly wanted you to do it, and you didn't. So thank you."

So she still didn't know, Kealey thought. She looked awkward, but her face was completely open, and that confirmed his initial observation. She didn't know that her father was responsible for all of it. He could have told her, of course, but now wasn't the time. Was there ever a time to hear something like that?

Probably not, he decided after a long moment. Machado's actions might have seemed reasonable in his own mind, but that was only because the Spaniard's sense of reason had been twisted, warped by eight years of grief for the loss of his eldest daughter and fear for the one he still had left. His actions would probably seem just as incomprehensible to Pétain as they did to Kealey.

"I don't know what it cost you," Pétain was saying. At this, Kealey felt his stomach clench, but he tried not to react. He still couldn't think about it. He had yet to come to terms with the decision he'd made at the substation, and he didn't know if he'd ever be able to.

"But I'm grateful," Pétain said. "I really am."

He looked at her. There were no tears in her eyes; that was the first thing that struck him. She was completely composed, and that, he had to admit, was an amazing thing. Javier Machado had clearly misjudged his daughter; Kealey had never been more certain of anything. He sensed that she would be able to hold her own on any undercover assignment; she was easily one of the strongest people he'd ever known.

And that, he suddenly realized, was just another thing that could be traced back to her sister's death. He had never seen a family so thoroughly destroyed by one incident. He didn't understand the internal dynamics—he had never been especially close with his own family—but one thing was clear: there was a lot of pain running below the surface with all of them, and that was something he *could* identify with.

"What did it cost you, Ryan?"

The question was nearly inaudible, but it shook him, and she saw his reaction. Kealey wanted to pretend that he hadn't heard, but they both knew that he had. He looked into her eyes for a long moment, then looked past her without answering. A car had just emerged from the trees and was coming down the hill. Kealey could see a familiar face behind the wheel.

"Looks like it's time to go," he said.

She turned to look at the approaching vehicle. "I guess you're right." And to Kealey's relief, she left it at that.

Walland was the man behind the wheel. He pulled up 10 feet behind the Subaru and shut down the engine. As the 4 men climbed out of the vehicle, Kealey reached into one of the holdalls and pulled out a pistol, a compact Beretta 9mm. He handed it to Pétain, along with two full magazines.

"What is this for?" she asked. She tapped the butt of the Makarov, which was tucked into the top of her linen pants, as if to remind him that she still had it.

"Just in case," he told her.

She accepted the weapon as the rest of the team approached. Kealey zipped up the holdall he'd taken the Beretta from and got to his feet.

"Is this all of it?" Owen asked, gesturing to the six holdalls piled at Kealey's feet.

"Yeah, that's it."

"So we're set?" Owen was looking past them to the unconscious form in the front of the Subaru; clearly, he was uneasy with the whole situation, and Kealey couldn't really blame him.

"Yeah, everything's fine. Listen, I've got to tell you something. . . ." Kealey briefed the other man quickly on his plan. Pétain was going to hold Fahim until they could verify that Mengal, Saifi, and Fitzgerald were all at the house in Sialkot. Then she would call his subordinates and tell them where to find him before leaving the country herself. When he was done with the short explanation, Owen nodded his agreement.

"We need to move," Kealey told him. "Let's get the equipment loaded."

Owen relayed the instructions to Walland. As the former ranger shouldered two of the holdalls and moved to the second car, Owen stepped away to address Manik and Massi, leaving Kealey and Pétain alone by the back of the Subaru. They stood there in silence for nearly a minute, but neither felt any particular need to speak. The others, engaged as they were in their separate tasks, didn't seem to notice the strangely intimate moment. For some reason, Kealey had the sudden sense that she had known all along, that on some level, at least, she knew who had been on the other end of that phone. But he couldn't ask her, and he doubted she would have admitted to it, anyway.

"Good luck," she said finally, glancing at him quickly. "I hope you find her."

Kealey nodded and turned to walk to the second car, but as he reached for the handle on the passenger side, her last words seemed to echo in his head, and he suddenly found himself wondering, looking deeper into her parting statement.

Who had she really been talking about? Was it Fitzgerald? He wondered if he was just imagining things, if he was reading too far into what she had just said. He could ask, of course, but what was the point? If she had known all along, would it really make a difference?

No, he decided after a moment's thought. *It wouldn't.* If Naomi was really gone, the blame would rest with just one person, and it wouldn't be Marissa Pétain. Even if she knew—or even suspected— what had really transpired at the substation, she was not at fault. Simply put, she wasn't responsible, and she could not be held accountable for what her father had done.

He could not help but wonder how much she really knew, but Kealey tried to remind himself that it didn't really matter. Either way, that particular bill would be paid in full. He had already made that promise to himself, and he fully intended to keep it.

Moving to the passenger door of the Toyota, he climbed into the car as Owen—who was now behind the wheel—started the engine. As they pulled away, Kealey looked in the rearview mirror and saw Pétain looking after them. He watched her as the car rolled over the uneven terrain, and for a few seconds, he thought he felt their eyes connect. Then they passed into the trees, and she disappeared from sight.

CHAPTER 38

SIALKOT · SOUTHERN PORTUGAL

The nightmare was as real as anything she'd ever experienced, and seemingly endless, a sickening montage of fire, blood, and death. It had been playing on a continuous reel in her mind, and no matter how hard she tried, she could not force the images from her subconscious. They seemed to dwell there, in the deep, dark recesses of her imagination; only she knew they were not a creation. Everything she was seeing was real. At least, it had *been* real. Now, she was no longer sure what was real and what was false. The hours, days, or weeks of horror—she couldn't be sure how much time had passed—had stripped her of certainty. Of hope.

Of her very identity.

She didn't know if she could trust her own thoughts. Was she still sane? It seemed that she was, at least for brief stretches of time. There were short, fleeting moments that seemed to work, times where she found herself able to focus, or at least conjure a lucid thought. But those moments never lasted more than a couple of minutes. Then her rational thoughts would slip away, just out of reach, and she'd begin the long slide back into the abyss. The tape would start again in her mind, and she'd open her mouth to scream, but all she could hear were the sounds of death and destruction: the screech and the sickening thump as the rocket tore into the car; the crack of the shot as it ripped its way through Lee Patterson's brain, and the nameless woman's cries for help, which she'd uttered a moment before the Algerian had fired that final, fatal bullet into her pleading face. She could see it, too—an endless display of what had to be hell, or at least the earthly equivalent.

Brynn Fitzgerald wanted it all to stop, but she knew there was no hope of reprieve. If there were any hope at all, she would have gladly endured the pain she was feeling. As it stood, she just wanted it all to end, even if that meant the end of everything. She didn't want to die, but it seemed like the only escape. She would give anything to know that she had something to look forward to, that there was even the slightest possibility of returning to the world she had once known. If there was only a light at the end of the tunnel, she felt she could go on for as long as she had to. . . .

And suddenly, there was.

"She's awake," Said Qureshi announced, stepping back from the bed.

On hearing the words he'd been waiting for, Benazir Mengal moved off the wall of the surgical suite and stepped forward to see for himself. The second surgery—the pericardial window—had ended eighteen hours earlier, and Fitzgerald had been out the whole time. The pain medication, which Qureshi had been administering every couple of hours, had played a part in keeping her under, but much of the sleep was natural as her body worked to regain its strength. At Qureshi's suggestion, Mengal had ordered a few of his men to bring a bed down from one of the second-floor rooms. They'd set it up in the suite, and once the surgeon was sure she was stable, they'd transferred Fitzgerald from the operating table to the bed.

Now, as Qureshi busied himself checking the monitors, the former general leaned over the acting U.S. secretary of state. His face was less than a foot from hers as he watched intently, waiting for a sign of life. Her eyelids fluttered, then opened, and for the first time, he looked directly into the sea green eyes of the woman whose abduction he had helped orchestrate four days earlier.

Their eyes locked for a few brief seconds, but Fitzgerald did not react. She seemed confused, distant, and completely unfamiliar with the man she was staring at. Mengal knew this should not surprise him; there was no way she could know who he was. Still, he felt oddly let down by the moment, which struck him as anticlimactic.

Fitzgerald's eyes drifted shut. Mengal hovered over her for a moment longer, then straightened and let out a low, disappointed grunt. Brushing past him, Qureshi approached his patient and touched her arm gently. She let out a soft groan, but otherwise, she didn't react.

"Ms. Fitzgerald, can you hear me?" Qureshi asked gently. "If you can hear me, please respond."

For a few seconds, nothing happened. Then Fitzgerald opened her eyes once more. Her lips parted, but no sound came out. Finally, she managed to croak a single, unintelligible word.

"Excuse me?" Qureshi asked. "I didn't quite—"

"Water," Fitzgerald said again, finding her voice. "Please . . ."

"Yes, of course," Qureshi said hastily. He hurriedly went to the sink and filled a glass, then brought it back as Mengal looked on silently. Setting the glass on his instrument tray, Qureshi turned back to his patient. "Ms. Fitzgerald, before I give you the glass, you're going to need to sit up. When I move you, it's going to hurt. If the pain is too much, just tell me, and I'll give you something for it. Do you understand?"

She seemed to consider his words for a moment, but she didn't acknowledge them. After an interminable pause, her eyes cleared and she said, "Where am I?"

Qureshi hesitated, then shot a glance at Mengal, who simply nodded his permission. It didn't make any difference if Fitzgerald knew where they were; in her current state, she was completely helpless to act on the information. "You're in a town called Sialkot. It's about an hour north of Lahore."

"Who are you?"

"My name is Said Qureshi. I'm a surgeon, the person who treated you." Qureshi paused for a moment. "Ms. Fitzgerald, do you know why you're here?"

Fitzgerald seemed to think for a moment, her eyes rolling up, as if she were trying to see the wall behind her. Then she regained focus. Hesitantly, she said, "There was an attack. . . ."

Qureshi waited for more, but Fitzgerald had lost her train of thought. "That's exactly right," he told her. "There was an attack on your motorcade in Rawalpindi. You were brought here, and I treated you for some injuries you sustained in the . . . incident."

Fitzgerald considered this for about ten seconds. Then, without warning, she tried to sit up. Immediately, she winced and cried out in pain. Qureshi quickly eased her back onto the bed. Mengal, who was standing near the foot of the bed, didn't react at all, his hard eyes fixed on his hostage.

"You shouldn't do that," Qureshi admonished her, checking to make sure that the catheter in her left arm was still in place. "Please, don't try to move without help. I haven't taken the chest tube out, so anytime you move suddenly, it's going to hurt."

"Chest tube?" she murmured. She looked up at him, her eyes filled with the obvious question.

"As I said, you were injured in the attack," he told her gently. Qureshi paused, thinking about the best way to explain it. In his experience, some patients needed to hear things in layman's terms, while others were capable of breaking down the most complicated medical jargon. He didn't know much about Fitzgerald, but she was obviously a very astute woman; otherwise, she wouldn't have risen to such heights in the American government. He saw no need to talk down to her.

"You suffered a pneumothorax of the left lung," he continued, "and a moderate hemopericardium. In other words, your lung was partially collapsed, and your heart was bruised, causing an accumulation of excessive fluid inside the pericardial sac. However," he said quickly, seeing the alarmed look on her face, "you're fine now. The operations—both of them—were a complete success."

Qureshi paused and shot a glance at his watch. She'd be complaining about the pain shortly, and he was already thinking about how much Dilaudid she would need. Probably less than a milligram, he decided, but it was too early to make the call. He'd see how she felt in an hour or so.

"Now," he continued, "I think you should—"

"Enough," Mengal growled. Surprised by the sudden outburst, the surgeon stopped and turned to stare at him. "Just give her the water. I need to talk to you outside."

Qureshi frowned but didn't respond. Murmuring a few quiet words to his patient, he helped raise her into a sitting position. Fitzgerald managed the best she could, Qureshi noticed, but it was obvious from the tight look on her face that the effort had caused her a great deal of pain. When she was finally sitting upright, he handed her the water, and she drank deeply, draining the glass in a few seconds. She immediately asked for more, and Qureshi went to refill the glass. Bringing it back, he handed it to her and watched with satisfaction as

she raised the glass to her lips again. Although she was clearly uncomfortable, she was alert, lucid, and coherent enough to ask the
usual questions, all of which were excellent signs.

At that moment, there was a sudden commotion outside the room,
the sounds of violent squabbling in English. Fitzgerald stopped drinking and pulled the glass away from her lips, a quizzical expression
coming over her face. Qureshi and Mengal both turned to look as
the door burst open, revealing a tall figure framed in the doorway.
Amari Saifi stormed into the room, followed closely by two protesting guards, both of whom immediately looked to Mengal, their dark
faces tinged with apologetic fear.

The Algerian stopped a few steps away from the foot of the bed.
Looking down at Fitzgerald, he smiled warmly, his brown eyes glittering with the wrong kind of happiness. "So, she's finally awake," he
said in a syrupy tone. "How do you feel, Dr. Fitzgerald? It's good to
see you've come back to us. We were starting to worry."

Qureshi looked from the Algerian to Fitzgerald and, in that fraction of a second, saw something that would stay with him for the rest
of his life. Her eyes were wide and round, as if a camera flash had
gone off right in her face, and her eyebrows were pinched together
and raised to the edge of her reddish brown bangs. Her mouth was
slack and gaping, her body completely still. Her face was a mask of
pure terror. As Qureshi watched in mounting horror, the plastic glass
slipped from her hand, rolled off the bed, and hit the tile floor. The
second it hit the ground, Fitzgerald released a prolonged groaning
sound, as if she were straining to lift an impossibly heavy load. Then
her eyes rolled up into her head, and she went completely limp, her
upper body slumping to the right side of the bed.

For a few seconds, there was nothing but frozen disbelief as everyone stared at her unconscious form. Qureshi, a veteran of ER wards
in Seattle and London, was the first to snap out of it.

"Get him out of here!" he screamed, flinging a finger in the in-
truder's direction. He rushed to his patient's side as Mengal pulled
the Algerian from the room, the guards babbling their apologies to
the general the whole time. Qureshi could hear arguing in the hall as
he rearranged Fitzgerald's position on the bed, then quickly checked
her vitals. He was relieved to see that everything was in order. Apparently, she had not suffered an aneurism or a heart attack, as he'd initially feared.

Once he was sure she was in no immediate danger, the anger kicked in. For the first time since the general had shown up with Fitzgerald, fear was not an issue for the diminutive Pakistani surgeon. He crossed the room in five quick strides, pulled open the door, and stepped into the hall. The Algerian was nowhere in sight, but Mengal was standing a few feet away, berating the guards in rapid-fire Urdu.

Catching sight of Qureshi, Mengal dismissed the guards and turned to face the smaller man. As the guards sulked down the hall, Qureshi stuck a finger in the general's face and snarled, "What the hell did he think he was doing? We're lucky she didn't—"

Before he knew what was happening, the words died in his throat. He felt a hand crushing his windpipe, then a sharp, bursting pain as the back of his head bounced off the plaster wall. Suddenly, Mengal's face was less than an inch from his own, his small eyes filled with rage and contempt.

"Who the fuck do you think you're talking to?"

Qureshi couldn't respond; he was too focused on trying to breathe. It had been less than a few seconds, but already it felt like his lungs were exploding. He began struggling involuntarily, his entire body screaming for air. His hands came up of their own free will and began clawing at Mengal's iron grip, but it was no good. The man was just too strong.

"You will do as you're told, Said . . . nothing more, nothing less." Mengal's voice was low and harsh, like a shovel scraping across cement. "If you ever question me again, I'll kill you without a moment's hesitation. *You* work for *me*. Is that understood?"

Qureshi nodded frantically, his chin moving against the coarse flesh of the general's right hand. Finally, Mengal released his grip, and Qureshi slumped to the floor, choking for air.

"Now," the general said, shooting an idle glance at his watch as though nothing had happened. "How long will it be until the woman can move?"

"I don't understand," Qureshi rasped, once he could manage the words. "What do you mean?"

"It's not a difficult question," Mengal growled. "How long until she can move? Until she can walk?"

Qureshi thought quickly, dismissing the first numbers that came to mind. He didn't want to do anything else to incur the general's wrath, but at the same time, he wanted to do what he could for Fitzgerald.

"Eight hours," he finally said. Mengal's face darkened instantly, but Qureshi didn't back down. He desperately wanted to escape this situation with his life, but the woman was still his patient, and he had to speak up for her. No one else was going to do it, and the thought of putting his own welfare ahead of hers didn't even cross his mind. "She can't move with the chest tube in place," Qureshi explained. "I have to take it out, but I can't do it safely until the intrathoracic space is fully drained of excess fluid. I—"

"I saw the tube," Mengal snapped. "There's nothing in it. The machine stopped draining an hour ago."

"Yes, but—"

"Stop talking." The general squatted down on his haunches so they were almost eye to eye. "I want you to listen very carefully, Said. It's been eighteen hours since the surgery, and I'm tired of waiting. I know you've been stalling. If you think you can trick me with your superior medical knowledge, you're mistaken. I've seen every kind of injury you can imagine, and I've seen how they're treated. I warn you, if you try to fool me again, you will not live to regret it."

Qureshi took a few shallow breaths, then gave a small, quick nod, showing he understood.

"Now," Mengal continued in a calmer voice, "once you take out the tube, how long until she can move?"

This time, Qureshi didn't even hesitate. "Four hours. She should be ambulatory in four hours."

"Fine. Then go take it out, and don't give her anything else for the pain. I need her to be coherent when she wakes."

Qureshi muttered his agreement. Shakily, he got to his feet and, without another glance at the general, reentered the suite. He closed the door behind him, then stood motionless for a moment, thinking it through.

As he started across the room, he realized his hands were trembling uncontrollably. It was the first time Mengal had ever verbally threatened him. It was also the first time he'd put his hands on him, though Qureshi had always known the threat was there, lurking just beneath the surface. It was not a natural relationship—he was the healer, Mengal the killer—but somehow, he'd fallen into the trap. It was the money, of course. The money and the fear of what would happen if he didn't comply. He hadn't done enough to sever their ties when he still had the option, and now he was paying the price.

As was Randall Craig, he thought, with a surge of guilt, but there was nothing he could do about that now. Hopefully, his old friend would forgive him for involving him in this mess, assuming they both managed to survive it.

As Said Qureshi stood next to his patient, who was still unconscious, it occurred to him, and not for the first time, how far he had fallen. It was not for want of effort; for the most part, he had always tried to do the right thing. It was just that he'd come up short on so many occasions. He couldn't help but feel that Fitzgerald was his last chance at salvation. If, by some miracle, she managed to survive this scenario, he would be able to take some pride in that. He knew it was asking a lot, that she should survive, but it was all he wanted. If she could just make it through, he would feel he had done something right for the first time in years.

With this thought in mind, he began moving around the surgical suite, collecting the items he would need to remove the tube. He was preparing to act against his better judgment, but the whole time he was fixed on what Craig had said earlier. *They want her for propaganda value, Said. In the end, they'll probably kill her. And if they're willing to kill her, we don't stand a chance. You must know that. . . .*

Qureshi had known as much from the start, but he had tried to remain optimistic. Now, given what had just transpired with Mengal in the hall, he could no longer ignore the truth. At some point, he was going to have to take a chance. There was no other way, not if he wanted to live, and he was surrounded by potential weapons.

For some strange reason, the last part of this thought didn't register—at least, not right away. Then he said it again in his mind, and this time it clicked: *he was surrounded by weapons.* They had given him full access to his surgical tools, and Mengal had never followed through on his decision to keep one guard in the surgical suite at all times. Inside the large room, no one was watching; Qureshi was able to do as he pleased.

As he considered the full implication of this realization, the possibilities coming together, he temporarily forgot about his assigned task. He found himself drifting toward the counter, his eyes passing over the assorted equipment. His gaze quickly settled on the tray bearing his scalpels. For the first time in his career, he was looking at the tools of his trade in terms of the damage they could inflict, as opposed to the good they could do. It was an unsettling change in perspective, but completely necessary. He knew that now, just as he knew that Mengal would not allow him to live. He simply couldn't afford to: Qureshi had seen and heard too much.

Shooting a quick, furtive glance back at the door, Qureshi steeled his nerve and started to move. He quickly gathered the things he would need: a pair of shears, a roll of surgical tape, and an aluminum cot splint with a U-shaped, clip-style design. Using the shears, he cut the finger splint into two nearly identical pieces, cutting at the rounded point where the tip of the finger would be. With that done, he began looking for the largest scalpel he could find. After a brief search, he settled on a No. 20 blade, which was mounted in a sturdy titanium handle. The No. 20 was a larger version of the No. 10, a long, curved blade primarily used for cutting through skin and muscle. If he had to use it, it would do the job.

Moving as fast as he could with his trembling fingers, he wedged the sharp part of the blade between the two cushioned halves of the splint, then wrapped tape around the entire contraption. Holding the makeshift sheath in his left hand, he practiced pulling the scalpel out with his right. He saw that it moved freely; if he had to use it, he would be able to draw the blade quickly. Satisfied, he positioned the scalpel so that the only part protruding from the sheath was the handle. Then, after rolling up the sleeve of his shirt, he awkwardly taped the modified splint to his inner left forearm.

Pulling his sleeve back down, Qureshi looked at his arm and turned it from side to side, trying to determine if the slight lump beneath the fabric was noticeable. After a few seconds of careful, objective consideration, he decided that it wasn't.

Having accomplished his goal, Qureshi gathered the leftover evidence—the remains of the splint, the tape, and the shears. With a sweeping move of his arm, he slid all of it into an open drawer directly beneath the counter. Then he resumed attending to his patient. As he prepared to remove the tube from Fitzgerald's chest, he felt a little stronger, a little more assured. Deep down, he knew he was deluding himself; if he was forced to use the weapon, he would likely die before he could do any real damage. Still, he felt better just knowing it was there. Now, all he had to do was wait for the right opportunity.

Randall Craig didn't know how long he'd been locked in the small room. For the most part, the past day was a blur, as was the previous evening, but he'd done his best to piece it together. He had a vague, troubling recollection of what had transpired after the truck had arrived. The guards had congregated around the vehicle, and they'd begun unloading it, lugging what appeared to be camera equipment into the small barn that stood next to the house. He could recall the moment of clarity, the knowledge that came with the sight of the cameras. In that moment, he'd seen what they intended to do with him, and he had decided to act.

That was when he'd gone after the Algerian. It had been an instinctive reaction, completely unplanned, and with predictable results: the guards had stopped him before he could finish the job. He *did* remember hitting the man, knocking him to the ground. He'd been about to hit him again when the first guard had arrived on the run. A split second later, he'd felt the blow. The butt of the rifle—at least, that was what he assumed his assailant had used—had struck him in almost exactly the same spot he'd been hit before, when they'd first taken him, and he was feeling the effects.

The pain was bad, but not nearly as bad as it had been that morning, when he'd first opened his eyes. Craig didn't know how long he'd been out, but it had been just after dawn when he had regained consciousness. His makeshift prison didn't offer much, but it did have a window, unlike the first room in which they had held him. Looking out, he could sense the gathering darkness. His brief attempt at resistance had occurred around nine the previous evening. Based on those two facts, he guessed that he'd been locked up for about twenty hours, maybe a little bit longer.

There was nothing to do in the small room, and the time had passed slowly. Although he'd searched the entire space, he'd found nothing that might serve as a weapon. Clearly, they had stripped the room before locking him in. There was a metal-framed bed, on which he was currently sitting; a small nightstand; and a bucket in one corner, which was obviously meant to serve as a crude toilet.

Craig had examined the bucket thoroughly. He had wracked his brain, searching for a way to take it apart, but it didn't seem possible. If there had been a handle, he might have been able to snap it off. It probably wouldn't have done him much good, but obviously, his captors weren't taking the risk; they'd thought to remove it beforehand. Later, his thoughts had shifted to the springs in the mattress. If he could find a way to dig one out, that might suffice as a weapon, but the covering was too thick to tear, and he had no way to cut the fabric. It seemed they had left him with nothing; they had even thought to remove the drawers in the nightstand. There was the window, of course, but it faced the rear of the house, and there were two guards stationed outside at all times. If he were to break it, they would know immediately, and one way or another, he would pay for the act.

He wasn't afraid to take them on, but the repeated blows to the head had slowed him down, and he was no longer eager to fight. When he'd first regained consciousness, the pain had been intense, almost unbearable, but that was secondary. When it came to recurrent concussion, Craig knew what to look for, and pain was not his main concern. Neurologic sequelae, a condition resulting from injury to the brain, was the real threat, and it could manifest in any number of ways. Some of the major symptoms were cognitive impairment, seizure, focal deficit, and persistent headaches. Temporary paralysis was also a possibility, but so far, Craig had yet to experience anything worrisome.

Still, he was leery of incurring his captors' wrath; in that respect, his reckless abandon was gone. He was prepared to resist, but next time he would not act impulsively. Attacking the Algerian had been a mistake; he should have held off until he was sure. At the same time, he knew he didn't have long. If he were going to move, it had to be soon.

His mind kept returning to what he had seen the previous night. It was clear that Mengal and the Algerian were erecting a film set in the barn, and it didn't take a great deal of imagination to figure out what it was for. Craig did not think they were preparing to kill Fitzgerald on tape. She was too valuable to them. On the other hand, he was nobody special, and he knew they would not hesitate to take his life. In that respect, he wasn't alone; once Qureshi had removed Fitzgerald's chest tube, his life would likely be forfeit as well.

He could feel the seconds ticking away, and it was becoming increasingly difficult to think through his fear, which was steadily rising. He kept drifting back to what the Algerian had said the night before, when Craig had first seen the cameras.

Doctor, you didn't think you were brought here for just one reason, did you? You've performed admirably so far, but your work is far from done. You're going to be famous, my friend . . . more famous than you ever dreamed possible.

The words had merely confirmed what he'd already known. Craig didn't want it to end that way, with him pleading into the camera as they spouted their rhetoric. Anything was better than that. If they shot him as he tried to run, at least he would die like a man, on his own two feet. At this point, that was all he wanted. There was no escaping his ultimate fate; all he could do was choose how and when it happened, and he intended to do just that.

Getting to his feet, Craig moved to the window. He stared out, not really seeing the lush, fertile landscape, the broad acacia that dominated the back garden, the fields beyond, and the gentle rise of the Kashmiri foothills. It had been overcast all day, and a light rain was still falling, but Craig could feel the night coming on. It would be dark in an hour or so, maybe less.

They'll come for you tonight.

Involuntarily, his breathing quickened, and his hands balled into fists by his sides. The thought had struck him suddenly, out of nowhere, but he knew it was right. He didn't know how, but he knew they would come.

And when they did, he would be ready.

As the truck rolled over a deep, unnatural pitch in the road, the vehicle shuddered violently, and Naomi Kharmai shuddered in turn. She wrapped her arms tightly around her calves, closed her eyes, and lowered her head to her knees. She had no idea how long she had been in the dark, dank bed of the cargo truck, but she didn't think she could handle it for much longer. It had been tolerable when they were on the main roads, if only just, but she could tell that Machado had left the A4 behind, as the ride had become progressively bumpier. It was only adding to her nausea and her headache, which was bad enough to bring real tears to her eyes. The headache had started several hours earlier as a dull throb at the base of her neck, and it hadn't stopped there. Now, it felt as if a pair of strong fingers was digging into either side of her spine, pinching the tender nerves that resided there.

The nausea was even worse. She'd vomited several times, and she'd tried a half dozen more, but she hadn't been able to bring anything up. She could feel the sweat all over her body; her arms were slick and coated with grime from the floor, and the perspiration was running over her face and stinging her eyes. Her clothes were completely drenched, and she was still sweating, despite the fact that her mouth was completely dry. She had tried drinking water to quench her unremitting thirst, but it simply refused to stay down. She was starving, but food was out of the question. Her entire body felt as if it had been carefully and methodically worked over; there were no bruises, but the pain could not have been worse if she'd actually suffered a physical beating.

It had been thirty-three hours since she had taken her last pills, and she'd been awake for fourteen of them. As a result, the withdrawal symptoms had been hitting her hard and fast. It had been ten times worse than she had expected, and for the past several hours, she had been cursing herself for getting rid of them. What a stupid, spur-of-the-moment move that had been. It wouldn't solve anything, and it certainly wouldn't assuage the source of her inner turmoil. In fact, the pills had been the only thing she could really depend on. At that moment, she would have given anything, absolutely anything, for just one more, if only to settle her nerves.

But they were gone, and that was that.

The truck hit another pothole. Her body came off the metal floor for a split second, and then she landed hard, her tailbone stinging with the impact. She groaned and slumped to the side, her chest and stomach tightening in a now familiar routine. She started to dry-heave, and though she could hear the choking, strangled noises she was making, they seemed very distant, far beyond the steady groan of the truck's diesel engine. It went on for several minutes, and then the nausea began to subside once more.

She waited for her stomach to stop convulsing, and when it did, or at least came as close as it was going to, she eased herself back into a sitting position and rested her head against the metal wall that divided the cab from the cargo area. *This was a bad idea*, she thought, the notion arriving like a load of wet sand on the back of a broken-down flatbed. *I should have stayed in Cartagena. I should have let it go. I shouldn't have flushed the pills. . . .*

Driving that last thought to the back of her mind, she steeled her resolve and reminded herself that it had been her decision to leave. Or at least, her decision to push Harper for another chance. When Machado had returned to the house that afternoon, he had given her back her sat phone, explaining that Harper had called while she was sleeping. When she called him back, she'd noticed that the call log was deleted, but she had let it go. She didn't know who Machado might have been calling on the phone, or if deleting the log was just force of habit, but it didn't really matter to her.

What *did* matter was that Harper had agreed to put her into play. He hadn't exactly agreed to send her to Pakistan, but she knew it was just a matter of time. He couldn't shut her out forever, and before long, he would realize that he needed her. That *Ryan* needed her. Hopefully, it would happen sooner rather than later. She knew— both from Harper and televised news reports—that nothing major had happened in Pakistan, which meant she still had time to change the deputy director's mind. He had sounded odd when she had talked to him earlier, as though he was holding something back, but she'd decided it was nothing, and she'd let it go.

Naomi had been somewhat surprised when Harper had asked Machado to help get her out of the country. She was even more surprised when the Spaniard had readily agreed. He had made a few calls, once again using her phone, and the truck—a Mitsubishi Fuso with a canvas tarp strapped over the gated cargo area—had arrived in record time. Then he'd said something that caught her completely off guard—that he would be taking her across the border personally. It seemed like a huge risk, and she'd told him as much, but he'd waved away her concerns. Still, there was something about his manner that was bothering her, something she couldn't quite shake. She'd had hours to think about it, though, and she had finally hit upon the change in his demeanor. For one thing, he refused to look her in the eye, even when he was speaking to her, and he seemed nervous. *No*, she thought to herself, *that wasn't quite right.* He didn't seem nervous. It was more like he was . . . resigned.

But resigned to what, she didn't know. When he returned her phone before they left Cartagena, he mentioned that the battery had died at the end of his call with Harper. She tried to power it up without success, and she'd been unable to find the backup battery, despite an hour's worth of increasingly frantic searching. In the end, she'd reasoned that it didn't really matter, as her next stop—if all went well—would be the U.S. embassy in Lisbon. From there, she'd be able to get in touch with Harper and Ryan, and then she could start angling for a seat on the next plane to Pakistan.

She heard a voice behind her. For a second, she thought it was the dashboard radio, and then she decided it was Machado. A cold chill swept through her body when she realized what was happening. They had reached the border, and Machado was talking with the entry officials. Lost in her thoughts, she had missed the jerky stop-and-go movements that the vehicle had made as it moved forward in the queue.

Pressing her ear to the thin metal wall, she held her breath and listened hard, trying to catch the gist of the conversation. Machado's voice—a quiet, confident baritone—was easy to recognize, and she couldn't detect a hint of unease; he seemed as relaxed as he had the day before. She wondered if she had imagined his strange mannerisms earlier that afternoon and decided that she probably had. She wasn't herself, she knew, caught up in all that had happened, and she was just seeing things that weren't really there.

The Portuguese official was saying something, but even though he was speaking in English, Naomi couldn't decipher the words, which were distorted by the metal wall of the cab and the vibration of the engine. Machado said something back, which was followed by a burst of shared laughter. Then the truck dropped into gear and jolted forward. Naomi slumped to the floor and closed her eyes, as relieved as she'd ever been. She was well concealed by a group of rough wooden boxes, which Machado had told her contained automotive parts bound for Peniche, but even a casual search would have resulted in her arrest. She couldn't believe they had gotten away with it, but the truck was still rolling forward, and now it was picking up speed. . . .

They continued on for another twenty minutes or so, the Mitsubishi rising and falling over a series of gentle hills. The ride was much smoother than it had been on the Spanish side of the border, and with the crossing over and done with, most of Naomi's tension had faded away, leaving her utterly exhausted. She didn't feel the sleep coming on, but it did, and when she woke with a start a short while later, she realized that they were no longer moving. In fact, the engine was shut down completely; all she could hear was the sound of cicadas or tree frogs, or whatever it was that they had in Portugal.

Rubbing the sleep from her eyes, she heard a movement at the back of the truck and tensed, her breath catching in her raw, parched throat. It hurt to breathe, let alone speak, but she relaxed when she heard Machado saying her name.

"Yeah, I'm . . ." She cursed as her knee banged painfully against one of the wooden boxes. "I'm here," she said, the words coming out in an awkward rasp. She moved blindly through the cargo area, hunched at the waist to avoid the tarp, which drooped overhead. She extended her arms and moved them back and forth in an effort to detect any obstacles before she ran into them. A blinding white light suddenly pierced the darkness, catching her full in the face. She squeezed her eyes shut again and glanced away, but not before she caught a glimpse of Javier Machado's bulky profile. Someone was standing next to him, a smaller, slender figure, but she couldn't see his face, as she was still blinking the dancing spots from her vision. She had seen something else in that brief moment, something that looked like . . . a gun in the smaller man's hand, but that didn't seem right. Still, she hesitated before moving forward, and Machado seemed to catch her reluctance.

"Come on, Naomi," he said quietly, but there was something in his voice that touched off her internal alarm. "It's time to go."

"Go where?" she said. She could hear the nervous tension in her own voice, and she hated it. The last thing she wanted was to appear weak in front of them, even though she knew that Machado had already seen her at her worst. "I thought we were—"

"Change of plan, Ms. Kharmai," he said. "Now please, get out of the truck."

Naomi hesitated again, but there was nothing to do but follow his instructions.

Carefully, she edged forward, the spots still dancing in front of her eyes, and Javier Machado stepped up to offer his hand.

CHAPTER 39

WASHINGTON, D.C.

It was just after one in the afternoon as Jonathan Harper entered the secure conference room beneath the West Wing of the White House. It had been a long couple of hours—a long couple of weeks, actually—and the stress had been building steadily. Now, judging by the lingering ache in his chest and the perspiration building beneath his arms, it had finally reached its peak. *At least the timing is right,* Harper thought sourly, but he pushed the distracting notion aside. Now was not the time to focus on minor things, as everything they had worked for boiled down to the next few hours. At last, the end was in sight. With any luck, this operation would mark the end of the strain that had gripped not only the people in this room, but the entire country for the past four days. Wiping his damp hands on his suit pants, he looked around the room slowly, examining the people who had gathered to take part in the administrative and logistical side of Brynn Fitzgerald's recovery.

There were about 20 people in the room, he guessed, not a huge number, but that was only because the confined space could not fit more, at least not comfortably. He knew maybe half of them by name; the rest were technicians and assorted aides, many of whom were in military uniform. Kenneth Bale was seated at the large table, engaged in quiet discussion with Robert Andrews. Stan Chavis was seated across from them, on the president's right. Both men were listening to a briefing being delivered by a brigadier general in army uniform. The west wall, Harper saw, was dominated by three large monitors. Shooting a quick glance at them, Harper was drawn first to the second monitor, which displayed hundreds of lights spread over a large landmass. After staring at the multicolored lights for a second, he realized they denoted the location of ground-based radar stations in Pakistan, along with confirmed SAM missile sites and areas of concentrated troop movements.

The first monitor displayed what Harper guessed was a higher-resolution view of a specific point on the ground—probably the Afghan-Pakistani border itself, he decided after a moment—and the third showed nothing but a test pattern. That one would display the feed from the 8X recon satellite that was currently moving into position over Sialkot. Harper was not surprised to see it was still en route to its new destination. Unlike the smaller Keyhole series of satellites, the 8X weighed close to 22,000 pounds, and though it had been positioned over the Kashmir Valley that same afternoon—a relatively short distance from Sialkot—it would still take some time to reach its destination. Adjusting a satellite's orbit was no easy feat to accomplish, particularly in the space of a few hours, but it was certainly easier when the satellite was already fairly close to its new objective.

Despite the obvious tension, there was an air of anticipation in the room, and that—in Harper's mind, at least—was cause for concern. It was too early to get overly excited. They had yet to confirm that Fitzgerald was in the surgeon's house, and if she was not, it wouldn't matter what else they managed to accomplish. Fortunately, Harper had managed to talk the president into letting Kealey and his team move into position prior to the insertion of the assault team. With any luck, they would be able to verify the secretary of state's presence before the lives of dozens of men were put on the line. Given Pakistan's escalating conflict with India, just entering Pakistani airspace without permission was a huge risk. Unfortunately, Mengal's connections to ISI and the Secretariat itself were not factors that could be safely overlooked, and the only solution was to keep the entire Pakistani government in the dark.

Once the president had approved the rescue operation, things had moved with incredible speed. Ninety minutes after he'd called with Mengal's location, Kealey had called back with additional info, including GPS coordinates for the surgeon's house in Sialkot. Harper had since relayed all of that information to the Pentagon's National

Military Joint Intelligence Center. From past experience, he knew that the material would be used for "IPB," or Intelligence Preparation of the Battlefield. This consisted of examining known enemy locations, force size, and possible extraction points, all in the hope of minimizing risk, while at the same time increasing the probability for success once the op began.

The assault team—an amalgamation of 24 SF operators that had been culled from three different units, including the 1st SFOD-D—was probably doing that right now, Harper realized. And when it came to IPB, Kealey's team on the ground would continue to play a vital role. Once they were in position, they would be able to send updates regarding the enemy's force concentration—where the guards were situated on the grounds. Their primary task, however, remained the same: to verify whether or not the secretary of state was even in the building.

Thinking about Kealey and the rest of the surveillance team, Harper shot a quick glance at his watch. They would still be prepping as well, he realized, even though it was already dark in Pakistan. They wouldn't even try to approach the house until they were completely ready to move, and even then, it would likely take them several hours to get into position. From that point forward, it would just be a matter of watching, relaying updates as needed, and trying to stay out of sight until the assault team arrived.

They were still hours away, Harper realized. And now there was nothing to do but wait. Resigning himself to this fact, he drifted over to join the DCI at the conference table.

Andrews was still talking intently to Bale, but stopped when he spotted his deputy. "John, take a seat." He waited until Harper was situated before asking the obvious. "What's the word from your man on the ground?"

Harper knew he was referring to Kealey, but by extension, that included the men he was working with. "They're at the last staging point, getting ready to move. That might not be for a few hours' time, and they probably won't make contact again until they're ready to go."

"Why not?"

Harper looked at the DNI, who'd posed the question. "Well, there's just no point, sir. If they have nothing to report, then they're only wasting battery time by continuously transmitting. Remember, the one thing they don't have is a satellite radio, which means they're stuck with a phone. We can only expect them to make contact when it's absolutely necessary, such as when—and if—they lay eyes on Secretary Fitzgerald."

"Or when something goes wrong," Andrews pointed out quietly.

"That won't happen," Harper said, but it had come out forced. He had faith in his people, especially Ryan Kealey, but like everyone else in the room, he knew what was on the line. Looking around, he wondered how many of these people would let Fitzgerald go—just walk away from her completely—if doing so meant sparing their jobs. As a patriot, he wanted to believe the number was small, but twenty years of government service had taught him otherwise. The men and women who really cared would be the CIA officers on the ground in Pakistan, as well as the elite soldiers of the 1st SFOD-D, the pilots of the 455th Air Expeditionary Wing, and the dedicated support troops, all of whom were waiting on the green light out at Bagram Air Base in eastern Afghanistan.

"And where is the staging point?" Bale asked, snatching Harper out of his short reverie. Bale looked worried. He had picked up on his forced confidence, Harper thought. "Because if they're spotted before they even—"

Harper cut him off by holding up his hand. "It's not a problem, sir." He managed to sound reasonably sure this time, and he saw some of the DNI's lingering doubt slide from his face. "They're about three hundred meters away from the building itself, and they've got cover. It's close enough to maintain a loose vigil, but not so close as to risk being caught. Believe me . . . They know what they're doing."

"Let's hope so," Andrews murmured under his breath. "For all our sake."

CHAPTER 40

SIALKOT

Balakh Sher Shaheed stood to the rear of the surgeon's house, staring across the dark field, eyes fixed on the column of Type 85-II main battle tanks moving into the foothills. Beyond the tanks, over the crest of the highest peaks, he could see the occasional flash of light, purple yellow blooms against the pitch-black sky. It could have been lightning, but Shaheed knew it was something more, and the thought filled him with an excitement he could barely contain. He had seen the same muted flashes eleven years earlier, not far from the place he was standing in now. As he pulled his last cigarette out of a crumpled pack and fumbled for his lighter, Shaheed was overcome with pride, but also with a sense of burning jealousy. He wanted nothing more than to be in that column, working his way toward the fight and a place in the great history of his country, like his father before him, and his before him.

Balakh Shaheed came from a long, distinguished line of career soldiers. He took enormous pride in this fact, and he had always measured himself against the great patriarchs of his family. His grandfather had fought in the Indo-Pakistani War of 1947, the first major conflict between India and Pakistan after their near-simultaneous seccession from Britain. When the traitor Hari Singh—the last ruling maharaja of Jammu and Kashmir—broke ranks and acceded his kingdom to India in '47, Hafeez Shaheed had been among the first to join the Azad Kashmir forces, the local militia supported by the Pakistani

Army. His bravery in that conflict had earned him the respect and admiration of the top Pakistani commander, Major General Akbar Khan, and his son—Balakh's father—had continued in that tradition, earning the Nishan-e-Haider, Pakistan's highest decoration for an act of bravery in combat, during the Battle of Asal Uttar in the Indo-Pakistani Kashmir War of 1965.

Given the heroic precedents set by his forebears, Balakh Shaheed's destiny seemed predetermined. He was meant to join the Pakistani Army at the earliest opportunity, and that was what he had done, enlisting on his eighteenth birthday, along with 6 other men from the village of Tarnoti, their shared home high in the mountains of the Northwest Frontier Province. The following years had seen him successfully apply to the Special Services Group and then Inter-Services Intelligence, which he joined in 1995. That was when he had first encountered Benazir Mengal.

At the time, Mengal had been a major general in ISI and the head of JIN, Joint Intelligence North. He was already a legend, owing to his actions during the Siachen war, and Shaheed admired him tremendously right from the start. The general had taken the young Special Forces *havildar* under his wing, and Shaheed had returned the favor by carrying out numerous acts of brutality at Mengal's bidding. Then, when Mengal had been forced to resign his commission in 2001, he had asked Shaheed to join him in private enterprise. Shaheed had done so without hesitation, and he had never really regretted the decision.

He had earned a small fortune over the years that followed, much of it accrued through Mengal's cross-border smuggling activities, but for the most part, they were standard deals, arranged in advance with reliable customers. The most dangerous part was the border crossings themselves, and even then, bribes to the right people all but negated the risk. Shaheed had begun to miss the army, so when the general had revealed his plan to abduct the U.S. secretary of state, Shaheed had jumped at the opportunity. Mengal had never revealed his overall objective, but that didn't matter to Shaheed; he was once again in the heat of battle. He had been one of the assaulters during the strike itself, and it had been the defining moment of his life.

But it had been five days since they'd taken the secretary, killing a dozen American security officials in the process, and the thrill of that attack was already starting to fade. The real action was taking place less than 100 kilometers to the north, and Shaheed wanted nothing more than to be there, fighting for his country as he had in the Kargil district eleven years earlier.

Taking one last drag on his cigarette, he flicked the butt into a clump of sod, then adjusted the strap of his weapon, cursing as the fabric rubbed over the raw patch of skin at the back of his neck. He knew he should not have the weapon slung, but it was hard to take the Americans seriously. Their senior diplomat had been snatched in broad daylight, and according to the Western media, little progress had been made in locating the people responsible, or the secretary of state herself, for that matter. The general was making the tape at that moment, and when it was done, it would be routed through an intermediary to the U.S. embassy in Islamabad. Soon after that, it would find its way into the hands of the U.S. president, and once that happened, the whole world would see how serious they actually were. If the first tape had made their demands clear, the second would undoubtedly complete the cycle. The content would effectively destroy any lingering notions of defiance still being entertained by the American government.

With this thought, Shaheed smiled to himself. He wondered how the general was planning to illustrate the steadfast nature of his resolve. Perhaps he would remove a few of the woman's fingers for the benefit of their American audience, or maybe he would settle on some other useful part of her anatomy. Either way, Shaheed knew it would not end there. Mengal had not revealed what he intended to do with the woman when it was all over, but Shaheed had no doubt that her life would end in Pakistan. He only hoped that he would be there to witness her final moments. Perhaps, if he was feeling charitable, the general would even give his senior lieutenant the honor of pulling the trigger.

Adjusting the strap of his AK-47 once more, he sighed and cast another longing glance to the lights in the north. After a while, his mind began to drift, finally settling on the first interrogation he had conducted after his acceptance to ISI. The prisoner had been an Indian sergeant, a *havildar* much like himself, except this man had been in the wrong place at the wrong time, captured after Pakistani troops had surrounded an artillery position in the Mushkoh Valley. The sergeant had proved all but useless. He was simply too low in the chain of command to have access to any actionable intelligence, but

Shaheed had enjoyed the experience nonetheless. He could remember the first time he had lowered the blade to the man's skin, preparing to shear it from his body, and the rush he had felt as the blood spilled onto the earthen floor, the Indian *havildar* screaming, screaming. . . .

As Balakh Shaheed, a third-generation soldier of the Islamic Republic of Pakistan, reveled in the memory of his first murder, he was completely unaware of the man lying prone less than 80 feet in front of him. He was also completely oblivious to the 3 other men in the field, all of whom had their eyes and weapons trained on him and the second guard standing watch at the back of the house.

Ryan Kealey was the closest, the man directly in front of Shaheed. He had watched intently as the guard had wandered out of the house, the screen door slapping shut behind him. Then he had moved under the canopy of the large tree in the garden. Kealey had watched in disbelief as he lit a cigarette, cupping his hands to keep out the rain. That single act was almost enough to throw a blanket of doubt on the whole thing. Surely, a man as unprofessional as this could not be involved in the abduction of Secretary Fitzgerald, which had been carried out with consummate skill. Nevertheless, the AK slung round the guard's neck seemed to verify what they had learned from Fahim's copious notes, and Kealey had felt a surge of adrenaline the moment he saw it. Now, for the first time, he was completely certain that Brynn Fitzgerald was somewhere inside the house.

Kealey was partially concealed beneath a juniper shrub in the broad, grassy field. He waited, watching through the AN/PVS-17 night-vision scope mounted to his rifle. Finally, the guard directly in front of him turned away for a split second, his head swiveling toward the second guard at the back of the house. Kealey used that stolen fraction of time to check his watch, cupping his hand over the illuminated display. He saw it was 2:36 AM, which meant they had been watching the house for just over three hours.

They had waited for dark in an abandoned factory outside Sialkot, studying the surveillance shots that Fahim's men had taken. Kealey's initial impression of the Afghan's organizational skills had only been supported by the quality of his intelligence. They had verified, through distinguishing physical characteristics picked up on film, that Mengal had at least 10 men on the premises. They had also managed to verify that the general himself was present, along with the Algerian, Amari Saifi. In short, all the major players were on-site. For this reason, the assault itself had been moved up, and the helicopters were already en route.

The core of the assault force consisted of two MH-53 Pave Low Combat Search and Rescue (CSAR) helicopters. Each MH-53 was carrying 12 Special Forces operators, in addition to the standard flight crew of four—2 pilots, 1 flight engineer, and 1 gunner on the platform-mounted 7.62mm minigun. The Pave Lows were being escorted to their destination by four AH-64 Apache gunships, each of which was armed with a full complement of thirty-eight HYDRA 70 rockets, eight Hellfire missiles, and the standard 30mm nose cannon. Kealey thought that the size of the rescue operation—at least in terms of the number of people the Pentagon had sent, as well as *how* they had been sent—was perfect for the current mission. The size of the aerial force was small enough to evade Pakistan's outdated ground-based radar, and the Apache gunships guaranteed a modicum of protection from everything except fixed-wing fighters. And if they showed up, the whole thing would be over, anyway. The size of the incoming force would certainly be enough to get Fitzgerald out, assuming she was even there to begin with.

And that was the problem. The only person they had not been able to locate was Brynn Fitzgerald. Kealey felt sure that she was on the grounds, but he needed to know her exact position. She was either in the house or the barn, which was located less than 30 feet to the left of the house, as viewed from the rear. The lights were on in the barn—a man had walked out earlier, and his silhouette had been plainly visible, even without NVGs—but there were no windows, and moving closer in hopes of catching a glimpse inside would entail too great a risk. At least, that was what had been decided in Washington.

Their role was still strictly limited to surveillance. Harper had set the rules of engagement several hours earlier, just after they had moved to the last staging point, a ridge overlooking the back of the farmhouse. They were not permitted to engage without provocation, and they were to take all steps to remain undetected. In short, they were there only to keep track of things until the assault team arrived. According to Harper, the National Security Council had arranged for a select team of SF operators to be assembled in Afghanistan

shortly after the abduction in Rawalpindi. These were the same soldiers who were currently inbound to Kealey's location. The foresight, above all, was what had impressed the younger man when
Harper had briefed him a few hours earlier. The members of the NSC
might not have expected to find Fitzgerald, but they had certainly
been prepared for it, and Afghanistan was as close as the operators
could get without a direct invitation from Musharraf. Of course, that
was no longer a consideration, and now all they had to do was carry
the mission off without a hitch, which was usually the hardest part.

During their last conversation, Kealey had pointed out that he
and his men were more than capable of getting the job done, that
there was no need to bring in an entire assault force. Harper said that
he had suggested as much to the president, but Brenneman had decided to err on the side of caution. Besides, they had to fly in to re-
trieve Fitzgerald, anyway, so there wasn't much point in leaving the
operators behind. After relaying this piece of information, Harper
had reemphasized the mission objectives. The deputy DCI knew him
too well, Kealey thought. Admittedly, he had considered the pros
and cons of "engineering" a little provocation. Once the first shots
were fired, all bets would be off, and he'd have no option but to go in
after her. He felt confident that they could pull it off, especially after
what he'd seen with Mengal's guard and the cigarette, but he wasn't
about to contradict Harper *or* the president. Not with the secretary
of state's life on the line.

Shifting his weight ever so slightly, Kealey peered once more
through the night-vision scope attached to his rifle. He was grateful
for the scope's rubber eyecups, which served to keep the rain off the
glass. The weapon was a SIG 550, an assault rifle manufactured by
SiGARMS, a company based in Exeter, New Hampshire. Kealey had
never used the 550, but he knew it was favored by police snipers for
short-range work, and he liked the heft and feel of it. The weapon
featured an integral folding bipod; a side-opening, skeletonized polymer stock; and a detachable mount, which had been modified to accept the AN/PVS-17.

Despite its quality, the rifle was a secondary tool, as he didn't expect to use it. Of far more importance was their communications
gear, which, regrettably, wasn't quite up to par. The encrypted Motorola radios, which Owen had picked up at the embassy, were fine,
but they were lacking the ability to communicate directly with their

controllers via satellite radio. That would have required additional equipment, which Fahim's organization had been unable to provide. As such, they were forced to use the Globalstar sat phone that Owen had brought into the country. As the team leader, Kealey had the phone secured in a pouch designed for the PRC-148, a portable radio of similar size and shape. A thin cord ran from the phone to a hands-free headset. Unfortunately, the phone's battery lasted only nineteen hours on a full charge, and that was on standby. They could count on no more than three hours of actual talk time, so Kealey had kept it on standby, powering up only to relay updates when needed.

Harper was his contact on the other end. To the best of Kealey's knowledge, the deputy director was still in the Situation Room at the White House, where he had immediate access to satellite coverage. One of the four 8Xs in orbit had already been retasked and was now positioned to provide a live infrared feed of Qureshi's house and the surrounding area. Unfortunately, even the 8X was incapable of penetrating clouds, which rendered it useless until the storm had moved on. The government *did* have satellites that could see through cloud cover, most notably, the Lacrosse radar-imaging series, but like the KH-12s, they moved too low and too fast to really prove useful in tactical situations.

The guard beneath the tree was distracted again. Kealey checked his watch again and decided to check in with the other operatives. The rain, while lighter than it had been that afternoon, was still heavy enough to drown out the sound of his voice as he checked in with each member of the recon element. He started with Manik, who had nothing new to report, then moved on to Owen and Walland. He was about to move on to Massi when several things happened simultaneously. The barn door creaked open, then opened all the way, revealing a large square of yellow light. A tall, bearded man in flowing robes stepped out of the barn, pausing to light a cigarette. Kealey, tracking the man through his scope, immediately recognized the face from the photographs Harper had shown him in Oraefi. Although Fahim's surveillance photographs had already placed Amari Saifi at the house, this was the first time Kealey had actually laid eyes on him. As he was processing this new development, he missed the calm but urgent transmission coming over his earpiece.

Cupping his hand over his ear, he murmured, "I didn't catch you, Massi. Say again."

The other man came back a split second later. "She's in the barn. I repeat, Fitzgerald is in the barn. I just got a positive ID, over."

For a split second, the words didn't register. Kealey had known she was on the grounds, but it still came as a shock to hear it confirmed. For a moment, he wondered how Massi had caught sight of her. Then he remembered that the operative had begun adjusting his position two hours earlier, once it became clear they didn't have a good view of the barn's main door. It had taken Massi the whole two hours to move a scant 30 feet, but the payoff had been more than worth the time-consuming adjustment.

"Kealey, do you copy?" Massi asked impatiently. "I repeat, do you—"

"I copy," Kealey said. "Stand by."

Kealey was thinking hard as he peered through his scope. He watched the Algerian terrorist move toward the house, leaving the barn door open behind him. A few seconds later, he disappeared from view, and Kealey heard the distant sound of a door slamming shut. Once Saifi was inside, the two guards behind the house returned their attention to the dark field in which Kealey and the rest of the team were lying in wait.

Making his decision, he powered up the sat phone, dialed Harper direct, and waited impatiently for the satellite to make the connection. Once he had the deputy DCI on the line, he quickly relayed the new developments.

When he was done with the thirty-second explanation, Harper said, "Thank God she's there." Kealey could hear genuine relief in the other man's voice, as well as a sudden surge of voices in the background. Kealey suddenly wondered if he was on speakerphone. "What kind of shape is she in?"

Kealey hadn't asked before, so he put the question to Massi, who answered promptly. Then he got back with Harper and said, "She appears to be unharmed. She's secured to a chair—we can't see how— and it looks like they've erected some kind of film set. Massi can see cameras, portable lights, and a flag in the background."

"But she's still in one piece?"

"Yes."

There was a long delay, the only sound that of the rain, the distant rumble of diesel engines, and the slight hiss of the satellite connection in Kealey's ear. He could almost hear the argument that must have been going on in the Situation Room. Finally, Harper said, "We need to know more, Ryan. Can you get closer without being spotted?"

"Probably not," Kealey said impatiently. "Look, John, we're right there—"

"I know. You want to get her, and we will. Just maintain your position. The assault team lifted off from Bagram an hour ago. ETA is thirty-five minutes."

"No, we need to get her *now*. We can do it. We have the advantage on all fronts. These guys are not—"

"Hold your position, Ryan. That's an order."

"Fuck." Kealey muttered the expletive under his breath, but he wasn't trying to hide his anger; Harper would have caught it over the line. Slightly raising his voice, he acknowledged the order, then ended the call.

Less than five seconds later, he heard Owen's voice in his ear. "Kealey, what's happening?"

Kealey relayed what Harper had said, then checked with each operative to make sure they were all on the same page. That done, he returned his attention to the back of the house. Through the night-vision scope, the green-tinted guard beneath the tree was incredibly clear; magnified, his head was about the size of a small pumpkin. All it would take was one gentle squeeze on the trigger, Kealey thought. It was incredibly tempting. Owen, Walland, or Massi would drop the second guard a tenth of a second later, and then they'd be down from ten hostiles to eight, a very manageable number. . . .

Kealey pulled his eye back from the glass and took a deep breath, shaking it off. His finger had actually been tightening on the trigger, as if of its own accord, and now he made a conscious effort to move it outside the trigger guard. The urge to fire was overwhelming. She was right there, less than 100 feet away, and the enemy had no idea they were being watched. It would be so very easy. . . .

He took another deep breath and wrapped his right hand tightly around the plastic grip of the rifle. Part of him wanted Mengal to try something. Part of him wanted the guards to spot the surveillance. Part of him wanted to end it now, but he forced himself to relax, knowing that Harper was right; it just wasn't time. All they had to do was hold on for another half hour, and then it would be done.

CHAPTER 41

SIALKOT

From the moment Benazir Mengal first laid eyes on Said Qureshi's home, he had been holding out possibilities for the barn. It was a fine two-story structure, built with the same fieldstone Qureshi had used on the house, and topped with the same slate roof. The only thing it was missing was windows, but for Mengal, that was part of the building's appeal; after all, he didn't want to advertise the things he was planning to use it for. There was a solid oak staircase against the north wall, which led up to a hayloft, but otherwise, the ground floor was completely empty, which made it ideal for the film set.

As far as sets went, it was extremely crude, but that was fine by Mengal. No one who watched the tape would be worried about the quality of the production. The tripod-mounted camera was bracketed by a pair of portable halogen lights and centered on a white flag bearing the symbol of the Salafist Group for Call and Combat. The oval-shaped symbol depicted an open Koran resting on a wall of gray stone, which was topped by a turquoise sky. The Koran was framed by a sword and an AK-47, and directly above the open book, a sun bearing seven rays seemed to illuminate the glorious teachings of the prophet Muhammad. There were also scrolls bracketing the central image. The banner beneath the wall marked the name of the group, and the banner above the Koran read, "And fight on until there is no more tumult or oppression, and there prevail justice and faith in Allah."

It was, Mengal thought, a thoroughly ridiculous symbol. Almost as ridiculous as the aims of the group itself, but using the flag was better than the alternative, which was to face the camera himself. It was the same reason he had recruited Saifi in Algiers. When he had first arranged the interview with Saifi in the Algerian prison, he had, for the most part, explained exactly what he intended to do, leaving out only the specific identity of his target. In return for Saifi's promise of assistance, Mengal had offered him freedom, which he could arrange through his friends in the Algerian government, as well as money and arms, everything Saifi would need to rebuild his faltering terrorist network in North Africa. He had also promised the Algerian center stage in the attack on the motorcade, the kind of attention that would guarantee instant fame, equating him with the top figures in international terrorism—Carlos, bin Laden, and Abu Nidal—virtually overnight.

Saifi had leaped at the opportunity, which wasn't surprising, Mengal reflected, given that the alternative was another twenty years behind bars. So far, the terrorist leader had proved reliable, but there was something about his manner that Mengal found distinctly unsettling. Qureshi had caught it as well, and while Mengal had deflected the surgeon's concerns, they had secretly added to the doubt he was already feeling. Mengal had very few moral qualms; he would gladly kill Fitzgerald if and when the time was right. The Algerian, on the other hand, was unpredictable, and that made him dangerous. Mengal had been careful about this; he'd never left his hostage alone with the Algerian, and now, as he glanced at the man whose freedom he had arranged for eight weeks earlier, he saw a perfect example of what had piqued his concerns to begin with.

The Algerian was standing to Mengal's right, next to one of the portable lights. He was staring intently at Fitzgerald, who was bound to a chair in front of the flag. Fitzgerald, in turn, was staring stubbornly down at her lap, her battered face contorted with pain. At first, she had refused to speak into the camera, and Saifi had been eager—perhaps overly eager, Mengal reflected—to elicit her cooperation. Still, her bruised, bloody appearance did little to deter the Algerian's interest. Saifi's expression was constantly shifting and hard to decipher, falling somewhere between lust, admiration, and pure hate. His eyes were slightly too open, his mouth fixed in a permanent smile. His gleaming white teeth were constantly visible, it seemed, fixed in the center of a tangled black beard, and his hands, with their long, spidery fingers, were wrapped in the folds of his robes. Mengal had to speak his name several times before he turned, and even that was unnatural. His head was the only thing that moved, swiveling slowly as if it were mounted on a fixed platform.

"Go and get the American doctor," Mengal instructed quietly, leveling his gaze on the bridge of the man's nose. He could not meet the Algerian's eyes: he was worried the man might see his concern and mistake it for fear. "Get him and bring him here."

"We're going to use him?" Saifi asked in Arabic, one of their several shared languages.

"Yes." It was a decision Mengal had been weighing for the past several hours. They had already performed several takes using only Saifi and Fitzgerald, and it just wasn't working. They needed something more to get the message across, Mengal thought. They needed something that would leave an . . . *impact* on the American government, and the secretary of state herself was not expendable.

At least not yet.

"And what of the surgeon?"

Mengal considered briefly. Balakh Shaheed, his top lieutenant, had locked Qureshi in his surgical suite several hours earlier, and he saw no reason to bring him out now. For the moment, Craig would suffice.

"Leave him. Just get the American."

The Algerian nodded, then pushed open the heavy door and stepped out. A minute later, a sudden crackling noise brought Mengal back to reality, and his eyes moved to the opposite side of the large room, where his two-way radio was resting on a rough wooden table. As he walked over to pick it up, he crossed in front of the barn door, which was still hanging open to the rain and the warm night air.

"I've got Mengal," Massi said suddenly. "He's inside the barn. He just passed the door. I guess he was on the north side of the building . . . I couldn't see him before."

"Got it," Kealey said. "You see a weapon?"

"Negative," Massi said, "but I can't see the whole room. He might have it leaning against a wall or something . . . We'd better assume he's got one close."

"Roger. Everyone get that?" Kealey asked.

In the order they had decided on earlier, the other members of the team reported in the affirmative, their voices scratching over Kealey's earpiece.

"Good," Kealey said once they had all checked in. "Maintain your positions. Massi, if he picks up a gun, you know what to do."

"Roger that," the other man said calmly. No one queried the order, and they didn't have to ask for clarification. Massi was the only one with a clear line of sight, and if Mengal approached Fitzgerald with a weapon in hand, the former USAF combat controller was going to take the shot, regardless of the consequences. It was a weak excuse to initiate engagement, and if it went bad, it would never hold up. Nevertheless, they had all agreed to take the opportunity if it presented itself. None of them were inclined to wait for the assault team, but neither were they willing to blatantly violate their standing orders, especially given the stakes.

"Where's the Algerian?" Owen murmured over the net.

"I have no idea," Kealey muttered back. He had been wondering the same thing. Saifi had been inside the house for nearly two minutes, but he'd left the barn door hanging wide open, which seemed to indicate he would be returning shortly. He should have been back by now, Kealey thought, but maybe there were more hostages in the house. Maybe Saifi was preparing to bring them out to the barn, or maybe they were already dead . . . There was no way to tell.

"So what do we do?" Manik asked.

"Hold your position," Kealey repeated. "Just stay where you are. Massi, anything?"

"Negative. He went back to the north side of the building . . . I can't see him."

"Okay. Keep your eyes open. Let's see what's happening here," Kealey said.

Randall Craig was lying awake on the narrow bed, his hands clasped over his stomach. Ever since his abduction, his thoughts had been coming nonstop, so fast he feared his head might explode with the pressure. Over the last few hours, though, things had changed. His mind had been blank, almost as if he had slipped into a meditative state. He was struck by the irony; the end was drawing rapidly near, and yet he was becoming less and less concerned with the thought of escape. Simply put, he was mentally and physically exhausted, almost to the point that he no longer cared. At the same time, sleep was out of the question. He was caught in a strange limbo that was draining his body and mind with each passing minute.

As a result, he didn't hear the footsteps in the hall. Nor did he hear the key as it scraped in the brass latch. The first time he was aware of the man's presence was when the door swung open, revealing a tall, slender figure framed in the doorway.

Craig immediately swung his feet to the floor, then stood to face the Algerian. The man didn't move into the room; instead, he merely stared at Craig and smiled.

"Doctor. It's good to see you're awake. How are you feeling?"

Craig looked at him warily. "I'm fine."

"Good. If you don't mind, the general would like you to step outside. He has something to show you."

Somehow, Craig was able to maintain his neutral expression, though his knees nearly gave way when he heard the word *outside*. It took every ounce of self-control he possessed, but he didn't reveal what he knew: that this was the end. He had seen them carrying the camera equipment into the barn, and he knew what was coming. *Jesus,* he thought to himself, *they're actually going to do it.* Somehow, he was astonished by the possibility, even though he had known it was coming all along. He was suddenly struck by the same vision he'd seen the day before. He could see himself sitting in front of the camera, bound to a chair, with the obligatory flag tacked up behind. He could see the blade coming down, and he wondered if Fitzgerald would be forced to watch, if she would witness his final moments along with the rest of them.

He knew what was coming, but somehow, he managed to maintain his composure. Nodding dutifully, he stepped past the Algerian and walked down the hall. He was watching the whole time, taking everything in; with the end so near, his vision seemed unnaturally sharp. There was an armed guard at the end of the hall, and as he passed the open living room, he saw another man concealed in the shadows, standing next to the grand piano. Clearly, they'd thought he was going to run from the room. They'd been prepared to stop him, but as he passed the two men, he saw them relax, their shoulders drooping with the sudden release of tension. In their eyes, Craig was the threat, and the threat had just walked past.

Too soon, he thought to himself. He had to wait until he was out of the house, and then he would run. He probably wouldn't get more than 10 feet, but he had to do it; there was no other choice. No one was going to help him. He briefly wondered where Qureshi was, then cursed himself for caring. After all, the surgeon had put him here. By giving his name to Mengal, he had sealed his fate. Were it not for Qureshi, Craig would still be working at the hospital by day, watching old movies by night, and anxiously waiting for the day he could fly back to Seattle, with a few good stories under his belt and another gold star to stick on his resume.

Fuck you, Said, Craig thought, the anger flaring up to engulf the fear. He was lashing out at the most convenient target for reasons he didn't understand. Subconsciously, he was building up his nerve for what he was about to do. *Fuck you. I hope they do kill you, and I hope you see it coming, you traitorous little bastard. . . .*

He was nearing the end of the hall. Sweat was pouring down his face in fine rivulets. His damp shirt was clinging to his torso, and his feet were mired in invisible mud. The door was just a few feet away, and once he stepped outside, there was no turning back. . . .

"Who the hell is that?" Walland asked, his voice cutting over the static. Kealey shifted his aim, peered through his scope, and watched as a tall, pale man came out of the house, the Algerian trailing a few steps behind. "Is that a hostage?"

"Got him," Owen announced, ignoring the question. "Saifi's right behind him."

"That's a new face," Manik reported. "Doesn't look like he's armed . . ."

Kealey ignored the radio traffic as he studied the unknown subject through his 2.25 power scope. Even with the green tint, it was clear that the man was Caucasian. He looked scared, but the fear was mixed with something else, something that Kealey could not decipher. He studied the man for a few seconds more, trying to figure it out. Then it hit him; the look on his face was fear mixed with utter resolve. It was one of the most dangerous combinations that Kealey knew of, and he had seen it before, most recently with Naomi in Madrid.

He was still weighing this discovery—and trying to push her face back out of his mind—when Manik asked, "Where are they going?"

"Back to the barn," Massi said. "Looks like they're putting him in with Fitzgerald. I still don't see a weapon. . . ."

"Hold your positions," Kealey said, cupping his hand over his lip mic to limit the sound. He shivered suddenly, a chill running down the length of his spine. He wasn't sure where that had come from, but he was guessing it had something to do with the scene unfolding before him. The whole thing seemed fake somehow, scripted, as if one or both of the participants were only pretending to play his role.

Still looking through the scope, he watched as Saifi prodded the hostage forward. Kealey didn't know why that word was sticking— the man could have been there of his own accord, and they had no proof either way—but it seemed to fit. There was just something about that look on his face, the tension in his shoulders, and the wooden way he was moving toward the barn. In fact, it looked as if his legs might give out at any moment.

But again, it seemed fake, somehow. Almost as if . . .

The hostage was halfway to the barn when he stopped, turned on his heels, and launched a short, wild punch at his captor, catching Saifi high on the right cheek. As Kealey looked on in disbelief, the Algerian stumbled back, then tripped and went down hard. The radio traffic started up instantly, but Kealey heard none of it, his eyes glued to the man standing over Saifi. The hostage stood motionless for a few seconds, staring down at the Algerian like a deer caught in the headlights. He was clearly unsure of his next move, and for a moment, Kealey thought he might try for Saifi's gun. But then he turned and started to sprint, running hard for the nearest safe ground.

Running hard for the dark field in which Kealey and the rest of the team were lying in wait.

CHAPTER 42

SIALKOT

When the screams reached the back of the house, Balakh Shaheed thought—for a fleeting instant of pure, uncomprehending shock—that the general had decided to kill Fitzgerald. The screams were high-pitched, almost feminine, but not quite, and as he listened hard, he realized it was not a woman screaming, but a man. Moreover, he was screaming in Arabic, which ruled out most of the guards. Apart from Mengal, Amari Saifi was the only one in the house who spoke Arabic. Before Shaheed could properly absorb the situation, a dark figure streaked down the back of the hill, running hard away from the house.

Shaheed was the first to react. The second guard was actually closer, but he had been relieving himself in a flower bed when the alarm was raised and was still fumbling with his zipper when the figure ran past. In the dark, it was impossible to tell who was trying to flee, but Shaheed, thinking quickly, decided it had to be Craig, the American doctor. Qureshi was still locked in his surgical suite—Shaheed had seen to that personally—and Mengal was in the barn, watching over the secretary of state.

It had to be the American.

Cursing viciously, Shaheed grabbed his weapon, which was slung across his chest, and raised it to his shoulder. The safety was already off, a full 30-round magazine locked into place. The doctor was already outside the arc of the building's lights; Shaheed did not have a visual, but he fired, anyway, the wooden stock of the AK-47 banging against his shoulder as he squeezed off a dozen rounds. As the echoes faded away, he cursed again and started running down the hill, going after the man who was trying to escape.

Ryan Kealey winced as the guard's 7.62mm rounds plowed into the earth, tearing up the waterlogged soil a scant 20 feet in front of him. It took all his self-control not to fire back, but he knew the guard wasn't aiming at him; he was trying to hit the man who had run down the hill just seconds before. The hostage was about 25 feet from Kealey's position and closing fast, his outline clear against the lights in Qureshi's garden. Kealey knew the same lights would impede the guards' vision, which was why the recon team had approached from the north. He didn't know if Mengal's men had access to NVGs and were just too lazy to use them, or if they didn't have them at all, but either way, they would be coming into the field. That much was already clear, and Kealey knew he had to be ready.

The hostage was still running hard, but he was moving without direction, and through his scope, Kealey could see that he was waving his arms in front of his body, as though searching for obstacles. Kealey realized that after running through the well-lit garden, he was essentially operating blind in the pitch-black field. His biological night vision wouldn't fully kick in for about two minutes, which would give the guards plenty of time to circle around and cut him off. Kealey could already see them streaming out of the house. They were congregating around Saifi, who had since climbed to his feet, still screaming his outrage. A quick head count yielded eight guards, not including the man who had fired after the hostage. That one was running into the field, his weapon at the ready.

The hostage—if that was indeed what he was—had made his play, and it had failed. He was already dead; he just didn't know it yet. He had been dead from the moment he decided to run; Kealey had never been more certain of anything. Now only one question remained, and that was how many people he was going to take with him in his failed bid for freedom.

He was now less than 10 feet away, stumbling forward, cursing and breathing hard. Kealey shifted his body carefully to the right, trying to get as far under the juniper as he could. At the same time, he raised his arm, propped his rifle in the thick branches of the low-lying shrub, and felt for his secondary weapon.

At the abandoned factory outside of Sialkot, Kealey had handed out the weapons. He still didn't know the overriding aim of Fahim's organization, but one thing had been clear from the start: the group was extremely well funded, and a sizable portion of their budget had been devoted to arms. And if their primary concern was smuggling, as Machado had indicated, then they had kept the best stuff for themselves. Kealey had selected the SIG 550 with the night-vision scope—mainly because the weapon shared many characteristics with the M4 carbine, which he had trained and fought with extensively—but he had also found a suitable replacement for the knife he'd lost at the substation. It featured a flat-ground, drop-point, 6-inch blade. The steel itself was tapered—thick near the sturdy rubber handle, thinning down the spine to a uniform tip—and coated with matte black paint, which rendered it all but invisible in the dark.

Now, as the hostage drew near, Kealey tensed and wrapped his right hand round the thick rubber grip, preparing the pull the knife from its sheath. He didn't intend to harm the hostage, but he couldn't save him, either, and Fitzgerald's life took precedence. It wasn't supposed to, but it did, and Kealey suspected that everyone on the team felt the same way. They had come too far and risked too much to lose her now, and for the most part, their sacrifices had been minimal. At least one other person had given much, much more to save the secretary of state's life, even if she hadn't intended to do so.

Pushing that troubling thought from his mind, Kealey lay perfectly still, his chin sinking into the damp earth as the hostage stumbled past, completely unaware of his presence. Thankfully, the other members of the team had enough sense not to transmit. That didn't mean they weren't watching. Kealey knew all four operatives had their weapons trained in his direction, waiting to see what would happen. One or two of them might be tracking the second guard at the top of the hill, but for the most part, they'd be focused on the immediate threats: the hostage—who had become a threat the minute he decided to run—and the guard coming after him. The hostage was already behind Kealey's position, moving north, and the guard was approaching fast from the south.

Kealey could hear the man's feet slapping the wet soil as he drew near. Without warning, the guard raised his weapon and fired again, the rounds whining 5 feet over Kealey's head. Five, six rounds total. Kealey heard a grunt to his rear, a pregnant pause, and then a wet, heavy thump as a body fell face-first into the mud.

The guard had stopped moving; apparently, he had heard his target fall. He began inching forward, and Kealey, lying nearly motionless beneath the juniper, drew his knife and waited, praying the man would pass him by. He could not believe the disastrous turn the mission had taken, but it could still be salvaged. If the guard walked by without incident, then no harm done; they would be able to maintain their positions, and the op could proceed as planned.

It all came down to what happened next, and the footsteps were coming closer. . . .

CHAPTER 43

WASHINGTON, D.C. • SIALKOT

In the Situation Room beneath the West Wing, there was mass confusion and no small amount of panic. All eyes were fixed on the infrared feed from the 8X positioned in GEO 22,237 miles over Sialkot. The clouds had cleared enough over the past several hours to provide a limited picture, but even with the distortion, the fact that something had gone badly wrong on the ground was abundantly clear.

"Christ, who the hell is *that*?" Brenneman demanded over the chaos, not realizing that he was only contributing to the problem. He was pointing directly at the first heat signature, which had just stopped moving after a hard sprint north of the house. "And who is that going after him? *What the hell is going on out there?*"

There was no immediate response, not that anyone had heard the question. Harper stared at the satellite phone plugged into the room's audio system, waiting for Kealey to call and tell them what had just happened, but it stayed silent. He wondered if he would even hear it ringing over the cacophony in the small conference room. On the screen, the heat signature moving away from the house was drawing ever closer to one of the men lying prone in the field.

"Jesus, whoever that is, he's going to trip right over one of them," Andrews said, his voice laced with undisguised tension. He was standing a mere foot from Harper's left shoulder. "How far out are the helicopters?"

Harper opened his mouth to answer, but he was beaten to it by a USAF major, who held up a handset and lifted his voice to get the attention of everyone present. Strangely enough, he found success where the president had not, and once it was quiet enough, he said, "The word is coming in from air traffic control at Bagram. Eagles 1 and 2 report they are still ten minutes out."

The room fell silent for a moment; everyone present, even the most junior aides, understood what that meant. In the end, it took an army colonel standing frozen with a phone to her ear, not 3 feet from the grim-faced secretary of defense, to voice what everyone in the room was thinking. "Christ," she murmured. "They're not going to get there in time."

Harper silently agreed as he stared at the heat signatures moving into the field. He had never felt more impotent. There was nothing he could do but watch as disaster loomed. He could only pray that the separate signatures would not converge, but even as he thought it, he knew that they would. The only question now was how the men on the ground would handle the unexpected change in plan.

Shaheed was sure he had heard the American go down, but he wasn't taking any chances. He waited for a moment, listening, but he couldn't hear anything over the falling rain, the tanks in the distance, and the outraged screams of the Algerian at the top of the hill. Cursing the man's stupidity—*the general should never have brought him into this*—Shaheed slapped a fresh magazine into his weapon and began moving forward slowly, each step planned and deliberate. He swept the ground with his eyes, searching for a lump that might represent the doctor's body. He kept his right hand around the grip of his rifle as he used his left to brush aside the damp, waist-high grass. As his eyes started to acclimate to the dark, he picked up a few things he hadn't seen before. There was a pine tree approximately 10 meters to his right, and to his left, nearly within reach of his arm, there was a small, low-lying shrub.

And beneath the shrub, he could see something that looked like a rock, or maybe a log. Shaheed hesitated. He was almost certain the American had fallen farther to the right, close to the pine, but as he stared at the dark shape beneath the vegetation, he could have sworn he saw it move. . . .

As the guard was firing his last barrage at the fleeing man, Kealey had taken advantage of the noise to adjust his stance. He'd planted his left hand in the damp soil and brought his right leg under him, wedging his foot against a large, partially buried rock. If he had to use it, the rock would serve as a starting block of sorts. It was all he could do without revealing his position, but it would give him a chance to move quickly and decisively if the guard stumbled over him. Right now, things were not looking too good. He knew he had to call in and tell Harper what had happened—the situation had changed drastically, and the helicopters might be forced to turn back—but it just wasn't possible, and he could see the other operatives in his mind's eye, swearing under their breath, wondering if they should take the shot.

Don't do it, Kealey thought, hoping they could somehow hear his silent, urgent plea. *Don't fire. Just let him go. He doesn't know I'm here. Just let him walk on by. . . .*

It wasn't going to happen; Kealey sensed as much in the last crucial seconds. As the guard drifted past the juniper, he seemed to hesitate. With his head turned to the left, Kealey could see the outline of the man's head, and he could tell from the profile that the guard was looking in his direction. Then he turned, took a few steps forward, and reached down with his left hand, his splayed fingers moving directly for Kealey's left shoulder. . . .

When he saw the contact coming, Kealey's mind shut down, and his body took over. Operating on pure instinct, he launched himself up and batted the rifle aside with his left hand, pushing the muzzle away from his body. At the same time, he whipped the knife around in a short, controlled arc, plunging the blade deep into the guard's neck, directly beneath the hinge of his jaw.

Even in the dark, Kealey could see the man's reaction. His head jerked back and to the right, partly from the impact and partly in an effort to pull away from the knife. Blood and spit sprayed out of his mouth as the tip of the blade delved into his opposite cheek. His face tightened into a grimace, and his mouth fell open, his partially severed tongue protruding between bloodied teeth. He was obviously trying to scream, but all that came out was a wet, guttural hiss. He dropped the rifle and lifted his hands to grip Kealey's right arm. It was a completely instinctive reaction, but there was nothing he could do; the damage was already done, and the wound was fatal. The guard just didn't know it yet.

The knife was buried up to the hilt, and Kealey had to pull hard to extract it. The man automatically started to fall, and Kealey followed him down. He landed hard on his back, and Kealey was on top of him in an instant, ready to finish the job. As the man stared up at him, his face contorted with rage, pain, and fear, Kealey drew the knife firmly across his throat, severing the trachea, the carotid artery, and the connecting muscle tissue with one deep, powerful cut. Blood sprayed out of the wound immediately, splashing onto Kealey's face, arms, and hands, but he repeated the process, then did it again, determined to extinguish the stubborn light in the other man's eyes. Once he was sure the guard was dead, the strange ringing noise in his ears began to subside, and gradually, he picked up on the traffic coming over his earpiece.

"Ryan, are you there?" It was Owen, his tone controlled but urgent. "Goddamn it. What the fuck just happened? Where's the hostage . . . ?"

"He's down," Kealey rasped. The short, one-sided fight had left him breathless, though the adrenaline was still pumping hard through his veins. He rolled off the dead guard, crawled the short distance to his hiding spot, and felt for his rifle. It was right where he'd left it, in the lowest branches of the juniper. "The hostage is dead, and so is the guard."

"How the fuck did that happen?" Owen demanded. "Why did you . . ."

Kealey ignored the rest of the question as he planted his right knee in the sodden earth, lifting the rifle to his shoulder. Peering through the scope, he saw that the guards—all eight of them—were fanning out, preparing to enter the field. The figures were blurred for some reason, and Kealey realized he had blood in his eyes. Wiping it away with the back of his hand, he flicked it into the grass, then resumed watching. One of them had a portable radio up by his face; clearly, he was trying to raise the missing guard. There was no sign of Benazir Mengal—Kealey assumed he was still in the barn—but the

Algerian was standing behind the cluster of armed men, screaming incessantly after them.

"The guards are coming in," Massi said, almost as if he could read Kealey's thoughts. The air force veteran sounded completely calm and in control. "Looks like we're missing a few."

"I count eight," Kealey said. He thought back to the detailed notes that he had acquired from Fahim's men. "Eight plus Saifi. Mengal's in the barn . . . That leaves at least two unaccounted for."

"So what the hell do we do?" Manik demanded. He sounded shaken, which didn't surprise Kealey at all. While Massi was a hardened combat veteran, Manik was on the other end of the spectrum. He had undergone some kind of paramilitary training—otherwise, Harper wouldn't have sent him—but he was easily the least experienced man in the group.

Kealey was torn. A hostage was dead, and he had killed a guard, which dramatically limited their options. The op was blown regardless, but now he had a decision to make. Should he violate standing orders and go in after Fitzgerald, or should he wait and hope that the guard wasn't found until the assault team arrived? That didn't seem likely, as the assaulters were at least . . . He checked his watch and swore under his breath. They were at least eight minutes out. Part of him fantasized that he could already hear the sound of rotors chopping the damp, humid air, but he knew all too well how long eight minutes could seem in a combat situation.

A third option occurred to him: he could put the knife in the hostage's hand. With any luck, the guards would buy into it, but Kealey dismissed the idea after a few seconds. They would never believe it. For one thing, the dead guard had suffered numerous well-placed wounds. How would the hostage have been able to inflict those wounds if he was already fatally wounded himself? Besides, how would the hostage have gotten his hands on a knife like the one Kealey had used? Even if the guards bought into it, Mengal would see through the ruse. He would know right away that something wasn't right, and he would either flee the farmhouse, with Fitzgerald in tow, or kill her on-site, then flee by himself.

And that was what it came down to; if they waited for the assault force, the secretary of state was either dead or gone. In Kealey's mind, neither option was acceptable. They had to go in after her, and

they had to do it before the dead guard was found. Once that happened, they would lose the element of surprise, and their odds of
success would drop dramatically. Worse still, one of the Pave Lows
was slated to set down in the field behind the house, and it wouldn't
help to have the enemy on top of them before the ramp even came
down.

Once again, Aaron Massi seemed to read his mind. "We've got to
go in," the former combat controller said, his words cutting over the
static. "They're going to comb this field until they find him, and in
the process, they're bound to stumble over one of us. We've got to
fire while they're still grouped in the clear."

"What about the other two?" Walland demanded. "At least two
guards are unaccounted for. And what about Fitzgerald? Mengal is in
there with her . . . If we reveal our position, he might kill her before
we can get to the barn."

Good point, Kealey thought, but he said, "Massi's right . . . We're
going in. These guys are operating without NVGs, so wait until
they're outside the arc of the lights, then hit them while they're trying to acclimate." Kealey was thinking about what he'd seen with the
hostage, the way the he had lost his bearings once he could no
longer see. He wasn't thinking about the fact that the hostage had
died when he could have stopped it from happening; at the moment, that was completely irrelevant. "If we wait until they're all the
way in, they'll be able to pick out our muzzle flashes. We have to time
it right."

"I've got the Algerian," Owen said.

"No," Kealey shot back, "we need him alive, Paul. He knows where
the rest of the hostages are, so in Saifi's case, shoot to wound only.
Same with the general."

"And the others?" asked Manik.

"You all have your fields of fire," Kealey replied calmly. "You know
which sector you're responsible for, so when they come in, you
know who to hit. Here's what we're going to do. . . ."

He outlined a quick plan, allowing for several contingencies. He
had his weapon trained on the enemy force the entire time he was
talking, tracking their every move. The guards at the top of the hill were
still fanning out, but they had yet to enter the field. When he was
done with the short explanation, the other men voiced their understanding and agreement.

"Wait until I give the word," Kealey reminded them, "and then start taking them down. Remember, guys, we're only going to get one shot at this, so let's do it right."

When Benazir Mengal heard the Algerian screaming, he resisted the urge to run outside and see what was wrong. Instead, he backed farther into the barn, doing his best to stay away from the doors. He saw the hopeful, defiant expression in Fitzgerald's eyes, but he ignored it and raised the two-way to his mouth. "What the hell is going on?" he hissed. "Balakh, what do you see? What's happening out there?"

There was a long delay, during which Mengal screamed the question several more times. He heard a long burst of automatic fire, then nothing, then another, shorter burst. He was about to transmit again when one of the guards came on. In a shaky voice, he said, "General, the American doctor knocked down the Algerian. He escaped. He . . . ran into the field, and Balakh went after him. There were shots. . . ."

"I heard them, you idiot!" Mengal screamed. "Where is the doctor?"

"General, I . . . He hasn't come back. Balakh hasn't come back, I mean, and we can't raise him on the radio. I don't know where the doctor is."

"Send some men after them," Mengal shouted. "I want you to comb the entire field until you find them, and I want the doctor alive, you hear me? The man who kills him will answer to me. Is that understood?"

"Yes, I—"

"Where are Amir and Qazi?"

"They're inside the house, General. They're guarding the surgeon, as you instructed."

"Do they have radios?"

There was a brief hesitation, then, "No."

"Bring them two radios. In fact, give Qazi yours. Tell them to circle around and flank our men, and make sure they go out the front, where it's dark. Tell them not to fire unless they are fired upon. If anyone is out there, we must be able to hold them off until we can get the woman out of here. Understood?"

"Yes, General."

"Then go."

Release the TRANSMIT button, Mengal swore under his breath,

closed his eyes, and resisted the urge to hurl the handset across the room. *This is all Saifi's fault,* he thought to himself. *How could he have let this happen? How could he be so careless? How fucking hard could it be to bring one man from the house to the barn . . . ?*

Opening his eyes, Mengal inadvertently caught the eye of Brynn Fitzgerald. They had covered her mouth with silver duct tape between takes. It was still in place, so she couldn't speak. At the same time, her eyes seemed to convey everything she was feeling. It was a strange mixture of hate, satisfaction, and relief. Mengal didn't understand the source of the second two emotions, but then it hit him. She didn't speak Urdu, so she didn't know that her fellow hostage had tried to escape. Apparently—based on the commotion she had heard—she was under the impression that she was about to be rescued.

When he realized what was running through her head, he laughed, then watched as the confusion spread to her eyes. Walking over, careful to keep away from the open doors, he crouched so that their faces were nearly level. When she met his gaze, he said, "Ms. Fitzgerald, did you really think they were coming to get you?" He gave another mocking laugh, the sound rising up from deep in his chest. It was partly forced, but at the same time, he was genuinely amused. "If that is the case, I'm afraid you were wrong . . . Nothing so dramatic has happened. You see, your fellow American tried to run. My men are tracking him down right now, and he won't get far. That is all that you heard. I'm sorry to let you down, but no one is coming to get you. I'm afraid it's just you and me, Dr. Fitzgerald . . . just you and me. I think you had better get used to that idea."

He saw the spark of hope in her eyes begin to fade, and he couldn't restrain another bout of contemptuous laughter. *How pathetic,* he thought. People with Fitzgerald's kind of power always seemed so assured on television, so sure of their place in the world, but put them into any sort of danger, and they folded right up on themselves. It wasn't just American officials, either; he had seen the same thing the previous year, when he and his men had kidnapped a low-level Indian minister. The man had been attending talks in Islamabad, and his security had been all but nonexistent, which allowed them to grab him without firing a shot. They had taken the minister's eight-year-old son as well, and the boy had proved to be an excellent bargaining chip.

It had not taken much to extort the money they wanted; in fact, they hardly had to cut on the child at all before the man caved in. That event had netted Mengal a decent sum, but it was nothing like the windfall he would reap if his current plan was seen through to fruition. It all came down to the next twenty-four hours. By then, the American president would have the tape in hand, and he would have no choice but to accept their demands. Either that, or he would see how serious they actually were . . .

At that moment, Mengal's thoughts were cut off abruptly by the sound of screams and automatic weapons firing. He whipped his head toward the sound but saw only the stone wall of the barn. After a moment of stunned disbelief, he raised the radio to his lips and shouted for a situation report, but there was no reply. Swearing loudly, he didn't register the renewed glimmer of satisfaction in Brynn Fitzgerald's eyes as he moved to the doors of the barn. He hesitated before looking out. He desperately wanted to see what was happening for himself, but experience and caution got the better of him, and he stayed where he knew he couldn't be seen.

Holding the radio an inch from his face, he demanded once again to know what was happening. Finally, he heard the voice of one of the men he had just ordered to join the search.

"General, this is Qazi." The man sounded shaken, but still in control. "There are enemy soldiers in the fields. At least three, maybe four, and they've taken down most of the men. Only three are left, not including Amir and myself."

"What about Shaheed?"

"Shaheed is dead."

Dead? My old comrade and most trusted lieutenant, gone . . . ? Mengal let that sink in for a moment, and then he dismissed his natural, emotional response. That was one thing he'd always been able to do, and this was not a time to indulge in sentiment. "Where are you?"

"Approaching from the other side of the barn. I can't see the enemy fighters, but once they fire again . . ."

Mengal nodded to himself, knowing what he meant. The moment the enemy soldiers fired again, they would reveal their positions, which would make them easy targets for the men he had just dispatched. Amir and Qazi were two of his best. Both had served on a sniper-observer team in the Special Services Group for years, and like Balakh Shaheed, both had fought in Kargil in '99. Combined, they had thirty enemy kills to their credit, twenty of which they had racked up during a two-week reign of terror in the Drass sector of the Kargil Mountains. The snipers carried identical custom Sako TRG-22s. Each .308-caliber rifle was fitted with an ATN night-vision scope, as well as a muzzle brake to reduce the weapon's powerful recoil.

In retrospect, Mengal realized he should have had them in an overwatch position to begin with, but he had been too caught up with Fitzgerald's agonizingly slow recovery—as well as the preparations being made in the barn—to deal with security around the house. That had been a mistake, he realized, but he didn't see how the Americans could have tracked him down so easily. And if it *was* the Americans, why were there so few of them? It just didn't make sense. . . .

Lifting the radio, he said, "Qazi, tell me when you have acquired a target, but do not fire until I give the order."

"Yes, General."

Mengal was about to say something else when Amari Saifi stumbled through the open doors. Mengal raised his weapon in alarm, then stopped when he saw who it was. The Algerian was bleeding from a small hole in his left arm, his right hand clutched over the wound. Despite the obvious injury, he was smiling madly, his face drenched with sweat. The AK-47 was still draped round his neck on a black fabric sling.

"What the hell happened?" Mengal hissed, his eyes fixed on the other man's crazed face. "How could you let him escape?"

"The Americans are here," Saifi gasped, ignoring the question. Somehow, he was still smiling, even though he was clearly in a great deal of pain. "We have to leave. If we wait, they will have us surrounded, if they do not already . . . We have to leave *now.*"

Mengal stood frozen for a few seconds, but he knew the other man was right. Perhaps Craig's escape had caught the Americans off guard while they were still moving into position. Perhaps his men had eliminated more of them than he'd initially thought. Either way, Mengal knew he was only seeing the first wave. If the Americans knew that Fitzgerald was in the barn—and he assumed they must—they would risk as many lives as it took to get her back. They certainly wouldn't be put off by the resistance they had encountered so far.

Pulling a small knife from his belt, Mengal unfolded the blade with one hand, then moved behind Fitzgerald. Crouching behind the chair, he began cutting the ropes that bound her. Glancing over her shoulder, he snarled, "Get away from the door, and pull the plug on those lights. You still have the keys to the van?"

"Yes," Saifi said. He pulled the plug on the halogen lights, and the barn was plunged into darkness. "I have them."

"Good," Mengal said. Still cutting fast, he felt the last of the rope fall away. Placing both hands under her arms, he pulled Fitzgerald roughly to her feet. He heard her scream through the tape that covered her mouth, then start to fall as her legs gave way. She was still weak, too weak to walk on her own. Pushing the muzzle of his pistol into the base of her spine, he said, "You had better start moving, woman, because I'm warning you, if you pass out now, you will never wake again."

He felt her stiffen; then the weight on his arms began to lighten somewhat. Clearly, she was trying to move under her own power, though it still took all of his strength to move her while keeping the gun wedged into her back. He had just reached the door when Qazi's voice came over the radio. Pushing Fitzgerald against the stone wall, he kept the gun in her back with his right hand and used his left to grab his two-way, which was hooked to his belt. Lifting it to his mouth, he said, "What is it? What's happening?"

"I have a target, General."

"What about Amir?"

The second sniper's voice came over the radio. "Still moving into position."

Mengal didn't reply right away. He knew he should wait until both snipers were in place, but the window for escape was rapidly closing. Looking through the open doors of the barn, he could see the Toyota van on the drive in front of Qureshi's house. The vehicle was parked directly behind the surgeon's Mercedes, which was closer to the house. If they could get to the van, they might have a chance. It all depended on whether or not the Americans were approaching from the front as well as the back. That was all that mattered; if they had the house surrounded, then it was all over, anyway.

The Algerian was standing just inside the doors, a black silhouette against the light leaking in from the back garden. Looking over, Mengal said, "When I give the word, step outside and start firing toward the field. Don't worry about hitting our men; just keep moving toward the car. Don't stop for anything."

The Algerian murmured his consent, and Mengal lifted the radio to his lips once more. "Qazi, are you there?"

"I'm here, General."

"We're ready to move. You still have your target?"

"Yes."

"Then take the shot."

CHAPTER 44

SIALKOT

There were 3 guards left in the field. Kealey had taken down 2 of the original 8, not including the man he'd killed with his knife, and now, as he snapped a fresh magazine into place, he could hear the elevated voices of the surviving men over the falling rain. Although he didn't understand the language, he could tell they were arguing, probably about whether or not they should return to the house. At that moment there was another burst of automatic fire, and as the sound faded away, Kealey heard panicked voices shouting in Urdu. Fewer voices this time. Raising the rifle to his shoulder, he peered through the scope and saw that whoever had fired had taken down the man to the left, leaving two guards standing between them and the barn.

"Got him," Manik said in a tight, excited voice. "Two left."

Kealey acknowledged this silently as he found his next target. His finger slipped into the trigger guard, and he let out a long, slow breath, preparing to take the shot. His finger was tightening on the trigger when he heard the supersonic crack of a high-powered rifle, and the two guards dropped into the waist-high grass. Kealey froze, marking their approximate locations in his mind. He didn't think either man had been hit; they had simply dropped of their own accord, which probably meant that the shot had been intended for somebody else.

"What the hell was that?" Owen demanded a few seconds later. "Who's doing the shooting?"

Kealey was wondering the same thing. Deep inside, he felt a sense of rising unease. The single shot sounded unlike anything he had heard so far in the short battle. The guards they had seen so far were all carrying AK-47s, so it couldn't be them; besides, they were all accounted for. A cold wave of fear clenched his gut when he hit upon the only other possible explanation: someone else had joined the fight, and if the weapon he was using was any indication, he was not to be taken lightly.

Kealey was about to relay this thought when he caught a sudden movement up by the barn, followed by a prolonged burst of automatic fire aimed in their general direction.

"Mengal is moving," Massi reported urgently, his voice crackling over Kealey's earpiece. "He just came out of the barn, and he's using Fitzgerald as a shield . . . It looks like he's trying to run. Saifi is covering them."

"Do you have a shot?" Kealey demanded.

"No, he's too close to Fitzgerald. *Fuck!*"

"If they get to a car, they're gone," Owen said urgently. "We've got to get up there."

"Yeah, but he wouldn't run unless he was covered," Kealey replied. "I think there's a sniper up there."

"What makes you—"

"You heard the shot, Paul. That was a long gun, so just hold your fire . . . Is anyone hit?"

Owen and Walland came on and reported in the negative, as did Massi. He could hear the same nervous tension in each man's voice, and Kealey knew where it was coming from. The prospect of a sniper lying in wait was enough to inspire fear in any man, even a hardened combat veteran. Husain Manik didn't respond, even after Kealey tried numerous times to raise him.

"Where the fuck is he?" Kealey finally demanded. "Can anyone see him?"

"Negative," Owen said. Walland and Massi echoed the single word. Then Owen said, "Did anyone see where the shot came from?"

Again, they all replied in the negative.

"That's a Pave Low," Walland suddenly said. "You hear it?"

Kealey listened hard, and sure enough, there was the sound he'd been waiting for: the steady, distant thump of approaching helicopters. His relief was short-lived, as Owen came back on a moment later, ready to point out the overlying problem.

"Kealey, we've got to get up there," he pressed. "They might not come down on the first pass, and if they circle, it gives Mengal a chance to run."

"They *could* come down on the first try," Walland pointed out quickly, his voice laced with tension. "That house is lit up like a Christmas tree. Even without infrared on the ground, they should be able to spot their landing zones."

"Maybe," Owen allowed, "but we can't afford to sit here and wait."

Kealey thought about that for a few seconds, then made his decision. "I'm going after them. Walland, watch for the two guards in the grass. Did you see where they dropped down?"

"Yeah, but I don't think—"

"If they stand up, take them out. Owen, you watch the ground to the left of the barn. Massi, you've got the other side of the house."

"Kealey, you can't—"

"Just *listen*," Kealey snapped, cutting Massi off in midsentence. "When I move, watch for a muzzle flash. It'll probably come from the top of the hill, and when you see it, pull the trigger. Don't fuck around . . . It doesn't have to be a perfect shot. Just squeeze the trigger, and keep firing until you run out of ammo, okay? I want suppressive fire, not a single round in the ten ring."

"This is a bad idea," Walland said. "If there *is* a sniper up there, you won't get more than a few feet. You know you can't—"

"Let me worry about that. Just watch for the—"

Kealey stopped talking when he heard the distant but unmistakable sound of an engine turning over. It was hard to tell with the rain and the rumble of tanks in the hills to the rear, as well as the sound of the incoming helicopters, but he was almost certain the sound was coming from the other side of the house. His muscles tightened involuntarily, and he swore viciously over his lip mic when he realized what was happening. "They're running . . . We've got to go now."

"Wait," Walland said urgently, "Kealey, you—"

Kealey didn't hear the rest; he was already moving. His right foot was already wedged against the same rock he'd used earlier. Launching himself up and forward, he began running hard for the edge of the field, eyes flickering over the wet, waist-high grass in front of him. He hadn't taken more than a few steps when he felt the air flutter over his right shoulder. The strange sensation was immediately followed by the crack of a high-powered rifle. Massi said something like, "I see him, I see him," and then Kealey felt the same sensation of another near miss, and Owen screamed, "Got another one. There's a sniper on the left as well. . . ."

Kealey dodged to the right, ran hard for two or three seconds, then dodged back to the left, trying to make himself a harder target. His heart was thumping against his ribs, and he couldn't breathe. He felt sure that death was imminent, just seconds away. He heard the rattle of automatic fire, then the crack of a bolt-action rifle, but the sounds seemed distant somehow, as if by running, he had removed himself from the ongoing battle, even though he was sprinting toward the enemy. It was a stupid thought, he realized; if one or both of the snipers had him in their sights, they wouldn't hesitate to pull the trigger, and they were probably tracking him right now. . . .

"Got him," Massi shouted over the earpiece. "I got one. . . ."

Owen: "Can't see him . . . The fucker is down in the grass. . . ."

Walland said urgently, "Your left, Kealey. *Watch your left. . . .*"

Still running hard, Kealey started to bring the rifle to his shoulder, but Walland was faster. Kealey heard a 3-round burst to his rear and got the scope to his eye in time to see a man dropping into the grass, the green-tinted image bouncing crazily against his face. Swinging the rifle back to the right, he saw a second figure rising up, a dark silhouette against the lights in Qureshi's back garden. Kealey squeezed the trigger without looking through the scope just as the guard depressed the trigger on his AK-47. The man screamed and fell back, firing a half-dozen rounds in the process, but Kealey didn't break stride.

He reached the garden a few seconds later and ran at a dead sprint up the hill. When he got to the top, lungs burning, he ran between the barn and the house in time to see a black van moving down the rutted path, the tires struggling to gain traction on the flooded dirt road. Suddenly, the vehicle swerved onto the highest point on the road, the tires caught, and the van lurched forward. He did a quick range calculation and placed the rapidly accelerating vehicle at a distance of 75 meters.

"They're running," Kealey shouted into his lip mic. "They're running. . . ."

Lifting the rifle to his shoulder, he aimed for the tires and started to fire, the collapsible stock thumping steadily against his shoulder. He saw the rear tire go on the passenger side. The van swerved sharply, went off the road, and hit a depression in the grass. The vehicle flipped onto its side with a wet thud, the sound of crunching glass dampened by the overgrown grass in the field. Kealey was tempted to fire again—he had a clear view of the passenger-side door, which was facing up to the sky—but he didn't know where Fitzgerald was in the vehicle, and he could risk hitting her with an errant round. As he moved slowly to the left, his rifle up at his shoulder, his earpiece came to life.

"Kealey, what's happening?" Walland demanded. "Where are they?"

"They are in a van," he shouted. "But I knocked out the tires. Get up—"

Kealey dove to the ground as soon as he saw the flash, but he wasn't fast enough. He never finished the rest of the sentence. He felt an impact in his left side, but he couldn't look: he was too busy rolling right to avoid the rounds kicking up the ground around him. *Where the hell was it coming from?* The question was right there, like someone was shouting it repeatedly inside his head, but then he figured it out, and it all came back in a flash of memory. The back of the van had popped open at the same time he had been distracted by Walland's radio call, and at least one person had tumbled out of the cargo area. *Or had it been two . . . ? And if so, which two had it been?*

Kealey was still trying to decide when something large and dark swept over the house, accompanied by the unmistakable roar of twin General Electric T700 turboshafts operating at full capacity. Still lying prone, he tilted his head up to the dark, rainy sky and watched as the big helicopter came in to land. The Pave Low dropped with surprising speed toward the large, open field in front of the house, but before it could touch down, Kealey was back on his feet, his attention riveted on the scene unfolding before him. For the moment, he was lost to the sound of the Apaches providing cover overhead, the guttural roar of the Pave Low landing 200 feet to his left, the radio traffic coming over his earpiece, and the stinging pain in his side. He was entirely focused on the struggling pair 50 yards in front of him.

The rifle came up of its own accord, but before he could fire, his target spotted him, and with one swift move, he had his hostage wrapped up in his left arm. In his right, he was holding a gun, and he had it against Brynn Fitzgerald's head before Kealey could squeeze off a shot he was comfortable with. The captor—along with his hostage—was less than 10 feet from the open rear doors of the disabled van.

"Don't shoot!" Amari Saifi screamed over the roar of the helicopter. His attention was clearly torn between the helicopter and the lone soldier in front of him, but he knew enough to keep his body mass behind that of his hostage. "If you fire, she dies! Do you hear me? *She dies!*"

He continued to scream random orders and threats, but Kealey didn't hear a single word. In his peripheral vision, he could see Delta troopers streaming out of the gaping hole in the side of the MH-53, but for the moment, he didn't care what they were doing, even though he knew that a good number of them undoubtedly had their weapons trained on his head.

"Drop your gun!" The Algerian shouted again. Kealey didn't respond, and he didn't move. He was still waiting for his opportunity. Gunfire erupted to the rear of the house, and the soldiers were screaming something at Saifi—at both of them, Kealey realized—but still, he refused to shift his aim. Through the AN/PVS-17 scope mounted to his rifle, he had a quarter moon of a target. . . .

And that wasn't enough. The thought hit him on a subliminal level; the decision to hold his fire was not a conscious one. It didn't occur to him that he had been in a similar position twice before, and that it had ended badly both times. He didn't think about the possibility that he might miss, and he didn't consider the full extent of what would happen if his round hit the hostage instead of the target. The target was all he could see; for Ryan Kealey, Amari Saifi's head was just a sliver behind the pale, frightened face of Brynn Fitzgerald. In his mind, she was no longer the acting secretary of state, the most powerful woman in Washington. She wasn't even an innocent bystander. She was simply something in the way of his target.

At that moment, one of the Delta troopers fired. Kealey didn't see where the round went, but he caught the flash from the corner of his left eye, and it had the desired effect. Saifi, distracted by the muzzle flash, turned his head a few inches to the right, and Fitzgerald jerked away from the gun, giving Kealey the fraction of a second he needed to act.

He squeezed the trigger once, which was all he had time for. The bullet hit Saifi just forward of his left ear and went straight through the intracranial space, removing the top right quarter of his skull as it exited on the other side. A fist-sized mass of bone, tissue, and blood spun out into the wet, waist-high grass, and Saifi dropped like a stone to the waterlogged soil, his body disappearing into the grass. He was dead before he hit the ground.

Fitzgerald was already moving; Kealey watched as she staggered away, her hands fluttering in front of her face, which was covered with the remains of her captor. The thing she was doing with her hands was strange, he thought. It was a fleeting notion, but nevertheless, the sight left an indelible impression. It was almost as if she were trying to direct traffic for the first time. He saw her mouth, which had formed a perfect oval of surprise and suspended disbelief, and the wide, uncomprehending look in her eyes. Even in the dark, he could see the blood spattered over the right side of her face. . . .

As he watched her, some innate instinct told him to drop his weapon—that the soldiers moving in from the left would not be able to tell him from their enemies. He wondered why they had held their fire this long, then realized that some of them might have recognized him, even through the low light of their NVGs. He had worked extensively with the 1st SFOD-D, and it was a small, tight-knit community; the possibility that a few of them had picked him out was not as far-fetched as one might believe.

Still, it would be better to lose the weapon. His body reacted instantly, and his hands sprung open. The rifle fell to the ground, but instead of falling to his knees and raising his hands, he found himself stumbling forward. The pain in his side was still just a dull ache, but he could feel a spreading warmth on his front and back. Ignoring it, he kept moving toward the van, one hand pressed over the small hole in his torso. He still had to find Mengal; the former general was the only one left who knew where the rest of the hostages were, and Kealey hadn't seen him get out of the van. It didn't occur to him that he had just dropped his only real means of defending himself. All he could see was the van, and that was his target.

Suddenly, he was hit hard from the left, and he felt his legs being kicked out from under him. As focused as he was on the incapacitated vehicle, he had been blind and deaf to the soldier's rapid, near-silent approach. He felt a foot land on his upper back, holding him down, and though he couldn't see it, he knew the muzzle of a high-powered rifle was aimed directly at his head.

"I've got him," a voice called out. Then, to Kealey: "Who are you? Identify yourself."

Maybe they *didn't* recognize me, he thought, and then it hit him; they were under orders to take Mengal and Saifi alive, and they might have mistaken him for one of the two men. "I'm with the Agency," he managed. It was hard to speak; the foot wedged between his shoulder blades was preventing him from getting the air he needed. "There are four other guys behind the house. Listen, you—"

"How do I know that? How do I know you're not with them?"

A fair question, Kealey thought. Thinking quickly, he reeled off the Pentagon's code name for the operation and a few other salient points that had come straight from the White House. It took about twenty seconds to convince the soldier standing over him that he was who he said he was. At that point, the man reached down and helped him to his feet.

"You're hit," he said, once Kealey had turned to face him. The CIA operative glanced down at the hole in his left side, but he waved it away.

"It's nothing." Which wasn't strictly true, but he couldn't address it just yet; there were still things to be done. First, he checked in with Owen, who told him that the rest of the team was already aboard the MH-53 to the rear of the house. Caught up in his attempt to stop Mengal from escaping, Kealey had forgotten about the second helicopter. "What about Manik?" he asked his former CO.

"He's dead," Owen said grimly. "So is the hostage."

Shit. Kealey supposed he had already known, but now he had confirmation, and nothing made it hit home like hearing the words. Owen started to say something else, but Kealey had already turned his attention to the scene unfolding before him. Four Delta troopers had reached Fitzgerald and were escorting her back to the Pave Low in front of the house. *Escorting* wasn't exactly the right word, Kealey thought absently, as the four men were practically carrying her at a dead sprint back to the waiting helicopter. At the same time, a series of dark shapes were moving toward the incapacitated van, weapons at the ready. Kealey couldn't see them, but he knew there were other soldiers lying prone between the MH-53 and the house, covering the secretary's evacuation.

The trooper who'd pushed him to the ground was standing a few feet away, murmuring calm, authoritative orders into his lip mic. Kealey suddenly realized that this man was probably leading one of the elements. He was about to ask a question, but it was gone before he could get it out. In fact, he couldn't seem to fix on any one thought; it was as if his mind was bleeding out, just like his . . .

Kealey glanced down at the gunshot wound on the left side of his abdomen. It didn't look too bad—just a neat hole surrounded by a large circle of blood—but then he reached around and realized why his vision was starting to blur. The hole in his back was significantly larger than the one in front. The exit wound, he realized, with a sense of sudden fear, had to be at least 6 centimeters in diameter. He briefly wondered how the soldier standing next to him could have missed it; after all, he'd been looking right down at his back a scant forty seconds before. But then he realized that the blood would have been hard to spot on his dark clothing, especially since it was still dark and raining. He had not felt the pain when the man's foot had been wedged into his upper back. The adrenaline had been pumping too hard for that, but he was definitely feeling it now. The dizzying waves of pain were radiating throughout his abdomen, and they were only getting worse. . . .

As he brought his hand away from the wound, he saw it was dripping with blood. Glancing in his direction, the soldier—who was still on the radio—did a double take and started to turn in Kealey's direction, his eyes opening wide. He had seen it, too, Kealey realized.

It was his last conscious thought. The Delta trooper lunged out to stop him from falling, but Kealey's legs were already going. The night sky started to fade, replaced by something much deeper and darker, and then the world was gone completely.

He was unconscious before he even hit the ground. He never heard the master sergeant's urgent call for a medic, and he didn't see the look of utter despair that crossed the young staff sergeant's face when he arrived on the run twenty seconds later. The medic had seen this kind of wound before, and he knew the odds. Still, he had to try, and he set to work, frantically pulling items out of his rucksack, wondering if he had even the smallest chance of saving this man's life.

CHAPTER 45

WASHINGTON, D.C.

It was just after one in the afternoon when Jonathan Harper was shown into the Oval Office by the president's secretary. It was the first time he'd ever been alone in the room, and he knew that Brenneman probably wouldn't arrive for another ten minutes. The president was just a few hundred feet away, speaking to the dozens of White House correspondents camped out on the South Lawn. It was a good day for it, Harper had to admit, and in more ways than one. At least, that was the predominant feeling in Washington on this warm Tuesday afternoon. Through the towering colonnade windows positioned behind the president's desk, Harper could see the sunlight streaming through the trees and the brilliant blue backdrop beyond. But try as he might, he could not appreciate the picturesque view.

The previous day's operation had been labeled a success, in spite of the many mistakes that had marked its execution. Even Harper had to admit that when viewed objectively, it looked like a win on every front. Brynn Fitzgerald had been recovered intact, Amari Saifi was dead, and Benazir Mengal was in custody. The former Pakistani general had already revealed where the remainder of the hostages were being held—a secluded village in the Karakoram range—and a second rescue operation was already in the works. Best of all, it had all been accomplished with minimal loss of life. But that, Harper thought soberly, was the objective version, and when one looked at the value of the lives that *had* been lost, the mission didn't seem like such a great success. However, he had to admit the truth: for the president—and for the general public at large—success rested with the recovery of the secretary of state, and that had been accomplished.

When the assault force had returned to Bagram, they had found the State Department's customized 757 standing by, along with a full medical team and eight newly appointed members of the secretary of state's protective detail. From there, Brynn Fitzgerald had been transported to the military hospital at Ramstein Air Base in Germany, where she was currently being treated in a closed, secure wing of the building. For the most part, she was still in one piece, though doctors had discovered evidence of recent injuries, at least two of which were potentially fatal in nature. At least, they *would* have been fatal had they been left untreated. Those particular injuries—a partial pneumothorax of the left lung and a mild to moderate hemopericardium—had been adequately attended to by Said Qureshi in Pakistan. The doctors at Ramstein had grudgingly admitted as much, but the surgeon's efforts had not been enough to satisfy them, and they had made it their personal mission to find the things that Qureshi had missed.

A full workup had been ordered on the secretary of state's arrival, and it had already revealed two cracked ribs, a cracked cheekbone, a hairline fracture on the left tibia, and the beginning stages of post-traumatic stress disorder, accompanied by possible psychotic depression. Only time would reveal the true extent of the psychological damage Fitzgerald had suffered at the hands of her captors, but the psychiatrists who'd examined her on arrival had already expressed some serious concerns. The preliminary reports of what she had gone through had leaked that very morning, and they had been graphic enough to provoke a large-scale emotional response. Hundreds of thousands of citizens from across the nation had been flooding the major news outlets ever since with calls to express their outrage. Harper was one of the few who had *not* felt a sense of personal outrage, partly because he was able to keep it all in perspective. Overall, Brynn Fitzgerald was a very lucky woman, especially compared to some of the people who had worked so hard—and suffered so much—to bring her home.

Harper collapsed onto a couch in the seating area and rubbed his eyes with the balls of his hands. He was exhausted, but more than that, he was weighed down by what had happened in Sialkot. All things considered, he knew he should have been pleased. The director certainly was. The Agency had performed an important role in Fitzgerald's recovery. Indeed, were it not for Ryan Kealey's misplaced trust in Javier Machado, they would almost certainly still be tracking down false leads in Pakistan. But it hadn't turned out that way. They had managed to find her and bring her back, and because they had succeeded, the accolades were pouring in.

So why, Harper wondered absently, *do I feel like we failed?* He had been weighing that question for the last eighteen hours, and he had yet to come up with a satisfactory answer. At that moment, the east door leading out to the Rose Garden opened, and the president stepped into the room, followed closely by Robert Andrews, Kenneth Bale, and Stan Chavis. As Harper wearily stood, the first thing he noticed was the exultant, satisfied look on their faces. He could see right away that the press conference had been a tremendous success, but there was nothing surprising in that; the media was always kind when the news was good. He had been asked to attend by Brenneman himself, but he had been unwilling to submit himself to the adoration of the press. Praise from the media was something that senior CIA officials rarely received, but that didn't make it any more enticing, especially when so much had been sacrificed to make it possible.

The president crossed the room and extended a hand, grinning broadly. He was dressed immaculately in a navy suit with a pale yellow tie, but he was typically groomed for the cameras. There was nothing unusual in that; naturally, the most powerful man in the free world was expected to look presentable at all times. But the others had clearly made an effort, as they were dressed with more panache than usual. Even Chavis, who usually resembled a harried accountant in his standard rumpled dress shirt and Dockers, had taken the opportunity to sharpen his image in front of the Washington press corps. This afternoon he was dressed in a charcoal single-breasted suit with a patterned navy tie, which was only slightly crooked. For once, the man looked almost presentable. Bale was wearing his customary dark suit, as was Andrews.

"Thanks for coming, John," Brenneman said, as though the deputy DCI had a choice in the matter. They shook hands briefly, but with clear enthusiasm on the president's part. "I'm sorry you opted out of the press conference. There are a lot of relieved people out there today, and you helped make that possible. You should have been there . . . You deserve the credit."

"Thank you, sir," Harper replied, not knowing what else to say. He felt the complete opposite, of course, but one did not contradict the president, especially not in the Oval Office.

"Let's take a seat, shall we?" Brenneman said. Harper resumed his place on the couch, and the other men took their customary seats, Brenneman with his back to the fireplace. A Navy steward entered with coffee, deposited the tray, and left without a word.

"So," the president began. Harper saw that his face had taken on a sober expression, which was fitting, since he knew what Brenneman was about to ask. "Let's start with the obvious question. How is Ryan doing?"

So it's Ryan now, Harper thought silently. In the past, the president had always referred to the young operative by his last name, and that was on the rare occasion he referenced Kealey at all.

Harper cleared his throat. "It's touch and go, sir." He saw their shoulders slump with relief, and he knew what they were thinking: *at least he's alive.* He couldn't blame them; he'd felt exactly the same way when he'd received his last update forty minutes earlier. "He might make it, and he might not . . . There's no way to know for sure, and we probably won't have definitive word for another few hours. The major problem was the hemorrhaging, but there was some internal damage that has proved . . . well, sort of hard to seal off. Still, it could have been much worse. If that sergeant hadn't been thinking . . ."

The other men nodded slowly; they had already heard the story. Shortly after Kealey had lost consciousness outside the house in Sialkot, the master sergeant standing nearby—an eight-year Delta veteran by the name of Deakins—had remembered that the house belonged to a board-accredited surgeon, a scrap of information he'd picked up during the pre-mission briefing. A quick search of the house had turned up Said Qureshi, who'd been locked in his own surgical suite. It had taken only a minute to explain the situation, and a confused but compliant Qureshi had instructed them to move Kealey into his OR on the ground floor. He'd set to work immediately, his efforts helped enormously by the fact that both MH-53 Pave

Lows had been preloaded with bags of plasma of every blood type, as was standard operating procedure in any CSAR mission.

A quick call to Langley had verified that Kealey's blood type was O+. From there, it was just a matter of luck and skill, and Qureshi was very skilled indeed. Harper had personally talked to the medic— the first man who had worked on Kealey—and the young sergeant had made it abundantly clear that Qureshi had saved the CIA opera- tive's life. And for that, not to mention his work on Brynn Fitzgerald, the Pakistani surgeon would be handsomely rewarded, although he probably didn't know it yet. Harper was going to enjoy making him the offer, though. He had read through Qureshi's background, and he thought that the man deserved another shot at practicing real medicine, along with a tax-free annual sum deposited in any offshore bank of his choosing.

"And where is Kealey now?"

Harper, still thinking about Qureshi, snapped back to the conver- sation. He looked at Bale, who had asked the question, and said, "He's en route to Ramstein, sir. Said Qureshi agreed to accompany him that far; he's keeping him stable until they arrive in Germany. That should happen sometime this afternoon."

"He's a good man," Brenneman pointed out quietly. For a second, Harper wasn't sure if he was talking about the surgeon or Kealey. "I don't think I ever realized just *how* good, but if he makes it through this, he will have the gratitude of an entire nation. Hell, he already does. I, for one, would like to see Ryan Kealey receive the recogni- tion he deserves in person."

Harper nodded along, knowing full well that even if Kealey *did* survive, he would never set foot in front of a camera. Nor would he dream of attending a press conference, regardless of its purpose. It wasn't his style to bask in his accomplishments. Part of this was due to his intensely private nature, but mostly, his dislike of the limelight could be traced back to his training, which had drilled into him the need for secrecy, deception, and operational security from day one.

Harper suddenly realized that the room had gone quiet. Looking up, he saw that the president was watching him steadily, and the other three men looked suddenly awkward. It occurred to him that the mention of Kealey had reminded them all of what Javier Machado had done to Naomi Kharmai. Or presumably done, anyway. He had briefed them all on the specifics that morning, focusing on the means through which Kealey had acquired Benazir Mengal's location to begin with. There had been no word from Kharmai or the retired Spanish operative since Kealey had refused to heed the Spaniard's bizarre order in Pakistan, and there was little doubt in any of their minds that Machado had carried out his threat.

Privately, he wondered if they were secretly pleased that Naomi was no longer a threat to the administration. What had taken place in Madrid three days earlier was still a hot button issue. So far, the president had stuck with the story he had fed to Miguel Vázquez, and though it was only a matter of time before the Spanish government unveiled their evidence, they still didn't have a personal admission of guilt, and now they never would. If they couldn't produce Kharmai in person, the story would die a quick death in the media, and what had transpired in Madrid would soon fade from the collective public consciousness. Harper had no doubt that everyone in the room had already considered this, though none of them would ever admit to it.

As if reading his mind, the president cleared his throat and said, "So, still no word on Kharmai?"

"No, sir," Harper replied neutrally. "Nothing yet."

"But I assume you have people watching Machado's house in Cartagena," Brenneman said.

"Yes," Andrews said, making his first contribution to the conversation. "We have people talking to Élise Pétain now. She's been moved to the embassy, and she's proved very cooperative, though understandably, she's also very upset."

"How much does she know?" Brenneman wondered aloud.

"Not much," Andrews admitted. "Just the basics. That her daughter was in line for an important operation, and that her husband was willing to do pretty much anything to prevent Marissa from taking that assignment. She's already told us everything she knows, but none of her information has really panned out. At the moment, nothing has changed. Machado is still missing. Obviously, Kharmai is also missing and, I'm sorry to say, presumed dead." Andrews fell silent for a minute, then added, "I doubt that she ever really had a chance."

The president absorbed this silently. "How long," he eventually asked, "will you wait before you call off the search?"

"It depends," Harper said. "If anything comes up to indicate she's still alive, we'll wait as long as we have to, and we'll keep diverting resources. But eventually, we'll have to call it off. It might be three months, or it might be a year, but we can't look forever. We just don't have the ability."

"As far as I'm concerned, her actions in Madrid are forgotten," the president said, a note of command authority entering his voice. "I remember what she did for us last year in New York City, and the year before that right here in Washington. Any way you cut it, she gave her life for this country, and I want it noted, right here and now, that I intend to award her the Presidential Medal of Freedom, whether it's posthumous or not. We'll do it in secret, given her background, but it *will* be done." He looked around slowly, searching for signs of dissent. "I assume no one has any objections."

They all murmured their approval, not that anyone would have been brave enough to object. The Medal of Freedom, first established by Harry Truman in 1945 to reward meritorious acts during World War II, was generally considered to be the nation's highest civilian honor, the kind of thing that most people would have been thrilled to accept. Privately, though, Harper sincerely doubted that Naomi would have wanted a medal after what she had done in Madrid, even if she had acted only with the best of intentions. Besides, despite Brenneman's forceful tone, Harper didn't put much stock in the president's words. If Naomi were to suddenly reappear, which she wouldn't, she would never see a medal of any kind.

He was also fully aware that he himself had played no small role in her death; by using her to bait Kealey into the search for the missing tourists in Pakistan, he had essentially set her on the path to her own demise. Worse, he had done so knowing full well about her addiction to painkillers, which only compounded his guilt. And she *was* dead; Harper didn't doubt that for a second. The search was merely a formality. He could not pretend that this didn't bother him, but the fact that *Kealey* might know the extent of his duplicity was something that scared the deputy DCI more than he cared to admit. Not to the point that he wanted the younger man to succumb to his wounds— he had not fallen to that level and knew he would never allow himself to do so—but still, it was frightening to acknowledge the possibility that Kealey might someday decide his old friend and trusted employer was as guilty as the man who had actually arranged for Naomi's death.

"What about this other woman?" Brenneman was asking. "Machado's daughter . . ."

"Marissa Pétain," Andrews offered.

"Yes, Pétain. How much does she know about what really happened in Pakistan?"

"That isn't clear," Harper said. "But she knows that her mother is being questioned, and she's smart . . . I'm sure she'll be able to figure it out, if she hasn't already."

"And where is she now?" Brenneman asked.

"On her way back to Andrews," Harper said. He didn't add that Pétain, on hearing about what had happened to Kealey, had demanded to see the injured man immediately. Even over the phone, Harper could detect real emotion in her voice, but he had declined her request, and she had immediately launched into an angry tirade. Harper had been too surprised to hold her accountable for the things she had said, most of which were bitter insults directed at him. Besides, the fact that she had been tied to the success in Pakistan was enough to earn her a pass, and she was a promising young operative with the necessary skill set. He couldn't dismiss her for what amounted to a minor infraction, not that he particularly wanted to.

The rest of the meeting primarily revolved around the issue of Benazir Mengal. Currently, the former Pakistani general was being held in detention at Bagram AFB, though this information was known only to a select few. The president had already called Pervez Musharraf to inform him personally of the unsanctioned operation. Normally, this would never have happened; in matters of such delicacy, diplomats were usually used as buffers to lessen political fallout on both sides. But in this case, given what had transpired in Sialkot, there wasn't much the Pakistani president could say. The simple fact was that a senior U.S. government official had been kidnapped in his country, and he had done almost nothing to help find her.

Still, in the name of diplomacy, the president had extended an olive branch, albeit a branch heavily tilted in favor of the United States. Once Musharraf agreed to fast-track Mengal's extradition proceedings, the press had been informed that the U.S. rescue operation was, in fact, a joint mission accomplished by U.S. and Pakistani forces. For this consideration, Musharraf had also agreed to stop making noise regarding the impending Indian-Israeli arms deal. Additionally, he had quietly agreed to start moving Pakistani forces back across the Line of Control in Kashmir. Harper thought it ironic that

Fitzgerald's kidnapping and subsequent rescue had almost certainly ended the burgeoning conflict in Kashmir sooner than if she had not been taken at all, but he wisely kept this thought to himself.

When the meeting ended twenty minutes later, congratulatory handshakes went all around, and then the men began filing out of the Oval Office. As Harper moved to the door, the president stopped him with a hand on his arm, then smoothly pulled him aside.

"John, I just want to thank you again for all your hard work. You did as much as anyone to make this operation a success, and I'm deeply grateful, as are the American people. I'm sure Secretary Fitzgerald will want to thank you personally once she's up to it."

Harper nodded and murmured his appreciation, but the president had already expressed his gratitude. He suspected he had been held back for a different reason, and the president confirmed this a moment later. "John . . . with respect to Kealey. You've known the man a long time."

"Yes, sir," Harper said, wondering where this was going. "I have. Nearly ten years."

"He's survived some serious injuries before, hasn't he?"

"Yes, he has. But he's not indestructible, sir, and this is probably the worst of the lot. Still, I wouldn't bet against him."

"And if he *does* survive?" Brenneman was genuinely curious. "What do you think he'll do? When he recovers, I mean. Have you given that any thought?"

Harper considered the question for a long moment. He knew what the president was really asking, and it had nothing to do with the possibility of Kealey resuming his work with the CIA. Harper *had* given it plenty of thought, and while he had yet to come up with a definitive answer, there *were* a few things he thought he knew for sure.

In the end, it all came down to Naomi Kharmai. After what had happened to her—or at least, after what the Agency *thought* had happened to her—Kealey would never resume his work with the CIA. There could be no question of that; contrary to popular belief, even the Directorate of Operations was an organization hampered by certain rules on what was and wasn't acceptable. Operatives did not have free rein in the field, and they couldn't just kill anyone, especially not when the operative in question was driven by nothing more than the need for revenge. Instead, Kealey would do things his own way. He would single-handedly go after the men who had betrayed him in Sialkot, and then, when he had exhausted every avenue of retribution, when he had finally decided there was no one left to kill, he would go after Javier Machado. Harper was sure of it. In fact, he had never been more certain of anything in his life.

Of course, that was not the answer the president wanted to hear. Looking Brenneman square in the eye, he said, "Sir, I honestly don't know. I just know that if he makes it through, he's not going to let it go, and I, for one, would not want to be in his way once he's back on his feet."

And, Harper thought grimly, *I would not want to be Javier Machado, wherever he is.*

CHAPTER 46

PUERTO SAN JULIÁN, ARGENTINA, FIVE MONTHS LATER

The old café was a modest establishment at best, but thanks to its location, the center terrace in a row of dirty brick buildings overlooking the port of San Julián, it catered to a steady stream of customers. Nearly all of them were men, because it was that kind of place. For the most part, they were large, grizzled individuals who earned a hard, dangerous living on the unpredictable waters off the southern coast of Argentina. The young waitress who moved through the tightly grouped tables was tired of the work, tired of trying to repel their interest, which usually presented itself in the form of lewd comments, lascivious stares, and even the occasional grope as she dispensed their food, drink, and more hard liquor than even they could handle. For the most part, she thought they were scum, and for the most part, she was right. However, even in this grubby place—and she knew what it was, because she had once lived in Buenos Aires and often wondered why she had left in the first place—there was the occasional person worth serving with a genuine smile.

She offered one now, though it temporarily froze on her face as she skirted a table surrounded by four burly, drunken fishermen, doing her best to give them a wide berth. Ignoring a slew of crude sexual advances, she made her way to the lone table by the large plate-glass window overlooking the pier. As she approached, her smile resumed its natural warmth, and her dark eyes shone with genuine pleasure. The man who sat there was about seventy, she surmised, with an iron gray beard and bushy, overgrown eyebrows. He had been coming in for about a month now, and she had never found him to be anything other than quietly respectful. She always looked forward to his visits, just as she was always sorry to see him go.

In appearance alone, he did not differ much from the men who occupied the other tables. He dressed in a similar fashion: thick woolen sweaters, tarpaulin rain pants, and black rubber boots. Despite his rugged appearance, something told her he had never worked on the ocean. It was his demeanor, though, that really made him stand out, the way he carried himself with quiet dignity. She often found herself watching him when business was slow, wondering about the sad look on his face and the defeated slump of his broad shoulders. He looked at her, too, but not in the way the fishermen did. Rather, he looked at her the way her grandfather once had, and for this reminder of happier times, as much as his polite manner and generous tips, she found herself visiting his table as often as she could get away with.

As she approached now, she was more than disappointed to see him place his money on the table. It was too much, as always; she didn't have to look to know that. She asked him, almost with a sense of quiet urgency, if he wouldn't consider staying for one more drink, but he shook his head and politely declined. As he stood, she stepped back to let him pass. She told him it was on the house, but still he refused. He returned her smile, bid her good night, and walked through a haze of blue smoke to the door. As she watched him leave, the waitress felt a sense of deep, unaccountable sorrow. She stood there for a moment, deaf to the cruel snickers of the men sitting behind her, and wondered if she would ever see him again. Somehow, she doubted it, but she didn't know why. It wasn't until later that evening, as she gratefully locked the door behind the last drunken customer, that she realized what had triggered the thought.

It was the smile. Before he'd walked out, he'd given her a strange, sad parting smile, and she didn't have to think about where she had seen it before, because she already knew. Her grandfather had given her that very same smile two years earlier, on the night he had died.

After the old man left the café, he wandered along the pier for an hour, looking out at the lights bobbing up and down on the gentle swells of the South Atlantic. It had rained heavily that afternoon, and the pier shone with large puddles, the still water reflecting the lights from the buildings across the road. There was almost no activity at this late hour; the pier was largely deserted, which was when he liked it best. It gave him the time and solitude he needed to think things through, to weigh the life he had led, as well as the many thousands of decisions he'd made along the way.

With increasing frequency, he found himself regretting the things he'd done, and one thing above all. At the same time, he did not regret the reasons behind his actions, and he knew that he never would. After all, how did one apologize for loving his children? How could he regret wanting to protect them by any means necessary? The answer, of course, was that he could not, and in the end, that was what it all came down to. That was the simple truth that allowed him to sleep at night, secure in the knowledge that if nothing else, he had at least acted with the right intentions all along.

He stopped at the end of the pier and stared into the black water, listening to the sound of slow waves swarming around the sturdy cement pillars that held up the pier. He had been standing there for about ten minutes when he heard a sudden noise behind him. A very deliberate noise. He froze for a moment; then he slowly turned, arms away from his body, to face his killer.

The American was hardly recognizable, and it wasn't the fact that the pier was draped in shadow. Even with the low light, Javier Machado could see that the young man had lost a great deal of weight, perhaps as much as thirty pounds, and there were lines in his gaunt face that should not have existed for another ten years. Machado was so focused on the incredible changes in his physical appearance that he nearly missed the gun in his right hand, which was extended at arm's length, the muzzle centered on his chest. Without even looking, he knew that the weapon was a .22-caliber Beretta, a competition-style handgun fitted with a 6-inch suppressor. He had used the same weapon himself on countless occasions, and while he was aware of the irony, it didn't mean a thing to him. After seventy-two years, there wasn't much that still surprised him.

Machado waited for the American to speak, and when he did not, he said, "You've been a busy man." He was surprised by how steady his own voice was; he had always thought that when the time came, he would be afraid. "You killed my colleague in Karachi."

"I assume you mean Fahim. Isn't that what you called him the last time we spoke?"

"And Rabbani in Paris. I assume you're responsible for that as well." The knowing look on the young man's face told Machado that he was, and he didn't feel the need to list the half dozen other business associates of the Afghan smuggler who had died over the past eight weeks. Machado had seen the pattern after the third man, a money launderer in Antwerp, had disappeared without a trace three weeks earlier. He had seen it then, but he had not tried to run, and when Fahim had died in Karachi the week before, he had known it was just a matter of time.

And now his time was up.

"Where is she?" the young man asked. He might have been asking for directions, for all the emotion in his voice. "Where is Naomi? What did you do with her?"

Machado cupped his hands in front of his body, palms up, and opened them slowly. "I told you she would disappear if you disobeyed me, and you did. I'm afraid she's gone."

"Her body—"

"There is no body." Machado shook his head in a barely noticeable manner, as if the younger man should already know what he was being told. "Don't you see? She never existed to begin with. That's all there is to it . . . I don't know what else you want me to say."

There was no reply. Machado knew he had just seconds to live, and there was one thing he had to know. "Does my daughter know what I did? Does Marissa have any idea?"

"I don't know. I haven't spoken to her in months." There was a long, unsettling pause. "Why, Machado? Why did you do it? You had already lost, so what was the point in killing her? I don't understand it."

At last, Machado caught a hint of emotion, a slight catch in the younger man's voice. He thought for a moment, then lifted his arms out by his sides.

"What can I tell you?" he finally said. "Would you really be satisfied with any explanation I have to offer?"

"Probably not."

"Then why ask?" Machado said. "Just do what you came here to do. Just finish it."

He closed his eyes, but nothing happened. He waited, but still, there was nothing but the sound of wind sweeping in from the ocean. He opened his eyes in time to see a pair of brief flashes, followed by a sharp pain in the center of his chest. He staggered back, then tumbled into space. He was falling, plunging toward his final resting place, and the last thing he saw before he hit the water was a face in his mind. It was Caroline's face, the unmistakable image of his long-dead daughter, and as he took his last breath, pulling the black water into his lungs, he saw her open her arms and smile.

She was bringing him home.

Kealey stood at the edge of the pier, holding the Beretta against his right thigh, staring down at the churning surface of the ocean. He stood there for several minutes, waiting for the weight on his chest to lift, waiting for the sense of relief that Machado's death should have brought, but nothing changed. And then he realized that it never would. Naomi was still gone, and there was nothing he could do to bring her back.

There was no point in hurling the gun into the ocean; there was no one around to witness so dramatic a gesture. Instead, he simply dropped it over the side.

Then he turned to walk away.